On Twisting Tides

Val E. Lane

wave song publishing

ISBN 979-8-9874248-0-3

Cover Art: Stefanie Saw/Seventh Star Art
Editing/Proofreading: Danielle Fowler
Header design: Etheric Designs

This is a work of fiction. Unless otherwise indicated, all the names, characters, businesses, places, events, and incidents in this book are either the product of the author's imagination or used in a fictitious manner. Any resemblance to actual persons, living or dead, or actual events is purely coincidental.

This work of fiction contains scenes and events set in an alternate 18th Century time period. Names and places may differ from actual historical names and locations, and it is not meant to depict historical events, myths, or figures accurately.

To those watching the horizon, waiting for their ship to come in.

PLAYLIST

Scan the code or click to listen. Each song corresponds to the chapters in order, plus additional songs at the end. You can also search for the playlist on Spotify by book title.

1. "Do or Die (feat. Kinn)" by Neon Feather

2. "feel it all" by sød ven

3. "Shipwreck" by Otherwise Fine, Emily Rowed

4. "Man's World" by MARINA

5. "Sailor's Heart" by Zyke

CONTENTS

1

CLEAN SLATE

KATRINA

T he nightscape blurred past us in streaks of midnight and indigo. Humid air rushed over me, dancing through the tangles in my hair as the bike sped through the streets. Even in winter, the evenings were mild. Sixty degrees was still plenty warm enough for a quick joy ride on New Year's Eve to watch the fireworks over the bay.

I clung tightly to Milo as he skillfully guided the motorcycle through the crowded roads, allowing us to dodge stopped traffic and blockades. Once we crossed the stone bridge over Matanzas Bay, he finally settled on a spot with a clear view of the glassy water below and the horizon into which it flowed. As he flipped out the kickstand with his foot, I pulled my helmet over my head and braced against his shoulder as I swung myself over to dismount.

It had been just over a month since I dove into the sea, breaking Milo's curse, and subsequently, mine. His ship and crew rested at the bottom of the ocean, along with the memories of the past, the darkness that had haunted us for so long, and the magic that started it all. Thankfully, my love for Milo had saved him. The legend says a mermaid—er—siren's heart could allow a man to cheat death. I'd technically given him my heart, I could admit to that part, but I still didn't like to think too hard about what else that implied. But ultimately, it didn't matter, I supposed. No more pirates. No more mermaids. We were free.

Milo removed his helmet with swiftness and shook his dark honey locks loose. His dark jeans and brown leather jacket offered a subtle nod to his past to my eyes only, but no one else would have ever guessed he'd been a literal pirate for 300 years.

"What do you think of this spot?" Luckily his accent wasn't going anywhere. It was something I never got tired of hearing. "We should be able to see them perfectly."

"I think I trust your navigational skills much more than my own," I uttered with a chuckle.

"Then here it is." He nodded, placing an arm around my shoulder as we turned to face the water.

A small chime in my pocket made us both glance down. I pulled out my phone and read the text from my dad out loud. *"Happy New Year from both of us."* Underneath the message was a grainy selfie with horrible lighting of both of my parents, smiling together. Even given the terrible quality, I couldn't help but smile at the photo, knowing Mom was finally going to achieve her New Year's Resolution of staying sober this time. She hadn't had a single slip-up since Thanksgiving, so I knew this time it was real. Out of habit, I reached up for my necklace, but was met with emptiness. Somehow, I kept forgetting I had tossed it into the ocean like a pebble.

Good pic of you two. Happy New Year! We are about to watch the fireworks.

I typed out my response quickly. I could tell by the rise in the voices of the crowd around us that the fireworks would be starting soon. Milo glanced over my shoulder at their picture.

"I still can't help but feel that your father thinks I'm an idiot," he groaned.

"I don't know why you're so paranoid about that," I laughed. "I thought it went great when you met them at Christmas." I thought back to their introduction, when I'd brought Milo back to Arkansas and he'd stayed with us for the holiday. My dad had taken to him right away when he found out Milo knew how to work on motorcycles. Mom was just happy to be back home and sober enough to enjoy the festivities.

We'd picked out a tree together, and my dad had given Milo a tour of his shop, where they both had spent hours talking about engines. We'd even gotten a light dusting of snow.

"You didn't hear some of the things he asked me. He wanted to know things like my plans for the future and what I intended to do with myself. I don't even know those answers myself yet. I couldn't tell him that I've spent the last 300 years on a ghost ship." Milo put his hands in his pockets, shifting from one foot to the other as he looked out toward the water.

"I'm sure he didn't think too hard about it. He likes you, really." I reassured into his ear, playfully grabbing his shoulder as the bustling crowd around us grew.

"Maybe he likes that I can hold a conversation about alternators, valve covers, push rods, clutches, piston bearings. But beyond that, I made a fool of myself to him." Milo glanced down at me, something in his hazel green eyes tugging at my depths.

"No, no. My dad trusts my judgment. And if I'm with you, he knows it's for a good reason. Don't be so hard on yourself. Just think of what you've got going for you at the shop with Noah. You're already building a life here." I smiled, thinking of Noah, which subsequently led to thoughts of McKenzie. My high-spirited roommate had been getting suspiciously close with Noah, who spent his time at his uncle's auto restoration shop when he wasn't working his weekend shift at the antique store. Thanks to McKenzie's persuasion skills, Noah had now found himself including Milo in his car restoration projects. Milo had even somehow convinced the shop into letting him take on a few clients just for motorcycles. It had been going well from what I knew.

"I'm doing the best I can." He nodded. "My father was such a great merchant and businessman. I hope I can continue his legacy. It might look different here, but I hope to find a way to make my way just as he did."

As the last word drifted from his lips, an explosion of colors lit up the night sky. Beside the moon, a burst of red and gold glittered in a thunderous rumble before cascading down to the watery surface below. More colors began to rain down in a symphony of snaps, pops, whistles and hisses. I stole a glance at Milo, who was watching them with intent wonder.

"I've seen these many times over the decades," he finally uttered, "But not like this. Not this close." He looked at me and then tenderly reached for my hand with his pinky finger, curling it around mine. "Not with cause for celebration until now."

As my eyes drifted over the scene of colors, I thought of my own palette of pigments waiting for me back at my dorm. Perhaps I could make an attempt at fireworks over the water for my next painting. Perhaps...

But then, I shook myself from the reverie. I'd promised to take a break from painting until the start of the spring semester. It seemed like a healthy idea, but my mind couldn't help but see the world through watercolors. So I shelved the idea for later. Naturally, my thoughts drifted to the note I'd been left with at the end of last semester. "I know I probably shouldn't bring this up now," I started, looking down. "But I went to Tesoro Del Mar again yesterday. I thought maybe Cordelia would have to be there for their New Year celebration or something."

"Oh?" Milo raised an eyebrow as he looked down at me through dark brown lashes. "Any luck?"

I shook my head. "No. Same as always. They said there is no Cordelia. I even showed them the letter. They just keep telling me it must be some mistake. It's so weird." I had to speak a bit louder than I would have liked over the sound of the fireworks.

"Very strange, indeed." Milo looked ahead at the fireworks, the gold, red, and white glows flashing across his handsome face.

"I mean, if she's alive after all this time, what does she want?" I grabbed the railing of the bridge in front of me, pressing my palms into the cold metal. "And why has she waited until now to reach out to me? Has she known about me this entire time?"

"I think we'd both like answers," Milo said. "Perhaps she'll contact you again. It's only been a month."

"I know," I sighed. "But it just drives me crazy. She didn't seem like the rational type."

"She wasn't." As Milo spoke, the hum of the fireworks began to die down. The crowd around us began shifting and dwindling as some people left their spots early in a hurry. "At least not once her heart was broken."

"Any chance it's healed by now?" I joked, though deep down I was serious, and I didn't like the answer I already knew.

We both turned away as the leftover smoke from the fireworks drifted across the night sky, creating a spooky smog over the dark water. Hand-in-hand and dodging throngs of families and couples, we made our way back to the motorcycle. The wind from the ocean was giving me a chill, so I closed my jacket tighter around myself as Milo started the engine. I knew he noticed when he looked me over up and down.

"Cold?" he grinned. "Hopefully holding onto me will warm you up."

I shook my head with a playful grin as heat flooded my face as I swung a leg over behind him. Gripping his shirt beneath his jacket, I clutched the fabric in my fingers and pushed my hands against his waist. With a snicker, he started off, and we headed back to Isabel School for the Arts. With my body pressed to his, I breathed in his scent. He still smelled of leather and amber, and no longer of salt. I remembered how I'd thought I'd lost him, but somehow, he was still here, and with him, I was home. And normally, I felt like together we could outrun anything as we'd done so many times astride this motorcycle. But tonight, as we left another year behind, I couldn't help but feel that the haunting of Cordelia was the one thing catching up to me. And it knew exactly where to find me.

2

SLEEP LIKE A SAILOR

MILO

The cool of the night might as well have been icy ocean waves splashing against my fingers as I drove the bike onward. Katrina's arms wrapped tightly around me fought away the chill. Even though I'd been free from my curse for a month, every sensation still felt like new. I'd almost forgotten the feel of the sticky night air, the taste of sweetness and bitter, and the feeling of a touch that could make my body flood with warmth and desire. In this strange new world, I had three centuries worth of feelings and experience to make up for, and I couldn't have been more grateful for it.

I managed the turns gently and kept our speed slow. I knew Katrina wouldn't let me know she was freezing, but by the way she was tensed and buried into my shoulders, I could tell she was fighting the wind. When we pulled to a stoplight, she lifted the face shield of her helmet and uttered something into my ear.

"On second thought, you don't have to take me back to my dorm. I'll stay with you tonight."

"You know you're always welcome," I tilted my head back toward her.

"I know. I just feel like I'm not ready to be back in the dorm. McKenzie still isn't back yet, so I don't want to be alone." She squeezed my core tighter.

"Whatever the reason, I'm never going to be opposed to spending the night with you," I reassured. My breath mixed with the heavy, wet air, and it reminded me how much I looked forward to showering and feeling clean—a sensation that brought comforts I'd long forgotten.

When the light turned green, I gave the throttle a nudge, and we lurched forward on the motorbike. The way Katrina gripped me as she steadied herself made me warm. I longed to reach the apartment so that I could return the favor. Noah's family was kind enough to offer me the room above the restoration shop in return for my apprenticeship with them. I couldn't have asked for a better start to my second life.

I parked the motorcycle in the garage, double-checking the locks and securing the alarm system, which still fascinated me, before heading upstairs to my apartment loft. Katrina followed, using her phone to light up the darkness as we managed the metal steps. I still needed to get one of those for myself. But it wasn't exactly as though I had anyone to call or who needed to call me.

Taking her hand, I turned on the light to awaken my quaint living quarters. To me, it was a palace. Framed by the sloping roof, industrial lights hung from the ceiling. A small television hung on the wall opposite the bed, while a small kitchen counter wrapped the corner, parallel to a square table and chair set just big enough for two. One would hardly expect a former pirate now dwelled here, perhaps except for the compass hanging from the metal bed frame. A token I'd found had somehow survived in my pocket when I awoke on Katrina's island.

"You've got to get some more chairs in here," Katrina teased, placing her helmet on the kitchen table next to mine. "I've still got some money left over from the painting. We could buy some more."

"As if I'm one for inviting guests over for get-togethers?" I chuckled at the thought.

"Well, maybe not, but there's plenty of time to bring out your extroverted side." She walked over to me, crinkling her nose mischievously. "But on second thought, maybe not."

"Well, if I'm going to be adding anything to this place, it would be a swinging hammock. Now that I've made up for 291 years of lost sleep, my body can't seem to adjust on this flat mattress."

"You still want to sleep like a sailor?" Katrina raised a skeptical brow at me.

"Aye." I winked, pecking her on the cheek as I walked past her toward the small bathroom that adjoined the room in the center. "But I don't want to smell like one."

Without another word, I tossed my jacket onto my bed and pulled my shirt over my head. I'd yet to find anything more comfortable than V-neck cotton T-shirts. As I crossed the threshold to the bathroom, a gentle hand stopped me. Katrina's delicate fingers gently pulled me back by my bare shoulder, tugging me towards her. I turned to face her without hesitation.

"What if I like it when you smell like the sea?" She smiled, drawing into me, and placed her head in the space between my chest and chin.

I grinned, traces of my hair falling into my eyes as I looked down at her. "Then I suppose I'll have to start bathing in the ocean."

When she looked at me like that, it was as though time stood at a standstill in her eyes. The deepest trenches of the ocean knew no depth of peace like those dark brown pools of molten mahogany. Like smoking coals just before turning to diamonds, they burned into me, and yet soothed me all the same. Her hand remained still on my shoulder, and the other one firmly planted on my waist. As the moment commanded me, I embraced her more, pulling her small frame snug against my body and meeting her lips with mine. She stepped backward, taking me with her.

"You know better than to take your shirt off in front of me." She giggled softly under her breath. My thoughts flashed back to the first night I'd kissed her, when

I'd pressed my bare skin to hers against the lighthouse. When I'd caressed every inch of her for fear it would be the only time I ever could. But now, my only fear was that she'd wake up one day and realize she was worthy of so much more than someone like me.

She deepened our kiss, dancing in my mouth with hers. My blood ran hot, and I couldn't help but swell with desire as I pushed against her gently. She didn't realize what she was doing to me. I lived in a constant state of craving her more and more with each passing day. And she was feeding the ravenous inner beast with the heat of her body against mine.

I slid my hand beneath her sundress. I traced her hips and the beautiful shape of her spine. She ran her fingers through my hair, pushing it back out of my eyes and tracing the scar across my eyebrow like she so often did. I needed her.

Another moment and our bodies had found the edge of the bed. Her muscles tensed against me as she lowered herself down onto it, as if falling gently. I brought my hand behind her shoulders, supporting her as I leaned over her. I breathed in her sweet scent of apricot blossoms and honeysuckle mixed with the midnight air. I wanted to taste more of her. I wanted to show her all the ways I could love her.

The kindling flame coursing through my body grew to a wildfire as I slowly unzipped the back of her sundress. I kissed her up and down, the taste of her salty, flowery skin tingled on my tongue. She circled the skin just above my belt with her fingertips, sending me rigid. With both hands, she reached for my belt; then slid her hands upward along the skin of my heaving chest with a gentle brace.

"Wait." I barely made out her weak whisper. "I'm sorry."

I pulled away, fighting the desire that I'd been working so hard to suppress these past few weeks. I imagined kissing her again and making her change her mind and lose control just as much as I wished I could. "Don't say sorry," I muttered, keeping my tone as gentle as I could. "You said 'wait.' And that's all right." I took a deep breath, then forced it back out through my lips to help settle myself. Katrina sat up, holding the top of her dress close to her chest with a worried expression. Her shining dark eyes settled on me in a wave of guilt.

"It's stupid. I know I love you. And I know you love me..." She sighed softly. "But I've seen the way my dad stayed by my mom, even when she was at her worst. It was so bad for him...But he stayed no matter what. Even when it was destroying his life. What if I do that to you?"

"You won't, Katrina. It was the curse..."

"What if it wasn't? What if it just really is who we are—who *I* am? After all, I have Cordelia's blood." She paused to swallow down the emotions she was trying to hide. "I don't want to fear forever with you. I don't know what I'm capable of, and it scares me."

"You're not Cordelia. And you won't destroy my life," I said, adjusting my jeans. "You've made my life feel worth living. Without you, this would all feel meaningless."

She put her hand to her forehead and groaned. "I don't know. It's stupid. I'm sorry."

Before she could say more, I knelt down beside her, taking her free hand in mine. "Katrina," I locked my gaze with hers. "I've waited three centuries just to find you. If there's anything I think I've mastered, it's patience. I love you, no matter what you need from me today, tomorrow, or forever."

I leaned in to kiss her, and she gently brushed my lips with hers. She always reprimanded herself like this. As if she didn't trust herself. She feared her own desires, and she was held captive by the eerie hold Cordelia had on her. I wished I could make her understand that though I wanted her more than anything, I would never compromise her or make light of what she felt. But I desperately wished I could set her free from herself.

I kissed her forehead without another word before walking away to the shower. Once the door was closed behind me, I rubbed my thumb along my jaw, feeling the steely facial hair as I tried to will the remaining lustful yearning in my veins to die down. All it took was one look in the mirror.

The rugged man staring back at me was tall and well-muscled, with dark ink decorating his arms and chest. A man who, even in this new era, looked all too much like his father. My flesh was still flush from the moment, and my dark golden hair had grown a touch longer in this first month of this second life. A life that, though I was grateful for, I knew I didn't deserve. A life that Bellamy had lost. It hardly seemed fair. And I couldn't make sense of it. We'd both had difficult lives dealt to us, but his—his was cruel. Yet I was the one granted another. No matter how strong my efforts to reassure myself were, I couldn't rid myself of the feeling that it should have been him.

3

ADRIFT

KATRINA

I watched him disappear behind the door. The way he'd touched me had left me breathless. I wanted him. All of him. But wanting him wasn't enough to overpower the worry that I'd somehow lose him again. I don't know why, but something still wouldn't let me believe all this was real.

But this all was clearly real. And I couldn't deny everything that had happened to me—to us. Even the parts I didn't want to be real. Like the strange vision I'd had at the bottom of the ocean after jumping into the maelstrom. Everything was real, but just because my mind believed it didn't mean my heart could accept it. But I did know that I loved him. Fiercely. Shouldn't that be enough?

It *was* enough. And I wanted to let him know. Standing up, I slipped out of the rest of my dress, letting it crumple to the floor and turned my feet to the bathroom door where the faint rushing sound of the shower beckoned me from the other side. But just as soon as I'd taken a step, I hesitated, feeling a strange sense of paranoia creeping in. I glanced around the room, without even knowing what I might be expecting to see.

"What is wrong with me?" I muttered out loud. I truly hadn't recovered from the sense that someone was watching me. And knowing Cordelia knew how and where to contact me had made me all the more bothered. But I felt it was beginning to get out of hand. After all, what could she possibly do to me? What could she *want* to do to me?

Just then, my eyes wandered to Milo's jacket that he'd tossed onto the bed. I caught a glimpse of a white edge peeking out—a piece of paper. I lifted the jacket, revealing a small envelope. It was addressed to me, handwritten, but the envelope was stamped with a seal of Tesoro Del Mar Club and Marina. I knew the seashell insignia all too well from all the research I'd done on the place, desperately looking for any trace of Cordelia. I quickly threw on one of Milo's clean T-shirts and a pair of leggings I'd left there previously, and then reached for the letter.

My fingers traced the envelope flap with careful movements as I sat back down on the bed. I stared down at the paper in my lap, a torrent of thoughts whirling in my mind. It was difficult to decide if I should open it yet. I'd been yearning for this clue for weeks, but now the joy of finding it was replaced with the pang of betrayal. Why did Milo have this letter? And why hadn't he mentioned it beforehand when I brought up Cordelia?

When the sound of shower water stopped, my eyes shot upward toward the bathroom door. For a brief second, I considered sneaking the envelope away, and not telling Milo I had found it. But I decided that secrets almost always do more harm than good. So I held it, turning it over in my hands nervously as I waited for him to emerge.

Steam filled the small loft as the bathroom door opened and he stepped out in boxers and a new plain white T-shirt. If I hadn't been wrangling my confusion and sudden feelings of betrayal, I wouldn't have been able to tear my gaze away from his solid, well-formed build. But instead, I looked at him, then dropped my focus down to the white rectangle in my hands. I was going to ask him what it was. But I could tell he understood me clearly without me having to say a single word.

"You found it," he said, shifting uncomfortably as he put his hand behind his neck.

"I did." I confirmed, locking my eyes with his. "Where did you get this? It's addressed to me."

"I—It was on your door when I picked you up from your dorm this morning. I was going to tell you. I swear I was, but..."

"But what?"

"But I wasn't sure yet. I wanted to make sure it wasn't something that would put you in danger."

"Danger?" I stood up, trying to keep my shaky voice even, despite the fact that a tide of emotion was welling up within me. "This is about keeping me safe?"

"Yes." Milo looked away, scratching his head and ruffling his wet hair. "I mean no. I mean—Yes, of course I want to keep you safe. I wasn't intending to keep that from you. But I know Cordelia, and I wanted to see what game she's playing now before I let her get to you. Think about everything she's done."

"So you thought you'd just take it home and read it without me? Then you'd decide if I could handle it?" My voice cracked.

"No, not exactly..." Milo grimaced, turning his head as though trying to shake off something. "I don't know what I planned to do. It was just my first reaction. My first reaction is always to protect you." He paced the floor as he spoke, his words coming faster with each thought, until finally, he stopped and looked back at me. "I should've told you about it immediately...and...and I'm sorry."

I wanted to be angry with him. And I was. But I also remembered what happened the last time I didn't trust him and jumped to conclusions. When I thought he'd murdered an innocent girl, and the truth couldn't have been further. But still, this was different.

"You don't need to protect me," I finally said. "Especially if it means lying to me or keeping things from me. Haven't we been through enough for you to realize sometimes I have to fight my own battles?"

"I know, I know," he sighed, sitting down next to me on the bed. "I'm just a bit worried that tracking down Cordelia hasn't been good for you. You're nervous all the time. You can't stop talking about it. You want to find her so badly. And I understand. But if I'm being honest, I'm a little afraid of what will happen if you find her."

"Just because you're afraid for me, doesn't mean you can keep things from me like this." I glanced down at the envelope.

"I was going to tell you..." He looked down, his damp hair falling across his forehead. "I just didn't know how or when. I panicked."

"If it was on *my* door, it wasn't for you to decide," I uttered.

"I'm sorry, Katrina. I acknowledge that I didn't handle this correctly. I promise I won't be so foolish next time." He leaned toward me, desperation in his voice.

A long sigh escaped my lips, as I pressed my gaze into his. "Weren't you the one who told me 'You probably shouldn't make promises you can't keep?'"

He blinked in response and looked down at his hands.

"I'm trying to undo a lifetime of lying, cheating, and deceit. And I'm sorry that I've already faltered with the one I care about most." He paused, staring directly past me at the compass hanging from the bed frame. "I always admired the way my father loved my mother, but it was such a different time. He was able to protect her from everything but the complications that took her. She died while pregnant with my brother. I wasn't there, but I know he would've saved her if he could." He paused, blinking as if in thought. "How do you love someone and let them risk themselves at the same time?"

"You trust them," I said firmly, "Now it's your turn to trust me. Trust that I know what I'm doing. I solved Cordelia's curse. I can handle whatever else she thinks she can do to me." I spoke with confidence in my voice, but inwardly I was still trying to convince myself as much as him.

There was an awkward silence between us. I didn't know what else to say. I still felt flustered by his decision to take the letter that was meant for me. But my desire to know what the envelope contained overpowered my twisting emotions.

"Let's just open this thing," I said, tearing the paper. "No sense worrying about it when we don't even know what it says."

My desperate eyes scanned the letter, absorbing every word.

Dearest Katrina,

I hope you've enjoyed the holidays. Now that my schedule has freed up a bit, I'd love to meet with you. I have a very special commission of high importance that I'm certain is only suitable for someone with your abilities. I'm inviting you to my private business dinner at the Tesoro Del Mar so that we can discuss the details. The time and place are below. Formal dress. I look forward to meeting you in person.

-Cordelia

"Seven o'clock, January 3rd," I uttered, reading the details below the message. "I wonder if this invitation is good for two?" I looked up at Milo.

He tilted his head, making his hair fall in front of his eyes in a way that never failed to make me melt, regardless of what else I was feeling. "You want me there?"

"I do," I said inching closer to him. "I always do."

He kissed my forehead. "I'll be by your side whenever you need me."

"That's all I need." I sighed, resting my head against his shoulder. The sound of fireworks outside continued, muffled through the walls.

"Want to go watch some more? I bet we can still see the amateur fireworks on the beach from the top," I said.

"You go ahead," he whispered. "I'm feeling a bit tired."

"You? Tired?" I raised my eyebrows and stood back with crossed arms.

"I'm making up for 300 years of no sleep." He laughed, but something about his voice sounded lifeless, as though the air could barely carry it to my ears without it slipping away.

"Okay," I sighed. "Then I'll see you tomorrow." Just as I took the first step upward toward the roof of the loft, I hesitated, looking back at Milo, who had sat down wearily on his bed. "Is everything okay?"

He nodded before lying down to close his eyes, but it wasn't convincing for me. "Shipshape."

As I walked upstairs, I clutched the railing. I suddenly realized I didn't want to watch the fireworks. But I knew that even though I wanted to close my eyes and forget about everything for a while, there was no way I could sleep right now. Though I didn't want to let Milo know it, I was terrified of what Cordelia wanted with me.

4

AN ILL WIND THAT BLOWS NO GOOD

KATRINA

I can't wait to see you!

I read the text from McKenzie with tired eyes as I fought with my unruly hair in a sad attempt to secure it with Bobby pins. If she were here, this would've been so much easier. She would've had my hair in the perfect, elegant updo in no time. But left to my own devices, I wasn't capable of creating quite the same masterpiece. But it would have to do. I wanted to look my best when I met with Cordelia this evening. I needed her to take me seriously.

Milo stepped into the dorm behind me, reminding me of the night he appeared at the gala, in his slacks and suit jacket, and his dark gold locks tucked back within a secure tie.

"You look handsome," I said with a smirk. "Think we look like we belong at an elite ocean club dinner?" I ran my gaze up and down my reflection, standing in my teal blue cocktail dress, wishing I still had the mermaid scale around my neck to add a dash of sparkle.

"I hope so because this is the most polished I'll ever look." Milo's mouth curved into a small smile. Despite his attempt at humor, I'd noticed his dampened energy and his shortness of words lately. Something about him seemed off ever since our conversation about the hidden letter two nights ago, but he relentlessly swore he was fine.

"Well, it's 6:30," I pointed out. "We'd better get to the resort."

"Agreed." Milo nodded, and together we made our way to my Jeep. The Cherokee was still running strong as ever, even if I never could manage to keep the sand-filled floorboards clean. I'd accepted it now as just a normal part of Florida life.

The resort club wasn't far, just on the border of Constantine and St. Augustine, and a chill ran through me just like it did every time I came here looking for Cordelia. To think that all this time, she was just a mere handful of miles away, made me wiggle with unease like a worm on a hook.

Clutching the invitation in my hand as though my life depended on it, I stepped out of my vehicle as Milo held the door for me. We walked down the ramp to the entrance together, my heels clomping on the narrow wooden boardwalk that led straight into the vicinity of the enormous white beachside building. I read the large sign carved in stone on the front gate entrance where the boardwalk ended, and the walkway became a pristine sidewalk leading to the doorway of a grand two-story resort and marina. Yachts of luxurious sizes lined the borders of the building around the back, bobbing calmly in the water of the Matanzas inlet.

Tesoro Del Mar. Treasure of the Sea.

This gate that was normally closed and required me to identify myself when I'd come looking here was now wide open, hosting a pathway leading to the front door of the marina resort. Strangely enough, I didn't see any other guests arriving. The parking lot had only been a few cars shy of being empty.

Milo squeezed my arm and I glanced at him with tightened brows. The churning in my chest wasn't stilling, but I was so desperate to finally meet this woman who had plagued both sea and land for centuries. I had written down the names of all my ancestors who'd fallen to her curse. I hoped they'd help me remember why I *had* to confront her.

"I don't have a good feeling about this," Milo said, his bicep tensing against my arm that was hooked through his.

"Where is everyone? It's six-fifty. We're not exactly early. Maybe I read the invitation wrong?"

"No, you read it correctly. Your reservation is at seven, not six-fifty." A withered voice startled both of us.

A man who looked to be in his sixties appeared from behind us, dressed in a tailored light gray suit. His thinning silver hair and wire glasses hooked over his wide nose made him look wise, but he spoke with sharpness.

"Ms. Black will be here in a few minutes. And she requested your presence. Not his." He turned to glance at Milo with narrowed eyes.

"Ms. Black?" I repeated, ignoring everything after that.

"Yes." the man nodded. "The owner. Dahlia Black."

"But she—"

"Do you want to meet her or not?" He asked before I could finish.

"Yes..." I calmed myself and ensured it showed in my voice. "Yes. I want to meet her."

"Then wait here." The man replied in one short breath. "Alone."

With a worried glance, my eyes found Milo's and he pressed his lips together with concern as the man turned to walk away.

"I'm worried about leaving you," Milo whispered.

"I know, but what choice do we have? I have to meet this 'Ms. Black.'"

"I understand this is important to you. I do. So for you, I'll stay behind."
He glanced toward the resort door through which the man had walked a few
seconds earlier. "But be careful. I'll be close by in case anything goes wrong."

"If I'm not out in a half hour, come check on me." My nerves were rioting
as the suspense hung in the air. I watched Milo leave, praying I wouldn't need
him. I didn't exactly know what he meant by "close by," but I trusted he knew
where to be.

Minutes ticked by like decades. I glimpsed down at my phone to check the
time. 6:59. I tapped the heel of my open-toed pumps and bit my lip. At the exact
stroke of seven PM, I heard a click as the resort door behind me slowly opened.
It was the old man from before who poked his head through the opening, letting
out a draft of cold air-conditioned wind.

"Ms. Black will see you now."

Without a word, I nodded with the slightest tilt of my head and stepped
forward into the building.

It was a venue, set up for what looked like a grand convention or wedding,
with round tables draped with fine royal blue linens and empty champagne
glasses placed around elegant place settings. Elegant orb lights hung above from
coiling metal chandelier-like settings, each reminding me of a menacing octopus
clutching a pearl. But it was desolate, devoid of any human presence.

Soft piano music played faintly in the background from a source I couldn't
identify. I turned to look at the man who'd guided me here. When he noticed my
confusion, he only gestured with his hand, pointing to the far end of the room.
I squinted as I looked again, focusing on one particular table in the distance.
There she sat. A woman, with her back to me.

I swallowed and did my best to keep my breathing slow and steady. The walk
across the room felt like it would never end. As I approached, I noted her raven
hair pinned up in an elegant fashion, with just enough left over to hang over her
shoulder, and I immediately recognized it as the same style she wore at the art
gala.

As I stood only steps from her, I expected her to turn around, but she never moved.

"Have a seat, please." Her voice almost made me jump, but I held my composure. The sound of her words still rolled over me like a graceful lullaby. It was like a sweet warm glaze, and I felt like a fly in a honey trap.

"Of course," I said, fighting the quiver in my voice. I pulled out the chair across from her, and sat down, smoothing my dress as I settled. I still hadn't looked her in the face yet.

"Katrina."

With an upward glance, I saw her, and her crystal blue eyes caught me. She looked younger than my mother, but older than me. Dressed in a costly dark grey dress and midnight blue blazer, she radiated sophistication. Her flawless skin seemed to glow beneath the rosy blush on her cheeks. With a wickedly beautiful smile, she spoke again. "Katrina Delmar. How nice to finally meet you in the flesh."

I tipped my head at her, still processing the place settings in front of me. A plate of decadent seasoned fish taunted my tastebuds as the scent reached my nostrils. Both my champagne glass and water glass were full. I reached for the water, desperate to hydrate my dry throat before speaking.

"It's...nice to meet you, too," I said in my most confident tone. "He called you Ms. Black?"

"Ah yes," she breathed, picking up her champagne glass. "Most people here know me as Dahlia Black. Cordelia was getting a bit outdated. Though I'm sure that's no problem for you, seeing as you have such a penchant for things of the past."

I forced a dry laugh out of politeness, surprised at her statement. It almost seemed like an insult, but she'd said it so beautifully.

"Don't worry, angelfish. I know you know who I am," she uttered with her lips millimeters from the champagne glass' rim. "You don't have to keep pretending."

"You're Cordelia." I spoke lowly, even though we were completely alone in the room. "Why did you ask me here? And how are you still alive?"

"Because I'm in need of something only someone with your...talents...can accomplish." She cut a small slice of the fish on her plate while she spoke, not answering my last question. "Besides, can you blame me for wanting to meet my own 7th great granddaughter?"

I shook off the eerie feeling I got from her last sentence. "My talents? What do you need exactly?"

Ignoring my question, she simply laughed softly in that melodic voice and guided the fork to her mouth. "Don't let your plate get cold, dear. That's the finest bluefin tuna."

Without knowing how to respond, I glanced down and forced myself to take a bite. It was delicious; the best seafood I'd ever tasted, in fact. But my nervous stomach wouldn't allow me to enjoy it.

Cordelia's words struck me suddenly. "I know you broke my curse."

I swallowed the last bit of tuna in my mouth as I looked up. "It had to be broken eventually," I said.

"I might've disagreed with you some years ago." She dabbed her mouth with a napkin, looking up at me through sharp, perfect brows. "But now I'll admit you're right. At some point eventually that curse was bound to become a waste of power. It had to be broken so that I could use the scale's magic for..." She paused, taking in a deep breath as she looked up at the chandelier before finishing her sentence, "...better things."

"Like what?" I asked

"Look at the world, dear. What do you see? Wars, diseases, destruction, greed. Things are getting out of balance. The world of men is collapsing in on itself."

"Yes, the world sucks. But that's nothing new." I set my fork down. "What about it?"

"You ask how I'm still alive? It's because our kind were given a much longer lifespan than mortals. Hundreds of years. Because we don't possess souls. When we finally die, we simply turn to seafoam."

I shifted in my seat, unsettled at her words, though I didn't know how much of them to believe.

"Katrina, the sea is angry. *We* are the sea, you and I. And mankind has taken too much from it. First it was the mermaids, soon it'll be everything else."

"With all due respect, didn't you help Valdez hunt the other mermaids?"

Cordelia slammed her hands down on the table, rattling her silverware. Her eyes became piercing shards of ice beneath dark brows before I could even regret what I had just dared to say.

"Don't say his name!" She spat the words out like arrows fired from a bow. "He tricked me. He *used* me to get to them. And not a day goes by that I don't regret it. I was just a foolish, curious mermaid who broke the laws of the sea by falling in love. And you dared to set him free from his prison."

I was speechless. I couldn't fathom what I could possibly say as she denied her own part to play in the demise of her kind. She watched me with her jaw tensed and her pointed fingernails digging into the table linen. I nearly jumped when she stood up without warning. With a menacing swagger, she moved toward me, walking around my chair and standing behind me.

"Which brings me back to why I need that scale. That last bit of my magic was being used to hold the curse. But now that it's broken, I have something much better in mind."

"What are you saying?" My voice cracked.

"I'm saying, it's not just about James anymore." Her words slithered out like shadows. "Mankind. Men. Man is destroying this world. And the sea groans because she knows she can stop it. If we would just let her. Think of it like a reset, if you will." She leaned over and placed her hands on my shoulders. I recoiled at an ice-cold touch I didn't expect. "You see, we mermaids—sirens—draw our power from a source as ancient as the moon and tides themselves. But we have limits. Within the sea there is a power even greater. One that can release the tides from their bonds so that the sea can unleash her vengeance on mankind."

"You want to flood the world?"

"Clever girl. This deplorable world is in need of a bit of a restructuring, don't you think?"

"No," I gasped. "No. I mean, yes, there is a lot wrong with the world. But you can't wipe out humankind."

"Katrina, you're not understanding. You can't think clearly because you, too, have fallen into the trap of man." She reached down and placed her hand over my chest. "I can feel it. Your naïve little heart beats for one." I wanted to free myself from her grip, but something held me frozen in place as she seemed to read my heartbeat before continuing. "Milo Harrington...hmm. I remember him. Always the guilty one. Always longing to be the hero. But I see through his façade. They are never what they claim to be. They are all selfish, greedy, and manipulative. He'll use you like James used me."

"No, he's done everything for me," I said. "I'm sorry Valdez hurt you, but you've let your pain turn you into someone just as bad as him."

Her grip on me tightened. Those nails dug into my shoulders, cutting into my skin as she put her lips to my ear.

"That's no way to speak to your great-grandmother." Her words bit like steel. I fought against her hold, trying to stand up, but she began to hum, and I somehow lost the ability to fully control my body. But I recognized the tune, and it sent shivers through my soul.

"Stop singing my mom's lullaby."

"Your mom's lullaby?" She laughed, still gently humming her siren song. "Angelfish, where do you think it came from?"

I swallowed, processing everything she'd said thus far. About Milo. About Mom. About me. Then she went on, adding to my mental burden.

"There's a trident deep in the ocean. An oracle of power thought to have been left behind by the gods. Resting beneath the place the humans call the Bermuda Triangle, its power has been unconfined for centuries. It would be the thing responsible for all those unexplained disappearances and souls lost at sea."

"What does this have to do with me?" I struggled against her hold.

"Sirens come from the same source of power. So only a siren could wield the trident for herself. But to do that, a siren must sacrifice a piece of herself—something more precious to her than anything—in the trident's hold. But sirens are selfish. They're nearly incapable of giving up the thing that means the most to them. That's why we aren't supposed to fall in love. Because it taints our nature... Hmm, I guess that was Poseidon's funny little way of keeping things in check." She drew in a breath, hesitating before going on. "But I... I no longer have anything left to be selfish over. Nothing but a wretched scale with the last bit of my magic. So, I'll be needing it back, angelfish."

She held out her hand slowly in front of me. I could move now, but I no longer wanted to run. I needed to finish this conversation. I had to know exactly what she was planning.

"I...I don't have it."

"Where is it then?" Her voice hardened.

"Somewhere at the bottom of the ocean. I thought offering it to the maelstrom was the way to break the curse. I threw it in the sea before I realized it wasn't the answer."

"You did what?" She released me, her voice rising.

"How can you be angry with me? You caused all of this."

She stepped back, holding her stern gaze on me, clenching her fists. "I was shown the cruelty of man without restraint. I've watched mankind destroy this earth, but he has never been able to tame the sea, try as he might. And it's time the sea washes away these sins once and for all."

"You're playing God," I swallowed, letting the seriousness of her words sink to my stomach.

"I'm no longer playing, dear." She grinned. "And I want you to join the game. Help me do this. Help me get the trident once we find the scale. You're the only one of us who can reach it. We'll rebuild this world together. You can help me decide who is worthy to survive."

"Like you decided my mom and her mom weren't worthy to survive? Like how you plagued them? What about Marina? Whatever happened to her?" I slapped down the list of names I'd brought onto the table, each with their death years written plainly beside them. "You killed every single one of them with your curse. You tortured us with dreams, Cordelia. Until the torture became too much for them to bear. You are in absolutely no position to judge mankind."

Cordelia's eyes scanned the names in a split second of silence.

Lydia Gatlin - 2003

Nelda Gatlin Harrows - 1971

Esther Graves - 1952

Alma Whitlock - 1922

Edith Barnes- 1900

Martha James Shores - 1874

Sarah Shores - 1840

Marina Samuels - 1819

For a moment she seemed speechless, her lip quivering before she hardened her features again. "I did what I had to do to ensure justice was executed to those who deserved it. Sometimes justice requires sacrifice. Besides, if I hadn't, you all might've lived a few hundred years too long, and that would've attracted a bit too much attention, don't you think?"

"You let your entire family suffer just so you could get even with your ex-lover."

"He emptied the sea of my kind!" she cried.

"And you helped him do it!" I screamed. "And your guilt has consumed you. But you won't admit to that part!"

She didn't respond, only held her position, drilling into me with her gaze.

"Cordelia," I uttered. "Destroying half of mankind isn't going to bring the mermaids back. I'm not helping you do this."

"Suit yourself, angel." She stepped backward. "But whether you help me or not, I *will* get what I need. I've spent my time on land wisely. I have many connections. I've built my own empire already. I'll find the scale. And then the trident. I may have lost my tail, but I still have power. In many forms." She rubbed her fingers together, signifying her strength in wealth.

I couldn't find the words to say, so I only sat, shaking my head in disbelief while staring into her topaz eyes.

"Go on, Katrina. Refuse me." She nodded towards the door. "Go back to the man waiting outside for you. Perhaps once you see how filthy his soul really is, you'll reconsider my offer. But in the meantime, I won't wait for you. You'll see that I'm right. You may think you're upholding some sort of moral righteousness, but just remember at the end of it all, you're just as soulless as me."

5

LONG SHOT

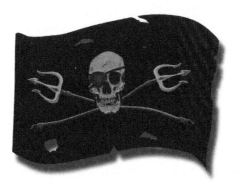

MILO

I watched the harbor, looking out at the great yachts docked there as the last bit of the fiery orange from the sunset bled out from the water's surface. Two more minutes and it would be a full hour. I couldn't stand it anymore. Not when I knew who Katrina was up against. Alone.

Cordelia was cold. She was manipulative and could demand anything she wanted with a simple melody from that voice of hers. But she never forced Valdez to love her. She would never have accepted a false love. I suppose that was her one redeeming feature, though it probably would've saved us all a lot of heartache if she did.

The longer I resurrected my memories of her conniving, dangerous nature, the more impatient I grew. I didn't know what she could do after all this time. Or what she *would* do. And if Katrina didn't return in one more minute...

Fifty-nine, fifty-eight, fifty-seven...

I turned to walk toward the entrance. I had to make sure she was safe. I'd probably already waited too long. With steps forceful and quick, I trudged through the gate entrance where we'd come earlier.

Just before I reached the door, it opened slowly, revealing my Katrina, standing in silence, staring straight ahead, her usually tanned, flushed skin pale as I'd ever seen it. I hurried to her. "Are you alright? Did she hurt you?" I swung a protective arm across her shoulder and guided her forward.

"She…" The words barely crept from her lips like a whisper before she shook her head. "Not here. Let's go home first. To my dorm."

"Where is she?" I glanced around, looking for any sign of the siren within the building she'd just exited. But there was no one. Not even the undertaker of an old man who'd greeted us.

"It doesn't matter."

"It does. Katrina I—"

"Let's just go home. Please." Her voice rose as she looked up at me with desperate eyes.

I nodded, forcing myself to take a breath. "Okay."

The ride back to her dorm lacked a single word from either of us. Once there, without even bothering to change out of her dress, she slumped to the floor, her head and shoulders hanging low in a defeated position.

I followed her, taking a seat across from her on her rug. "What happened?" I asked as gently as I could.

"Cordelia…" She hugged herself, leaning forward and staring at a spot in the floor. "She knows I broke her curse. She wanted the scale back." When she stopped and looked at me, I nodded for her to go on. "And when I told her I didn't have it, she said she's going to find it. She said she's going to use a trident to flood the earth."

I shifted and pressed my lips together, trying to soften my reaction. "She wants the trident."

"So it's real?" Her brows tensed.

"It's a legend. But if it's real, it's meant to be somewhere impossible to reach. Otherwise, I'd imagine it would've been found by now. After all these centuries."

Katrina took a piece of her hair and began twirling it between her fingers. "She said it's beneath the Bermuda Triangle. And that it requires a sacrifice to use. That's why she wants the scale. She's going to exchange her power for the trident's."

"And she thinks a simple scale would suffice? That hardly seems like a sacrifice to me."

"But think about it." She gestured with an open hand. "That scale is all she has. It's her last bit of magic. What else does she care about in this world?"

I tilted my head in acknowledgement. It was certainly a perspective I hadn't considered. I brushed a stray hair from my forehead with my thumb and noticed Katrina's focus settle on me. Her gaze deepened as she spoke with a somberness in her voice I hadn't expected.

"Milo, do you think Cordelia will find the scale?"

I willed the muscles in my face to remain expressionless. I couldn't let my concern show. But Katrina had to know what she was up against.

"I know she will," I uttered. "It's only a matter of when."

With a weak shake of her head, Katrina stood to her feet. "Then I guess we have to find it first. We'll go out tomorrow morning and start looking."

I could think of nothing more to say. She was right. So I stood up, too, and took a small step toward her.

"Aye aye, Captain." She turned away, trying to hide the small smile I knew was there. If she only knew how I'd follow her to the depths of the ocean if she asked.

"I'll see you in the morning at the docks." She closed the space between us and kissed me lightly on the cheek. I knew she wouldn't ask me to stay with her. She hadn't since the day she'd found Cordelia's note. And I couldn't blame her. I turned to go.

"I—" As I reached for the doorknob, I looked back over my shoulder. Frail fragments of a word barely escaped my lips before I stopped myself. Instead, the only thing I managed was, "Goodnight, Katrina."

6

MISS THE BOAT

KATRINA

I couldn't sleep that night, so when my alarm went off at 5:45, it was no challenge to get up and face the day. The only thing lingering on my mind was finding that scale, no matter how overwhelmingly daunting it seemed. I didn't even know where to start. But I knew starting was my only option.

Cordelia had taken so much from my family and left so much damage in her wake. The curses she left behind had more than proven her ruthlessness, but if I needed any further confirmation, the meeting with her had done the job. And I was sure I couldn't let any more power fall into her hands.

I pulled on my swim leggings, merino sweater and a beanie. On the way out the door, I snagged an extra hoodie just in case the January winds were especially ruthless on the water today. The air was cool and damp. The periwinkle twilight of morning was just beginning to peek through the canvas of clouds stretching across the flat Florida landscape. An ominous morning fog already blanketed the ground, sending a shiver through me despite my snug spot in the driver's seat.

The lone motorcycle parked at the harbor reassured me Milo was already here. I climbed out, double-checking my bag with water bottles, keys, flashlight and air tank. I'd bought it for novelty from the antique store where Noah worked, but I really hadn't expected to actually put it to use. At least not yet.

I crossed the dock where Milo was already waiting, his back to me and the shore as he watched the sunrise, wearing a dark brown windbreaker. I stepped beside him. He didn't turn to look at me, but he reached for my hand.

"I don't even know where to start." I breathed, fog forming in front of my mouth with each word.

"Neither do I," he said. "But the important thing is we're starting somewhere. It'll be alright." He gave my hand a subtle squeeze.

"If you did know where to find it, would you tell me?" I knew I shouldn't have asked, but I couldn't hold it back.

The look on his face twisted into one of confusion and hurt, but I could tell he was trying to keep it from showing by the way he swallowed and bit his cheek. "I promise I'm not keeping anything from you."

"I like to think that. But I'm just making sure." I forced a weak smile. I'd never anticipated how difficult it would be to move past the letter incident. But for some reason, I couldn't manage to get it out of my head. And I knew it was hurting us both.

He walked away toward *La Esperanza* bobbing on the water and stepped over, hoisting his own bag of supplies over the hull. I followed and made my way to the helm where I turned my key and started the engine. After allowing it a minute to run, we both untied the mooring lines securing the boat to the dock, and then I returned to the wheel to ease us out into deeper waters.

Though we hardly spoke, it seemed clear that we both knew our destination—the island—or at least the waters surrounding it where I had thrown in the scale. My fingers began to numb as the cold moist air mixed with the sea spray and chilled them. But I held tightly to the wheel, burying my nose into my pullover. By the time the last bit of sun had finally climbed over the horizon, the island was dead ahead in front of us.

Milo tossed out the anchor once I hovered the boat over my best guess as to where the *Siren's Scorn* had last sailed. With nausea rising in my throat, I leaned over the edge and gazed down into the lapping water below. The morning tide had brought with it some harsh waves, that lifted my old boat up and down as it charged through the swells.

"Now the question is," Milo said, turning to look at me, "how do we plan to get down there?"

I reached into my backpack and pulled out the vintage air tank and regulator. Milo's eyes widened.

"Katrina, that thing looks older than me."

"Noah said it's from the seventies or early eighties," I uttered, fully aware of how sketchy it was to be using, "but it should still work...I think."

"The air is probably stale. When was it last filled?"

"I—I don't know," I grumbled. "But what else can we do? Do you have a better idea?"

"Not necessarily." Milo crossed his arms and held his gaze on mine. "But if the legend about a siren's heart was true then that should also mean..."

With a grimace, I quickly blinked, looking away. "Okay, don't be ridiculous."

"What? Katrina, how else did you survive going down into the water after you jumped into the maelstrom? Don't think I didn't figure it out. If you're truly descended from Cordelia, at some point you'll have to accept what that means."

"It doesn't mean I'm a mermaid!" I shouted. The absurdity of the statement flooded over me like the waves cresting below. And I had to switch my thoughts before I gave into them.

Milo's eyes softened and his shoulders dropped. Without another word, he watched as I took off my shirt, revealing my swim top. I strapped the air tank onto my back and checked the PSI, which still looked good from what I could tell. But it didn't matter. I knew this was a horrible idea, about as irresponsible and reckless as it could get. I didn't know what awaited me down there, but I knew I was the only one of us who stood a chance with this rickety old gear. I walked to the boat's ladder, but a firm hand caught me by my arm just as I began to step over.

"Katrina, I can't let you do this. Do you know how deep it could be down there? You could die from the pressure if you don't drown first."

I knew he was right. I was terrified. But I was more afraid of Cordelia. "I have to try, Milo. I know this is dangerous. But we have to find that necklace before she does." I looked up at him, and a warmth came over me as I concentrated on his hazel irises that were reflecting bits of honey and teal from the seawater and sunrise.

"Then let me do it. I'll go under."

"No. No, it *has* to be me."

"Why?" He spoke with a grit of desperation I recognized. It reminded me of when he told me he loved me on the ship when I came to tell him goodbye.

"Because..." I took a deep breath and pinched my forehead. "Because I know this ancient air tank isn't enough to make it. So, if something goes wrong down there...it has to be me."

There. I said it.

Milo released his hold on my arm. "So, you *do* admit it."

"I..." I searched for words, but they were as lost at sea as the scale. I knew in my heart what had happened when I woke up at the bottom of the sea months ago after jumping overboard. I knew what I saw. But that didn't mean it was something I wanted. I had never told Milo how I survived. And he had never asked. Something unspoken within the bond between us assured me he knew. That's why he'd offered to dive instead. He knew it was the only way to get me to confirm what he already suspected.

As we sat in silence on the boat's edge, the faint sound of an engine trickled in somewhere from behind us. We both glanced out to the open water, where a mid-size yacht cut through the water like a knife, sending wakes our way and rocking my little fishing boat.

I scanned the deck to see some divers packing up their equipment, their wetsuits still shiny from the water. My blood ran cold as the boat neared enough that I could see the lone figure standing at the front of the stern, overlooking the water as though it was at her command. In a royal blue skirt and blazer, Cordelia stood, like a queen. Even the meters between us couldn't keep me from catching her deathly stare. She fixated on Milo, narrowed her eyes, then looked back at me as her scowl turned into a mocking smile. She lifted a closed hand with a silver chain dangling from it.

No. Impossible.

As her yacht whisked past us at a dangerously close distance, she opened her hand to reveal the scale still secured in its pendant on that damned necklace I fought so hard to get rid of.

"She has it!" I belted out, nearly falling forward if not for grabbing the ladder rail at the last moment. The boat zoomed out into the distance, fading away as I caught the lettering on the back. "*Belladonna*" it read.

Milo reached out to steady me as the wake of the rolling water tossed me off balance. With anger welling up in me like a cresting wave, I let myself fall into his arms and let out a groan of defeat. "She hired a dive team. She got the scale." I cried into the slick exterior of his windbreak jacket as he closed his arms around me.

"Shhh," he said softly, "That doesn't mean she's won."

"We shouldn't have waited," I said. "We should've come out here last night. Immediately. We would've been first."

Milo pulled back gently and looked me in the face, stilling me as I focused on that lock of honey hair falling over his scarred left eyebrow like it always did. "We never would've been able to find it in the dark. Cordelia clearly has more resources than we can imagine, and you can't put the blame on yourself that she doesn't play the game fairly."

I nodded, trying to reel in my swirling thoughts. "You're right. But that doesn't change the fact that if I can't stop her, the consequences will be so much worse than just losing a game."

"We." I looked up at Milo's sudden correction. "*We* can stop her. You're not alone. You have to stop putting everything on your shoulders. I'm here, too."

I rubbed my temples with my cold palms. "Then what do *we* do now?"

I didn't expect a response, but Milo's silence cut through me like a knife. I knew there was only one answer. The cool sea air filled my lungs as I pulled in a deep breath before answering my own question.

"We find the trident."

7

FILTHY PIRATE

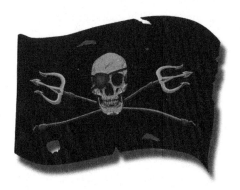

MILO

"**I**f we're going to sail to the Devil's Triangle, we'd be in much better shape with a bigger boat." I gestured to the small vessel on which we stood.

"Well, I've done greater feats with much less." The way Katrina spoke felt like a foreign language. There was a coldness in her words that I didn't recognize. She was so focused on her own thoughts that I felt she was a million leagues away. "And there's no time."

She started the boat with haste and set off back toward home. I watched her at the helm. Her eyes never wavered from the straight ahead gaze she held looking out at the stretch of sea before us. The last time I'd seen a determination so fierce on her face was right before she dove overboard from Valdez' ship. And I secretly feared what we'd be diving headfirst into this time.

"Will you help me get supplies? I want to leave by tonight." She turned to me as she stepped over the hull and onto the dock after we pulled the boat to port.

"Tonight?" Of course I knew time was of the essence, but the fact that we still lacked a suitable vessel made me hesitant.

"You're the expert. How long do you think it'll take us?"

"In this," I sighed. "Six days at the least, I'd think. In something with a stronger engine, maybe half that."

"Well unless we can find a bigger boat in a few hours, looks like we'll just have to do with a couple of extra days."

"Then part of my preparations will include praying for fair weather. If we hit any storms out that far, I doubt she'll fare so well." I patted the rope as I pulled the hitch knot tight.

Katrina paced across the dock, and then suddenly stopped. "I'm going to pack food and supplies. Can you get the fuel and anything else we'll need?"

"I'm going to get fuel and some spare parts from the shop."

"Okay," She nodded and then stepped toward me to give me a peck on the cheek, but it felt cold.

I hadn't realized Noah was in the shop this early until the sound of rollers started me as he slid out from underneath a car. He must've heard me come in, though I did my best to enter quietly.

"Morning, Sandy," he uttered, his voice throwing a cold echo into the garage. I was never fond of that nickname he chose for me. "I must've missed you on your way out this morning. Early bird today, yeah?"

I shook my head. It would be difficult to get what I came for with him here. "Just here for some things."

"Oh yeah?" He stood up, wiping his hands on a towel smudged with black hanging from his front pocket. "What are you working on?"

"It's sort of personal." I walked over to one of the toolboxes, rummaging through the parts bin for spark plugs, screwdrivers and sockets, and whatever else I could think we might need if something were to go wrong on that ancient engine.

"Well, you can't just come in here taking all this stuff if you're not gonna tell me. How am I supposed to explain to my uncle why all this crap's missing when he gets back from his vacation?" He leaned over me, his elbow propped up on the toolbox.

"Tell him it was a bit of an emergency. Boat engine."

"Pssshhh, what kind of boat emergency you got going on, Sandy?" He chuckled slyly.

"You wouldn't believe me even if I told you."

"Bro I knew you were weird, but come on. This is a whole new level, even for you."

"Katrina and I need to find something. Something far away." I packed the tools and parts I'd gathered into my tool bag. Then headed to the oil shelves to find what I needed, despite the increasing difficulty to focus with Noah yapping in my ear.

"How far are we talking? You're not planning on taking my grandpa's old boat, are you?"

"Your grandpa?" I stopped with my hand just over the quart of oil I needed.

"Yeah, my grandpa sold her that boat. She told you about Russell, right?"

"Yes, but..." I tensed my brows as I made the connection. "Your Russell's grandson?"

"Yeah, I am. So I know what an old shitbox that boat is. I don't know how far you guys are going, but I wouldn't be taking that if the word 'far' means what I think it means."

"Trust me, I know," I sighed. "But Katrina is determined. And honestly if we don't make this trip, something bad could happen."

"Believe me, I get it. I know these chicks can make a lot of bad things happen when we don't do what they want."

I couldn't help but smirk. "I know it's crazy, but we have to do this. I can't exactly explain why. But trust me."

"Okay well, I feel really guilty about turning a blind eye while you guys commit suicide."

Just then I turned around, still chuckling at Noah's typical uptight tone. A picture on the garage wall caught my eye, surrounded by other framed images I'd seen dozens of times now. But this was the moment an idea began to form. My eyes focused on the picture of Rob standing on his motorsailer with a massive swordfish in hand. "Is that your uncle's boat?" I asked over my shoulder.

"The big sailboat? Oh yeah, he bought it just a couple of years back and—" He stopped as though he'd sucked his words down mid-sentence. "Why?"

"No reason."

"I don't like what you're thinking."

"How do you know what I'm thinking?" I turned around, heading toward the office of the shop with the tool bag slung over my shoulder.

"Because I'm not an idiot," Noah snapped as he trailed behind me with nervous steps. "He doesn't keep his keys in there."

So that's exactly where he keeps them.

I opened the door without looking back, but I could sense Noah's presence behind me.

"Calm down," I said, carefully scanning the office. If Rob was anything like Valdez, those keys would be in the back of a drawer locked in a box of some sort. "I'm only leaving a note of the things I'm taking. He can take whatever the cost is out of my pay."

"Man, I don't believe that. You're freaking me out." He crossed his arms as he stood in the doorway protectively. I quickly used my fingers to slide the pen on the desk up into my sleeve. Then I began rummaging through the drawers.

"What're you doing?" Noah stepped forward.

"Just looking for something to write with." I smiled, moving my hand around in the drawer and using a slight of hand to snag the keys I felt tucked away in the drawer's corner. I didn't know for sure if they were for the boat, but I didn't mind taking my chances. As I pulled my hand from the drawer, I leaned over at just the right angle to produce the pen from my sleeve and quickly swapped the keys to my other hand.

With Noah's suspicious glare burning into me, I scribbled the note on a piece of loose paper, listing out the items I'd taken and my signature. With the keys tucked away safely against my forearm, I walked out and up to my loft to get something I couldn't leave behind. Grabbing the compass hanging from the bedpost, I made my way back down the stairs and out of the shop. And Noah was none the wiser that he'd just been robbed blind by a pirate.

8

SINKING

KATRINA

I stood at the edge of the dock beside *La Esperanza,* waiting for Milo, and thought about the irony. Somehow, I always ended up here. On a pier, looking out at the water, waiting for Milo. As much as my heart beat for him, a part of it felt a bit broken, but I could no longer pinpoint what was responsible.

The breeze blew back my hair, giving me a clear line of sight to the approaching figure looming on the water's surface. A bright white boat with high slanted sails, headed in this direction but still a way off. I didn't recognize it, but I secretly wished it was mine as I watched it effortlessly cut through the water. Footsteps from behind tore my focus from the boat.

"I knew I'd find you here." I didn't expect it to be McKenzie who'd walked up on me. I smiled, a little nervous about her untimely visit.

"Hey," I offered her a hug, noticing the rolling luggage still at her side. "Happy New Year."

"It is now that I'm back." She tossed a lock of red hair back behind her shoulder as she spoke in her signature lilt. "Ugh, my family was about to drive me insane. I drove past here on the way back from the airport and figured I'd stop to see if you were here."

I chuckled. "You couldn't even wait to unpack to see me."

"Well duh! Anyway, you about to go on an excursion?" She lifted her eyebrows as something caught her attention behind me. I turned around to see what had caught her eye out on the water.

The big sailboat I'd seen in the distance was now easing in to moor at the dock next to my boat. I watched in awe as its massive hull drifted near and dwarfed my little fishing boat in its presence. And to my utmost surprise, Milo stood proudly at the helm, his expression focused as he maneuvered the thing.

"What is this? Where did you get that?" I cupped my hands around my mouth as I called out my words so he could hear me from his place so far above me.

"Let's just say Russell isn't the only one in his family with a liking for boats." He yelled back with a smug look.

"What does that mean?"

"Noah's uncle—Russell's son—sort of lent it to us."

"Really?" I put my hands on my hips. "I didn't know Noah was Russell's grandson. This seems like a big deal. Does he know how long we're going to be gone?"

"Well not exactly," Milo said, "But let's bring the supplies aboard and I'll explain. But the important thing is that we'll be much safer traveling in this one."

Something felt off, but I reached for the cooler handle and overstuffed backpack at my side and lugged them on.

"Where are you guys going?" McKenzie asked.

"Ummm, we're just taking a sailing trip for a couple of days."

"Days?" Her eyes lit up and flashed blue like the water below us. "That sounds so cool. Can I come?" Suddenly she recoiled, grabbing her arm like she was embarrassed. "I mean I'd stay on the other side of the boat or whatever because I'm sure you guys want your privacy so like obviously I'd stay away, ya know? But this just seems so cool. And that boat is so freaking nice."

A subtle sigh escaped my lips and mixed with the salty air. How could I tell her no in the nicest way?

"Well—um…" I scratched my head and bit my lip. "The thing is…this could be a rough trip and I'm not sure—"

I was unable to finish my statement when an oddly familiar voice tore through the air and frantic footsteps wobbled the wooden deck beneath my feet.

"Hey! I'm calling the cops if you don't get down from there right now!" I was startled to see Noah rushing across the pier, shouting in a panic directed at Milo.

"What?" I cried, glancing up at Milo, who looked completely unconcerned with the accusation as he stood leaning over the ship deck's railing.

Just then, I noticed a boat cruising out into the horizon, navigating swiftly through the outer banks toward the open ocean. A memory flashed before my eyes. I knew that boat. It was unmistakable for the bold dark blue stripes along the sides and the name on the back.

Belladonna.

Suddenly, however Milo managed to acquire this boat didn't matter. Noah didn't matter, and I knew I didn't have time to talk McKenzie into going home. Cordelia was already steps ahead of us, and if she found the trident first…

"Sure, come with us! Get your luggage." I grabbed McKenzie's arm and pulled her onto the hull as Noah stood yelling on the dock.

"Get off my uncle's boat! He's gonna kill me!"

"I'm sorry, Noah!" I shouted. "I swear it's an emergency! We'll bring it back!"

"No! Get back here!" He stepped back, as though surveying the scene of his uncle's boat adrift as the space between it and the dock widened. With obvious hesitation, he took a running leap and found himself dangling from the side of the boat. McKenzie and I rushed to pull him up.

"What the actual hell is wrong with you? All of you?" He brushed himself off as he clumsily got to his feet, struggling to balance with the boat's motion.

"It's a lot to explain," I panted as I caught my breath, "but you have to believe me when I say that your uncle's boat missing might not be the worst of our problems if we don't set sail *right now.*"

"That's it, I'm calling the cops," Noah reached for his phone. McKenzie shot me a worried look before lunging forward to stop his hand.

"Noah." In one of the calmest tones I'd ever heard from her, she spoke to him, looking straight into his face before looking back at me for a split second. "If Katrina says it's this important, it must be. She doesn't lie."

I blinked back a flood of guilt as I realized the depths of McKenzie's trust. She would blindly follow me like this, without even knowing why. And yet lying was all I'd ever done to her. I hid everything from her. But how could I tell her the truth?

It was to keep her safe. Mostly.

To my surprise, Noah seemed to listen. As though letting her words sink in, he looked at me, then back at her and finally up to Milo, who was too busy at the helm to notice.

"Why do you really need this boat?" His voice was pure. The question was genuine.

I took a breath. "This is going to sound absolutely insane."

"Well, you've already kidnapped us." McKenzie giggled. "Might as well spit it out."

"We're going after something. Something that could cause the end of life as we know it if we don't find it first."

"Man, I should've known you were crazy when I found you hiding in the back of my car. I knew something was up, but this is a whole new level of deranged." Noah threw his hands up in defeat.

McKenzie's expression began to darken, and her eyes narrowed as she pressed her brows together. "Katrina, where are we going? You're being so cryptic."

"To..." I swallowed and clenched my jaw. "To the Bermuda Triangle. To...to find a trident."

They both stared at me in silence in a way that made my gut flip like a fresh-caught fish in a net. By now our boat was far enough out that there was no chance they could get off now. They were in this whether they believed me or not.

Just then, Milo's voice broke the tension from above. "Can someone give me a hand with the sails? We need to get the mainsail up if we want to maintain speed against these headwinds."

"I'm gonna go help him," I uttered, using the excuse to slip away before one last pathetic attempt to reassure them. "You guys have to trust me. Make yourselves comfortable because this won't be a short trip."

Praying Noah wouldn't change his mind about calling the police, I climbed the short stairs up to the deck to help Milo, leaving our two new reluctant crew mates standing in silence at the stern.

"You *stole* a boat?" I grabbed the line to the mainsail, tugging it as I tried to figure out what to do with it. "From your boss?"

"If we took *La Esperanza* we might not make it back. We might not even make it there," Milo gritted his teeth, pointing at the sails. "I already unfurled the jib, now you just hold the line here and make sure it keeps tension on the winch."

I tried to follow, but this was my first experience with sailboats. I took the line in his hand and held it taught as he began to pull the seemingly endless rope out and the large sheet above us began to drop slowly.

"But you stole it, Milo! You're not a pirate anymore. You can go to prison for things like this."

"And I would've been hanged for it back in 1725." He froze for a second as his eyes sharpened at me. "Can't you see I'm trying to help? If we don't find this trident, there's a lot more at stake than incarceration, Katrina."

I groaned as I squeezed the rope in my hand. "I know..." I sighed. "I just don't want things to end badly."

"You think I want to risk my second chance at life by getting arrested? I wouldn't have done this if I didn't have to."

He wasn't wrong. I knew what it was like to be forced into something wrong in order to do the right thing. Like lying to McKenzie. Or when I had to make Dad believe I'd given up on him and Mom. But no matter how much I understood, something kept me from telling him that. So, I was silent as he walked out of the helm station and went to secure the sail into the sail bag up top.

I looked out at the water ahead. Six days of this. And once we got there, then what? How would we even know where the trident would be and how would we get to it?

I heard the banter of McKenzie and Noah below, and I knew I couldn't avoid them forever. I hurried back down to them, watching my step as the waves of the open ocean danced beneath me. They watched me with suspicion as I approached timidly.

"It's only fair that I explain to you both what's going on."

"Please do." McKenzie crossed her arms.

I asked them to sit down, because I knew there was no possible way I could give an explanation that didn't make me sound like I'd lost my mind, and I knew I'd talk in circles trying to do it. But there, as the sun rose higher in the sky and cast its glittering white diamonds across the sea's surface, I told them how I'd uncovered a mermaid's curse on an undead pirate crew last semester, and also how I broke it, and how now Cordelia was still alive and ready to take out her vengeance on the world. And I made sure to explain how we were now in a race against her to find the trident. Though I did leave out the part about me possibly being a mermaid.

"Wait," McKenzie looked down at her lap, holding out her pointer finger as though she was connecting the dots on an invisible piece of paper. "So, all those times you were out at night so late...you were meeting ghosts by the ocean? Bellamy was one of them, too? And those men who chased us downtown were...pirates?"

I nodded. "In a nutshell, yes." Noah hadn't said a word, but his wide eyes and disgusted expression were enough to tell me he didn't believe a word of it.

"You mean to tell me you actually believe her?" He turned to McKenzie.

"Well...I mean yeah, it's a little out there...but it technically makes sense. That necklace was pretty freaky. And besides, who are we to say we know what's out there? Pirate ghosts and mermaids could be entirely possible. I always say there's a reason for the stories."

"This isn't Pirates of the Caribbean, McKenzie! Your friend is just on some hard drugs." Noah stood up and began jogging up to the deck. "I'm taking this boat back right now."

"Noah, no!" I cried, shooting to my feet and running after him. The floor beneath us bobbed and rolled, making for difficulty going faster than a quick walk.

He took off, sprinting up to the control cabin. When he grabbed the wheel, I lunged forward, using the railing along the boat to pull myself forward faster. Reaching the helm, I tried to pry him from the steering wheel.

"Stop, Noah! I know it sounds impossible, but it's true! You don't understand how important this is!" I cried.

He shoved me off him and I stumbled into the control panel. I went for him again and knocked his hand from the wheel just as he had begun to turn the boat, sending us rocking and flying off balance before he regained his grip. A thud startled me as Milo leapt down from the masts and landed in front of the cabin doorway with skilled agility.

"You have to stop." His voice boomed in an authoritative way I'd only heard before when he stopped Bellamy from taking my necklace on the beach. He stepped in front of the wheel to readjust it as Noah held on tightly and resisted.

Noah flinched. He shoved Milo backward in a panicked motion. Milo shook his head as he stepped forward without losing his balance. "Calm down."

"Calm down? I need to calm down? You've kidnapped us!" He yanked the wheel to the side, tossing our boat and making me slip and tumble into the wall. When Milo pulled back on the wheel, Noah threw an unexpected punch at Milo's jaw. He then went to throw another jab. Though the first blow had caught him by surprise, Milo caught the second swing in in his palm with ease, closing his hand around Noah's fist. He pulled Noah's arm around, putting him in an armlock that left Noah grimacing.

"I said, you need to calm down." He loosened his grip on Noah after turning him around to face him, and then gave him a light shove backward. I stood tense, bracing against the doorway threshold as I watched.

"If you think you still have a home in the shop loft, think again," Noah hissed.

"Whatever you need to do, Noah. But here's the reality. You're stuck on this ship anyway. If we get to our destination and it turns out there's no trident and we're all insane, you can call the police. Send me to prison. I'll accept my punishment, however severe. But leave Katrina out of it." He looked at me as he smoothed back some stray pieces of hair falling across his eyes, only for them to fall right back. "Agreed?"

Noah's nostrils flared as he met Milo's gaze. I could see the veins in his neck as he tightened his shoulders and jaw. "Agreed. For now."

Milo stepped back, surveying the ocean before us. McKenzie had made her way up the control cabin now, a look of fear frozen on her face. I'd never seen her look so undone.

"How long are we going to be on this boat?" Her voice came out in a hoarse whisper as she hugged herself in the cold open wind.

"A few days." I shuddered.

"I think I need a minute." She turned away, making her way down into the lower cabin belowdecks.

I looked at the two men before me, my gaze catching on Milo as he stood firm, still breathing hard from the altercation. "Please stop fighting," I said.

With heavy steps, I trudged out of the helm area and followed McKenzie. Once I entered the interior below, I examined our living quarters for the next week. A high-end kitchenette wrapping along the length of the left side of the boat gave way to a small table and bar, where McKenzie sat with her head in her hands. As I made my way to her, I caught a glimpse of the sleeping area around the corner.

"I'm sorry I didn't tell you about this." I told McKenzie, taking a seat next to her softly. "It was just too fantastical of a story."

"So Milo...he's...?"

"He's a pirate. He *was*." The words felt foreign on my tongue, but it was far from the strangest of things I'd said lately. She didn't say any more, so I sat there in silence with her as the boat rocked us gently.

As I sat there thinking how I'd hidden the truth from her, I understood why Milo had hidden the note from me. He wanted to protect me. Just like I wanted to protect McKenzie. But now it had only hurt the both of us. And somewhere in the back of my head I hadn't been able to turn off the ever-present echo of Cordelia's bell-like warning.

"Always the guilty one...He'll use you like James used me...you'll see how filthy his soul is."

What had she meant? And how could I ever truly know? Milo could hide centuries of himself from me and I would never know it. Even if he truly was different now...what was he *really*? Who was he once upon another time? And did it even matter?

With these thoughts heavy as an anchor in my soul, I gave McKenzie's hand a squeeze and then stood to go, grabbing a wool blanket on the way out.

Back out on the deck, Noah kept his distance from Milo, but continued watching him like a hawk. It was cold out, and I knew Milo must've been freezing by now. Clutching the blanket in my hand, I found my feet taking me back to the control cabin.

I didn't speak a word as I draped the blanket across Milo's strong shoulders. I knew I should say something, but I just didn't know what.

"You're taking care of me, now." A ghost of vapor formed in front of his mouth as he spoke.

"We take care of each other." I corrected. The corner of his lips lifted into a smirk.

There was a long stillness before I noticed the compass in his hand.

"Does the boat's GPS work okay?" I asked. I felt him follow my gaze to the compass

"It works just as it should. But I never sail without this, no matter the century."

I should've known that. I knew his father had given it to him as he took his last breaths after Valdez shot him. That's what he'd told me. It was more to him than just a compass. As I studied the old tool intensely from where I stood, I didn't expect Milo to start speaking again.

"But right now, I have no need of a compass to tell me that something doesn't feel right between us." He turned to me keeping one hand on the wheel.

"Things are just a little intense right now. A lot of stress." I spoke fast, trying to suppress the nerves bubbling up within me.

"Well, I don't want to be just another thing that's causing you stress. Is this still about the note?" My thoughts flashed back to Cordelia, as if she was standing right there beside me whispering in my ear like some devil on my shoulder.

"*You'll see how filthy his soul is...You'll see through his façade soon enough.*"

With a shake of my head, I rubbed my eyes as I searched for my next words. I chose them carefully and spoke them as confidently as I could manage. "No, I love you, Milo. I get why you hid the note. I understand why you thought stealing the ship was a good idea. I know why you do the things you do. I think I do, at least. But sometimes I just feel like there's so much of you I'll never know.

You lived a whole lifetime before this. And for some reason that's never scared me until now."

"Then I'm glad it's not just me who feels we are sinking." His words struck my heart like a harpoon, and I wished I knew how to bring us both back to the surface.

9

All Hands On Deck

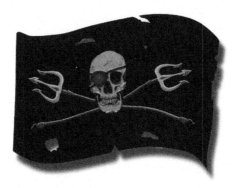

Milo

The grip of the wheel in my hand was the only thing grounding me as I stood with Katrina's molten eyes pleading with my soul. I always feared one day she would wake up and realize the man she was in love with wasn't worth her devotion. But I suppose I always hoped a fear was all it would ever be.

"You're right to wonder who I was, Katrina. But I can't change the things I've done under Valdez's command. I regret them. And I've repented of them as best I can."

"What about before Valdez? Who were you before you joined his crew?"

"I...I was just a boy. An apprentice with my father. Learning his trade. Mourning his mother." I let go of the wheel and stepped toward her gently. As I closed the distance between us, I touched her chin. "Don't start doubting me. Please. Not when we've just begun."

"I'm sorry." She squeezed her eyes shut, as though snapping out of some sort of deep daydream. "I don't know why I keep thinking about it so much. Maybe it's just the possibility that we might have the FBI waiting for us when we get back. It's not exactly easy to relax."

"That's not going to happen." I wrapped the blanket around us both and pulled us close. "And if it does, you know I'll keep you out of it."

I stared out the window, watching the blue grey water stretch before us as the boat tore through it at full speed. This was the first time in a while that I'd sailed in open water during the day like this, knowing there was nothing ahead and nothing below for leagues. A shiver met my spine as all at once I was back on Valdez' ship again, only for a split second, binding the hands of mermaids and dragging them to their temporary holds beneath the ship. I barely remembered it. I'd black out during those moments to keep myself from succumbing to insanity from the guilt. I'd often vomit afterwards, unable to eat for days. But I couldn't forget their cries and the blood-soaked deck as Valdez' men cut out their tongues to keep them from singing their songs. And worst of all I couldn't forget how powerless I was to do anything about it.

"We have a long trip ahead. I've brought enough fuel for the trip and for the journey back. But we'll have to maintain full speed if we are to reach the Triangle before Cordelia does. We might be lucky to have the extra hands aboard if the seas get rough."

I regretted that Noah and McKenzie had become unwilling participants in this voyage, but there was no room for choice now. Between the four of us, I hoped maybe we might just stand a chance. I glanced through the cabin doorway at the stern, where Noah sat bundled in his heavy dark green jacket with his back to the deck. We had almost been friends until this morning. Just when I'd started to settle, I was already ruining my chances at this new life. Perhaps I didn't belong here after all.

"I'll see if I can win them over," Katrina muttered. "But for now, they need their space. Seems like I'll have plenty of time to try."

"We should be there January 10th, and depending on if we find the trident the same day, we can be back in Constantine by the 16th."

"Classes start the 15th." Katrina's eyes widened as she groaned. "But I guess if we don't do this, there won't be a class to go to before long."

"No," I sighed. "There won't be."

She pulled away from our blanket and kissed me on the cheek with lips that felt tired. As I watched her walk back down the steps of the ship, I prayed to feel the warmth between us once again before the world ended.

Our time on the ship was lonely. My space became the helm cabin, not by choice. With a crew of only four, it was easy to stay separated on a boat of this size. Katrina came to check on me from time to time, and sometimes she would take charge of the wheel, but I was never gone from the helm for long. I made a few attempts to talk to Noah, but he refused to acknowledge me. I kept a watchful eye on him, though, because I didn't trust him not to sabotage the engine. He knew just enough to be dangerous.

Even McKenzie was quiet around me, but she was an excellent cook for all of us, being more resourceful with our food supplies than I ever would have expected. I managed without sleep. I'd had centuries of practice. But when my eyes grew heavier than I could handle, Katrina would station herself at the helm while I slept in the hammock I'd hung for myself in the cabin.

On the morning of the 10th, I stretched with a weary yawn as I studied the horizon and the stars still visible in the twilight above. According to my coordinates, we were almost there. The twinkling markers in the sky gave me their reassurance that the Devil's Triangle lay just ahead.

I nudged Katrina, who had fallen asleep in my hammock this particular evening. She sat up with a weary groan and looked ahead, pulling her blanket around herself to fight off the chill of dawn at sea.

"There it is," I said.

"How do you know?" She yawned again.

I pulled out my compass and aligned my fingers with the sky. "We're, 25 degrees north and 71 degrees west. Right where we need to be. Or at least we will be by the time the sun's fully risen."

Katrina slid out from the sling and stepped closer to the cabin window, becoming more alert as she spoke. "Do you see any sign of her boat?"

"No." I frowned. "I haven't seen the *Belladonna* once. But maybe that means we're ahead of it."

"Or that we're too late." She pushed her hair back behind her ears in a way that made heat rush to my core. "We're screwed if she got there first."

"Don't worry," I said softly. "Even if she made it there first, she can't dive down that far to look for it. She lost her tail, remember?"

"I just hope th—" her voice caught in the air, as though a ghost had clasped a hand over her mouth mid-sentence. "Milo?"

At the utterance of my name and her eyes growing wide, I turned to see what she saw. The light of dawn had vanished in an impossible instant, obscured completely by some black storm cloud growing more threatening by the second. They puffed up like giants, swallowing the line between the sky and sea whole.

"That came from nowhere," I uttered. I studied the clouds with suspicion and noticed the waves rising in the distance. I'd spent a great portion of my life weathering storms at the mercy of the ocean. But this storm looked unlike any other I'd ever encountered. It looked like the legends every sailor had heard but had yet to ever lay eyes upon.

It can't be...

A strike of white lightning sent me rushing to the deck shouting. Noah and McKenzie were already out, watching the surreal scene before us from the bow.

"Don't just stand there! All hands on deck! I need to get the sails down as quickly as possible!"

I rushed to the mast as Katrina hurried to grab the lines in the control cabin. If this monster storm hit us, we stood little chance.

"Lifejackets!" Katrina cried, fetching the vests from the hatch and tossing them down to our two passengers. I hadn't even thought about them. We didn't have such a salvation back in the 1700s. As the cold sea air battered my skin, I fought the wind to the sails, which were already getting mangled in the gusts. The storm had darkened every inch of the sky. I strained to see. With trembling hands, I worked as quickly as possible, but every sail had been raised. I at least had to get the mainsail down. I had to...

I pulled the sail as Katrina fed the line, but the water below had already begun to toss the ship. I stumbled but held my ground with gritted teeth. No matter what I did, I couldn't win the wrestling match with the canvas sails. The storm had come too quickly. Desperate, I reached for my knife. I'd cut the damn thing.

Just as my blade touched the rope, a steady arm reached forward and pulled the flailing sail away from me. Noah.

"Don't think this changes anything, Sandy." He shouted over the wind. "I'm just trying not to die!"

With his added strength, we could fold the sail down as it lowered and keep it from coming undone in the wall of wind threatening to carry it—and us—away.

The ship was rocking madly now, and the sky was midnight. Wind beat against the waves, lifting the boat as though it were nothing more than a piece of driftwood. McKenzie screamed below, and Noah cursed into the wind. Oddly enough, there was no rain. Just like the rumors go...

"We have to get down. We're sure to get struck by the lightning up here!" I called out to Noah.

He nodded and we dropped down from the mast. I waited until he ran down to meet McKenzie and was out of range. There was no way we could get the other sails down. But I was going to try...

"Get down as low as you can! Go into the cabin!" I shouted to them on the deck. "The lightning is about to get worse."

Noah ushered McKenzie into the lower cabin, but Katrina stood watching me with eyes full of fear. "Go now, Katrina!"

Suddenly the boom of the mast swung around, knocked loose by the wind and struck me. The pole slammed into my back, throwing me overboard from the ship. I heard Katrina cry my name before I hit the water. A wave tucked me under. I emerged hurriedly, fighting the sting of ocean water in my eyes and lungs. When I looked up, the boat was vertical, rising up on a wall of a wave.

She lifted higher and higher until the tip of the bow looked as though it could touch the sky, and then through a horrific flurry of lightning strikes, I watched as she capsized, with Katrina, McKenzie, and Noah still on board. Then I went under, pulled into a sea of black.

10

CASTAWAY

KATRINA

My mind raced faster than the wind around us as I watched Milo drop into the raging sea. McKenzie and Noah screamed for me to get inside, but I only ran forward to the hull. I looked for him, searching the water in desperation for only a second before the boat began to lift and sent me stumbling backward. The skin of my palm pinched against the railing as I squeezed it tightly, begging my arm strength to hold out long enough to brace against this rogue wave.

But then I was dangling in the air. The deck disappeared from beneath my feet as the bow rose higher. The boat tilted in the air, then came crashing upside down. I fought to keep my grip on the slippery smooth railing as the icy water slammed into me like a freight train. I thought the weight of a sailboat coming down on me would crush me, but somehow, it felt like falling through frigid air once I hit the water.

There was a brief moment where I thought I blacked out, but I came to quickly, realizing I was still holding onto the boat, which bobbed above me on the top of the water. I swam out from underneath and upward, bursting forth up to the surface like shattering glass. I opened my eyes, expecting to see the underside of the capsized boat floating like a white hill on a blue plain, but instead, there were only fragments. The boat was gone. Bits of canvas and wood floated around me, scattered about.

Wood?

The motorsailer was made of fiberglass. But these planks and wooden pieces looked like...

Suddenly the water shook with a boom that made me shriek. Thunder, I suspected. Salt stinging my eyes like venom, I searched my blurry surroundings for any sign of the others.

"Milo! McKenzie!" I cried, turning in a complete circle to survey the endless water on all sides of me. I saw no one. "Noah! Milo!"

My breaths became rapid as the fear settled into my skin like a stone sinking to the sand. I was alone as far as I could tell. The boat was in gone...destroyed? And the sky...it was the brightest blue. Not a sliver of evidence remained of the storm that had just struck our boat seconds earlier. And I wasn't cold like I expected to be. The water was warm and calm.

I dove beneath the water, ignoring the sting of salt in my eyes as I forced them open. I looked around in the blue murk, desperate to catch a glimpse of any of the others. When I could hold my breath no longer, I darted back up to the surface. Then I shouted once more for my friends, praying they'd survived.

"Katrina!" A shrill voice in the distance made me whip around. I hadn't had a chance to put on my life jacket, so I was fighting my tired arms to stay afloat. McKenzie and Noah slowly came into view, huddled against each other a few yards away as they drifted along on a piece of floating debris.

"Are you guys okay?" The thunder struck again just as I spoke, rattling the sea and sky. "Have you seen Milo?"

They both shook their heads as McKenzie sniffed back what looked like tears as another crash of thunder exploded. But the sky was still clear.

"What is that?" Noah looked up with pressed brows.

"The thunder?" McKenzie chimed in, mascara running down her porcelain face.

"That's not thunder," Noah kept his gaze on the miles of outstretched sea before us.

I closed my eyes, becoming aware of the water around me. Somehow, I could sense its flow, its movements, and its currents. It carried vibrations as subtle as a spring breeze along the length of my fingertips. The rumble in the distance became strangely clearer to me as the sensation of the sea rippled around me. Noah was right. It wasn't thunder.

"It's a ship in the distance," I said.

"How do you know that?"

"I don't know. I can just...feel it."

McKenzie and Noah both looked at me through mistrusting eyes.

"Then let's swim toward it before it gets any farther away." Noah began kicking against the water to propel the piece of driftwood on which they floated forward.

"Wait," I said. "Milo's still not here. We can't leave without him."

"Yeah, I'm not so sure about Sandy. I'm sorry, Katrina," Noah groaned. "But we can't stay out here and miss our chance to be rescued."

I wouldn't let myself believe he could have drowned. No, he was used to shipwrecks. He *had* to have survived, somehow. At the mere thought of it, I plunged myself back underneath the water, swimming all around the area and taking in whatever my burning red eyes could. He had to be here. I had to find him. But I had to catch my breath again.

Once my head broke through the water's surface, I did my best to settle myself and cling to whatever hope I had left. I glanced around at the world of blue around me. Cerulean teal rolled calmly at the horizon's base for as far as the eye could see, stretching out to meet the pastel blue open sky. I shuddered, knowing there was no end within reach to this kingdom of sky and sea. And my heart beat quickly, frantic as I thought of this bottomless blue void taking Milo in its ruthless hold as it had once before.

There were so many things I wish I hadn't said to him, so many emotions I was working through at his expense. And now I'd lost him on the open ocean. I had to find him. I couldn't leave him behind.

Never.

I blinked back the hot tears pushing their way to my eyes as I called out his name once more.

"Milo!"

The boom in the distance made itself known once more. This time it was closer, and it was followed quickly by more sounds of the same thundering intensity.

"The ship's coming this way! There's two of them!" McKenzie's voice demanding my attention as I looked to see two dark masses on the water, approaching quickly through a dense patch of white smoke.

Boom.

Fire and smoke ignited along the side of the ship on the left, sending a swift shot into the side of the other. The smell of gunpowder mixed with sea salt and tickled my nostrils. Cannon fire. I squinted in disbelief at the sight of billowing sails and a black flag as the smog cleared just enough to make out the looming silhouettes.

More cannon fire erupted through the air, rattling my bones as the ships drew near. These were no modern-day yachts or sailboats. These were wooden warships. Galleons. One with a Spanish flag, and the other flying a black flag proudly.

In disbelief I stared as the ships neared slowly, both sides exploding from their own cannons and from the impact of the other. I glanced over to see Noah and McKenzie frozen in place and wide-eyed.

"What is happening?" Noah spat.

"I—I don't know yet." I stuttered. I was beginning to feel a tingle all down the entirety of both my legs, and I feared what might happen if I stayed in the water too long. I'd never swum this long. Except for once.

The battle between the two dueling ships continued until the Spanish ship appeared to retreat in haste. It seemed somewhat damaged, attempting to flee before it took a hit that could sink it. But as it turned, the opposing ship launched out a flaming barrel with an intense cry, then fired at the low point of the hull. The blast crippled the ship as it sent wooden splinters flying, and its stern began slowly tilting downward into the water.

"Is this some kind of reenactment? Way out here?" Noah swam closer to me, his eyes wide with disbelief.

"I...I'm not sure." I choked on the words. Nothing felt familiar out here. Not that the middle of the ocean was a familiar place. But even the air seemed different.

The battered Spanish ship turned its sails and pulled away as quickly as her battered body allowed. The victorious shouts of men reached my ears in the distance as the pirate ship followed, closing in quickly like a lion on an injured gazelle.

Even from our distance, we could make out the ropes shooting out like webs from the side of the pirate ship, snagging on the enemy's starboard side and pulling it in to meet their own ship's hull. Through the sounds of clanging and pistols blasting, my terrified companions and I watched with the realization that what we were seeing was all too real. A battle on the waves was unfolding right before our eyes, a brutal welcoming into a time long past.

"I think this is real," McKenzie whispered. "I think they're really fighting."

I glanced around once more for Milo. I was shaking now. The humid air wasn't enough to fight back the eerie chill penetrating my flesh as I processed the reality that he'd never come up from the water. And my heart was sinking.

I was so fixated on Milo's fate, lost in a watery trance of blue and grey melding together before my eyes, that I hardly noticed when the ships became silent as the pirate crew crossed back and forth across gangplanks, taking what they could from their defeated opponent with quick, confident steps.

"We have to flag them down." Noah's arm shot up, waving and shouting for help.

"What if they kill us?" McKenzie gasped.

"It's still a better chance than staying out here in the middle of the ocean."

Noah was right, but I couldn't seem to dig any words from the pit of my chest. I was speechless. Stunned. Because the ache in my core was enough to paralyze me as I realized that we might leave this wreck without Milo.

The ship with the black flag eventually loosened the ropes tethering it to the Spanish, its sails catching the wind like kites that carried it forward. It drew near to us, casting a looming shadow that made me swallow a lump in my throat.

"What's this?" An unyielding male voice shouted from far up on the ship. "Shipwrecked castaways? Well, bloody sink me! Throw the line."

A rope hit the water in front of me with a thud. Noah took it, handing it first to McKenzie, then looking to me to grab onto it second. I furrowed my brows at him in hesitation. He glanced out to the sea at our side.

"He isn't here. He's...he's gone." I was surprised when he looked down. "I'm sorry."

I nodded, my voice seemingly spent as nausea and dread rose in my stomach. The ocean all around me became mist as it spun in circles around me. Like mixing paints, the sky and sea became one blur, and I knew if I was standing, I'd be wobbling. The water around me was the only thing holding me upright in place.

"I can't leave him...I'll stay. You go." I sucked in a breath. "I'll stay."

"Look, I get it, but you can't stay here in the middle of the Atlantic."

I thought of what might happen. I could stay here. I could wait for him. Noah didn't know what I was capable of. If I stayed in this water long enough. If I dove down deeper...

"Hurry up or we'll leave the lot of you to drown!" A crewman called from the deck, manning the rope we were climbing up.

"Come on, Katrina," Noah tucked his arm through mine, pulling me with him as he gripped the thick rope. "You know you have to."

I could no longer tell if my eyes burned from the salt or from the tears I was fighting back. But I couldn't argue with him. I knew I couldn't stay, and I took hold of the rope, too. But my body wouldn't let me go on without my heart.

Clutching the rope as it hoisted us upward, I felt my hands slipping. Water cascaded off my body as we rose, but with each thought of abandoning Milo, my grip weakened. I felt my senses fading, and the sea pulled me back.

I could see only blurry figments of reality. I looked up at the giant ship towering over me. The sounds I heard were muffled, but I could make out a voice just well enough to catch the last bit of someone calling to the crew.

"Damnit, I didn't just scupper that galleon just to be playing rescuer. Get her up or leave her."

Someone dove in for me—it was Noah, I think. He wrapped the rope around my waist and then called back up to the men on the ship.

"She's just in shock!" He shouted. "Pull us up!"

I felt my weight sink into the rope as Noah supported the rest of me. My vision cleared slowly as I passed the wood carvings on the ship. The side was scuffed and scratched from cannon fire, but still the cedar siding looked sturdy, the armored hull just as carefully crafted as the mermaid bow ornament carved from the same wood. She faced outward toward the ocean, with both arms behind her as though she was cutting through the water with ease. But she wasn't as free as she looked. She was bound to this ship. And now so was I.

Noah helped me over the hull, and McKenzie rushed to my side as I gathered my senses. A few small coughs escaped my lungs, spitting up water I didn't realize I'd swallowed. In an eerie silence, I could sense the bodies standing around me. Heavy boots reverberated against the wooden floor. Wood creaked. Sails flapped.

"A woman aboard is bad luck they say." A calm but unwavering voice carried across the deck as footsteps neared. The crew around me parted as a man walked closer, his long black coat drifting behind him like a cloak. The captain, I imagined. He went on, his voice smooth and stern. I recognized it all too well. "But fortunately for you, I'm not superstitious. Because it looks like I'm your last hope, love."

I squinted, looking up at the brazen blue eyes staring down at me through locks of raven black hair escaping from beneath a leather captain's hat.

"Bellamy?"

11

WELCOME ABOARD

KATRINA

I shook the water from my hair and face, blinking in disbelief.

"*Captain* Bellamy, lass. Good on you that you've heard of me. Saves me the explaining." He looked me up and down, as if disgusted or confused. I couldn't tell which as he glanced away from me and toward my two friends.

"Do you lubbers have names?" he asked with an arched brow above kohl-smudged eyes.

"Is anyone going to explain what the hell is going on?" Noah shouted after an awkward pause.

"We rescued ya." A gruff crewman watching beside us spoke up. "What more is there to explain?"

Bellamy cocked his head with hardened eyes. "Aye, we did. You'd think these castaways would be a little more grateful."

"No, we are," McKenzie uttered, her voice shaking tenderly. "We're grateful. But we just don't know where we are."

"Does it matter?" Bellamy jeered. "Your safe for now, only because I lost some men during that little cannonball swap and needed replacements. You weren't exactly what I was hoping for, but..." He eyed us all up and down, no doubt confused by our jeans and hoodies with zippers.

Their voices faded from focus as I looked around, taking in the sight of the ship deck and the crew hustling to and fro, working on side repairs and rigging, polishing cannons and rolling barrels into place. I remembered what Cordelia said about the trident in the triangle and held my breath. Time. Life. Space. It controlled all three within the oceans.

Time.

"Bellamy," I interrupted, still watching the scene before me and remembering the sky above us was not the same one we'd been under an hour ago. "What year is it?"

Bellamy's perfect lips curled into a mocking smirk. "You must've hit your head in the wreck, love."

"Just tell me, please. Maybe I'm confused like you say. But just tell me the year."

Bellamy didn't speak, but reached into a leather pouch at his side beneath the folds of his coat and tossed a coin in my direction in one swift motion.

In an instinctive reaction, I managed to catch the coin and took one look at its rough bronzed exterior before the raised numerals caught my eye.

"1720?" I said the date printed on the coin's rim aloud, confirming my own horrifying suspicion. "The year is 1720?"

"Something like that," he chuckled. "But really who's keeping track out here on these waters?" A sudden drop hit his voice, as though veiling something serious.

"This is a joke." Noah jumped in nearly before Bellamy had finished speaking "This can't be real. Am...am I getting punked?"

"I'm so sorry. To both of you," I muttered, tucking away the coin in my pocket and flicking my gaze between the two of them. This was the quietest I'd ever seen McKenzie, and Noah's eyes were smoldering with frustration and fear. "You were never supposed to have been part of this."

"Part of what?" Noah screamed. "Time traveling?"

Without warning, a cutlass blade lowered down swiftly right between Noah and I, creating a barrier between us. I looked up at Bellamy, who was firmly grasping the hilt. "You still haven't told me your names."

"Katrina," I uttered, gesturing at the other two beside me as a sick feeling rose in my stomach. I wasn't sure if I should've given him my real name. Would it mess with things later on in the future? I didn't know. But it was too late by the time I'd thought otherwise. "It's Katrina. And this is McKenzie and Noah."

I studied Bellamy as he gave an approving nod. Did he know about Milo yet? Had his father forced him to join the crew? Or was this before their unfortunate meeting? And where was Valdez? Bellamy had never mentioned that he'd captained his own ship before.

"I've encountered strange things at sea, but you three are quite the odd trio. You don't seem cut out for a life of sailing. I'd be hard pressed to find a way to make you useful aboard my ship. So, you'll be disembarking at our next port."

"And where is that?" McKenzie chimed, to my surprise.

"Kingston." Bellamy nodded.

"What do you expect us to be able to do there?" I asked.

"I really haven't given it that much thought, love. Your affairs off my ship don't intrigue me enough to be concerned. Be grateful I didn't leave you lost at sea."

I sighed. I don't know what more I even expected. It didn't really matter where Bellamy took us. Because the problem wasn't where. It was *when*. And I didn't even know how to begin to remedy that. And Milo. Was he unable to come with us because of some obscure rule that wouldn't allow him to go back to the time he lived? Was he left behind? Or had he been brought here, too, only to not survive the wreck?

Please, no. Not the last one.

I prayed he was safe, whatever or however that may be. I just couldn't convince myself that he'd drowned. He had to be out there. Bellamy must've noticed the tension in my face as I stared at the wet woodgrain on the deck in thought. "Relax, lass." He patted my shoulder as he turned to walk away. "It's only a few days voyage for the *Widow*. And I promise my men don't bite." With a cold glimmer in his eye, he looked back at me over his shoulder. "But I might if you're not careful."

As I stood, my nerves jumbled within me like tangled ropes, still processing the impossible reality of it all. The crew members who had been watching us resumed their duties, scurrying across, below, and above the deck. And I stared, in the same insufferable silence as McKenzie and Noah, as the *Widow* caught the wind and rocked forward across the water.

12

Every Man for Himself

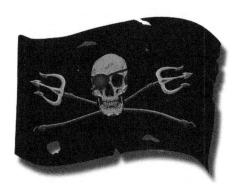

Milo

When I opened my eyes, I was face down in the sand. My arms ached from swimming. A few coughs quickly arose as I sat up to clear the seawater from my lungs. I let out a groan as my muscles flinched with exhaustion.

"Katrina," I muttered, only to realize she was nowhere to be found in and around this desolate place. "Katrina!"

I called out her name, standing to my feet and taking in the strange coast where the waves had carried me. It was a clearing at a jungle's edge. An opening lush with exotic greenery and twisting vines climbing rocky ledges contrasting with the white sands beneath. It almost seemed familiar, but then again, I'd seen just about every port in the Caribbean...even if it was three centuries ago.

I studied the untouched area, amazed at its wild beauty, already feeling the Caribbean heat I'd long forgotten as the white sun beat down on me. But a cold ghostly chokehold gripped me that no one else from the ship appeared to be here, too. I was alone. And I feared the worst.

As I walked around, surveying my surroundings and looking for any sign of survivors, I noticed a small sign of a campfire still smoldering beneath a lumbering palm. A joy rose within me, as I thought that perhaps they'd made it after all.

At least Katrina. God, Katrina has to have made it.

But one thing caught my eye that made me second guess. A rosary hung there on the sticks used for a hanging pot. My eyes followed the beads to the ground and noticed a small brown leather satchel. This wasn't McKenzie's or Noah's, and certainly not Katrina's. I glanced around, looking for any sign of the owner, and then reached down to see if there might be any fresh water at this campsite, driven by the coarseness of my parched lips. But as I leaned over, a man of my own size leapt down on top of me from the treetops above.

He collided with me, knocking me to the ground and pinning me there with his knee. A flash of silver glinted in the sunlight. I barely had time to glimpse the blade wielded as he plunged it toward my throat.

An instinct that I thought had long gone cold within me suddenly resurrected like embers from ashes. With speed I didn't recognize, I blocked the incoming dagger with a jab of my elbow, and with my other hand caught my assailant's wrist inches before his blade met its target at my neck.

My blood burned within me as I slung the man off me with and made a break out from under his weight. But he wasn't willing to let me escape.

"What do you want?" I grunted, dodging palm fronds and rocks as I kept my distance from him.

"I want to keep my dealings free from the likes of spies." His hoarse voice was like a snake's hiss, cunning and threatening. He was closing the space between us quickly, a look in his eyes I'd seen before. This man aimed to kill me. And he wouldn't stop until he had hit his mark.

He lunged at me, agile and skilled. This man was no brawler. His tactics demonstrated an adeptness best held by assassins or militiamen. Little did he know I'd had my fair share of stealthy combat. Valdez would send me aboard other ships to steal their maps or contracts often enough. If I was caught, I had to put an end to things quietly. This would be no different if need be.

The man leapt for me, curved blade in hand. I reached toward my hip for a sword that wasn't there. Foolish mistake. I'd given him a split second of opportunity to take advantage of my distraction. He swiped his knife across my cheek.

The blood mixed with salt and sweat, singing my skin. I blinked to refocus, catching his arm just as it came down again. This time, he blocked me too. Then he shoved me backwards with a roar of determination. I fought the pain that reverberated through the back of my head as he pinned me against a large rock wall. Wedging my foot, between his, I knocked him off balance, just enough that I could grab the hand that held the blade, turning it on him in a struggle that intensified with each passing second.

"I'm not a spy," I spat through gritted teeth. My jaw was so tightly clenched, my teeth ground together in pain. I could only see the tip of his nose and jaw, under the shadow of the hooded cloak he wore that obscured everything else above.

"You're one of Kellem's. I knew he'd stick his damn nose in this," he grumbled, pushing his forearm against my hold to force his knife closer. "I'll send him a message about meddling in affairs he won't be likely to forget soon."

"Kellem?" I knew that name. A rival of my father's...long ago.

"Stop! Just listen to me," I uttered under my strained breath, bracing with all my strength against the quivering arm pushing into me. A few more centimeters and he'd have my throat slit.

"Just face your fate like a man." With one sudden burst of energy, he fought his way through my defensive grip. I had to make a choice. If I continued to hold back, I knew he would eventually overpower me once I tired out. I released my hold, sliding downwards below him as fast as I could manage as his upper body flew forward into the now empty spot against the rock wall. He turned, grabbing me from behind before I could regain my footing and get farther away.

But a sharp metal clang against the rocks was music to my ears. He'd dropped the knife in his effort to seize me.

In our grappling, he held me in a tight chokehold from behind. I wrestled against him as he squeezed until my vision went blurry. My legs buckled and I used the momentum to toss us both to the ground, where his grip on my remained unbreakable. Prying his bicep from my throat was impossible in this position, so I blindly felt around me for the dropped blade. By some divine mercy, my fingers worked the blade into my hand as the last of my vision faded, and with the blade pointed back, I plunged it into the man's side.

His death grip on me loosened, as a short breath of surprise escaped him. I turned to catch him on the way down, my own vision still spinning.

"I'm sorry," I uttered, watching the life leave his surprised gray eyes. I eased him to the ground. This wasn't what I wanted. I hated killing.

With fresh blood staining my hands, I walked back to the campfire without looking back at the body. I took the rosary into my hands and said my penance.

"Forgive me." I clutched the red beads, staring into the ground as I thought of the final moments of the man's life I had just taken. My stomach turned.

He'd spoken of Kellem. Kellem Thatch. I hadn't heard that name in quite literally forever. Who was this man? I glanced over at his lifeless corpse meters from me. His clothing was old. Not in age, but in fashion. Beneath his leather baldric, the hooded vest cloak hinted that he wanted his identity concealed out here for whatever reason. His brown leather boots, loose tunic and breeches certainly didn't look to be anything belonging in the modern world. In fact, they were exactly the sort of thing I might've worn...back in my adolescence.

With a chill, my jaw tensed as I took another look at the landscape. I took out my compass and noted the North just to the left of the tree line. The longer I studied it—the shore, the channel leading out into the sea, the foliage and the barely visible trail leading into the tropical forest flanked by rocks and boulders—I recognized it. This was a clearing I'd come to a few times as a boy playing with the other village children. We'd follow the trail and pretend it led to some new world. But we'd only be met with another variation of the same coastline we'd seen every day of our lives. Just another shore. And we'd turn back and follow the trail that would lead us back to the filthy buzz of Nassau.

So why was this man here? And what secret business did he have with a cheat like Kellem? Or rather his rival...my father.

I hesitated before walking back to the man's body and pulling off his boots and the rest of his clothing. He was roughly my size. If I truly was where I thought I was, and *when* I thought I was, I couldn't be drawing attention to myself in the cargo pants and windbreaker jacket I wore. I swapped out my clothing for his, refusing to leave him unclothed out of respect.

In the vest pocket, I found a note that I was quick to unfold.

Henry,

The Company will be delivering your share of what I owe at Rock-shore Point anytime between the tenth and thirteenth of August. If you're not there, they will not come looking for you, believe me. This is a bit of an inconvenience for their route, so be grateful I'm persuasive. There are those watching me now that we're making a name for ourselves on these seas. The Company has made it clear they need me. My fleet can transport as many as they need. And their desperation is too profitable. So don't cause any uproars if you want this balance settled.

-Tiburón

Tiburón was a nickname my father called me. He'd picked it up from Spanish sailors on one of his many voyages to the West Indies. And it stuck.

Kellem was another merchant—a crooked one and my father's rival. And this man thought I worked for him. The signature was my childhood nickname. My father had written this note. And that meant I was back in Nassau before I became part of Valdez's crew. My guess was around 1720. I would've barely been fifteen years old.

I tucked my compass away along with the bloody rosary and took a step in the worn leather boots I'd now claimed as my own. There was no sign that Katrina or the others survived the wreck, at least not here. With my heart torn in a million ways, I pulled the hood over my head, drawing it close to hide my face in shadow as I followed the trail to town, where I prayed I'd find them.

13

CAPSIZED

KATRINA

We sailed on, the Caribbean sun showing no mercy as Bellamy's ship sliced through the water with surprising speed for a ship of its size. I sat on the deck floor with McKenzie and Noah, our backs to the hull as we did our best to stay out of the crew's way.

"If we're really stuck in the past, how are we supposed to get back to the present? How did this even happen?" McKenzie blurted out, her eyes red and puffy and her fair skin already beginning to turn pink from the harsh sun.

"It...It must've been the trident. Cordelia said it controls all time in the sea." I blew a lock of hair from my face in defeat. "I think we got too close or something."

Noah glanced at me, holding onto a long pause before responding. "So, all this time...all the mysterious disappearances of planes and ships...they were just going through some wormhole of time travel."

"I guess so." I shrugged. "But now I'm afraid of what that means in our time. If we're here—not there—that means Cordelia has nothing stopping her from getting the trident."

A spark of light lit up Noah's eyes. "Unless we get it first."

"So, you admit that I'm not crazy?"

"I mean I'm not sure denial would do me much good now. As much as it sounds like bullshit, it's clearly not."

McKenzie leaned in. "Then what do you mean?"

"I mean if we find it 300 years sooner, maybe we can hide it somewhere else."

"That actually makes a lot of sense," I uttered, "But *how* is another question. I don't even know how close or far we are." I looked down as a sudden sadness struck me in the chest. "Milo would know."

I could feel both their eyes on me, and I couldn't find the strength to lift my head.

"If he was here...he would know," I said. "He would know what to do."

A vision of the note left on my door flashed before my mind's eye. I'd gotten upset with him for trying to keep me safe. And now I would give anything to have him here to do just that. I'd asked him to trust me. Now I needed to be able to trust myself.

As McKenzie and Noah talked amongst themselves, I stood to my feet, over-looking the long stern pointing to the horizon. My eyes followed the line of the ship deck until they rested on Bellamy, talking to one of his men near the helm.

I studied him. His piercing blue eyes seemed softened here by the rugged dark stubble lining his jaw. His hair was unkempt, unlike when I knew him, but it suited him in this role. He seemed sprfrom helier, more youthful, and definitely cockier—which I didn't think was possible. But there was also a sternness about him that wasn't there before. He was captain of this ship and he made sure everyone knew it. I could see a version of Valdez in him here, but not in the worst way.

As he finished the discussion with his crewman, he casually turned his face to glance in my direction as I was observing him. I looked away, but I knew I wasn't quick enough. He'd seen me. Our eyes had met for only a millisecond, but it was one millisecond too long. I tried to focus on the horizon ahead of me as heat rose to my cheeks, burning hotter than the white sun above.

If only he knew we'd met before. If only he could remember his future with me. It'd be a lot easier to convince him to help us. But to him, I was just some stupid girl washed up in a shipwreck.

When night fell, we tried sleeping on the deck. It was much too stuffy for us belowdecks, and the smell wasn't very appealing either. I couldn't sleep, though. There were too many thoughts crowding my head, leaving no room for rest, despite the exhaustion in my body. I worried about Milo, and the trident, and getting back to the present—if there was even a present to go back to at this point. For all I knew Cordelia had already gotten her way and the modern world I knew was underwater.

I wanted to watch the stars, but the thin layer of clouds above hid them from me. The full moon, however, was bright enough to shine through, illuminating the deck enough. I could plainly see McKenzie and Noah lying limp as they slept, backs to each other on the wooden boards. Noah had sworn he wasn't going to sleep since he didn't trust anybody here, no matter how tired he felt. But the steady snore sneaking from his mouth said otherwise.

I stood up, examining the deck. It was mostly empty, with the exception of a few half-drunken sailors lying against barrels in a partial slumber. But surely they wouldn't notice—or care—that a castaway was making her way to take a look over the edge of the boat.

Taking a deep breath, I didn't spend too much time looking down at the water. I knew better by now. But as I strode along the hull, I inwardly groaned at what I was considering. But if it could help me find Milo...I could swim back to the wreck site and look for him. Sure, it was dangerous, but it certainly wasn't the riskiest thing I'd ever done for him. The only problem was that I didn't exactly know to bring out that special side of me. But it was the side I would need to survive a solo search and rescue in the sea.

The side with a...tail.

I swallowed. And with one last glance at my sleeping friends, I dove into the water, knowing they would be safer with Bellamy than with me. I couldn't leave Milo. I wouldn't believe he was gone until I saw it with my own eyes.

In the darkness I shuddered at the depth beneath me. I couldn't see through the black depths, and I wasn't sure I wanted to. I knew it wasn't enough just to be in the water. Nothing had activated a transformation in me the entire time we were floating about hours earlier. But I didn't know what else to do. The only time I'd changed, I was at the bottom of the ocean. Maybe I needed to dive deeper to take on the form of myself I was sure had taken over that night I jumped overboard from the *Siren*.

Instinctively, I drew a breath and swam downward into pitch blackness. Some part of me wanted to scream and scramble back to the boat, while another wanted to swim deeper, giving myself fully to the call of the depths. The sea around me terrified me with its mystery and nourished me with its embrace all at once. But nothing happened. I still had legs and I knew I couldn't swim across the ocean like this.

A panic swept over me as I realized this plan may not be working like I anticipated. I quickly swam upward to think more, only to come up short. I dipped back under the water, releasing my air in a string of bubbles from my nose. Sinking like a rock, I looked upward. Even the moonlight was too weak to break through the water's thick surface. So, I kept my gaze focused on the heavens I had no choice but to imagine, just knowing the sky was somewhere up above me. My lungs burned and my heart raced with fear. It wasn't working. I wasn't changing.

As the breath I was holding diminished, and my lungs begged me for oxygen, I started to regret this experiment. I quickly kicked my legs out and swam as fast as humanly possible upward. But I had sunk too far. I couldn't get to the surface fast enough.

My head grew heavy as crushing darkness closed in around me. I thought this was what I wanted, but now that it was happening, I was stricken with fear. The horror of the nothing below me wrapped around me like a smothering cloak. And I wanted out.

A shadow approached, and I flinched. Here, suspended in the shadow of the sea, there was no telling what sort of creatures lurked below. I thrashed, yearning to race upward, but I wasn't sure which way was up anymore. But something splashed above. I saw a stream of bubbles jet behind a shadow that had just shattered through the water. Just before I blacked out entirely, someone embraced me, and swam upward with me pressed against them. I still retained some senses, but if I knew if I opened my mouth to inhale, as I so desperately wanted to do, I'd be out.

Just when I thought I'd have to succumb to the instinct to breathe, I broke through the water's surface, wrapped in the arms of a heaving Bellamy.

"The bloody hell are you doing?" He panted, water snaking down the sleek wet locks clinging to his forehead.

"I might ask you the same thing." I choked. His grip on me tightened, and he pressed me to him in an aggressive manner as he guided us both to the hull of the ship.

"If you can't learn to watch your footing on this ship, next time I won't be so chivalrous."

I nodded, conflicted. My body was grateful that he'd pulled me from that torment, but my mind knew it was only through torment I could become who I needed to be. He'd ruined my only chance at going back to find Milo.

He grabbed a rope hanging from the side of the ship and handed it to me. "Ladies first." He cocked his head and rolled his eyes, seawater still dripping from his brow.

Reluctantly, I pulled myself up, clambering up to the hull with tired arms. I glanced over and saw that McKenzie and Noah were not where I had left them. Bellamy must have noticed.

"Don't worry," he grumbled, stepping onto the deck and walking past me. "They're safe belowdecks. I offered them separate arrangements when I saw your lady friend was drawing...unnecessary attention. And the boy wanted to go with her." I breathed a sigh of relief. Bellamy kept his back to me and strode across the deck, watching his own soaked footsteps as though he didn't trust where they might lead.

"And where are you going now?" I called out.

"Back to my quarters. I didn't expect to be going for a late-night swim."

"What were you doing out here anyway?" I asked. No answer. "Bellamy."

"You are to address me as 'Captain.'"

"You never told me you were a captain."

Bellamy stopped. "What do you mean? I just met you. And I would think it was obvious regardless."

"No," I said softly, not sure why I was telling him this. Maybe I just wanted to see if some part of his soul recognized mine. We never had a proper goodbye. "I think we met before."

With a sly step, Bellamy turned to face me.

"Trust me, love. I would never have forgotten that pretty face."

"Fair enough." I blushed, despite the cool air chilling my wet body. "But I thought your father was captain."

"You know my father?"

"Sort of," I shrugged. It then occurred to me that I had no idea what Bellamy knew at this point in history. I didn't know if he hunted mermaids yet, or if he even knew they existed. And suddenly I realized how dangerous things could have been if he had jumped into the water just a few moments later than he had, if my idea had worked, and he had found me as something...else.

"Captain Valdez," I uttered, the name sour on my lips. "He's quite the man so I hear." I hoped to press him to find out what I could. Maybe knowing *when* to start was the key to getting back home.

"He's a good captain. A poor excuse for a father, though."

"You don't like him?"

Of course, I knew Bellamy hated him in the future. But I had no idea he was at odds with him before.

"I respect him as a seaman. And as a result, he's given me control of this brig. It's all business. Nothing more."

"Oh," I sighed, not knowing what else to say.

Bellamy turned around swiftly, a move I didn't expect. He walked back toward me, the lanterns on the ship giving his skin a touch of a warmth I'd rarely seen on him. But the light only reached so far, and the rest of him remained cast in shadow. For a moment, he reminded me of a ghost, half of him pulled in by the darkness of the night. But his piercing blue eyes still shone through. "You're welcome," he uttered.

I realized I hadn't acknowledged that he'd saved me—even though he'd actually sabotaged my plan. But I couldn't let him know that, of course. "Sorry," I muttered. "Thank you. I'll be more careful."

Bellamy held those blue eyes on me like anchors that had taken their hold, and I pushed away the silent urge to say more. It'd be a lie to say I hadn't thought of him from time to time since the night I broke the curse. But I convinced myself this wasn't what it felt like. This wasn't meant to be a chance to tell him things I never got to say. This was just a fluke. And a huge inconvenience to stopping Cordelia.

I turned away, returning my thoughts to Milo and how I could possibly find him. I refused to think he hadn't survived. He had to be out there somewhere. And I'd brave that dark sea if it meant I could find him. Because I knew I couldn't stay here.

"You're cold." Bellamy's voice cut like a steel blade through the silence of the night. Keeping my back to him, I looked down, noticing the goosebumps along my arms.

"I'm fine. I'll dry."

"No, you can't stay out here like that. It'll only get colder."

"Since when are pirates such gentlemen?"

"Who said I'm gentle?" He grabbed my arm, yanking me forward without hesitation. "I just don't want a sick body aboard infecting my crew."

He pulled me behind him toward the cabin door, and I dug my heels into the floor, fighting his grip.

"Let go of me!" I cried, only to provoke a stoic chuckle from him. He stopped, turned to face me, and then scooped me up like I was no more than a child, throwing me over his shoulder as I wriggled to free myself.

"Don't worry, love. I just need to keep you healthy until we reach port and I can get rid of you. So, you'll be staying where it's warm till you're dry."

As he swung the cabin door open, he pulled me inside and swiftly released my arm, making me stumble. "Now stay here," he growled. He locked the door and sauntered to a hanging hammock bed in the corner, pulling a blanket down from it and tossing it in my direction. "Take this and don't argue."

I caught the heavy blanket with two hands. The threading woven within was soft like lamb's wool, and it smelled of sweet spice, rum, and smoke. I yearned to wrap my chilled body in it, but I resisted, eyeing Bellamy cautiously.

He ran his fingers through his damp hair, shaking it to dry, before removing his heavy, soaked coat. I glanced away when I caught sight of his wet tunic clinging to his chest, the shape of his pectoral muscles easily visible. As he began to peel his tunic from his waist and tugged it upward, I failed to stifle a sound that made my discomfort obvious. "Turn around if it bothers you, lass. I'm not sleeping in these wet clothes."

I searched for words as he continued to undress. The tattoos on his torso and chest held me captive. I felt a strange flutter in my chest when I realized the anatomical heart was there, inked onto his arm, but lacked the two arrows he would add 291 years later. Guilt washed over me as I let my eyes linger a little longer just as he began to undo his belt buckle. Milo was still in the forefront of my mind, and the thought of him was just the encouragement I needed to finally turn around and face the wall.

The sound of pants dropping and the jingling of a belt rattled on the floor. I steadied myself against the gentle ship's movement, trying to brush away the fact that Bellamy stood fully unclothed just a few feet behind me. My heart pounded and my muscles tightened as the air around me became thick. Without thinking it through, I reached for the door handle right in front of me. Though I'd seen Bellamy lock it, I thought maybe I could somehow get it open.

With an unsuccessful jiggle of the knob, I knew I'd made a foolish choice. Within seconds, a muscular tattooed arm from behind me snatched up my hand, pushing me to the wall, firmly enough to rattle me. I fought the conflicting sensation I felt as Bellamy breathed out against my skin, lingering by my ear. When he lowered his face to mine, I glanced down to see he was only clad in a pair of dry dark burgundy pants.

"Listen to me, love." The mocking pet name left his lips quickly and abruptly, as though he'd just chewed on something bitter. "Stop flattering yourself. If I wanted to do anything more with you, I would have."

If he wanted me to act afraid, he would be disappointed. He'd held a sword to my chest before, ready to cut out my heart. And he didn't do it. I wondered if with that perspective, I knew him better than he knew himself.

"Flatter myself? Take your own advice. I'm not worried about you." I narrowed my eyes at him. "I just prefer not to sleep in the same room as a filthy jackass."

Bellamy grinned. "You're on a pirate ship, my dear. You're surrounded by jackasses. Welcome aboard." He looked down, as if he was deciding whether or not to continue. When he spoke again, his voice was softer, more serious, but he still grinned at me as though he found something funny that was unknown to me. "Listen, I have no room in this heart for anything but the sea. And I'm loyal to only her. Now shut up, quit pissing about so much, and put that blanket around you before you catch a fever."

I eyed him suspiciously as he proceeded back to the trunk chest where the rest of his clothes lay, and pulled a billowy, loose-fitting tunic over his head. I internally chastised myself for the heat rushing to my face as I stood, my back still to the wall, watching the muscles in Bellamy's back and shoulders flinch as he worked his way into the thin shirt and then casually climbed into his hammock bed.

Secretly, I was glad for the blanket and warm area to stay, but I didn't want to make Bellamy think I wanted to be here. I slowly sat down, resting my back against the wooden wall behind me and closed my eyes as I wrapped the blanket around me tighter. My damp clothes were uncomfortable, and I yearned to peel them off, but I just couldn't bring myself to do it with Bellamy mere feet from me.

And it was then that the realization sunk in and settled like the wet clothes on my skin. I was really trapped here. In a ship in the literal 18th century, without a clue how to get back. Milo was missing, and my parents would be wondering what happened to me. My friends were trapped here too. All because of me. And Cordelia's words flashed before my mind as I fought away the unwanted, shameful desire I felt rising in me for the man sleeping across the room.

You're just as soulless as me.

The last thing I heard was the slightest hint of a snore from Bellamy's hammock. It was then that I finally allowed myself the luxury to sleep.

14

IN THE OFFING

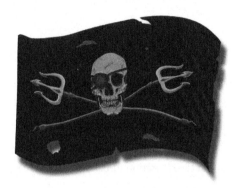

MILO

I'd been searching the island for hours, slowly accepting the harsh truth that my friends didn't seem to have ended up in the same place I did. But I had to find them. I *had* to find Katrina.

With a weary soul and aching body, as if by instinct, I wandered home. My feet couldn't help but carry me through the village where I grew up, knowing every one of my steps like I'd taken them yesterday. I wondered what awaited me should I find the courage to see my childhood home. A churning in my stomach quieted my racing thoughts.

Avoiding curious stares, I kept my head tucked low beneath the cloak hood, concealing most of my face. If this was the year I suspected it was, I couldn't risk people recognizing the face of a man who was meant to be a boy. And I certainly couldn't attract the attention of my father, or anyone who might've known us then.

Palm trees grew wild in every corner of the failed colony, poking up from the sand and rising higher than the small wooden houses plotted along the island. Shops like the fisher's stand, the sailmaker, and the tavern brought some sense of order to the place. It was an otherwise lawless place, with taverns and brothels plentiful. Disease was as rampant as the debauchery.

Diseases like that of the sudden infection that took my mother. I knew then that Nassau wasn't the place I wanted to make my home. I hated to admit I was even a citizen. The city was all I knew of a home outside of my birthplace in Portsmouth, England. And when my father was offered a stipend by the king to settle and maintain trade routes in a place the government refused to touch, I knew there was no escaping it. Not till I was old enough.

And yet, as these sour memories invaded my mind, I found some strange peace being back in the time of my adolescence. I smiled slightly at the thought that maybe I'd see my father here. Just to catch a glimpse of him before his untimely fate...

And that's when I caught sight of something that made me shudder in the harbor. Docked at port, it floated, proud and regal—the *HMS Regal Mercy*. A Royal Navy ship that I recognized without trying. I remembered that ship visiting on a very particular day.

I stopped at a nearby tavern by the name of *The Salty Crow*. It stood on the edge of town, frequented by pirates, visiting officials, and locals alike. I knew the owner, old Codface, well enough. With his tavern closest to port, he had the monopoly on fresh gossip from the harbor.

"I'll have a round," I uttered, and watched the withering man slide me a mug overflowing with cheap beer. He wasn't even that old. But his skin had been lost to the sun long ago. "How long has that ship been docked there?" I asked.

"Just got in last night." Codface wiped his face with the back of his arm. "Something about withdrawing funding or something or other. Some bloke going around offering pirates a pardon if they'll just be dumb enough to give it all up. Nothing but the damn king trying to screw us over as usual, I'm sure."

"Hmm. Benjamin Hastings," I said, trying to make it sound like a question as I took a swig from my cup. But I didn't need to ask. I knew exactly who was here and why. He'd helped found this republic, and now he was turning his back on those same pirates who helped him build it. "He's at it again, eh? Maybe Daven can hold him over just a little longer. Before they start hanging us in the streets." My father was one of the few liaisons left here willing to negotiate with both pirates and privateers. He'd be one of the first to report on the state of things when the government paid a visit.

"Aye, a proper mess it is," Codface coughed. "Now pay up."

I dug into my pocket and flicked a coin toward his open palm.

"You look an awful lot like Daven," he said with a strange smile. "You a relative here on business?"

"Something like that." I barely noticed what I was saying. I was too busy turning over the reckless idea forming in my mind. If Hastings was here, that meant Valdez wasn't far behind. I remembered this week perfectly. My father turned to working with Valdez because of the king's ever-growing threats to revoke stipends for tradesmen as the state of Nassau worsened and dealings there became less and less profitable. And Valdez would be here for his next trade deal. But I knew how it would end.

And that's when I thought it.

What if...?

What if I could stop my father's fate? The rosary in my pocket suddenly felt heavy, and I reached in to close my fingers around it. I was given this moment—this chance to be here, in 1720, the exact week my father was double-crossed. It would be the day after tomorrow. What if I could keep it all from happening?

I had to find him. I could hardly suppress the eagerness flurrying in my bones to get up and run home. But I had to. To keep safe the identity of the mysterious man under the hood, I had no choice but to sneak my way back to the house from my childhood.

When I crept inside, the place was just as I remembered. The smell of freshly tanned leather and the crisp scent of map parchment intermingled with that of rum and dust. The roof was still patched from the week before, when my father repaired it after a hurricane had blown through.

My gaze swept the space. My room was small, but it was all I needed as a boy. I was never in it anyway. As I wasn't now. There was no sign of a younger me here at the moment. But I knew he wasn't far. If I wasn't out sailing with my father or repairing the ship, I was out exploring and making my own secret maps of the island. I did wonder, though, if my presence here now somehow disrupted my existence in the past.

In the left corner of the house, near the hearth we never used, my mother's chair faced the center of the room. I could picture her there in it, singing slightly off-key and working her magic with a needle and thread. But the last time she'd sat in it was seven years ago, before the sickness took her. And that's why her portrait now took her place on the seat cushion.

I glanced upward, awakening a memory I'd almost succeeded at pushing away. The door to my father's room stood locked, a heavy padlock guarding the entry. It had been that way since the day Mother died. He said it was his way of protecting her memory. I never questioned it more than once. His reaction—the only time I'd ever seen him lose his temper—had been enough to keep me from prying.

And now, as a man walking in the shadows of my past, I still yearned to see behind the locked door just as much as I did in my adolescence. I walked to the lock, examining it carefully for any sign of weak points. I'd now had my fair share of practice lock-picking, and I thought this one could prove no more a challenge than the others.

But as I touched the lock, I heard voices from the outside. My father's. And someone else. I scurried to the small section of the house that acted as my room and slid underneath the bed, thankful for the silent leather boots I'd swapped out with my attacker earlier.

"I trust you found everything in accordance with what we agreed upon the last time we spoke?" My father's voice became clear as he entered the doorway, his heavy, strong steps as familiar as breathing.   "Aye," the other man's voice was one I didn't recognize, but I assumed him one of the many business partners of my father. "All but one. You were a vessel short. And I've arranged payment as such."

"You know why. My son was on board that ship."

"I don't care about your private affairs, Daven." I couldn't see the scene, but it sounded as though the man was now pacing the room. "All I know is that you wasted a whole ship that could've been carrying an extra hundred or two."

I ran through our voyages in my mind. He might've been talking about any of them. Countless times in my teenage years I'd joined my father with his fleet ships across the Atlantic. I didn't know what made this one any different. Nor what made this trip as wasteful as this man claimed.

"I used that ship to carry the textiles and dyes. There wouldn't have been room."

"You lie, Tiburón." The man chuckled, but there wasn't humor in his voice. "You can keep it up if you must, but I wouldn't if I were you. Remember the cost of keeping secrets."

"Don't speak of Mary Ann, not in my own house." My father's voice was rising, trembling as he held back an anger I'd only seen unleashed once. I wondered what my mother's name had to do with any of this.

The man with him snickered once more, and the sound of a slap like a pat on the back followed. "I didn't mention her name. You did." There was a pause. Even from my hiding space far away from them under the bed, the air was thick with tension before he spoke again. "Just hold your tongue like you always do and we'll all get along fine."

The creak of the door and the lock in place of the knob reached my ears before I'd heard my father sit down. The man had left. I couldn't see him, but I could imagine my father well enough. He was distraught, in the wooden kitchen chair, rubbing his face with both hands in frustration.

The sound of his hand slamming down on the table startled me, and I held my breath as I listened for his footsteps. He was up, walking around now. And then a rattling of something metal. He was unlocking the door to his room.

Once I heard him close the door and the sound of footsteps ceased, I let myself breathe again and crawled quickly out from under the bed and toward the house entrance. I'd be back later to find out what that conversation was about, and why it included my mother. And I'd be back to unlock that door. But for now, I just had to stay out of the way.

15

FLY-BY-NIGHT

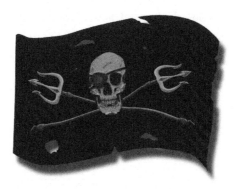

MILO

A s I wandered the streets, keeping to the shadows, my heart weighed heavy in my chest. What secrets could my father have been keeping? He was by no means a perfect man, but he was always just, fair, and hardworking. That man he spoke with, he seemed to speak with such confidence. But I knew my father.

The distant sound of thunder called my attention. The horizon was darkening, not only with the oncoming evening, but also with storm clouds on their way inland. I'd have to find a place to rest for the night. There was no more time for searching, and certainly not in a tropical storm. I'd planned to sleep in one of my father's ships at port, but that was no longer an option for tonight when the waves would soon be rioting. I reached into the leather pouch I'd taken along with the clothing from my attacker.

Thank God.

There was still a small handful of coins remaining. Enough to afford some lodging and maybe a warm meal for the night. As sorrow trickled across me, I added to my internal prayers that Katrina was somehow protected and safe. Her friends, too, of course, but most of all, *she* had to be all right.

I turned to put the dark sky to my back and began my walk toward one of the rougher streets of Nassau. I paid no mind to the drunken sailors brawling and cursing at one another in the alleyways, nor to the women calling to me through painted lips and sways as I passed.

Tugging at my hood, I entered *The Salty Crow*. Its weathered wooden sign swung in the coming wind as heavy raindrops started their descent.

"A room, please." I placed the coins on the bar counter, my head low. Codface wasn't around that I could see.

"I've got one left upstairs. Watch for the roof leaking in this storm." The bartender gestured to the staircase in the corner leading to the second floor above.

"I'd say a leaky roof trumps total lack of shelter."

"That it does, stranger." The bartender wiped his hands, took the coins and then pulled a pint out from behind the counter. "Something to warm ye?"

I nodded. "Aye."

The rum would do me good. I scooped up the pint no sooner than he'd placed it in front of me. I drank down the potent liquid, savoring every sting on the way down. But it wasn't enough to quell my empty stomach. I asked for a meal and tore into the flounder and chicken set before me. But a vaguely familiar laugh from behind made my stomach churn, and suddenly the food tasted quite foul in my mouth. That laugh was the same I'd heard in my father's house.

I turned to see a group of gamblers. The laughing man was ruddy and large—not overweight, but oversized. His bones must've been steel poles, and he carried the weight of his brawny flesh like armor. His laughter mixed with the thunder outside as he tossed the dice at his table surrounded by others small in stature in comparison. It was him.

The things he said to my father resonated in my mind, and though I knew better, I approached him. "You trade with Daven?" I uttered, careful not to sound wavering by masking my question as a statement.

"Who wants to know?" The man looked up, his voice like iron against a grindstone. I noted his missing hand, replaced with a hook as sharp as a scythe, as he peered up at me through hollow golden-brown eyes.

"I'm here on business. And Daven is my middleman of sorts. No one else. I must see to it that there is no breach of contract."

"That doesn't sound like it involves me," the man growled, returning his focus to his gambling game. "Whatever lines he's crossed with you don't concern me."

"What business do you have with him? At least help me find my lead." I forced my voice to calmness.

"Why would I disclose anything to you? I don't know you. I can't even see your face."

"I'm...Samuel...Holland. On behalf of...the Dutch East Trade Company." I used the first company name I could remember to quickly create my alias. "What business do you have with Daven?"

"Something about the way you're asking sounds personal. And you seem a little too enthusiastic to hear what I might have to say."

"Let's just say I have reasons that carry weight. If it's money you want in exchange for information, name your price and I'll get it."

The man eyed me up and down. "I don't want your money." He stood slowly, nearing me as his footsteps made the floor creak. He stood just an inch taller than me, an unusual occurrence given my near six-foot frame. "But you seem like the type to take on a fool's errand. I might could use a hand for a reckoning that's long overdue."

"I'm listening." My eagerness was getting the better of me. This was my only shot to uncover whatever business my father failed to mention to me.

"There's a sloop out in the harbor, the *Lark*." His voice lowered the longer he spoke. "Her captain's a shameless bastard who mutinied against me. I retreated and he called it weakness. He made his fortune from my losses. Took half my crew and forced me to rebuild from the bottom of the barrel. Let's just say I never completely made my peace with that." He looked bitterly at the hook attachment at the end of his arm where a hand should've been.

"And?"

"And a man hiding his face and begging for information seems like the perfect pawn to help me repay the favor."

"What do you want me to do? Spit it out." I shifted uneasily from one foot to the other.

"I want you to put that sloop at the bottom of the sea floor. If this storm doesn't get to it first."

I hesitated, knowing well who captained the *Lark*. Carl Thane. He was known for his cruelty to prisoners and sailors alike. I was sure it was him who'd taken this man's hand. He'd even tried to overtake Nassau a time or two. Before he'd disappear for months at sea. I didn't mind taking out his ship. But if it went wrong...

"I'll do it." My fist clenched and my heart dropped as the words left my mouth. "And in exchange you tell me everything you know about Daven Harrington."

"You have my word."

"What good is the word of a pirate?" I raised an eyebrow, remembering the time Katrina had asked me the same thing.

"Worth about as much as the word of a shadowy stranger...*Samuel*." He spat out the name with suspicion. "But I'm no pirate. I'm as honest a businessman as there ever was in Nassau. Just with a bit of bad luck." He winked and raised the hook he wore for a hand, turning it so it caught the light, drawing my attention to the jagged scarring around his slightly exposed wrist.

"Where can I find you once the job's done?" I uttered under my breath barely above the noise of the tavern chatter.

"I'll be here each night till I depart in three days."

"Give me your name." I knew it was a long shot to ask. But I needed something. I cursed myself for not asking sooner.

"Not part of the agreement, stranger."

"I gave you mine."

"And I know you're lying about it. So, looks like we both just have to have a little faith in each other." He grinned with a mocking air, revealing a toothy wide mouth that stretched across his broad face.

At least he was memorable. It wouldn't be terribly difficult to find a hulking one-handed man in these parts I knew like the back of my hand anyway. We shook on it, sealing the deal. Before I could say more, he turned and sat back down, resuming his gambling as though our conversation never happened.

I made my way back to my plate and pint. But the sight of the food turned my stomach. Perhaps the rum had clouded my judgment and boosted my confidence too much. I'd just agreed to sabotage a sloop. Because I wasn't sure if my father was the man I remembered. And the girl I loved was still missing. And for the first time in a long time, I didn't have a clue what else to do.

But, whether for better or worse, I had managed to acquire a task to keep me occupied until I figured the rest out. And if everything would go according to the plan I'd already devised in my head, by tomorrow night I'd have sunk Carl Thane's sloop.

16

By the Wind

Katrina

Throughout the night, I struggled to sleep. The rocking of the ship and the coldness of my wet clothing and hair kept me uncomfortable. Once I was sure Bellamy was asleep, I wandered over to the chest I'd seen him open earlier. I had to find something dry, or I really was going to get sick. I opened the chest to find what I expected—men's pants and tunics. But I didn't care. I was so cold.

I glanced over my shoulder to be sure Bellamy was still sleeping. As quickly as I could move my shivering body, I stepped out of my wet jeans and top. I kept my bra and underwear, hoping they'd hurry and dry. Slipping a tunic that was much too big for me over my head, I breathed a sigh of relief as the feel of dry clothing touched my skin.

"That's a bit big for you, love." I whipped around at the sound of Bellamy's laughter.

"Were you watching me that whole time?" I snapped.

"Hard not to when you decide to undress right here in front of me."

I shook my head, feeling the heat rushing to my face and a flutter in my stomach.

"Come here," he muttered, propping himself up in his hammock.

I hesitated but stepped closer. I flinched when he reached forward and touched my hand.

"You're half-frozen," he uttered. "Lie here with me."

"What?" I stepped backward, nearly tripping over my own feet.

"I don't believe I stuttered, lass. Body heat works wonders."

I rubbed my arms, unsure of how to respond.

"Get in. Now." His voice was solid as stone.

I choked down the feeling that this was wrong. That I was somehow betraying Milo. It was just to keep me warm, I reassured myself. Nothing more. It was either this or the cold floor again.

With careful steps, I pulled myself into the cloth hammock. Bellamy grasped me by both my arms and pulled me toward him, so that I was fully wrapped in this hanging cocoon of blankets with him. He pulled me close to him, pressing our bodies together, and I thought my wet hair would dry from the heat of my blood racing alone.

I searched for something to say, but nothing would come out. Bellamy rubbed my arms slowly, his blue eyes staring back into mine by the moonlight barely illuminating this small space through the small open slit of a window in the wall. I shivered without meaning to, and he drew me even closer. Face to face, we lay there in the hammock, so close that I could feel the warm air from Bellamy's nostrils against my neck.

"Now go to sleep," Bellamy whispered. I nodded.

What was I doing? Lying here with Bellamy alone in his quarters. All while I knew Milo was lost at sea. My conscience wouldn't silence itself, no matter how much I rationalized it. But before long my eyes grew heavy. My body was finally warm. And I finally fell asleep.

When morning came, I opened my eyes to find my head resting against Bellamy's chest, rising and falling with his slow, steady breaths. I jolted upright to see he was already awake.

"I have to go," I stuttered, scrambling out of the hammock. "I'm completely dry now." I shuffled my feet across the wooden floor to the door, nearly tripping over the long pants and swallowed by the man-sized tunic covering my upper half.

"Who is he?" Bellamy's question caught me off guard. Just as I reached for the door I stopped and looked over my shoulder, but I didn't meet his gaze. I stared at the floor. The weight of his eyes on me felt like stones tied to my ankles.

"Who is who?" I asked.

"The name you were whispering in your sleep all night long." Bellamy sat up in the hammock, dangling his sock-covered feet over them like a child on a swing. "Milo, was it?"

"I...I didn't know I said anything."

"Oh, you certainly did." Bellamy cocked his head. "Who is he? A lover?"

"Y...yes." I tried to think fast. I didn't know if saying too much about Milo here could endanger him or somehow alter the past. I was afraid to speak, not knowing how much I could safely say.

"Where is he?"

I hesitated, biting my lower lip as I fought against acknowledging the reality of what happened to Milo. "I...I don't know." Gripping the door handle, I went to open it, but forgot Bellamy had locked it last night. I waited for him to offer to open it, and when he didn't, I asked, "Can I leave now?"

"Whatever you want, love." He tossed me the key from wherever he'd been holding it. "Later we'll get you and your friends some proper clothing. I believe there might've been some women's fineries aboard the loot from the last ship we took. Surely there's something in there for you."

Great. Now he's going to make me squeeze into a corset or something.

I turned the key in the lock. Bellamy reminded me to leave it in the keyhole for him.

"Aye aye, Captain," I sneered with a roll of my eyes.

Outside it was brighter than I anticipated. After a moment of allowing my eyes to adjust to the blinding Caribbean sun, I scanned the deck for any sign of McKenzie or Noah. I was surprised when I saw them near the hull by the sail rigging. Noah was sitting on the boat's edge, and McKenzie stood listening to a crew member droning on about something.

I went to approach them, but never in a million years did I expect the crude terms that would be hurled at me as I made my way across the deck. But I don't know why I would've expected otherwise.

"Hey lads, Cap'n finally let his new wench back out and off the leash. Are we allowed to share?" One crew member called, drawing attention from the others.

"You don't know what you're talking about," I uttered. "I was just drying off. I...sort of...fell...overboard."

"I'm sure you were drying off alright." Another pirate chuckled.

With my fingers curled into a tight fist, I shook my head, trying to shake away the flush of redness I could feel flooding my face. Storming past the ogling crew across the deck, I made my way to McKenzie.

"Where were you?" McKenzie looked at me through eyes wrought with dark circles—whether from tiredness or just running makeup, I couldn't tell. Her voice still held every ounce of her usual sprightliness, however. Noah glanced at me over his shoulder, eating some type of jerky meat and porridge I couldn't identify.

"Bellamy made me stay with him." I uttered.

"Why?" An ocean breeze caught McKenzie's bright red hair and whisked it across her face.

"Because I was wet, and he didn't want me to get sick. I fell off the ship last night."

"You didn't fall," Noah interrupted from his seat on the edge of the hull. "You jumped. I saw you."

His forwardness caught me off guard, but I wasted no time snapping back at him.

"You're wrong." I tilted my head at him. "I fell." I didn't want them to know the truth of how close I'd almost been to leaving them behind for the sake of finding Milo. Noah already didn't trust me.

"You and Milo make the perfect couple." Noah looked away. I could now see he had been chewing some type of dry jerky. "Both liars and sneaky as hell."

My shoulders dropped. "Can you not, Noah?"

"I'm sorry," he sighed. "Maybe that was cold. But I'm just so freaked out right now. I mean where are we, and how do we get back home?"

"We have to get the trident," McKenzie chimed. "Right, Katrina? Do you think Bellamy could take us to it?" She glanced at me for reassurance, but I didn't even know what to say.

I looked out to the sea. It stretched out into miles and miles of nothingness, just as vast and endless as the blue sky above it. What could I possibly do from here? Could I convince Bellamy to take me to find some mythical trident? And where did that leave Milo? Even if I could find a way back, I couldn't leave without him...

"Maybe," I huffed, glancing down to my bare feet covered by the baggy pants. "But I wouldn't know what to do even if we find it."

Noah stood to his feet, tossing me a piece of jerky. "We use it."

"Cordelia said the only way to use it is to sacrifice the thing most precious to you. Are either of you interested in doing that?"

McKenzie and Noah exchanged a worried glance.

"No one had to sacrifice anything to end up here. I'm sure we can figure out how to make it take us back. But we don't stand a chance without it," Noah said.

"And how exactly do you expect me to convince Bellamy to deviate from his route and take us looking for a trident? We don't know what this could do to the future. I don't know this Bellamy."

"Oh great, so now we're following Back to the Future logic?" Noah groaned.

Something in me snapped. A thread of impatience that I hadn't even noticed weakening. But I couldn't manage the pressure crushing me like a tidal wave. How was I supposed to figure this out? How was I supposed to find Milo, get back to the present, keep us all alive, and save the world in just a few short days? Something in me shifted; darkened even.

"I don't know what the hell we're following!" I seethed. "If you have any better ideas, feel free to go ask Bellamy yourself."

"Ask me what?" Bellamy suddenly stood behind me. I whirled around, cringing at the sensation of my bare feet against the grain of the wood below.

I swallowed. "If...if you could help us."

"I am helping you lot, though be it regrettably," he shrugged, now fully dressed in a pair of loose pants tucked into boots and a loose hanging open-front tunic.

"Yes," I blinked, "And we're grateful, but..." I couldn't continue. As if on cue, Bellamy held up a hand as he squinted to see who'd called his name from the other side of the ship.

"Later," he uttered, walking away to deal with whatever matter it was. "Just stay out of my crew's way for now." Then he turned around and called out to me while still walking backwards and pointing at a crew member in the distance. "Except Tristan. See Tristan there about some clothes that actually fit."

I turned to see the boyish sailor Tristan lugging a crate in his arms near the stern of the ship. He was stacking them with others on board and looked like he'd rather do anything other than interact with me. But with an encouraging look from McKenzie, I approached and found myself handed a pair of small burgundy pants and a white tunic that looked to be much closer to my size. Taking the clothes belowdecks with McKenzie, I put on the new outfit I wrapped a brown sash of cloth over the seams at my waist, tucking in my tunic and pulling on the leather boots I'd found close to my size.

"You look like a pirate yourself now," McKenzie noted.

"Maybe you should put together something a little more century-appropriate, too." I suggested. "You know, it's probably best we blend in once we get to land."

"That's probably true." McKenzie uncrossed her arms and rummaged through the crate of clothing. "Though I just don't feel like any of these are my color." We both giggled at her comment.

"It feels good to laugh," I said. "Every moment feels like hell here."

"It's hard to see the bright side, I'll admit. But try to stop shutting us out so much. We're your friends, and we're just as much trapped here as you are."

"I think Noah would love nothing more than for me to shut him out."

"Well, who can blame him?" McKenzie's tone rose a bit. "Think about what's happened to him. To us. This is a literal impossible nightmare. Noah can be blunt, but he's just stressed. He's scared. And to be honest, I am, too." The air between us hung heavy for a moment, before McKenzie spoke again. "I'm so worried about what my parents must think happened to me. I wish...I wish I had listened to you when you told me not to get on the boat."

I looked down. She was right. I already hated myself for having caused all this for them. I just wanted to get them home, and to make sure there was even a home to go back to.

"I can't tell you how sorry I am that I've dragged you here. Trust me. I'm scared, too. Actually, I'm terrified. But we're going to figure it out. If we got here somehow, there has to be a way to get back."

"Well, we have a lot better chance of figuring it out if we're not all pissed at each other." She nudged me, but her voice was anything but playful.

"Maybe I was a little harsh with Noah. I'm just not myself here." I played with a piece of fraying thread on one of the shirts as McKenzie pieced together her own outfit.

"I've noticed." McKenzie's soft voice was barely audible over the creaking sound of the ship. "None of us are. We're just trying to survive." She sighed, holding up a pair of pants against her waist for comparison. "I just want to be back in our dorm drinking coffee and doing our makeup."

"What, you don't like playing dress up on a pirate ship?" I chuckled. "Don't tell me this ruffly shirt doesn't match my eyes." I batted my lashes dramatically.

McKenzie's lips formed the slightest smile for just a moment, but it quickly faded as her gaze met mine.

"What?"

"I'm just making sure I know what color your eyes actually are," she said gently. "When you yelled at Noah, I could've sworn they flashed blue. Like a deep blue. But now they're back to brown. Like I thought. I guess the sun is getting to me."

"Blue?" I glanced up. She nodded confidently.

"Hmm..." I said, mentally adding yet something else to my list of things to worry about. "That's...weird."

"Maybe it was just a trick of the light, but I don't know." McKenzie flicked her head to the side.

"Well, whatever it was, it's the least of our problems right now." I grabbed a pair of pants and shirt with a vest and tossed them to McKenzie. "Tell Noah to put these on. He'll do it if you ask him. If I try, he'll probably just throw them overboard."

McKenzie nodded and began to walk away. But she stopped at the steps leading up to the deck and looked back at me. "Hey Katrina," she said softly. "What if we never make it back?"

I looked her over in her loose flowing skirt and billowy tunic and cracked a small smile. "Then at least we'll look the part." I chuckled, but it wasn't enough to hide the worry in my voice.

With a half smile and another nod, she made her way back up top. I sat in silence in the darkness of the ship's innermost space. The smell of fish and salt toyed with my senses, and the muffled sounds of the crew above deck sounded distant, like a far-off dream. I thought of the last thing's I'd said to Milo. Was it something I said that made me lose him? Was this fate's cruel way of giving me what I deserved?

And Bellamy...What was I feeling when I was lying next to him? Something I didn't want to feel. Something I refused to acknowledge.

As I sat there, staring into the shadows and rat-chewed burlap sacks of grains on the floor, the sound of rushing footsteps above made me stand alert. Next came yelling, and before I knew it pirates were sprinting down the steps to get past me, running to the cannons lining the inside of the ship.

"Man the cannons! All hands!" A voice cried.

"What's happening?" I asked, rushing back above deck. It looked like a battleground already, with men running across the soaked floor to and fro, shifting sails and tying ropes.

Bellamy came storming past, sliding an arm into his captain's coat as he walked. He didn't stop as he spoke. "Get your friends and get belowdecks," he ordered firmly into my ear. I glanced across the water, noticing a massive warship approaching our direction with British flags flying proudly.

Bellamy yelled out to the crew. "She's too much ship for the *Widow* in this shape! But she's coming for us, nonetheless! Man those cannons and tar the barrels! Load them with whatever you can find! We can't take another hit after that last scuffle! I'll try to outrun her but be ready just in case!"

In the chaos and confusion, I whipped my head around, looking for my friends. Noah appeared suddenly, hand linked with McKenzie's, and he grabbed my arm as he led us both downstairs.

"Let's go!" He yelled, pulling me belowdecks with them. I don't know why, but I fought to catch one last glimpse of Bellamy before I lost sight of the scene on deck. He was at the wheel, still shouting orders and commanding the crew with a confidence in his voice that I found inspiring. This Bellamy knew who he was. And he loved it.

Tucked away underneath the ship's hold, we waited in fear of what would happen next. Any minute I expected a hole to be blown in the wall of the ship beside us. The minutes were agony. And eventually, silence fell.

"I think we outran them," I said.

But at the sound of incoming cannon fire, I immediately knew I was wrong. A distant boom followed by a brief silence warned us to brace. I held tightly to McKenzie and Noah, there kneeling on the floor of the ship's hold. I wondered if it was a good idea to be this low if the ship were to start sinking.

Within seconds, the impact of multiple cannons shook the boat, tearing holes across the deck and battering the hull to splinters. McKenzie screamed, and I bit my lip so hard I thought my teeth would tear right through it.

Once the rocking of the ship subsided and it seemed we had recovered from the hit, a long pause hung in the air.

"Somebody go check on the captain up on the gun deck! See what's going on up there." A crewman behind a cannon suggested.

Before any of them could offer to do the task, my hand shot up and I clambered to my feet.

"I'll go," I volunteered. Noah grabbed my sleeve as I stood to walk away.

"What are you doing?" He grumbled. "It's insane to go up there."

"I just want to see what happened," I said. "If we're going down, we're going down whether I'm down here or up there."

I climbed the steps quickly to find Bellamy at the helm, focused with an intense gaze on the open water in front of us. Behind us trailed the British warship, an intimidating sight through the haze of the smoke its cannons had left behind rising from the stern.

"Can you outrun them?" I called, rushing to Bellamy's side.

"I have no choice. If they hit us again, she's sunk." Suddenly, his eyes widened. "Why are you up here? Go back down!"

"I'd rather face it than go down hiding like a coward."

"It's not cowardly to keep yourself safe. I'm trying to protect you!"

Something in me stirred again. Bellamy's words reminded me all too much of Milo. I shook my head to reset my thoughts and fight the fire building within. Bellamy shouted another order to the crew, and the sails lifted higher. The same wind catching the sails caught my hair and swept it behind me, dancing across my neck and shoulders. As if a breath of fresh courage rippled through me, and along with it, a foreign feeling of power and strength. Like I could tear down anything in my path.

I stepped forward, past Bellamy, and planted myself firmly at the bow of the ship as we sailed on. I looked out into the stretch of blue before us and breathed in the briny air. We'd outrun that ship. We *had* to, if I was going to be able to get any of us out of here. And then with all the force in my voice I could summon, I shouted a command I could never forget as I finally embraced the fact that this was it. This was reality. I was sailing with pirates in 1720, so I might as well act like it.

"Under full sail!"

17

BURN THE SHIPS

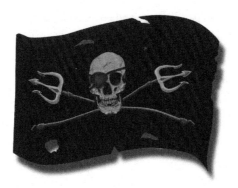

MILO

I dreamed of Katrina that same night. If only for a moment, I saw her face, calling to me from across the sea. And no matter how much I swam, I could never get any closer to her. And then nothing.

The next morning my head ached. Perhaps I'd gotten too drunk. I must have, stupidly, because my coin pouch was almost empty. Either someone stole it from me, or I'd spent it all on gambling. It seemed my old habits were quick to return. *Damn.*

I pulled on my boots and exited the tavern expecting to see a gray sky, but it appeared the night's storm had long passed. A bright blue horizon greeted me, the sun high over the Caribbean waters. Leaves littered the streets from the wind and the ground was still damp. But otherwise, it was a beautiful day for sinking a ship.

I made my way to the rooftops of the buildings nearby. It was important that I stayed out of sight, but I still needed to be able to watch the harbor and determine my point of entry. As the sun beat down on me, I gazed down at the bustling life below. I hoped that maybe, just maybe, I might be able to spot Katrina or one of the others if they'd made it here, too.

Something caught my attention. A whistle. And then the bark of a dog. I peeked over the edge of the roof I was utilizing as my perch and smiled. It was just as I thought. Me—my young self—with a scrappy brown dog at my heels. Peg. I'd named him Peg for the gimpy leg that did nothing to slow him down. The mutt could still outrun me and any other dog in the village. Father wouldn't let me "keep" him, but Peg knew he was my dog. He was a stray by definition, but he always found me.

I watched myself and Peg jumping about, playing with an old stick I'd found on the ground. It lasted only briefly, before I knew I had to stop playing about and tend to my father's work. I remembered that day, like so many others. I was always looking over my shoulder to make sure he didn't catch me playing with Peg when I was supposed to be patching sails or inspecting the hulls for any spots in need of repair.

The grin on my face faded when the pair walked out of sight. I remembered the dark fate soon approaching that young boy playing with his dog. This boy had already spent so many nights crying over his mother's death. If only he knew how many more tears would have to fall before he'd harden to it all. Perhaps it was better he didn't. Let him enjoy this short happiness with Peg.

I waited there until evening came. Unlike the one before, it was a calm night. Ignoring the hunger in my empty stomach, I climbed down once the port became quiet. I pinpointed the *Lark* with ease. She floated six ships back, with a blood-red flag raised high—a warning that the crew took no prisoners and left no survivors.

When I was certain I had a shot, I climbed down, keeping the path to Carl's ship I'd mapped out in my head close to the forefront of my mind. I shuffled through the docks, careful to stay hidden, using crates and barrels to hide behind whenever I sensed someone nearby. My boots were silent on the wet wooden boards.

There would be no easy way to reach the boat. I'd have to swim. Drawing a deep breath, I dove in, careful to keep my splash as subtle as possible. I was thankful for the calm waters as I swam toward my target. Once I reached the side of the sloop, I gripped the side of the hull, feeling along the sides for any section I could use to pull myself up. Once I found a hold, I climbed with all my might, fighting the added weight of my soaked clothing and boots.

Once aboard the ship, it was only instinct to look around. In the pale light of the moon, I could make out the barren deck of the boat. There wasn't much here, which made sense. Carl and his men would've returned from a looting expedition or a raid and had probably sold off everything by now, only to come here to recharge and reward themselves for a while. So, I expected this sloop to be empty.

I moved carefully in the darkness, taking a walk down into the galley and belowdecks. Every good sailor should have a tinderbox down here to light the lanterns in case of an emergency. The question was whether Carl was a good sailor.

I scanned the row of barrels along the back wall. Oil barrels. And two rum barrels. Perfect. To my delight, in a large chest by the bottom of the steps, there was a box, complete with flint, a steel striker, and some pieces of dry cloth.

I reached into my satchel and pulled out a bottle of liquor I'd swiped from the tavern. Quickly and quietly as a church mouse, I turned the bottle over and doused the innards of the ship with the pungent liquid, being extra careful to coat the oil barrels. I made a trail, using a small pile of tinder from the tinderbox as the starting point. I didn't have enough to lead all the way back up to the deck, however. So, I'd have to be fast.

With the trail of alcohol as long as I could manage to make it, I struck the flint against the steel until I saw sparks. With hands I fought to keep from shaking, I tossed the burning piece of tinder down to the pile, where it immediately caught, creating a ball of orange flames as it began to follow the line of alcohol to the oil barrels. I knew I had mere seconds to get out of there.

I rushed to the galley steps, darting up to the deck. My eyes locked onto the edge of the ship as I ran to leap overboard into the water. But there was someone there. On the deck. It wasn't Carl. But whoever it was, he was young. Older than me, probably, but still young.

"Hey, you!" He cried, holding up a lantern. "What are you doing here?"

"Get off the ship!" I yelled, still running and not slowing down.

With a nagging in my conscience that I couldn't ignore, I turned to his direction and ran toward him, counting the mere seconds in my head that I knew were left before this boat went up in flames. The old me wouldn't have saved him. But I had too many regrets now not to.

I leapt forward, pushing the frantic man overboard. He tumbled over into the water below, cursing and screaming on the way down, and I went to jump off, too, but I'd lost one second too many. Bright orange lit up the air behind me. The sound of wood splintering pierced my ears as a flash of light consumed the night. The force threw me into the water, even as I'd already dove into the air, the heat singing the skin on my back even through my thick shirt and hooded vest cloak.

Without looking for the man, I set my sights on the side of the harbor, where the entrance back into Nassau was unkempt, wild routes of nature. A place I could escape to quickly without being recognized. As the ship crackled and lit up the black water with yellow flames, I swam like a devil to shore.

There. It was done. Carl's infamous sloop was destroyed and the hook-handed man who asked me to do it had better be ready to tell me what business he had with my father. I planned to find him immediately. I didn't trust him not to try to make a quick escape once he saw that I'd actually gone through with his request.

I heard screaming from the distance. The lights of lanterns became visible, one by one, as people started to notice the ship aflame in the harbor. Though I hoped that man survived, I also hoped he didn't take note of my features or any part of me that might make me recognizable. Because I knew this town would soon be rioting with chaos and accusations trying to pinpoint the culprit.

No matter right now. I needed to get back to Hook-Hand. I didn't even know the time. Destroying that ship felt like it had lasted only a mere moment. But my sense of time passing was quite unreliable in this state.

Leaving the blazing port behind me, I fled back toward the city, dodging behind crates and wagons any chance I had. There weren't many people in my path, but I still did everything I could to keep my dripping wet clothing from leaving a trail in the dirt that had already dried from last night's storm. As I approached the tavern, I paused at the sight of Carl Thane himself bursting through the door, the look of a madman in his eye. He must've just heard the news of his ship's fate. He looked around, grinding his jaw as he addressed the crewmen in tow behind him.

"If anyone knows the fucker responsible for this, he'd be wise to speak up! Because when I find him, I'll paint my next ship with his blood after I peel the skin from his bones with my own teeth! And I'll feed it to whoever stayed silent about it!"

I shook away a shudder along my spine. A threat like that wasn't far-fetched at all for Thane. He was known to cut off the ears and lips of his enemies or traitors. Or he'd pry off their fingernails with wooden stakes. He was a twisted excuse for a pirate, and every one of us knew it. I'd even dare say he was more demented than Valdez.

I waited in the shadows for him to pass, and once he was out of sight, I quietly slipped into the tavern. It was almost empty. Except for Codface and Hook-Hand, who was leaning up against the wall near the back.

"Everyone's gone to see the fireworks," Hook chuckled, stepping forward.

I neared him so that I could speak low enough for Codface not to hear me. I didn't need anyone involved that didn't need to be.

"I did what you asked," I grumbled, keeping my face tucked downward. "Now tell me about your business with Daven."

"I have to say, I really didn't think you would—or *could*—do it." He grunted a bit before continuing.

"Your underestimation of me is not my problem. Now honor the code and tell me what you promised." I was growing impatient.

"Fair enough." He looked out into the tavern and shifted his weight from one leg to the other. "But know this. After tonight, don't come looking for me anymore. You'll mark us both as dead men if we draw attention."

"You're wasting my time." If he could see my eyes under the shadow, he'd know I was holding a gaze strong enough to burn through the flesh on his face. My fists clenched at my side.

"Allright, damn." He finally spoke. "Daven is my shipper."

"He's a shipper for many a company." I rolled my eyes, aggravated with the way this man danced around giving me the information he promised. "What does he ship for you? What merchandise it that was so imperative that he filled every last ship in his fleet to the brim with?"

The man looked shocked. He stepped backwards uneasily. "How did you hear my conversation with him?"

Dropping my guard, I lunged at this hulking man, pulling my knife from my belt and digging the tip into the skin of his neck. I no longer cared what Codface saw.

"I didn't just put a bounty on my own head for that shitty scrap of information." I growled. "I know more than you think already. Yes, I heard your conversation yesterday. So, tell me what it is Daven transports for you or I'll deliver you to Thane myself—piece by piece."

I could hardly believe the words coming out of my mouth. I hadn't negotiated like this for centuries. But this was how I survived then. And it was how I was going to have to survive now. A pirate's life was anything but gentle.

Hook grabbed my wrist with his good hand before speaking again. I pushed the blade against his skin, drawing a thin line of blood.

"You're just as unhinged as Thane." He laughed. "Daven transports shipments for me and my company—The West Royale Trade."

"You're a slaver?" I spat, knowing all too well that dreaded company name.

"Is that a problem?" The man coughed.

I didn't respond. I was too busy processing it all. As I loosened my hold on the man, unable to think properly enough to know what to do next. He shoved me backwards and sauntered past me, knocking me into a table, but I didn't care. I straightened and picked up my knife as I watched him leave. But I couldn't move from that spot. Because I couldn't believe my father—the man who'd always preached nobility and the value of life to me—was shipping *people* across the Atlantic like stock animals.

18

OVER A BARREL

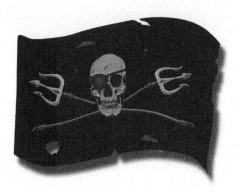

MILO

As I connected the pieces, it slowly made sense, no matter how much I
didn't want it to. Father's fleet was made up of large cargo ships, and at
some point or another, I'd been aboard all of them, however briefly. But more
recently, that year, he'd only assign me to the same ship—*The Marietta's Jewel*—
for the few voyages on which I accompanied. And each time I was ordered to
stay behind and man the vessel while he took the cargo ships inland for a "quick
exchange." Or I'd be sent to a different port to offload that ship separately. The
last voyage we'd made to the African coasts was supposed to have been a normal
delivery of textiles and rum. But clearly Father had arranged some additional
dealings. How long had he hidden it from me? When did he stop transporting
merchant goods and switch to being a pack mule for the slavers?

A pit formed in my stomach. My life had been a lie. I hated many things about
Nassau, but it was a place where every man was equal, free from the confines of

societal expectations. It was a haven of refuge built by outcasts and fugitives, exploited poor men and aristocrats turned rebels, men born free and men who fought their way free alike. No one was lower or higher. The only thing that owned us was the sea. So, I couldn't comprehend how my father was part of something that stood against everything I thought he'd always believed.

A part of me refused to believe it. My father wouldn't do this. He couldn't have been this desperate for money. I needed to see for myself. If not for the commotion going on at the harbor, I would've snuck aboard one of his ships right then to take a look at the other ships' cargo holds or his captain's log. But I couldn't risk being seen. Not now.

For now, I needed to get as far away from here as I could. For all I knew, the man I'd pushed overboard had told everyone that he saw me cause the explosion. What had I done?

I took off into the night, stealthy and silent, making my way to the farthest corner of the island. There was one building where I knew I'd be safe for the time being. The old church.

It was a symbol of refuge on this night as I saw the white stone cathedral contrasting against the midnight sky. The bell tower was cracked, and the doors to the sanctuary were barely still hanging on to their hinges. I stepped inside the small building, not expecting to see anyone else here this time of night. The candles were unlit, but by the light of the moon streaking down in bands through the bell tower opening, I could see the inside well enough. Old wooden pews lined either side of the aisle I trudged down with echoing footsteps. It stirred up the vaguest of memories.

My mother came here often. She loved to pray. I'd come with her a handful of times as a child, but it wasn't a place to which I typically chose to venture. How ashamed she'd be of the life her son had made. In some ways, I was glad she died before seeing what I became. She couldn't have prayed for my forgiveness enough. But she would've tried anyway, I knew.

And did she know of my father's sins? Maybe that's why she was here so much. *No.* If Father worked so hard to hide it from me, I'm sure he hid it from her, too. But why? Why did he turn to something so vile when our merchant business had always sufficed? I supposed for the same reasons he turned to Valdez. The need for money. But I wasn't aware of whatever great debt he owed that drove him to this.

I sighed, sliding down into the second-row pew just meters from the altar up front. It was a relief to finally pull the hood back from my face and let the cool air refresh me. My weary body ached, and I leaned forward, hanging my head over the back of the pew in front of me.

Suddenly I remembered the rosary I'd taken. With tired hands, I rifled through my pants pocket. I knew there was some method to this, but I didn't know it. I remembered bits and pieces from watching my mother in passing...Somewhat. With uncertainty, I took the rosary beads in my hand. It was easy to see the dark dried blood on them against their vivid red. Making the cross symbol across my forehead and chest, I bowed my head.

"Forgive me," I grumbled into the empty air, "for my sins and the sins of my father."

Of course, I expected the silence that came after I spoke. But it was painfully deafening. "Please. I seek forgiveness." I no longer knew if I was asking God or myself. I thought of killing that man on the shore. And nearly slicing open Hook's throat. And lying to Katrina and then failing to keep her safe through all this. And all the things I helped Valdez accomplish. And now here I was—a pirate with three centuries of guilt weighing on his shoulders, praying for forgiveness in an empty, rotting church with a stolen, bloody rosary.

19

OVERBOARD

KATRINA

Bellamy abandoned the helm, charging forward to where I stood on the boat's edge.

"Hold fire! What the hell do you think you're doing?" He yanked me down with a tug of my arm.

I stared at him in surprise, though it only made sense that he would ask me what I was doing. I wasn't even sure myself.

"Why did you leave the helm? I thought we have to outrun them." I glanced back at the ship in the distance behind us.

"We do. But I'm the captain. I give the orders. You don't even know how to keep from falling overboard."

"I didn't fall overboard." The words rushed out of my mouth faster than I could stop them. But I immediately knew I'd said too much.

Bellamy's eyes narrowed at me. "So, what then? You jumped?" He said sarcastically.

I cursed silently to myself. Why did I say it?

"Damn...You jumped." Grazing his hand across the back of his neck, he glanced down at the wooden deck below, then back up at me. "Why?"

Thankfully, the ship behind us quickly recaptured his attention again before I could think of a response. He whipped around, racing back to the helm. I followed.

"At least now I know why you were stupid enough to come up here. You've got a death wish." Bellamy spoke over the sound of the ship tearing through the foaming seawater below as the sails above us billowed in the wind.

"It's not like that," I said. "Just trust me."

"Trust you? I don't even know you."

Something about his words stung and I didn't know why. It shouldn't bother me that Bellamy didn't recognize me. There was nothing between us. There never had been. So why did it bother me so much to feel like I'd lost something I never had?

When the explosion of cannon fire rang out overhead, I ducked behind a mast and braced. But the impact never came. Instead, great splashes of water sputtered in the distance, just barely missing the back of our ship. I glanced up to see Bellamy grinning, a sly look set in those ice blue eyes and perfect teeth.

"We've sailed out of their range, and I've turned us into the wind, which will slow a galleon of that size down. That was their last attempt to stop us, and they missed. We're too far for them to bother catching up now. If we aren't easy prey, we're not worth the chase. We hold this speed till they're out of sight," he said.

I watched as the crew emerged from their spots beneath the ship's deck, cautious at first, but then eager and celebratory. Bellamy stood firm, still standing firm with his hand on the ship's wheel.

"Inspect her for damage. She took a few nicks on the starboard side," he ordered the men on board.

The crewmen scurried away, scanning the sides of the boat in a hurry. Some of them called out to Bellamy in a way that didn't sound positive. Bellamy shouldered past me, as though I was more of an obstacle in his path than another body aboard his ship. "Take the wheel and don't turn it even the slightest," he muttered.

"What? Really?" I stuttered, slowly and hesitantly reaching for the wheel. But Bellamy ignored me and walked off to further inspect the section of the ship that had been hit. When he came back, he wore a scowl that told me the damage must've been serious.

"That bad?" I asked.

"She'll make it a good few leagues just fine. But I can't risk her getting in another scrapple like that again like this." He paused, taking in a deep breath of sea air as he reclaimed his position at the helm. "We'll have to stop at the nearest port for repairs. It'll slow us down a bit, but don't worry, we'll get to Kingston soon enough."

"The next port," I muttered. "And where is that?"

Bellamy ruffled his hair, focusing his eyes on the glassy blue surface below us. "Nassau. Fortunately, it's not too far off our path. We should be there tomorrow afternoon if we can hold this speed and the wind stays on our side."

"Nassau?" I repeated, remembering what Milo had long ago told me about the pirate colony.

"Nassau. Paradise. One in the same," Bellamy confirmed with a grin.

Nassau. Milo had told me so much about it. And...and if Bellamy was here...did that mean Milo might be there? My shoulders straightened and I lifted my chin. It was foolish hope. But it was hope, nonetheless. I knew it was ludicrous to expect it. But I had to hold onto something. Because up until then, I was truly starting to fear I'd never see Milo again.

"Listen to me," Bellamy growled, his voice suddenly like gravel. "Don't ever disrespect me in front of my crew like that again. You're starting to make me regret saving you. Both times." And with that, he stormed off back to the helm.

If only he knew I didn't understand what had come over me then either. When I stood at the bow and yelled into the open sky, I hardly recognized myself. But I'd felt powerful with the sea in front of me and below me and behind me. I'd almost been tempted to dive in as I stood there overlooking the depths. And something in my head had told me I could command every soul on this ship if I tried. And I don't know why I wanted to.

I shook away the foreign feeling. It had to be the sea salt in the air getting to me. And the heat of midday wasn't helping.

Just then Noah and McKenzie came running over to me, frantic with just the reaction I expected.

"What were you thinking, Katrina?" McKenzie looked at me with eyes wide beneath a wrinkled forehead.

"I wasn't thinking," I uttered. "I just...I thought Bellamy was hurt."

"Why would you care about Bellamy?" Noah threw his hands up, and McKenzie touched his arm to settle him.

"Katrina had a thing with Bellamy before Milo. He was cursed too."

"We didn't have a thing!" I snapped, stumbling with the movement of the ship. "Neither of you have any idea what's going on with me." As I spoke my head spun. And I knew I'd said the wrong thing. But I had to get away from them. From everyone. Something was wrong.

Putting a hand to my head, I glanced between a shocked McKenzie and Noah. "I'm sorry," I stuttered. "I really am. I didn't mean that. I'm sorry." I turned away. "I think I just need some time to think. Alone."

The quick nods they offered in response reassured me that my apology was enough, but I could tell by their worried expressions that they were concerned. But what more could I say? I couldn't explain my dilemma because I didn't understand it myself.

I quietly walked to the stern on the forecastle upper deck above Bellamy's quarters. It was rarely occupied and seemed the perfect spot to escape the constant commotion of the crew. I curled up and brought my knees to my chest. Despite the blazing sun, I felt ice cold inside.

I watched the stream of churning water trailing behind the ship, foaming white froth dancing on a blanket of blue. Each curl of the waves beckoned me like fingers coaxing me in their direction, calling me, begging me. I yearned for my paintbrush to capture this moment as my eyes drank in the scene below. I wished I could paint. To remember. To understand. To escape in at least one way.

I wondered if I might find some kind of material that I could salvage enough into a makeshift paintbrush. There had to be something on board this ship that could work. I stood to my feet, looking for whatever I found that could have potential as a brush handle.

There was nothing that I could find that worked. The fishing rods and oars were far too thick to make use of. I felt like an idiot for worrying about painting at a time like this. But it was the one thing I could do something about. For now, I could only wait until we reached Nassau to do much of anything.

When searching the ship proved a waste of time, I thought of the one place that might have something. I'd seen writing utensils and navigation tools of the like in my time in Bellamy's cabin. There had to be something in there I could use.

With Bellamy at the helm, I did my best to go unnoticed as I scurried across the ship's length. The last thing I wanted was to give him another reason to make me stay the night in his bed again. I slipped between the crew members along the deck and to the captain's quarters, testing the door handle once I reached it. A grin stretched across my face as I realized the door wasn't locked and entering was just a matter of turning the knob.

It creaked open, reminding me faintly of when I'd snuck aboard the *Siren's Scorn* to steal Valdez' key. With footsteps light and a breath caught somewhere between my throat and my lungs, I crept forward, looking at the items all around me as I passed. A small desk of Bellamy's stood nestled beside the chest where he'd kept his clothing the night before. I didn't have the chance to get so close to it then, so I quickly walked over to examine it further. Rummaging through the mess of papers and half-burnt candlesticks, I was disappointed not to come across anything even remotely pen-like that I could convert into a paintbrush handle.

But when I looked a second time, I noticed something I hadn't at first—a charcoal pencil. It was long and blocky and awkward. But it would do. I tucked it in the sash tied around my waist and looked for a knife I could use for the brush. One of Bellamy's cutlass swords rested sheathed against the corner. I pulled out the blade, admiring it for a moment. I'd never held anything like it before. The clear steel reflected my own face back at me and I nearly jumped at the sight. I was ragged and worn, but I looked fiercer than ever. My face was the same, but something about it now seemed striking and intimidating. Something was happening to me.

I shook away the chilling realization and refocused on the task at hand. Selecting a thin strand of my hair, I pulled it taut with one hand and carefully guided the sword's blade with the other. Just a few inches should be enough for a thin brush head.

That's when I heard the door creak open.

20

MURKY WATERS

KATRINA

"I 'd ask you why you were in here," Bellamy said while he walked up behind me. "But there's no possible explanation you could give that would make it acceptable."

Something in me stirred again, like a whirlpool within that I couldn't control. I spoke before turning around to face him, still holding the sword firmly in my grasp. "You didn't seem to have a problem with me being in your room last night," I said calmly. "Make up your mind. Do you hate me or want to sleep with me?"

I was shocked at my own words. They were out before I'd even thought to say them. It wasn't like me to be so snarky and confident.

Bellamy leaned toward me, his unruly black locks falling around his eyes. "Maybe a bit of both." He gently took the sword out of my hand. "Now tell me why you're in here. And what you're doing with this."

Don't tell him. Make him wonder. Make him beg to know.

"None of your business," I snapped, fully attentive to the strange new inner voice in my head.

"My sword. My business," Bellamy smirked.

"Fine," I said, momentarily shaking my head to return myself back to normal. My voice softened. "I...I just wanted to paint."

"I must admit that's not at all what I expected you to say." Bellamy cocked his head. "You're a strange lass."

"You have no idea," I muttered. "Now can I have the sword back?"

"Not yet, love." Bellamy's ice blue eyes glimmered beneath sturdy raised brows. "See, you've got me thinking, Katrina." He spun the sword in his hand by the hilt, with no more effort than if he was flipping a pencil. "If we were to run into any more trouble along our route, you and your bilge-sucking friends are rather defenseless—dare I say *useless*." He raised the sword between us before continuing. "So, I'm going to teach you how to hold your own properly. Sunset. On the main deck. We're going to have a little lesson."

"What if I say no?"

"Then you can meet me at the end of the plank instead."

I lifted my chin. Bellamy had always been arrogant, but this surpassed even the Bellamy I thought I knew. "Fine. But I doubt you'd really do that. After all, weren't you the one who jumped in after me last night?"

"Don't push your luck, love. I'm less of a gentleman than you think." With a wink that made my blood boil, he placed the hilt of the sword back into my hand.

As he turned to walk away, he tossed something back over his shoulder. I caught it with a last-minute reflex. It was a paintbrush—a strange, awkward wooden brush with the finest tip—but a brush, nonetheless.

"Old mapmakers' brush," Bellamy said, still walking away. "Now as for paint, you're on your own. But rest assured you won't find it here."

With a toss of my head, I turned to go, taking a few scraps of parchment paper from the desk as well. I wouldn't let Bellamy get under my skin any more than I'd let him get into my heart.

Back out on the deck, I explored the bilge of the ship. I only knew the term because I'd heard the rest of the crew call it that. Down there I found cargo with crates labeled as spices, dyes, and fine silks. Stolen, I presumed. But this seemed exactly like the kind of place I could find something to use as paint.

I took a handful of powdered dye from a crate I managed to open at the corner. Any color would do. I was pleased to see a tablespoon's worth of deep indigo and red when I opened my palm. I tore a piece of fabric from my sash and dumped the powder in, being careful as ever not to mix it.

Satisfied, I scampered back up to the upper deck. Returning to my spot at the stern, I seated myself on the deck floor with my weird brush and makeshift pigments. I hardly had enough parchment to paint on. But I didn't care. I just needed the movement of the brush in my hand. The comfort of my strokes creating trails of color. It was the only thing that was still the same.

I needed water to mix with the dye powders. But the late afternoon sun had dried the deck completely. So, I sat there, feeling that, like everything else I tried, this wasn't going to work. And I suddenly thought of Milo and the warmth of his embrace. I remembered what it was like to kiss him goodnight. I remembered how I'd felt with him on New Years Day, when we watched the fireworks and made so many plans. And how I wish I'd given myself to him that night. If I had known I might never see him again, how I would go back in time—or forward—and I'd have shown him how much I loved him then. Because I was sure now. At least, I thought I was. Until something in me would take hold and make me wonder what reality was in this twisted place.

As I thought of Milo and my confusion, I blinked to catch the tears on my eyelashes. They fell perfectly, right onto the tiny piles of vibrant powder on the deck before me. So, I mixed the pigments with my tears, making just enough paint to swirl across the parchment's waxy surface with my brush. I did my best to create an outline of what I imagined would be a curling wave, but as I looked at it, tracing in the indigo color, the red I tried mixing in looked more and more like blood in the water. It all ran together as the water dribbled off the parchment and seeped into the deck, staining it permanently. As if a representation of the past few days, the perfect image I had before me quickly became a nightmare.

As if on cue, a low thunderous rumble sang out in the clouds. An afternoon rainstorm. Within moments, the rain came sprinkling down, washing away my bloody water painting like it was no more than sidewalk chalk. I decided to find McKenzie and Noah again.

"How's it going?" I asked shyly, feeling more like myself as I approached them leaning against the masts near the front of the ship. "Are you both okay?"

"As okay as we can really be," Noah said, looking up at me through the featherlight raindrops dusting his face. McKenzie nudged him. She must've thought I didn't notice.

"I thought I was a beach girl," McKenzie said. "But this has proven me wrong. I'm sapped. Katrina, how are you doing it?"

"Doing what?" I asked, raising an eyebrow as I sat down to join them.

"Looking so refreshed. You look the complete opposite of how I feel. This seems like a spa day for you."

"I have no idea what you mean. I feel terrible."

"Drink something." Noah tossed me a canteen and I chugged, but quickly coughed when the pungent taste of rum hit my lips. When I shot him a look to kill, he shrugged. "There's not much else to choose from here. Besides, might as well use something to numb the senses here."

"I know it feels hopeless," I said. "But I swear, we're going to find a way back to our time. I'll talk to Bellamy tonight."

We chatted more as the sun lowered and the rain clouds cleared. Our conversation felt as hollow as the ship below us. There was still just enough light left to cast a fiery red glow over the water. The deck shone with the glassy shine of a freshly wet surface.

Suddenly a gruff looking crew member approached us. Beneath his head rag he peered at us with dark, sunken eyes.

"Captain's calling for you three on the main deck," he uttered.

I glanced at McKenzie and Noah who both wore equally puzzled expressions. "I forgot to tell you. We have sword-fighting lessons." I sighed.

"Finally, something worthwhile," Noah sat up with more enthusiasm I'd seen in him probably ever.

McKenzie took his hand as he helped her to her feet. I stayed sitting, dragging myself to get up. I didn't want to interact with Bellamy anymore. I didn't like who I was when I was near him. But I knew if I didn't get up and go to him, he'd come find me. And that would be worse.

As a trio, we sauntered down the steps to the main deck, where half the ship's crew seemed to have assembled. A few lanterns placed along the deck lit the open floor space amongst them. Bellamy stepped out from the crowd, giving me a nod and a half smile that made my blood pump harder and my eyes want to roll into the back of my head.

"Step up, mates," he ordered, picking up three swords from an open barrel beside him. He tossed them to us, one at a time, hilt first.

"Um, dangerous!" McKenzie screamed.

"You're sailing with pirates, lass. Dangerous is all there is." Bellamy's voice drifted to my ears like thick smoke, smooth and bold. "First, watch how I hold it. Grip the hilt firm against your palm. Use your last two fingers to tighten your grip and provide power on a swing—but keep these two fingers loose to help guide the sword." He stuck out his index and middle fingers to emphasize. We all three did our best to mimic his movements and position as he walked around and corrected us individually.

"Decent enough start. Now for your stance." He stopped at me and lifted my chin as he spoke. I pulled my face away. "Stand with feet shoulder width apart, and eyes straight and focused. Be sure to keep one foot in front of the other. You don't want to become unbalanced."

He'd made his way to Noah now, and made an effort to shove him. Noah braced to steady himself, and that's when Bellamy swung his cutlass to the side without warning, clattering it against Noah's.

"And the most important thing to remember," he said with a chuckle, "is that pirates never play fair." He swung again, nearly knocking the blade from Noah's hand. But Noah tightened his grip at the last second and leapt to the defense. McKenzie and I watched wide-eyed as he sparred with Noah, yelling tips and suggestions as their blades crossed.

"Kind of hot, isn't it?" McKenzie leaned over and whispered over my shoulder.

I couldn't help but giggle. "I can't say I disagree."

I knew she was likely referring to Noah, but I had my eyes on Bellamy. I watched the way his body turned and twisted as he stepped deftly across the wet floor, as balanced and sturdy as the masts themselves. He moved with the subtle bobbing of the ship as though he and the sea were one. His raven hair, loose and flowing, whipped around his face just as fluidly as his movements.

You thirst for him.

What was that? I looked away, reprimanding myself for the way I was fixating on him. I looked at the last bit of setting sun remaining on the horizon.

"Katrina," Bellamy calling my name made me refocus on him. He was walking toward me with a fierceness in his eyes that made me shift uncomfortably. "Since you're so interested in what's out there, I supposed you already know that a proper swing isn't really a swing at all."

He lifted his sword at me. When I flinched, he lowered it, and then took my hand, pulling me forward, not at all in a gentle manner. I stumbled to the middle of the deck, gripping the hilt of my sword in my sweating hand.

"Swinging isn't effective. It'll make you tired before the salt's dried from your boots." He grinned, lifting my arm to set my sword up to brace against his. "No, instead, you want to conserve your energy in a fight. Use jabbing motions. Stab your opponent. Thrust forward." He demonstrated, pointing his sword at me with a poking motion. "Now fight me."

I felt a foreign heat building in me. Something else was intruding and I couldn't stop it. I lifted my sword as he'd shown me and swung it, and he caught it with his.

"Try to hurt me, Katrina," he commanded under his breath.

"Believe me, I want to," I growled. Stepping forward, I attempted to whack him with the flat side of my cutlass, missing as he dodged it effortlessly. I bent at the waist, trying to achieve more reach, but he deflected my attack yet again. With our swords still crossed, he pulled me forward with his free hand. I barely reached his nose, but he looked down into my eyes with a gaze as steel as our weapons. "I told you to *thrust*, not swing," he said under his breath. A tingle ran down my spine like fingertips across velvet.

"Like this?" I shook away the heat rushing to my face and shoved the point of the sword toward him as I spat out the rhetorical question.

"Good lass." He spoke low and slowly as he parried my blow with ease. "It's a start." His gaze swept over me from top to bottom and back up.

For the next few moments, he instructed me, and I did my best to follow. And when he would correct me with a repositioning of my arm or when he touched my waist to fix my posture, the voice within me told me he was everything I wanted. And I fought hard to shut it up.

With the setting sun at our backs and the open sea in front of us, we danced our waltz of blades, as I became more confident with my cutlass. I swung, nearly landing a hit against Bellamy's shoulder just before he flicked it away with the tip of his sword. So close.

"Left. Lean to the right. Now backwards." My footsteps followed Bellamy's every word like clockwork. Our steel blades began to move faster. And faster. Out sang a chorus of metal on metal as sparks flew across the deck. I was too confident. I was sure I could land a hit on him if I kept going. And just as I thought I saw an opening near his waist, I dove for it. But the clang of steel reverberated up my arm and made me wince. He'd knocked the sword from my hand. No sooner did it come to a sliding stop on the deck at the feet of his crewman did he have his own sword pointed at me.

"Not bad." His upper lip curved into a smirk. "But it appears I'm the winner here." He held out his hand, and Tristan stepped out from the group of crew members surrounding us and shoved a canteen of rum into his open hand. Bellamy took a swig, leaning his head back so that I could see the shimmer of sweat along his neck beneath his raven locks.

"Guess you can go celebrate now. Are we done?" I shrugged.

Bellamy tossed the rum to the floor and fixed his gaze on me. With a mischievous look in his eye, he stepped forward to me, and took my hand in his before yanking me forward against him.

"I won. So, you owe me a dance." He winked towards his crew, and music began to emit from the men. The vibrant, upbeat sound of a fiddle and flute filled the air as two crew mates with the instruments made themselves known.

I rolled my eyes, but if he could tell how fast my heart was beating, he'd know I was only lying to him. And to myself. He pulled me to him and began to follow the music. It reminded me of dancing with him at the gala months before—or centuries later—whatever made sense. But only, this dance was rugged, more lighthearted, and he carried me across the deck in his swift movements and lead me with grace and skill I didn't expect. He spun me around as the fiddle played faster and the flute's notes went higher. Soon the other crew members joined in, and I even caught a glimpse of Noah and McKenzie embracing each other as they danced, too. It made my heart happy, and for just a moment, that's all I wanted.

For so long my heart had been heavy. So much had felt lost and broken and irreparable. But this. This was just simple, real fun. And the more I watched the man in front of me, the deeper I found myself lost in him. But it was a good kind of lost. The kind that makes you forget all the bad things happening around you. And I wanted more of that.

I drew myself closer into him. I was all too aware of the secure brace of his hand against the curve of my back. The look in his eyes as they locked onto mine made me feel like I was looking into some unknown, beautiful depths of the sea that had yet to be discovered. And the way we moved together, stepping in time to the upbeat shanty music, gave me a feeling I was afraid to acknowledge, but at the same time was all too afraid to let go of.

I noticed his eyes as they moved from mine to my lips. He was close to me. So close that I could feel his quick breaths as he spun me around the open deck. A stirring in me caught my attention. I used every ounce of willpower in my body to ignore it, but it was too strong this time. I couldn't block it out.

Kiss him, it said.

I knew I couldn't. I knew I shouldn't. But I was compelled all at once by the other voice in my head and the temporary fleeting emotion of my heart. But I didn't have to make the decision. I still wonder if I would have done it or if I would've been strong enough to resist. But I'll never know, because Bellamy moved first. He let go of my hand and moved his fingers to lift my chin in one swift motion, and then crashed his mouth into mine.

As quickly as he dove in, he pulled away, grinning like he'd just won a prize. He turned to his crew, earning a jeer from the men on deck. I suddenly felt sick to my stomach. Everything about this situation was wrong and I couldn't believe I'd let Bellamy use me as his prize to show off in front of his crew. Noah and McKenzie stood flabbergasted off to the side, and Noah shook his head scoldingly.

As if I'd woken up from some sort of bad dream, I blinked, stopped the motion of our still-swaying dance, and tore myself from Bellamy's grip.

Without looking back, I disappeared into the dark side of the ship, praying no one would follow me. I threw myself between two cannons belowdecks, where I felt hidden enough to let myself cry until I lost all the tears I was holding in. The muffled sounds of the music and dancing above me lulled me into a strange sense of loneliness and comfort, where I let myself stay until it all died down.

21

Rats from a Sinking Ship

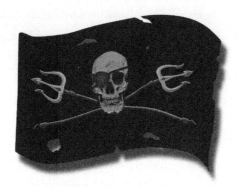

Milo

I tried to sleep there on the church pew. But I couldn't clear my head. I knew stepping outside this church would mean risking being recognized, but a realization struck me that I couldn't ignore. My father would've most likely been out at the harbor, joining in on the commotion as everyone worked to keep their own boats from going up in flames. Which would mean our house was unattended. This could be the perfect chance to uncover what my father was hiding. Or perhaps...just perhaps...I could find evidence that proved the contrary...that he wasn't hiding anything. That he was an honest man and had no part in such a nightmarish trade. I doubted it, but I hoped that maybe it could be true.

Besides, I needed something to do to keep me from going mad. If I wasn't thinking of my father, I was worrying about Katrina. I felt sick about it. I wanted her more than anything right then. I wanted to hold onto her and breathe in the scent of her. I yearned for her, and my heart screamed within me every time the thought crossed my mind that she didn't survive the wreck. But I knew better. She of all people could survive the sea. She would be alright, I told myself. I just had to find her.

In silence I moved out into the night, carrying the loneliness with me like a shadow. I arrived at my father's house—my house—as bells in the distance chimed. It was an hour past midnight. My father would eventually be back when he'd finished securing his own ships. I tried the door handle. As I expected, it was locked, but I knew all too well there was a window in my room I often left open as a boy because I loved the sound of frogs and crickets chirping in the night.

I made my way around to that window and leaned my head in. The sleeping boy—me—in the cot against the wall didn't stir. But the lone lit candle told me he was either awake moments before or pretending to be asleep. I'd take my chances.

I crept in through the window, careful not to make a sound as I cast a foreboding shadow on the wall against the candlelight. When my boots hit the floor, I let out a sigh of relief as the boy remained still. With feather-light steps, I made my way through the rest of the house.

"Finally," I muttered, approaching my father's door. I had longed to see what was behind it for so long, and now more than ever.

As I picked the lock, I found myself frustrated that I couldn't get it open. I'd never found a lock so difficult, as I'd successfully picked open countless others. But by the light of the moon through the window, I caught a glimpse of something on the door handle that seemed strangely familiar. Of course, I'd seen this door a million times. But where else did I see that symbol on the doorknob?

Then it struck me. It was the same symbol carved on the back of my father's compass. I pulled the compass out from my pocket, holding it up to the door to compare. The same exact mark. A cursive *H* for Harrington.

I fiddled with the compass in my hand, working the puzzle in my head. I shook it, hearing something rattling inside. I'd heard it before, but I'd never thought much of it, being a 300-year-old navigational tool. But then I wondered...

As quietly as I could, I used my knife to pry off the baseplate of the compass. And there was a small key. I tried it in the lock. When I realized it was a perfect fit, a shiver snaked through me. My father wanted me to find this. He'd given me this compass the day he died. Whatever was behind this door, I was always meant to know.

With a deep breath, I prayed this was all a misunderstanding. Maybe there was a chance my father wasn't really involved in this dreadful trade. Maybe it was just a one-time mistake or maybe he entered a deal he didn't understand.

I felt the lock's gentle click as I turned the key, and the door creaked open with just a touch. The room was dark. But I could smell smoke from freshly put-out candles. I reached for one to light it, carrying it with me to help me see. With nothing but the small flame's glow, I navigated this new room. A bed, larger than mine. A barrel-turned-table with liquors and rums of all makes on top. A chest with boots and sailcloth. Parchment and maps tucked away in the corner. Nothing I wouldn't expect in a sailor's bedroom. Until I turned. I turned and the candlelight illuminated a striking image of a woman on the wall. A charcoal sketch of my mother—pinned to the wall over a baby cradle. It would've been my brother's had he not died along with my mother.

I scratched my head, moving my candle closer to the empty cradle. There appeared to be something inside. A golden ring rested in the middle. I recognized it immediately as my mother's wedding ring on a thin gold chain. And lying all around it were notes. Scribbled notes of all sorts, scattered across the dusty blanket within. Some were old. Some looked like they were written yesterday. But they were all just random words and cryptic phrases.

Love.

I'm sorry.

Failed.

Forever.

Taken.

Regrets.

As I scanned the notes in confusion, a voice from behind nearly made me jump, but I held my stance. My back was to the door, but I didn't have to turn around to know who stood in the threshold.

"Did you come for my boy, too?"

I couldn't speak. In a mix of confusion and surprise, I stayed silent. Because there was nothing I could think to say to my father, especially not to a question like that. I stood there, refusing to face him, and glad for the hood over my head that I didn't dare remove, even as I browsed the house.

"Answer me, damnit!" He shouted. I didn't need to turn around to picture his green eyes flashing. "Are you going to take the only thing I have left, Henry? All for one empty ship?" With each word, his voice broke, going from stern and strong to choking back tears. I guessed the empty ship he was talking about was referring to his earlier conversation with Hook. And I remembered the name from the note I found on the man I fought on the shore. *Henry.* The man I killed. He thought I was him. But what did everything else mean? I had to say something...

"What do you think I'm here for?" I muttered, being sure to keep my face turned away.

"Did you already do it? You killed my son? Just like you killed her when you couldn't wait another damn week for your bloody pay."

"The boy is fine. For now." I did my best to keep up with the façade. "How do I know I can continue to rely on you?" I was hoping I could get answers.

"I'm working with the slavers now. I'm getting the word out with the companies, and I'm getting commissioned more often. God, Henry, was the arrangement at Rockshore not enough to tie you over? I can ensure they'll pay the remainder of what I owe if you just give me a little more time."

That was it. My father was somehow heavily indebted to this brute. For what, I didn't know. But this had to be why he'd turned to the slave trade for profit. He was in too deep with these dark affairs. I had to swallow down the lump in my throat before speaking again. "Time. Time is what we all need a little more of, isn't it, *Tiburón?*"

Suddenly, a startled voice shouted from the other room. My voice.

"Go tend to your boy. Before he finds out who you really are." I said, each word stinging like salt in fresh wounds.

I listened for the sound of footsteps as Daven hurried to the other room. I used it as my chance to make my escape, right after I snatched up my mother's ring from the cradle and tucked it away safely. My father didn't deserve to hold onto it. Not when he was the reason for her death.

Strangely, as I disappeared into the night, I realized I now had a sudden memory of this incident. One that hadn't been before. It became part of my mind in an instant, as if it was forming at that very moment. I was no longer in the house, but vividly I could remember my younger self after my departure, startled by the strange conversation I'd heard with my father and an intruder.

I stumbled to a tree and leaned over it, the memory clear before me as it was happening right then in the house I'd left behind.

"Who was there, Father?"

"It was just some bastard who came back with me. He was interested in joining my crew, but I told him we were full."

"Oh." Young Milo nodded, the sleep still heavy in his eyes. "Came back from where?"

"The docks." Father smiled a tired smile, the crow's feet in the corners of his eyes folding together. "There was an...incident down at the harbor. I was checking on the ships. But everything's right now. Go on back to bed. You'll be up early for the delivery tomorrow. And then we set sail for England."

"Is this the shipment from Captain Valdez?" Milo blinked.

"Aye. And you know how he gets. So be rested up."

I shook my head. I remembered it perfectly. My future self had altered my past and therefore altered my memories. So now I knew for sure the past could be changed to some degree. But at what cost? Because what my younger self nor my father didn't know was that Valdez would be a day late. And when he finally arrived, he would kill my father in front of me.

But that didn't matter at the moment. I still needed some time to process what I'd heard and piece things together. My father owed a debt, and he was doing whatever he could to pay it off. I should've known no reputable merchant would continue with his home base in a city like Nassau, with pirates practically running the place. But perhaps that was why he did. Perhaps he couldn't go back to Barbados for some reason. Maybe "Henry" had higher up friends elsewhere, keeping my father cornered here. All I knew was that my father was a liar and a cheat—all the things he made me believe Kellem was, and he was responsible for my mother's death. He told me she'd taken ill and passed and that my brother died in her womb along with her. Just like he never told me he was shipping humans like cattle right underneath my nose.

Suddenly, I was glad I'd killed Henry. And I was glad that I was a pirate. Because at least a pirate didn't hide his deeds. He bore them proudly as the tattoos on his skin. And a true pirate knew all were equal at sea. For the first time in my life, I decided pirates—maybe with the exception of Thane and Valdez—had more decency than the lot of them.

And then I wept that night. I couldn't remember the last time tears had fallen like that. Not since I was a child who lost his mother. But now I'd lost my father, too. And I watched as my tears washed away the dried blood on my rosary before I tossed it to the ground.

None of this mattered. I rebuked my foolishness once I shook off the anger. I wasn't meant to know these things. I was meant to be back in the 21st century, with Katrina, learning the names of car parts and lattes. Not here, reliving my life and uncovering the dark secrets festering beneath the surface about my family.

One thing I'd learned in these past few twisted days spent here was that whatever I did here affected the rest of time. I'd killed one of the thugs who came to collect my father's payments. There had to be a bigger fish coming. And he'd take it out on my father or my younger self. And if I tried to change what happened with Valdez and save my father like I thought I could, who knew what that could do to the future? I would probably live my life on the run from whoever was sent for retribution for Henry's death. My father would go on digging himself deeper in this mess of cruelty he called business. And I'd never become cursed and meet Katrina.

All my life, I'd hated myself for the coward I was on board Valdez's terrible ship. But by letting my father die like he was meant to, I was severing at least one small vein of the slavers' trade, even for just a little while. At least that could console me now.

I looked up at the sky above me. There was the North Star, clear as ever, watching over me. And I knew I had to let all this go. It was time I found Katrina. I didn't know how. But I knew where to start. If I was going to be trapped here in the past, I couldn't linger in Nassau for long anyway. I'd need to commandeer a ship from the harbor once things settled down. Because if Katrina was out there, I had no doubt she'd still be heading toward the Devil's Triangle. And who better to meet her there than a man already trapped in hell?

22

OCEAN EYES

KATRINA

When I awoke, the ship was silent. There was no trace of the merrymaking that had been going on earlier. The only sounds reaching my ears were the low creaks of the ship against the waves and the scurrying of tiny mouse feet in the shadows.

I lifted my head and let my eyes adjust, remembering that unfortunately this was all too real. I was still here, trapped on the sea, centuries in the past and miles from any hope of finding Milo. And the compass of my heart seemed to be spinning out of control. Maybe Cordelia was right. Maybe I didn't have a soul.

I stood up, balancing as the ship leaned in the rolling night waves. Making my way back up the top deck, I returned to my spot where I'd tried painting earlier. Sitting crisscross beside the stains from my earlier "painting," I tilted back my head and gazed heavenward. The light of the stars above was unlike anything I'd ever seen. The constellations shone brighter and more numerous than even when I'd watched them with Milo on the lighthouse.

He wasn't kidding when he said there was no better way to stargaze.

I smiled to myself, imagining him here with me, watching the stars on a sailing ship in the night. With a drawn-out sigh, I looked back down, tucking my knees up to my chest. What I would give to find him and sit under the stars with him one more time.

The sound of soft singing drifting in the air caught my notice. I glanced up, looking for the source of the sound. Shadows contorted every shape on deck, and even with the dim lanterns of the ship and the moonlight reflecting on the water, my vision was obscured. The only people I could make out were a handful of crew members on the night shift, and it the song clearly wasn't coming from them.

I leaned in the direction from which the voice came. It was male, but still gentle. It seemed to come from the stern. I followed it, my footsteps steady in the slightly too-large boots I wore. As I neared the stern, I saw Bellamy seated along the hull with a leg propped up to rest his elbow, a bottle of rum dangling in his hand. He was watching the water, singing softly with his back to the ship. I crept closer, stopping a few feet away to listen to the song as each word lazily drifted from his lips.

Lost out at sea
Do you dream of me?
By the call of the waves
I hear you and seek you
Till again the roaming sea
Brings you back to me.

I thought the tune seemed familiar, but my body stiffened when I heard the second verse.

Down by the shore
Meet me once more
By the light of the moon
Love me, then leave me
With the dawn rising
Haunt me forevermore

"What was that song?" I asked, my voice gentle to keep from startling him. I knew I shouldn't be striking up something else with Bellamy, especially not out here alone on the back of the ship. But I had to know how he knew that song centuries before he met Serena.

He turned to look at me, a tiredness in his eyes that seemed uncharacteristic for him.

"Aye, just a sea shanty."

"That was no sea shanty." I straightened my shoulders, stepping forward. "That song sounded...special. Am I wrong?"

"You're onto something, lass," Bellamy grumbled. "But you remember how I said I have no room in my heart for any mistress but the sea?"

I nodded with a raised eyebrow, noting his shining eyes and unguarded way of moving.

"That's because the sea keeps my secrets. It's always just between her and me."

"And what did you tell her tonight?" I climbed up onto the hull with him, dangling one leg over each side and turning to face him.

"You're too curious for your own good, love." Bellamy grinned, raising the bottle of rum to his lips again.

"Well, how about a deal? I tell you about where I'm from and I tell you a secret of mine if you tell me about that song." I crossed my arms. "Oh, and I'll forgive you for that uncalled for move back there."

"You mean the kiss?" Bellamy rubbed the scruff of the dark beard covering his jaw with his ring-covered fingers. "That was just for show. In front of my men. Have to keep up the morale out here and keep the reputation."

"Why? Don't your men trust the real you?" I leaned forward.

"I'd like to think they would." Bellamy looked down, tracing the rim of the liquor bottle with his fingertip. "But my father is a much fiercer man than I. He can command his crew with just one look and they cower. But I don't want to be like him. I want my crew to respect me, not fear me. So, I try to show them I'm one of them."

I listened to Bellamy's words intently. This was like meeting him all over again. It was a side of Bellamy I had no idea existed. "Well, they seem loyal enough." I shrugged. "You must be a good enough captain."

"I'll take the compliment, but we'll see what my father thinks when we make port tomorrow. He was supposed to be making a stop at Nassau for a delivery exchange." His eyes darkened as he spoke. He shifted his gaze from the rum bottle to the water below, hardening his expression.

"Well, I'm glad to be on your ship," I said, brushing a strand of loose hair behind my ear. "And if your father has a problem with how you've been running things, then he's the real jackass here."

I thought I saw Bellamy's lips widen into a small smile, but it quickly faded. He glanced at me. "He's not a bad man. He's just been blinded by the pursuit of wealth." He drew in a deep sigh as I listened, urging him to go on with a nod. "It's never enough. We have plenty to return to Spain and make a life now, but he doesn't see it."

Not a bad man, I wanted to say. *Until he tried to cut my heart out.*

"He promised my mother he would return when he'd made his fortune. Her parents didn't approve of their relationship because my father was just a poor sailor. And when I was born out of wedlock, they were the shame of the village. So, my father swore he'd become rich and powerful and come back for her. But he's never satisfied."

"I had to be away from my mother for a long time, too. I'm sorry. I'm sure you want to go home." I looked up at him longingly through my lashes.

"I don't want to go home. I want to spend my life at sea. But I want my father to return for my mother. It's only fair to her." He paused and shifted, readjusting himself along the hull in a way that put him a few inches closer to me. "She waits for him. I remember how her face lit up when she saw his ship coming in the distance when I was ten."

"Why didn't he stay?" I asked.

"He did for a short while, and then he said he needed to be richer than the king himself before he would have what he wanted. He took me with him. And he set back out to find something that could give him that kind of wealth."

"Has he found it yet?"

"I'm not sure," Bellamy shrugged.

I thought on his words for a moment. *Mermaids.* They were his key to power and riches. Milo had said Valdez used them to bargain with the elites and rulers of the world, making him more powerful than them. If Bellamy knew about that, he wasn't letting on. But of course, why would he expose something like that to some random girl he'd pulled from the ocean?

"Anyway," Bellamy looked down, his hair falling in a way that made me shift against the hull. The warmth I felt rising in my face was more than enough to fight the chill of the night breeze. Something was welling up in me again, pooling in my core and my head like an unwelcome visitor I was fighting to keep out. "That song, if you must know, was a song my mother used to sing. She'd wait for my father at the shore, hoping one day he'd finally return as promised."

Bellamy shook his head, as if trying to escape an invisible net. When he composed himself, he looked at me, strangely. "I don't know why I'm telling you this," he said.

Suddenly, I didn't like that he'd stopped. I wanted to know more. There was more. But not if he wouldn't tell me.

Make him tell you.

The voice in my head sang loudly, like a chiming bell in a hollow space. I leaned closer to him, and placed my hand on his knee, sliding it up to his thigh. "It's okay," I said gently, in almost a whisper. "You can tell me anything."

He narrowed his eyes at me, leaning toward me. "The strangest thing about it is that I swear I can hear a woman singing it on my father's ship when he's in his quarters. And it's not my mother's voice."

Cordelia. There it was.

I studied his face. He was rugged and handsome and the curve of his mouth drew me in like a rushing undertow. "Why don't you sing that song again, Bellamy?" I couldn't even recognize my own voice. The seductive way my words came out disgusted me. But I couldn't stop it. And without hesitation, Bellamy began to voice the words under his breath.

"Lost out at sea

"Do you dream of me?"

He paused for a gentle breath. One that I could feel along my cheek as there was now only a finger's width of space between us. I opened my mouth to sing the next line, softly as a feather against his nose.

"By the call of the waves

I hear you and seek you

Till again the roaming sea

Brings you back to me."

I heard the rum bottle drop from Bellamy's hand and roll away along the deck. He drew his body toward me as I finished the last line of the song.

He tilted his head and pushed his mouth onto me. I didn't stop him. I drank his lips with mine and tasted him like he was the fresh water I'd been thirsting for all day on this ship. The rum on his breath mingled with my own, and I searched deeper for the taste of it on his tongue. I let him pull me closer. My hand along his thigh continued roaming his body, until he reached down and grabbed it with his hand, guiding it where he wanted it. He groaned and I felt it in my throat, sending a shiver through my spine that I wanted more of.

I opened my eyes and looked up to see the brightest star overhead. The North Star. And in that instant, it was as if I snapped out of a dream I never wanted to be in. Bellamy had just finished a bottle of rum, yet I was the one who felt drunk. The starlit sky above spun as I took notice of Bellamy's lips against mine and my hands beneath his tunic. It was the moment some clarity finally found its way to me. There was no doubt I'd always felt something for Bellamy. But this was something I would never do. So why was I doing it?

Bellamy wasn't the one who survived the curse breaking, because Bellamy didn't have my heart. Milo did. I gave my heart to Milo. So, what the hell was I doing right now? This wasn't me. This wasn't Katrina. But as I fought against the voice in my head, I finally found her.

I pulled away quickly, and I slapped my hands over my lips. "I'm sorry," I stuttered. "I don't know what I was doing."

Bellamy seemed entranced. He reached for my face and placed a gentle palm against my cheek. "That one wasn't for show, love." He uttered with an intoxicated looking grin.

"I know, and I'm sorry!" I snapped, keeping my voice low.

Bellamy cocked his head, still locking his eyes with mine. "You know, it's the strangest thing. You have the most beautiful blue eyes. As blue as the sea. I bet that's why I told you everything. Because you look like the sea."

I felt my heart drop. My eyes weren't blue. Whatever was happening to me was clearly not something I wanted. But I didn't know how to stop it.

"But wait, aye. Now they're becoming brown again." Bellamy straightened, his voice rising and becoming clearer and more controlled. "You're—you're one of them?"

"One of what, Bellamy? Tell me what you know." I demanded. This time it was all me who spoke, full of desperation.

"You're whatever the woman that appears on my father's ship is...her eyes are blue like that. Always. But they turn the deepest blue. And he becomes her puppet. You're controlling me?"

"No," I said, "I mean, not on purpose. I don't know what's happening to me."

"That's why you jumped in the water that night, isn't it?" Bellamy stood up, eyeing me like I was some kind of alien. "You're a siren. You're real?"

"No. I mean, yes. I mean, I don't know." My words came in frantic gasps.

"That means I wasn't crazy. I know what I saw on my father's ship." Bellamy turned his back to me, taking a few steps away to the starboard side of the ship.

"What are you talking about?" I uttered desperately, following him. He ignored me. "Please!" I reached for his arm.

"Why?" He yanked it away. "You'll just manipulate it out of me anyway? Go ahead, turn me into your puppet again and put me under your spell."

"Bellamy, I promise I wasn't trying to—"

"No," he uttered. "Leave me alone." With his jaw tense and his forehead pressed, he gently shoved me away as he walked back down the steps toward his quarters. Once he was out of sight, I listened quietly for the sound of his cabin door slamming. With a burning in my chest, I looked up to the stars that had just watched it all. And I'd never felt more alone and lost.

23

Message In a Bottle

Katrina

I sat there wondering how I was ever supposed to earn back Bellamy's trust. And I wondered if I really even needed it. But some part of me at least had to know he didn't hate me.

Tomorrow we'd be making port at Nassau, and I hoped more than anything that somehow, I'd find Milo there. But how would I look at him after how I'd just kissed Bellamy? Even if most of it wasn't me...some part of it was. My siren side was stronger than I realized. But it didn't have desires of its own. It just made me act on the dark ones I already had. And that's what I hated the most. It made me bold, mean, and selfish. And it knew how to overpower me.

I went to find McKenzie. She and Noah slept somewhere belowdecks, but I didn't know exactly where. Stepping down into the depths of the dark ship, I looked for them, holding a lantern I'd taken from up top to see by. I passed rows of hammocks and sleeping barracks, until a hand motioning for me caught my attention. It was McKenzie lying on the floor on a pile of blankets. Noah was propped up with his back against the wall, his head hanging to the side as he slept.

"Care if I join?" I whispered.

"What were you doing?" McKenzie asked. "Getting another night of special treatment from Bellamy?" I could almost taste the sourness in her words. I sat down beside her, careful not to ruffle the blankets and disturb anyone sleeping nearby.

"No," I hissed. "I was trying to talk to him. But it didn't go as planned."

McKenzie shook her head. "So can Bellamy help us or not?"

"Bellamy's pissed at me right now for various reasons," I muttered, looking down at the dust on the blankets. "I think we're on our own. But I'm hoping tomorrow when we land in Nassau that maybe we'll find Milo and maybe he'll know what to do."

"I hope you're planning to tell Milo about all this quality time you've had with Bellamy." Noah's voice cut through the darkness as he leaned forward in the shadows. "Though God knows maybe he deserves it after all the shit he's put us through."

I opened my mouth to argue, but I couldn't think of what to say. Noah wasn't wrong. I'd betrayed Milo, even if I wasn't in control when I did. I was just as selfish as Cordelia. Maybe it really was my destiny to become like her.

"Noah," I finally managed to stumble out. "I would say 'it's not what you think,' but I know that sounds like such BS." I could see Noah's fed-up expression, even in the dark. His dark brows stayed pressed together, and he was nearly scowling at me.

"It does." He nodded. "But I mean, what's happened to us isn't normal. So, who's to say what even makes sense here?"

I turned my face away, the weight of Noah's condescending side eye. He went on, "Look, I'm the first to assume the worst about everyone. I was just starting to be Milo's friend before all this went to hell. But I'm starting to think maybe, just maybe, Milo wasn't the crazy one here."

McKenzie and I both exchanged a look of surprise. "There's something I should probably tell you both," I fumbled with my words.

"Well, go on then," Noah muttered.

I took a deep breath, worried this could make me sound even crazier. But it was the only way I could salvage the thin, quickly fraying thread between us. "Ever since we've been here, I've been hearing this...this voice in my head. It's like my own, but it tells me things I would never think. Sometimes I follow it, and I don't realize I am until it's too late.

"Is that supposed to make me feel better?" Noah crossed his arms. "Because all it does is tell me you're crazier than I thought."

"That's what I was afraid of. But I need you to listen." I clenched my jaw and leaned forward, making my words perfectly clear. "Something here has been controlling me. And I'm still trying to figure out how to stop it."

McKenzie looked at Noah, who still didn't seem willing to budge. "Noah, look at what's happened to us. We literally traveled through time. Maybe it's not impossible to believe something could be messing with our minds."

I was grateful that McKenzie was willing to give me the benefit of the doubt, but I knew my excuse wasn't enough. They needed to know the rest. Keeping secrets almost always did more harm than good.

"There's more to it than that. I think it's time I own up to it. I..." A lump rose in my throat, and I almost couldn't finish the sentence. I didn't want to hear myself say it out loud. But I forced myself to get it out. "I told you I was Cordelia's descendant back on the motorsailer, remember?"

They both nodded, and I blinked nervously before going on. "Well, that makes me a siren, too. And I'm starting to think maybe that side of me has a voice stronger than my own."

They both hesitated for a moment, and I hung my head. To my surprise, it was Noah who spoke first.

"At this point I'm starting to think I'm dreaming, but I mean if we freaking traveled back in time, who's to say you can't be a mermaid?"

"Trust me, it's not something I want. I wouldn't lie about this." I shrugged. "But I wanted you to know so that it means something when I say I'm sorry. I'm sorry for getting you into this mess, I'm sorry that I don't know how to save us yet, and I'm sorry that I'm making a fool of myself on this ship. But you're both all I have left. And I don't want to lose you next."

Noah's eyes softened just a touch, and McKenzie leaned into him, her arm against his shoulder.

"Apology accepted," McKenzie sighed. "We're not going anywhere." She looked at Noah, as if waiting for him to confirm what she said. He sighed and rolled his shoulders with a groan.

"It's fine. I appreciate the apology. And I guess if there's anyone we should wanna be stuck with in the middle of the ocean, it's a mermaid."

"Thanks." My lips formed a little half-smile. "I promise I'm trying my best."

"So are we," Noah said. "And while we're apologizing, I'm sorry for the way I acted about Sand—er—Milo. I guess he didn't mean to screw us over like this. But even if he did, I didn't want this to happen to him."

"I promise you, he only did what he had to do. To keep the trident out of the wrong hands." I straightened myself, ready to defend Milo. "And I refuse to believe he's gone."

"Me too, Katrina. He wouldn't go down that easily. He's gotta still be out there. And when we find him and get back, he owes my uncle a new boat." Noah spoke under his breath, but I could sense the lighthearted change in his voice.

"Fair enough," I uttered, my spirits lifting. "It's not every day you find out your coworker is a ghost pirate."

We all enjoyed a brief chuckle, but soon the space fell silent again. Together we leaned against the wall of the ship and closed our eyes as the sea's rhythm rocked us to sleep. And I clung tightly to McKenzie's reassuring words as I replayed them in my head: "*We're not going anywhere.*"

"Land ho!" The muffled sound of a gruff voice yelling above made me open my eyes. I sat up in the small space in which we'd all slept and looked down at McKenzie asleep with her head on Noah's shoulder.

I smiled. Things felt as though maybe, just maybe there was some small ray of hope starting to peek through. Clutching the wooden railing, I made my way up to the deck and wandered to the edge of the ship. I glanced around, surveying the horizon for any sign of land. But I didn't see anything but the never-ending stretch of deep blue rolling for miles.

"Land ho?" I said out loud, squinting in the morning sun as I looked upward to the sailor up in the crow's nest.

"Guess he can see something we can't with that thing," Noah stated, gesturing to the spyglass that the man held to his eye.

"I wonder how far away that means we are." McKenzie leaned on the railing. "I'm gonna go find us some food. I'll check the rations."

"I'm going with you," Noah added, "Remember last time how that guy in the galley got a little too friendly with you."

McKenzie nodded and they disappeared back down below the deck toward the galley. I'd catch up with them in a minute, but first, I wanted to try "painting" one last time, just to clear my head for the new day. I walked back to the spot on the deck where I'd painted the waves on the parchment before. The dye stains were barely still there, and I was impressed the colors had lasted through the rainstorm. I laid out my last piece of parchment and sat down, mixing a handful of dye from my pocket with some water on the deck. It made just enough paint for me to outline the shape of a message bottle among the waves. But as I formed the picture, I felt the ship rise with the crest of a high-rolling wave. Even sitting down, I had to grab the railing on the hull to steady myself and catch my balance.

As the ship came crashing back down, it nosedived toward the ocean with quite a splash, sending seawater lapping onto the deck and crashing over my artwork. As I watched the dye and spices fade into the water around them, I suddenly felt an intense fury—a reaction that was way too disproportionate for the situation. I locked my gaze onto the running colors as they bled off the parchment, onto the deck, and leaked off the side of the ship.

The longer I stared at the destruction, the more I suddenly felt that dark siren essence rising within me. And then I noticed the colors reforming into the blotchy excuse of a picture they were before. I watched the seawater trickling off the edge of the ship, but as I followed it with my eyes, it changed course right in front of me, flowing opposite the direction of gravity and returning to the outline of the painting. And I blinked, nearly stumbling backward at my own shock.

The water ran in reverse in little streams, following the path I'd laid out for it in my head, taking form of an image back on the parchment solely by command of my thoughts. I was controlling the seawater.

Suddenly it struck me as to why I'd always been so easily able to work with watercolors. I'd tried painting with acrylics and oils, but they never felt quite right to me. And now I knew why. I'd always had power over watercolors. I could tell the water how far to run and where to stop before it bled into a section I didn't want it to...all just by thinking about it. But it never made sense until today, when I painted an entire picture on the deck of a ship without touching it.

I ran to the edge of the ship and stared down at the water below. Could I control that too? I concentrated with every ounce of strength in me, drilling my focus into the water just as intensely as I did when I painted. But nothing happened. I wanted the water to rise up like a waterspout. But to my disappointment, nothing changed.

Controlling the sea must be something I'd have to learn to master. But for now, it wasn't happening. I tried my best to compose myself as I leaned against the edge of the ship. It had only been a few days, here, yet I felt as though I was losing it. Why had none of this happened back home?

I shook my thoughts away and pushed out the siren voice inside. To regain my senses, I hurried to find McKenzie and Noah. I followed the sound of crewmen singing sea shanties near the front of the ship. Mingling amongst them was McKenzie, and Noah was gripping the rope rigging attached to the masts and appeared to be standing amongst the crew as they worked to change the sails and direct the ship to land.

As I neared the crew, the gritty, salt-dried voices singing the jolly lyrics of their shanty became clearer. I caught a better view of Noah. And I couldn't believe the way he looked. He was actually...smiling. And as I stepped closer and closer, I chuckled at his musical addition to the song.

"Is he...beatboxing to a sea shanty?" I asked, stepping up beside McKenzie, who handed me some type of dry bread and a cup of water.

"Yeah," she laughed, nodding toward the crew. "They love it."

As I giggled at the scene before me, I thought about how grateful I was to be trapped back in time with two friends. Of course, I'd give almost anything if I could've somehow kept them out of all this, but in some selfish way, just for that fleeting moment, I let myself be glad that they were here.

The next moment, a dark scowl from across the deck darkened my mood. Bellamy emerged from his cabin, his heavy boots announcing his presence as he trudged across the wooden floor. He strode past me, his elegant captain's coat drifting behind him, and his icy gaze fixed straight ahead toward the open water.

When he turned to address the crew, the shanties stopped, and everyone became so quiet that all I could hear was the gentle flapping of the sails overhead. His eyes swept over me as he spoke, and I could tell he was intentionally avoiding looking my way. He clearly remembered last night. And he was still upset, understandably.

"We make port at Nassau in two hours!" He shouted. "Continue to man the rigging on the mizzen. See if you can't get some more speed out of these sails."

His eyes fell on me as he began to walk toward the helm. "I want to get this time waste over with as fast as possible."

"Bellamy," I tried to call out to him, but he kept walking. "Bellamy, please."

When he halted and tensed, a small flicker of hope lit up in me. I expected him to turn around, but he only looked back over his shoulder. "That's two hours until you and your friends disembark from my ship. And then I never want to see your faces again."

"You're going to leave us in Nassau?" I asked.

"Be lucky I don't leave you dangling at the end of the plank."

"What would it mean if I said I was sorry? How can I make you trust me again?"

"You can't. I know the kind of thing you are. I've seen what you're like."

"Well then you know more than me, because I still don't understand who I am." I threw my hands out to the side in a defeated motion.

"Ask the woman who keeps my father captive at sea. I'm sure she can help you hone your craft." Before I could even think of a response, Bellamy turned his back to me and stormed to the helm.

Shaking away the frustration I felt with Bellamy, I explained to McKenzie what I'd just witnessed with my watery painting.

"That's awesome! You can control water?" Her eyes lit up a bright cerulean as the waters surrounding her. They contrasted against her freckled pale skin, which by now had reddened significantly in the sun.

"I think," I said. "But just small amounts for now. I want to try practicing more though, with the time we have left."

McKenzie agreed and together we headed to the least crowded section of the boat.

"Can you cup some water in your hands?" I asked her. With her help, we lowered a bucket down into the water on a rope, scooping up a good amount of water to last us a few tries.

McKenzie held out her cupped hands, barely a quarter of a cup full. I stared into them, willing the water to do something...anything. Move up and down.

Slosh side to side. Trickle along the side of her skin. But nothing worked. We tried for what felt like hours, each attempt looking more foolish than the last.

"What the heck are you two doing?" Noah came trotting up, unsuccessfully trying to tuck his loose-fitting tunic into his pants.

"Katrina might be able to control water," McKenzie said nonchalantly. "We're trying to test her powers."

"Of course." Noah rolled his eyes playfully. "Why not?"

"So far it's clear I'm not very good at it." I tilted my head with a pout.

"Well, how did you figure it out in the first place? Is this part of your mermaid thing?" He asked, crossing his arms.

I lowered my gaze, blinking and thinking about the question. "Well..." I tried to remember every time I'd painted something difficult. Something that shouldn't have turned out perfectly the first time, but did.

There was the time I painted a flower, a beautiful withering rose when my mom had her first relapse. The petals had formed perfectly, and the paint drifted into all the right spots without a thought. Then there was the showcase painting. Each time I added something, I was thinking of my own hopelessness, or of failing Mom, or losing Milo. And most recently, the message bottle painting on the deck. Because I'd been thinking of how lost we were. And I was afraid Milo was dead...

"I think I figured it out," I gasped turning to McKenzie. I crouched down and scooped up my own tiny handful of water. I stared at it and thought of Milo. I thought of how much I regretted the way I'd spoken to him before we set sail. I thought of how angry he'd made me when he kept Cordelia's letter from me. But how now I realized it wasn't something that should've come between us. He swore it was a mistake, and I knew it really was, but I chose to hold onto it and let it break our trust. But he wasn't wrong. I had become consumed with chasing her. And he was right to be wary of it. Cordelia's influence had made fools of us all. And I was at the center of it. I'd pushed away Milo for it. And now I'd lost him and everything else.

"I'm sorry." The words quivered on my lips as tears came to my eyes, and at the same time, the tiny amount of water in my hand slowly began to creep upward in droplets, curling over my fingers like vines made of bubbles. I dropped the water in surprise, flinging it on Noah. My smile widened into a gaping grin.

"I did it!" I gasped.

"How?" Noah asked, wiping the water from his face with his sleeve.

"I think it's when I feel. When my emotions are strong. But especially when I cry."

"Interesting," McKenzie raised an eyebrow. "Like your tears are connected to the water or something."

"That theory sounds good enough to me," I exclaimed, still catching my breath from the excitement. "It works, whatever the reason."

"Well maybe that will come in handy somehow." Noah shrugged. "Maybe you can drain the ocean and find that trident."

McKenzie stepped beside him, wiping her wet hands on his arm as he gave her a disapproving look. "Don't be so sarcastic, Captain Asshole." She planted a kiss on his cheek. I couldn't help but laugh at them.

The rest of the morning, we sailed quietly as the *Widow* picked up speed and carried us onward. I looked out at the horizon just as the land mass came into view. A long stretch of island with rising green hills and sandy cliffs in the distance.

Nassau.

24

TURN A BLIND EYE

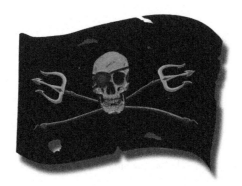

MILO

I t was morning. The morning my father would die.

I did my best to focus on my mission of stealing a ship for my own, but my relentless thoughts continued to tug at me. No matter how much I tried to convince myself he deserved it, another small voice in me wanted to believe that perhaps I was still wrong about him. Perhaps I'd just misunderstood everything. Perhaps I *should* intervene. Or at the least, I could be near the scene...just in case.

By the church bells, I knew it was 11 o'clock. Valdez would kill my father at the last stroke of noon. With my stomach full of fresh ale and bread, I stalked off to the harbor, where plenty enough men remained still clearing out debris from the ship I'd burned down the night before. But it was quiet enough.

With a full bottle of rum in hand and a woodblock in the other, I sat down on an overturned skiff by the harbormaster's shanty. It was a rough, creaking excuse for a shack perched high on level with the docks by its own set of stilts. No one would think twice about a poor sailor day drinking and whittling a block of driftwood in a spot that smelled of brine and rotting fish. So that's the part I planned to play.

It didn't take me long to spot Valdez's ship, already moored at the docks. Some of his crew remained on board, but I knew he wasn't on the ship. He would've been returning from a chat with my father soon.

I waited as the sun inched across the sky, taunting me with its unforgiving heat. I'd been so used to coming out at night in the cold Atlantic that I'd almost forgotten what it was like to bake out in the open Caribbean like this.

Damn. Hurry up, Valdez.

I didn't know what I wanted him to hurry for. I didn't know what I planned to do. But something in me wouldn't allow me to be absent for this moment. As if somehow, everything would make sense right before Valdez fired a lead ball into my father.

But assuming I did save him, what then? What would that change? I recalled how the instant I'd altered my memories by breaking into my own home as a boy. Whatever I did here clearly influenced what would happen in the future. Which could mean that if I stopped my father's death, Valdez might never have forced me onto his crew. And if I never became part of his crew, I'd never have been cursed. I'd never have suffered for 300 years. And I'd never have met Katrina.

I shifted, sliding the sole of my boot across the pier wood. With my small blade, I dug into the malformed chunk of driftwood in my hands as though I could punish it for the confusion racing in my head. I could save my father's life and spare my younger self the most tormented destiny. Or I could let him die, and live it all over again. I told Katrina I'd endure hell all over again for her. And it wasn't a lie. Was this God's cruel way of making me prove that?

"I told you, Daven, I can't explain to you what I have on board. You'd best have to see for yourself. The governor struck his deal with me, but the law don't mince words...no pirates in the British ports. 'Said I'd need a middleman to cross and carry the goods. But the price he's paying. It's worth the job, trust me."

I turned my head to the familiar voice that scraped against my soul like the knife in my hand against the driftwood. Valdez. I was careful not to reveal my face, so I kept my hood pulled low and my head down as I listened.

"Valdez, if this is as big of a job as you say, I'll need more than the usual share."

"Hmm. We'll talk prices after you've seen the cargo. I plan to pay you more, but don't think you can take advantage of the situation."

I kept a watchful eye as my father and the captain strolled across the dock, walking right past me, and onto the gangplank and up to the *Siren's Scorn*. It was silent except for the gulls around me belting out their constant cry.

I waited. And waited. Sweat rolled off my forehead and onto the blade I flipped back and forth between my fingers. My foot tapped nervously. I knew if I couldn't calm myself down, I'd start to look suspicious. But I couldn't get any of it back under control. These next few minutes were critical in whether or not I would alter the course of history.

Finally, my father and Valdez emerged, their pace much brisker than when they'd boarded. My father looked unhinged, pointing a finger threateningly toward Valdez as he uttered something much too low for me to hear. I expected this to be the part where he refused to do the job after he'd seen the captured mermaids in their glass tanks inside.

"You're out of your bloody mind if you think I'll pay any shipper that." Valdez spat. "What I offered you is more than fair."

"No, Valdez." My father spoke through a clenched jaw and bulging neck. "He wants these delivered *alive*. This isn't the usual chopped tail and heart in a jar shipment. I'll need triple the usual rate. At the least."

"Triple? For a voyage you can make blindfolded. Daven, hear yourself."

They continued arguing as my head spun with my father's words echoing in my mind.

This isn't the usual chopped tail and heart in a jar shipment.

He'd done this before. And he'd lied to me about this, too. He didn't refuse this job because he didn't want to ship mermaids. Why was I surprised? As the realization sunk to the very bottom of my soul, I understood that my father—Daven Harrington—was undoubtedly not the man he'd tricked me into thinking he was.

As they tossed words back and forth back on the docks, I looked up when I heard the running footsteps of a boy come all too late to stick his nose where it didn't belong.

"Tiburón, go back home! This doesn't concern you." Daven shouted. It was only now that I could detect the quake of nervousness in his voice. His desperation to keep his dealings a secret from his son was all too plain to see now. This warped hindsight allowed me to see what was right in front of me all along.

"I came to see if you need any help, Father." A naïve, lanky fifteen-year-old Milo approached the docks, oblivious to the doom that awaited him.

"He's in need of some help, boy, that's for sure." Valdez peered around at young Milo, his voice sour. "Maybe your boy can talk some sense into you."

"Don't bring my son into this!" Daven shoved Valdez backward, and I knew what happened next.

The captain would pull his pistol out without hesitation and aim it at my father. This was my moment to decide. I studied the teenage boy running to the feuding men, desperate to jump in and defend his father. And I saw what awaited him if I were to jump in and stop Valdez. Daven would live, and he would continue living a lie to his son, until eventually one day, his son would become too wise for the charade, and he'd figure it out. And if he wasn't smart enough to realize it was wrong, he'd fall into the same pattern of justifying the wrong thing just to please his father. And perhaps he'd even end up carrying on the business, unable to see the evils in it, or worse—choosing to ignore them.

And that, to me, was a fate worse than a thousand years at the bottom of Davy Jones Locker or wherever else Cordelia could send me. And I refused to let that young boy grow to become the same man as his father. So, I sat there in silence as I listened to the sound of a pistol firing and my younger self screaming.

Young Milo ran to Daven, frantic.

"Father! Father...no..." He hung his head, grimacing with glistening eyes from choking back emotion. "What happened?"

I couldn't hear Daven's dying response from where I sat, but I remembered exactly what he said to me.

"He...he wanted me to...to ship mermaids. *Mermaids*, Tiburón..." he coughed while straining for his last lying breaths. "Can you believe it?" I could still see him lifting his head as the blood began trickling from his mouth and his hand dropped from my shoulder. "But I wouldn't do it. And this is what he I got for it." He grunted out the words between his desperate gasps before reaching into his pocket and pressing a compass into my hand. "May this guide you better than it did me."

I hoped he'd be glad to know that it had.

25

WALK THE PLANK

KATRINA

Once we'd docked, Bellamy's crew wasted no time rolling up sails and grabbing whatever materials needed to be unloaded. They worked quickly, almost as if the ship would catch on fire any moment if they stayed on it too long.

"Come on, Katrina. I guess we have to get off here, too," McKenzie called to me as I stood observing the commotion around me.

"Your friend is wise. The sooner you get off my ship the better." Bellamy seemed to have appeared from nowhere. He walked past me with a crude bump of the shoulder.

I shook my head, watching him walk away with that sure, but heavy stride towards the lowered ramp leading down to the dock. I knew I shouldn't say anything. I knew the best thing was to just let him keep walking and get off his ship. So, I held my tongue.

With some strange reluctance and steps slower than they should have been, I trailed far behind Bellamy with Noah and McKenzie at my side. I took in the sights and smells of the port around us. Other ships just like Bellamy's bobbed in the harbor, all varying in size.

The stench of dirt, saltwater, and rum tickled my nose and reminded me of how Milo often described this place as a rancid haven for pirates. A paradise of free men, paid for in lawlessness and mayhem. By the looks of the rundown, bustling buildings and weathered streets, I could see why. Filthy fishermen ogling McKenzie and me, men chatting on the pier while chugging rum and yelling obscenities at us, and a strange, hooded man seemingly watching us in the distance all gave me an uncomfortable feeling. The siren side in me despised him right away, and I felt disgusted when I looked his way. Suddenly, I no longer knew if searching this city by ourselves for Milo would be wise. I sped up a bit to catch up to Bellamy, if only to ward off the creeps for a moment.

As I watched the sights around me, I almost didn't notice as I followed Bellamy right past a ship I didn't recognize in the daylight—the *Siren's Scorn*. I didn't mean to gasp, but I couldn't help it when I saw Valdez approaching. A slightly younger Valdez, with less harsh features and lacking the deranged, bloodthirsty look in his eye, hobbled near with laughter.

"Boy!" he cried with a hearty laugh, "I wasn't expecting to see you till Kingston."

Bellamy stopped in his tracks and replied with a coy air in his voice. "Yes, well, I didn't expect to be attacked by the Royal Navy twice. We're just here for repairs. Won't be long."

"Who's the girl?"

Bellamy glanced back at Katrina. "She's..." He hesitated for a long few seconds. "Just a lucky castaway. She was shipwrecked with her companions. They're getting off here and we'll hopefully never see them again."

The way Bellamy shifted when Valdez pat him on the back made me take notice. I couldn't tell if he was glad to see his father or repulsed. "Just stopping in for repairs," he uttered half-heartedly.

"Well, who did you pick up along the way?" Valdez's eyes snaked their way to me.

"No one. Just a few castaways." Bellamy stole a glance at me, but I didn't look away from him. I was too afraid to look at Valdez. He couldn't possibly know me yet, but something didn't feel right.

Valdez inched closer to me, and my heart went pounding in my ears. He questioned Bellamy about me, and insisted I was more than just a castaway.

"Shipwrecked, you say?" he asked, circling us.

I glanced at Bellamy, afraid he would give me up to his father. Why wouldn't he? He clearly knew his father hunted us. I fully expected him to tell him my secret after how clear he made it that he hated me. So, I was shocked when Bellamy stepped in front of me as his father approached.

"I said she's nothing special. Just a girl."

Valdez shoved him out of his way. "Look at her. She's got something more than usual beauty about her..." He paused and scratched his chin. "It makes me wonder...That face. Those eyes. She favors Lady Cordelia wouldn't you think?"

I went rigid at the mention of Cordelia. And I knew if Valdez thought my eyes looked like hers, the siren voice must be lurking in the shadows of my conscience, waiting to take control.

"I can't say I agree, Father. Perhaps you just can't get that woman off your mind."

"Hmm," Valdez growled, "Well don't send her away yet. I'd like to see what Cordelia has to say about her."

"What will that matter to you?" Bellamy asked, putting a protective arm across me. When his arm touched my body, the siren soul in me took charge and unlocked my dark desires once again. Unable to fight it, I wrapped my hands around his arm and pulled myself close.

"I love you, son, but I don't quite trust your judgment here. This girl just might be more...useful...than you think." Valdez turned and called for one of his crewmen to get Cordelia from her quarters on the ship to "provide her expertise."

I thought of running, but it would only make me look like I was hiding something. So, I stood there, waiting for Cordelia as I pressed myself against Bellamy, who continued to calmly argue with Valdez. Why was he trying so hard to save me when moments earlier he'd just seemed ready to throw me overboard?

I looked up at him, desperate to understand. "Why are you helping me?" I whispered.

He didn't answer me, but looked away as though he was trying to swallow down something bitter. I held onto his arm tighter, something primal in me wishing I could pull myself into him until I disappeared. My siren was taking over, and despite how inappropriate it was in a moment like this, all I could do was picture myself entangled with Bellamy, tasting the rum on his breath.

I glanced back briefly and noticed the man in the distance had pulled back his hood and seemed to be watching us closely. It gave me an eerie feeling, and I looked away quickly and recoiled further into Bellamy. His was the only face the siren allowed me to see.

But then I looked up to see the figure that emerged from the cabin, I shuddered, and my desires went cold. From the top of the ship she descended, like an elegant queen floating down the ship's ramp in her billowing dress of sky blue. She craned her head around, breathing in the fresh ocean air and then her eyes fell down to me. And she held them there as she walked down.

You're just as soulless as me.

Her words echoed in my head, but I fought against them and did my best to calm my breathing. I rubbed my fingers together in my sweating palms as she neared. There was no way she could know me, not in this time. I wasn't born yet. She might be powerful, but she didn't have the ability to see the future.

She joined Valdez, stopping at his side and placing her hand on his shoulder gently. "What did you need me for, darling?" she asked in a sing-song voice that matched the rest of her refined appearance.

"Take a look at this 'girl' would you. Is she one of yours? Maybe a runaway to land?"

Cordelia narrowed her eyes at me. "Ah, I could see why you might suspect that," she said. Taking a step toward me and holding out her hand, she addressed me for a moment. I glanced around, realizing Noah and McKenzie were gone. Did they abandon me? Or were they taken when I wasn't looking? My heart began to speed up so fast I thought it would be loud enough to hear. "Come here, angelfish." She spoke softly as she reached for my hand and pulled me from Bellamy's grip. "Don't be frightened."

I focused on my breathing, trying to keep from looking nervous. If I looked scared, she'd know I had something I was keeping a secret. As Cordelia circled me slowly, inspecting my face and body with her gaze, I fought every nerve going haywire within and told myself to stand still and relax. But my heart felt like it would explode through my chest.

I was shocked when she glanced at Valdez and said, "I assure you she isn't one of them. You won't find her of any use in your dealings."

It took everything in me not to breathe an audible sigh of relief. But when she turned her head back around to look at me, my stomach flipped, and I froze with a sinking feeling. She cunningly smiled at me with a look in her eye, in a way that communicated everything at once. And the way she fiddled with the mermaid scale necklace at her neck to draw my focus to it was no coincidence. She knew who I was. And she'd just saved me—whether because I was her granddaughter or because I was a pawn in her plan, I'll never know. Maybe both.

Whatever the reason, I watched her pull Valdez away and reassure him I wasn't who—or what—he thought I was. Bellamy turned to me as I stumbled around, steadying my shaking breaths that threatened to betray me.

"This is your chance. Go, now, and don't *ever* come back here," Bellamy said, catching me off guard. His tone was anything but gentle.

I turned around, confused. "If you hate me so much, why did you try to protect me just now?"

"I don't hate you," Bellamy mumbled, "but I could never be with a siren. I've seen the consequences of that." He glanced at his father, who was still busy talking with Cordelia. "Like I told you before, my love—my *only* love—is the sea. Not the demons within it."

"Well...thanks, I guess," I said, slightly offended at his last choice of words. "But don't worry, I don't belong here, so hopefully you'll never have to see me again."

"It would be for the best," Bellamy said, and he leaned forward, kissing my forehead. I'd never felt more confused and bewildered, but I didn't question it. Bellamy was as mysterious as the sea itself, and I'd never quite understand what he was feeling. But it didn't matter, I realized as I snapped out of my siren fog. *Milo.*

As if reading my thoughts, Bellamy added one more thing. "Besides, I wouldn't want your Milo to miss out on such a prize. Does he know what you are?"

I tilted my head as I thought how to best answer him.

"He knows better than anyone," I said. But something nagged at me. Of course, Milo was the one who insisted that I accept my mermaid side. But did he know of this selfish, conniving side that came with it? That, I didn't know. And I wondered what would happen when he saw the other side of me. The side that fed off intimidation and desire, showed no compassion, and made me do things I would never choose to do. The side I still didn't know how to control.

"Be careful out there, siren." Bellamy nodded knowingly, as I pulled my gaze from him.

"You do the same," I warned. The thought crossed my mind to tell him that I would see him again someday. But I thought it'd be best to keep that information to myself. And with one last look at Bellamy, I turned away toward Nassau, determined to set out to find Milo, the others...and hopefully myself.

I hadn't gotten far after I left the harbor when I couldn't shake the feeling that someone was following me. Footsteps trailed me, and I whipped around as shadows passed. And then, a brooding figure pulled me into an alleyway of rotting fish and old crates, a hand over my mouth to silence my screams.

26

BEDLAM

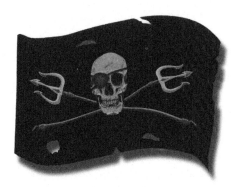

MILO

The church bell sounded its miserable chime, each one ringing out like another pistol shot. I couldn't listen to the boy's heartbreak any longer. Standing, I did my best to fight back the tightness in my chest and the burning in my eyes as I intended to leave this place of horrid memories. I shouldn't have come here to begin with.

As I walked away, I heard the desperate shouts of my teenage self. I didn't need to turn around to remember the dreadful scene unfolding at my back. I listened to the broken boy struggling as he fought against the crewmen pulling him onto the ship by his arms. One of the men grappling with him struck him across the face, splitting open the skin above his left eye. I touched the scar on my eyebrow as if I could feel it happening just the same.

"An orphaned lad needs a home, and the *Siren* needs a good sailing master and navigator." Valdez chuckled with a sharpness in his voice that made my stomach turn both then and now. "Welcome to the crew, Harrington."

"No!" I winced as I heard the break in my voice. "I'm not a pirate. And I won't become one!"

"Seeing as you have nothing left to lose here in this shit-ridden city, and you know just as much about charting as yer' father did, I'd say you're just about as much a pirate as my own son." Valdez turned to address the men taking hold of the boy on either side, dragging him away from the lifeless body of his father. "Put him in the brig hold for now, you swabs. He'll come 'round soon enough."

It would almost seem strange to think that this scene could unfold at a busy harbor—a kidnapping over a freshly slain man lying in his own blood. But this was Nassau. There were no rules. This type of madness was the norm.

"Don't worry, boy. Daven Harrington wasn't the man you think he is." Valdez followed behind the crewmen forcing my younger self up the gangplank.

"Shut up, you bastard! Keep my father's name from your lips!" As young Milo screamed in anger, another crew member of Valdez appeared to dispose of my father's body. He rolled his corpse into the water, kicking him as though he was no more than a bag of wet sand.

I had to look away. I forced myself to take another step forward. I couldn't bear it here another moment longer. And I needed to find a ship so I could get the hell off this cursed island and find Katrina. With my mind raging like the sea unchained, I thought of her. I wanted to tell her how she was worth every one of these painstaking memories. If it all brought me to her, it was worth it.

I kept the thought of her in the forefront of my mind. If—when—I found her, I would kiss her until she couldn't breathe. I would hold her so tightly Poseidon himself couldn't tear her away. She didn't want me to protect her, but I would never be able to let her go if I saw her again.

Just then, the sound of a different kind of bell caught my attention. It was the signal sound of a ship coming into port. It shouldn't have been a cause for me to notice. It was a sound I was used to hearing more often than not. But for whatever reason, this time, I turned to look.

The ship came in fast, and the sails were finally folding to slow her down. She was nearly rolling in waters far too calm for the strength at which she barreled into port. I wondered what the hurry was. Because this was one memory I didn't recall. Of course, I was being pulled to the gut of Valdez's ship by now, so who was to say what I might have forgotten in the fray.

It was a ship smaller than Valdez's galleon, but still mighty enough. I might've even considered it as a vessel with potential to commandeer, but by the battered sides of the hull, it was clear she'd been through a recent cannon exchange or two. So much for that idea. I hoped there was a good carpenter aboard for the captain's sake.

I watched as the anchor dropped and the crew rushed to close the sails and secure the rigging and everything else necessary before they came ashore. I counted a small crew of around fifty men as they flooded the docks, eager to step foot on land in who knew how long. But it was the captain who made me second glance.

My eyes narrowed as I strained to see in the blinding sunlight glittering on the harbor. The confident, brooding young man stepped out in a hurry, turning his head every which way as if he was looking for someone. His long blue coat fell to his boot-clad calves with an air of regality as he strode off his ship with an arrogance I could sense from here. I could hardly believe my eyes when he turned enough that I could see it was Bellamy. I had to resist the sudden urge to call out to him, remembering he wouldn't have known me yet. But it was the three passengers walking behind him that made me pause, sucking in a breath that caught in my chest.

I almost didn't recognize them. They were dressed as though they belonged on a ship as good as any. But the gleam of McKenzie's red hair, the sulking demeanor of Noah gave away their identities immediately. And then there she was. Katrina. She looked like a pirate herself, dressed in her own tunic and breeches and boots—delicate and fierce all at the same time. Her dark hair flowed behind her, full and tangled by the sea winds, and her eyes widened in wonder as she looked around at the harbor, taking in the sight of an entirely new world.

Of course, she didn't notice me. Not as I hid in the background waiting in the shadows. I wanted to run to her and show her my face. I needed her to know we'd found each other again. I desired so much that she knew how close I was to her. But I'd need to wait until she was closer, free from any influence of Valdez on the situation. Drawing attention could be dangerous.

I knew this Bellamy wouldn't let anything happen to her. He was always a hothead, but he'd never mistreat a woman. I briefly recalled our interactions after becoming part of Valdez's crew. Bellamy was the first one who spoke to me without commanding me to do something. He asked me my name and told me he was sorry for what happened to my father. Being five years my elder, he treated me almost as a brother for that first year on board Valdez's ship. He taught me to wield a cutlass as well as he could and showed me how to brawl like a sailor and raid ships like a pirate. I was sure it was only because he felt sorry for me. But my mind liked to pretend that he truly enjoyed my company. And I wished our ending had been better.

"Stay true north, and you'll never wander," he told me once over a shared bottle of rum. He was just intoxicated, speaking carelessly out of his ass, but those words never left me. And they finally made sense, three hundred years later.

When it came time to hunt sirens, he never seemed at ease in his conscience about it much more than I did, but he always convinced himself—and me—that it was necessary. Because like me, his duty was to Valdez. For obviously different reasons, of course.

I watched Bellamy saunter across the docks, making his way to the shore with Katrina and her friends in tow. But he veered around at the sound of his father's voice as Valdez greeted him from the docks.

Bellamy uttered something to Katrina, an almost threatening look on his face. She nodded and turned to walk away, but Valdez called out something that made me step closer. I tensed, ready for whatever strange thing may come next. My identity be damned.

Valdez slowly approached Katrina with an observant look in his eye. I wanted to react. To run and grab her, to rip her away from his filthy gaze. But I remembered Katrina's words that seeped like poison into my soul.

"You don't need to protect me...Haven't we been through enough for you to realize sometimes I have to fight my own battles?"

So, I restrained myself impatiently, waiting to see if maybe she had some plan up her sleeve.

Valdez circled them, studying Katrina up and down. The way his eyes moved over her made me want to rip his head from his body and toss it in the sea with my father's corpse. Any longer and I'd have to do something.

Valdez leaned forward and said something to Bellamy so lowly that I couldn't hear. But I fought with every voice in my head telling me to rush in and pull Katrina away. But where would that leave McKenzie and Noah? Did I even care? I only wanted Katrina.

But then I saw the way she was looking at Bellamy. Her eyes never left him, and she moved close enough to reach for his hand as Valdez continued speaking. And she clung to his arm like he was the last person in the world. And then she finally looked away from him, and then straight towards me, as if she knew I was there the whole time.

I ripped back the hood to show her my face, in case she couldn't see me well enough. But she hardly looked at me longer than a second before casting me aside through an indifferent gaze that stung like venom. No warmth. No welcome. Nothing. Then she drew her eyes back to Bellamy.

"You don't need to protect me."

Perhaps I truly didn't. Perhaps she had all the protection she needed in the arms of Bellamy. She seemed content enough. And seeing that I was alive clearly didn't matter to her. And what could I offer her at this point? I couldn't get us out of here. And I would have a bounty on my head soon enough, and it would only make things worse for her. Perhaps I was a fool for standing here hoping things would ever be the same between us again. Our ship had started sinking before we'd even set sail, but I didn't expect it to go down so quickly.

I shook my head, unable to think properly anymore. And the longer I stood by, the greater the urge to crush the compass beneath my boot and burn down every ship in the harbor grew. Ducking my head, I withdrew myself from the scene, my swift strides carrying me back into town where I escaped into an alleyway.

After I caught my breath, I looked at the nearest tavern, just meters away. It wasn't even noon yet, but I'd say I'd seen enough in the past hour to excuse my choice of remedy. It wasn't like me to act so rashly, but I no longer cared. Everyone I cared about had failed me. And I was tired.

27

TIDAL WAVE

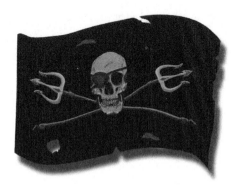

MILO

I downed the first pint as though it was fresh water after a week in the desert, and I immediately demanded another. The tavern keeper slid down another drink, as the bards sang shanties and the women danced around the tables of sailors immersed in their gambling.

When a hand touched my shoulder, I whipped around, pulling the blade from my sleeve and pointing it straight at the culprit.

"Noah?" I said with surprise as my eyes narrowed at his rugged expression. It was him, with a much more bold and unwavering air about him than before. "I'm surprised you didn't start crying." I muttered as I lowered my hand and put the blade away.

"Shut up, Sandy," he spat, but a small half-grin formed on his face. "It's...good to see you."

I shook my head and turned around, hunching over the bar. "I'll admit I'm glad to see you're not dead. Mostly."

"Look, man, are we really gonna still be like that after all this?" he exclaimed, sliding into the seat next to me.

"Consider me not punching you my apology. Why are you even here?" I took a swig of my drink. "You left Katrina and McKenzie to come here? I know they were with you."

"I saw you by the docks and followed you here." Noah hesitated for a moment. "McKenzie's right outside. She didn't want to come in here, understandably." When he paused to sigh, I looked up. "But Katrina..."

"What about Katrina?" I slammed my drink on the counter, my voice rising.

"That's why I followed you. Something's wrong with her."

I perked up, but I tried my hardest not to look too concerned. "She looked fine to me. In fact, she looked quite comfortable with Bellamy."

"That's my point, dude!" Noah leaned in, nudging my elbow with his. "She's been acting strange...but it's not *her*. It's like something is controlling her. She told us herself she can't stop it.."

"Go on." I didn't mean for the words to spill out so quickly, but they did.

"She's put herself in danger more than once, doing stupid stuff like running up on deck during a battle with another ship, jumping overboard in the night, just crazy stuff. And yeah, she's up Bellamy's ass, but when she does these things it's like she isn't Katrina. It's like she's...someone else."

A strange suspicion rose within me. If what I'd observed from the mermaids was true, then I supposed the things that lurked in their nature could be the same for Katrina. Perhaps it was diluted in her time...but here in this time when siren magic was aplenty in the seas, maybe somehow the ancient magic in her veins was awakened. And if what was happening to her was what I suspected, I knew I had to stop her before she lost herself completely. And if there was any small chance of keeping us afloat, I couldn't abandon ship now.

"Where is she now?" I stood up, fearing the answer, fearing I had just made the biggest mistake of my life by not ripping her away from Bellamy when I had the chance.

Noah dropped his gaze. "She's still back there. Valdez wouldn't let Bellamy let her leave. He called some woman out from his cabin to talk to her or something."

"What?" I took off before the word had even left my lips. I assumed McKenzie and Noah would follow, but I didn't wait for them.

I darted through the town, back through the streets and toward the harbor, hating myself for not thinking straight earlier and leaving Katrina. This Bellamy wouldn't have any idea that Katrina was a mermaid. He wouldn't have realized the danger he was putting her in.

When I reached the harbor, Bellamy, Valdez, and Katrina were nowhere to be found. They must've taken her inside. The gangplank was up, and there was no way onto the ship. I quickly realized my only option was to climb the side of the ship. Just as I leapt into the water below, Noah and McKenzie arrived, skidding to stop behind me at the edge of the dock.

"Keep watch!" I ordered.

Grabbing the siding of the boat, I began my ascent, my fingertips gripping the thin wooden ledges that barely stuck out along the ship. My soaking wet clothing and boots made the climb all the more difficult. But I couldn't afford to slip. The muscles in my knuckles ached as I held onto whatever I could manage to grab. When I reached a cannon, I sighed with relief, throwing my arm around it to haul myself up higher. It wasn't the first time I'd climbed up the side of a ship. But I certainly hoped it would be the last.

When I finally reached the deck, I swung myself over the railing and glanced around for any sign of Katrina. Not a soul was on board. Eyeing the captain's cabin, I wasted no time barging through the door, calling her name. But it was empty.

"Who are you and why are you looking for Katrina?" The voice that asked the question accompanied a shadow that darkened the doorway at my back.

I spun around to see Bellamy, standing with that arrogant demeanor I remembered so well. He watched me like an eagle locking onto its prey. I couldn't show him my face, especially not that my younger self was locked on board below.

"Are you Milo?" His question nearly caused me to stumble. How could he know?

I stayed silent, still trying to figure out how he could recognize someone he'd never met yet. When he stepped forward, I drew the blade at my side.

"So you *are* him then." With another step toward me, he placed his hands behind his back in a formal sort of manner.

"How do you know my name?" I uttered, knowing the less I said, the better. But I had to know.

"She called out your name in her sleep...No. Don't worry, mate. It wasn't like that...I made her sleep in my cabin to keep her safe." He must have noticed the way my jaw clenched, and I tilted my head in a threatening way at his words. "After she jumped in the ocean trying to find you."

I swallowed, taking in this information and trying to decide what to make of it.

"Where is she now?" I asked, doing my best to stay at an angle that hid my features in the shadows of this cramped wooden room.

"The hell I know where she is by now, but my father let her go so I'm assuming she went into town."

I nodded my thanks. It was all I could give as I still processed the strange interaction between a brother-like figure I'd once looked up to, who was now younger than me and naïve to what life held in store for him.

He stepped aside so that I could leave. With my wet clothes sticking to my skin and making moving quickly difficult, I stepped out onto the deck. It had been so long since I'd seen this ship in this condition. Like new and modified with cannons and new sails, ready to conquer the world. How little I realized how many decades I would spend a slave on board here, rotting away with it as eras passed.

Shaking myself free of the strange memory, I stepped to the raised gangplank and sliced through the rope holding it back with my knife. It dropped with a heavy thud and slammed onto the dock below, bringing memories to the forefront of my mind I'd rather have not faced as I walked across. McKenzie and Noah awaited me, both wearing looks of disappointment when they saw that I'd returned without Katrina.

"She can't be far," McKenzie stated. "She probably went looking for us when she saw us leave to get help."

"Then let's not waste time finding her," I ordered, shaking my head. "I should never have let her go."

I paced forward, scanning every inch to the left and right of this port. As we walked along the main dock back to the town entrance, I thought I saw her. My spirits lifted as a woman with dark, full hair tumbling over her shoulders approached, heading back toward the piers. But when she came closer to me, I could see that she wasn't Katrina. It was Cordelia.

Walking with a regal stride in her layers of fine skirts and corset, she neared. I didn't expect her to know me, or even notice me. So, when she looked up and grinned at me with a dark, sly smile, a bolt of ice struck my core. She passed by me as if on purpose, turning her head just to hold her cruel smirk on me just a bit longer. And I noticed around her neck was the scale hanging from its silvery chain, and all at once I felt sick.

I shook her chilling stare out of my mind and refocused on finding Katrina. The last place wanted to imagine her getting lost in alone was Nassau. Not that she needed me to protect her, I reminded myself. But I would be there just in case she did. We would find her.

So as we rushed along the dirt road into the belly of Nassau, I stopped dead in my tracks when someone called out to me from a section of a building on the coast blockaded in by barrels and crates. And in between them stood three men, obviously trying to stay out of plain sight. McKenzie shrieked in horror at the scene. Two men stood on either side of a brooding figure in the middle—Carl

Thane. And he was pulling Katrina's head back by her hair to expose her neck as he pressed the edge of dagger against it.

28

OF THE CODE

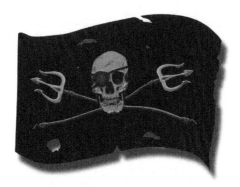

MILO

I wanted to scream. I fought back the wave of panic rising in my veins. My nerves shook, and it took every ounce of my focus not to let it show. I had to appear unshaken, despite my world crumbling before me. I had to draw this out as long as I could. There was a good bit of distance between us—too much distance for me to make it in time if Thane decided to swipe the knife across her neck. Katrina held my gaze, a wide-eyed look of terror in her trembling face. And I remained still. Because I knew Thane would slice her throat without a second thought if I made one wrong move.

"You're the bastard who set the *Lark* ablaze," Thane grunted.

My eyes flicked to the man at his right. It was the one I had pushed into the water to save. And all at once I regretted that mercy. I should've let him burn.

"It was nothing personal. You should be looking for the man who assigned me the mission," I uttered, hiding the ever-growing fury in my voice.

"Well don't consider this personal when I spill her blood out on the ground in front of you," he dug the point of the blade into Katrina's skin, and she winced with a yelp.

"Wait," I pleaded. To my surprise, he stopped. I spoke through a tight knot in my chest that nearly left me unable to breathe. "What do you want? I'll restore your loss with a new ship. Take your pick from my fleet." It was the perfect bargain now that my father's ships sat without a captain in the bay.

"I'll take the whole fleet."

Fine by me. He could have them all. "Done. Now let her go."

"Tsk, tsk, stranger. I'm not done bargaining." Even from where I stood, meters away from Thane's position in the shadows, I could see the way his eyes darkened.

"What else?" I stiffened, stepping forward and clenching my fist, hoping it wouldn't set him off.

"I want to know who you are, so that I can ensure every minute spent on this island is devoted to hunting you down. Take off the hood."

I tilted my head at the strange request. "Why don't you and your men just kill me right here?"

A grim smile stretched across his thin lips. "Because where's the fun in that? I want you to spend every day forward in fear, ne'er knowing when I'll finally strike, but always knowing that one day I will. If I spare your whore, I'm coming for you." This was exactly the sort of sick game Thane would relish. A chance to enact his sadistic tendencies by hunting me down like an animal. But I was more than willing to play along if it meant saving Katrina. After all, I'd been killed before.

"So, you'll let her go?" I reached for the top of my hood, not fully convinced he wouldn't kill Katrina after I showed myself anyway.

"I'm a man of the code," he grinned, lifting his knife off Katrina's neck, but still holding her by her hair, nearly lifting her from the ground.

"If you hurt her, I swear I'll send you back to hell myself." I watched his hand like a hawk tracking its prey.

He laughed a laugh that sent fire flashing before my mind's eye. I longed to watch this man bleed and burn. "I'm waiting," he crooned.

I glanced at Noah and McKenzie, who stood firmly on either side of me, before slowly removing my hood. As we stared at each other in silence across the alleyway, I waited with bated breath for Thane to release Katrina as he studied my features.

"I won't forget that face." His words made me uneasy, but I reassured myself it wouldn't remain here much longer for it to become an issue. Whatever he wanted, I'd agree to, as long as he'd release Katrina unharmed. I watched him hesitate, then lift the blade above Katrina's chin.

"Such a pretty girl," Thane growled. Then he sliced his knife across the side of her face.

Her scream reached my ears like the sound of every failure I'd ever made crying aloud in my soul. I ran to her as Thane shoved her to the ground, but my feet couldn't move fast enough. He turned away with his men in tow as a cloud of dust arose around us from their movements.

I locked my target onto him, reaching for the dagger at my side. I'd kill this man if it was the last thing I ever did for what he'd just done to her.

"Stay with her!" I shouted to McKenzie and Noah who followed fast behind me. Damn my conscience. Damn my soul. Damn it all. I would have Thane's blood for this.

I turned and climbed the building bordering the alleyway, clinging to the trellis and ivy crawling up the side as I scrambled upward. Once atop the roof, I scanned the streets for Thane and his men. There were few places they could have escaped to this quickly.

My gaze roamed the alleys below. The sounds of Nassau's usual chatter and buzz filled the air, carried along by the wind across the rooftops. But in the midst of all the laborers, sailors and drunks traveling below, I finally caught sight of them—a glimpse of that matted copper hair of Thane's between his two henchmen walking back toward the main strip of town.

I surged forward, my legs aching as I pushed my stride to its limit, racing along the edge of houses and dilapidated buildings as silently but quickly as I could manage. I needed a good angle. Good enough to leap down and plunge my knife into Thane's back before he even realized what struck him. I slid down to a low hanging balcony and waited overhead. They'd have to take a turn and pass by it to get back into town.

One... Two... Three...

I counted their footfalls and held my breath. I flexed my fingers around the bone handle of the knife in my grip. And just as Thane walked past below, I pushed myself from my lurking spot and pounced.

One of Thane's men caught sight of me just before my knife reached its target. He shouldered Thane out of the way and disrupted my concentration. With a stumble I landed, but I found my footing quickly and took a stance to fight the man at Thane's side. He drew his cutlass and swung it around toward my neck. I ducked with ease and plunged the knife into his abdomen. As he dropped to his knees, I ripped his sword from his grip. It was then that the other man—the one who I'd saved from the *Lark*— whirled around to come far too late to the defense. I dodged his attempt to strike me by furiously ramming my new blade into his shoulder. Hot blood spattered out, raining on me like crimson sea spray. As I realized Thane had escaped and was nowhere to be found, I heaved in anger that I'd lost him.

"Next time I suggest keeping your mouth shut," I snarled. And as I thought of Katrina, an unconfined fury rose in my bones that I couldn't snuff out. So, I twisted the blade as the man groaned in pain, driving him to the ground where I planned to deal him one final blow. "Tell your captain if he plans on hunting me like some kind of animal, it's an animal he'll find."

"Milo! Stop it!" Katrina's voice tore me from my rage. I shook my head and placed my boot on the man's hip to pry him off the edge of my sword. I dislodged the weapon from his flesh, and watched him clamber up to flee, bleeding and wounded. I looked down at the body of the man left behind. Then at Katrina, who stood a good distance away, clinging to McKenzie and Noah shielding them both.

Straightening as I caught my breath, I brushed my hair back from my eyes, only to smear my hands with the blood on my face. "They hurt you." I panted.

She watched me with uncertainty, like I was a poisonous viper. And I couldn't blame her after what she'd just witnessed. The right side of her face was stained red with blood just beginning to dry across her cheekbone. I stepped toward her, feeling the weight of my compass and my heart.

I wanted to run to her, but I knew it wasn't my place after what I'd just done. She'd never seen me like that. And she very well may never trust me again. But she had to know. She had to know I'd do anything to keep her safe. Past, present, or future.

Without warning, she took off past Noah and rushed toward me. She threw herself into my arms and I closed myself around her. The world around me faded. The stink of Nassau, the burning sun above, and the sweat and blood dripping from my brow. None of it mattered in her embrace.

"Don't become like them," she uttered into my shoulder. I nodded, squeezing my eyes shut tightly.

"This is a life long past I thought you'd never have to see," I sighed, pulling back from her and touching her injury with my fingers. It would scar. "I'm so sorry he did this to you."

"A scratch on my face is not our biggest problem right now. I was so afraid you were dead." She shook her head. "We all were." She looked back over her shoulder at McKenzie and Noah, who stepped near as she motioned for them to join.

"It's good to have you back." Noah rolled his eyes, but his words were genuine. "Now maybe you have some kind of idea of how we're supposed to get back to our time?"

"I'm afraid the trident is still our only hope. If it took us here, it has to be able to take us back. But we'll have to figure out how. But the first step is getting to it."

"So, we just sail right back over the Bermuda Triangle again in a wooden ship?" McKenzie raised an eyebrow. "That didn't work out so well last time."

"I'm open to any other suggestions, but he's right. What other option do we have?" Noah leaned in. It felt strange to hear him agree with me.

I reached into my coin purse and produced enough gold to show them. "Give me enough time to secure a ship. I have just enough money left to buy us lodging for one more night. I'm sure we're all in need of a good night's rest."

We wandered into town, far enough away from the incident with Thane's men to avoid suspicion—not that anyone would have cared. I couldn't lead them to Codface's tavern. He already knew too much, and I wouldn't make us targets more than we already were.

There was another inn on the far side of town. It was a bit of a trek, but no one complained. I did find myself watching my back for any sign of Thane or anyone else who sought to do me harm, but I tried my best to appear calm and unbothered. If I was the reason something happened to Katrina or the others here, I'd never forgive myself. I couldn't continue my father's legacy of destroying those around him by his own mistakes.

29

SHIPWRECKS

KATRINA

Milo led us to a tavern on the edge of town. I stayed close to him, watching with suspicion as strange men ogled McKenzie and me, and rogue beggars teetered near us in their drunken state. No one said much, still in shock after our brush with danger moments earlier.

As we walked, I looked at Milo and thought of him in the alley. I'd never seen him like that. Something had broken free from him. Something animalistic, dark, and feral. And it terrified and fascinated me all at the same time. But I had to remind myself, this place was no Constantine. This was a pirate-ridden city in 1720. Of course, there had to be things Milo had to do to survive that I could never comprehend. But I still felt an uneasiness when I remembered the expression in his eyes when he turned around, covered in another man's blood.

"We can stay here tonight. In the morning we can set out at first light." Milo took my hand and gently guided me up the steps to the entrance. How moments earlier those hands drove swords into flesh without mercy, but now caressed mine like a dove.

McKenzie, Noah, and I waited while Milo went to talk to the innkeeper. The smell of liquor, salt, roasting meat, and bread filled the air, making my stomach growl. I longed for a meal more filling than the watery stew and jerky on Bellamy's ship.

"What if we never make it back?" McKenzie uttered all of a sudden, a shakiness in her voice. "It sucks here. What if we're trapped here?"

"McKenzie," Noah reached for her shoulders, leaning down to look her in the eyes. "I promise that no matter what happens, we will be all right. I'll make sure of it."

I smiled a small smile as I watched them from the corner of my eye. McKenzie nodded and then threw herself into him for a hug. I was glad for her to have someone as stubborn as Noah. But secretly I feared the same as she did. And Cordelia's haunting words that found me even in my sleep certainly weren't helping me feel any better about it.

Milo returned and gestured to us to follow. "There's a room left."

We made our way upstairs to a small room with one bed, a wash bucket, and a small table, all of it barely big enough for one person, let alone four.

"Okay, I'm going back down there for some food," Noah announced. "Anyone else?"

Based on the way McKenzie jumped to agree, I must've not been the only one who felt like they were starving. I breathed a sigh of relief at the thought of filling my empty stomach.

"I'll be down in a minute. I want to clean up my face," I said, touching the cut from where it ran from the bottom of my jawbone back up toward my ear.

"I'll stay with you," Milo uttered, and then hesitated, looking at the door. "That is...if you want me to."

"I'd like that," I nodded.

"I'll go get something to clean the wound, then."

As the wooden door closed behind McKenzie, Noah and Milo, I sat down on the floor where I dipped a rag into the water bucket. It wasn't long before Milo returned with a cup of liquor.

"Here," he said, taking the rag from my hand as the candle fire flickered its light on his tanned skin. "Will you let me?"

I nodded, brushing my hair back behind my ear so that he could better access the injury. He gently pressed the rag over the mark, soaking away the dried blood. I winced at the burn.

"I'm sorry, Katrina," he muttered, cleaning the cut with soft strokes.

"It's okay," I bit my lip. "At least I can hide most of it with my hair."

"No." He pulled the rag away and held my gaze. "I'm sorry for everything."

"Who were those men?" I asked.

Milo parted his lips and released a heavy sigh. "There's so much that's happened in my few days here. I sabotaged that man's ship for information about my father. Turns out he's not at all the man I thought he was. It wouldn't be a stretch to say I'm ashamed to be his son."

"It can't really be that bad, can it?" I watched him with worry.

Milo pulled out his compass from his pocket. He spoke as he stared down at the tool in his hand with a hardened gaze and traced his finger and thumb along the rim. He told me about his father and the slave and mermaid trade, and everything else he'd been through since waking up on the shores of Nassau.

"He's the reason my mother and brother are dead. He got in over his head in a the details of a deal I never quite figured out. And they paid for it." He put the compass away and straightened his shoulders. "And now I've caused you to pay for my mistakes."

We sat in silence as he reached up to touch my face. He caressed his fingertips delicately along the scratched skin on my cheek. "I could never say I'm sorry enough times," he whispered.

"I'm the one who should be sorry," I said, looking down. I wanted to tell him how I felt like I was losing myself. I wanted him to understand why I should be sorry. But I didn't know how to put it into words. But I tried anyway. "I'm sorry that I pushed you away. Before any of this even happened. Before we ended up here..." I looked up at him. "But it has been worse since we've been here."

"What do you mean?" Milo cocked his head at me and raised an eyebrow.

"I mean it's almost like...like there's a part of me that wants to be cold and cruel. A part of me that only wants to do things I would never do. And sometimes it wins."

"What kind of things?"

"Like telling you I don't need you. And like flipping out on McKenzie when she's just trying to help. And like trying to take control of a whole pirate ship right in front of its captain. And like...like..."

My voice trailed off. I couldn't tell him about Bellamy. The voice inside me told me not to.

Secrets won't hurt anyone. But telling him will.

"That's it?" Milo leaned forward.

Knowing it was wrong, I nodded. Milo almost looked crushed. He straightened and looked away. "So then...does that mean that you and Bellamy...that was all you? The *real* you?"

Something took hold of my heart, clamping down on it like fangs. "How do you know about that?" I hissed. The siren side was back.

"I saw you. At the docks. You two looked...close. And you looked right at me, like you hated me."

"I...I don't even remember doing that. I thought I might've seen someone, but I wasn't sure. I didn't see your face. It must've been controlling me then."

"Well, I left after that. It crushed me. But then Noah told me you were acting strange and so I thought maybe—"

"Bellamy saved me. What did you expect?"

Oh no.

Milo stood up, his gaze hardening. "I don't know. I don't know what I expected. Maybe you'd tell him you didn't want or need his help like you told me."

I heard his words, but that dark, terrible side of me relished in the hurt I sensed welling up within him. I shot up to my feet and stepped toward him, into the low light of the candle burning in the room.

Don't say it. No. Yes. Say it.

"Maybe I *did* need him. Maybe I *wanted* him."

Milo stomped toward me, with his jaw clenched, and gripped my shoulders with each hand. "Why? Why would you say that, Katrina?" Even through his gritted teeth and steel eyes, I could tell how hard he was trying to hide the pain he felt from my words.

He lowered his gaze to match mine, as if studying my eyes. When he paused, I knew he'd noticed them. But I was glad. I was glad he could see the other side of me was there and in control. I wanted him to know it wasn't me who had said that to him.

"Your eyes," he growled.

"You see it, then." I smiled, knowing he'd caught a glimpse of my cold blue irises. "You see why I don't need you? I have all the power and protection I need, right here."

Shut up.

I closed my eyes. I couldn't let her win. I'd never fought the siren in me so hard. But I thought of Milo and for a moment...just a moment...I broke free of her. "Milo, this isn't me! Don't listen to her...me...*anything* I say when my eyes are blue." My words came out so desperately I nearly choked on them. I didn't know how long I had before the voice came back.

"I know," he sighed. "I was afraid this is what happened to you when Noah said you've been acting weird."

"What? What happened to me?"

He hesitated, looking around the room like he wasn't sure speaking here was safe. "Let's go downstairs to eat with the others. I'll explain there. They deserve to know, too."

"Okay." I hugged myself, ashamed of the monster I became when I least expected it. But I had it under control. For now. But I'd still need to repair the damage that had been done. Because as much as admitting it felt like fire on my skin, there was always the smallest inkling of truth in whatever I said when the siren took over.

Back down in the tavern, we stayed to ourselves, keeping to the darkest corners of the place to stay out of sight. But we gobbled down the pork and vegetable stew like it was the best thing we'd ever tasted.

"We'll have to make this last," Milo noted. "I've only enough left to purchase our food rations for our journey. Unless the ship we commandeer happens to have some on it already."

We all nodded, too ravenous to worry about it right then. McKenzie gave him a quick thumbs up and continued slurping her stew. I ate, too, but something heavy was still clouding my mind. I feared at any moment I could lose myself again to the other version of me that constantly lurked in wait. It was just a matter of when something happened that gave me a reason to be selfish.

"Something else," Milo added, and I perked up to listen. "As we've all noticed by now, Katrina is dealing with something that makes her...well, not herself." McKenzie and Noah nodded, pressing him to go on. "Back on Valdez's ship, when we would capture mermaids, I noticed the longer they were out of the water, out of their siren form, the more vicious they became. Eventually Valdez contained them in special tanks of seawater to keep them more...agreeable." All eyes at the table flew to me. I wanted to crawl away and hide.

"So, you're saying Katrina needs to go full mermaid to snap out of it?" McKenzie asked, tearing into a piece of bread.

"I'm saying I think it would make sense based on what I know about mermaids." Milo placed his hands on the table and looked at me.

I wondered if that's what made Cordelia so ruthless. She physically couldn't return to her mermaid form, and she'd been forced to be on land for centuries.

So maybe that's why her heart had grown dark beyond repair. When I finally found the courage to speak up, I put my spoon down and addressed him.

"I tried to do it when I jumped overboard on Bellamy's ship. I wanted to look for you. I was ready to do anything to find you. But I also had the strangest feeling...like a need...a pull to just...dive in. I wanted to be in the water, and I couldn't ignore it. But I didn't change."

Milo looked at me as if I'd just given him a riddle. But he finally placed his elbows on the table and spoke. "There's a place I know of that might be a good place to try again. It's too small a body of water for ships, so it's quite useless to most here. It should be safe."

All at once, I felt three pairs of eyes on me, waiting for my next words. Was I supposed to just agree to go practice turning into a mermaid in front of them like it was completely normal? I suppose for us, it was probably the most normal thing about these past few days. With hesitation, and maybe even a bit of fear, I nodded once. "Okay," I breathed, closing my eyes. "I'll try. But only because I have to beat this thing."

"Then I'll take you there as soon as you're ready," Milo said.

Cordelia's taunting voice rang out in my head, reminding me how little time may be left back in our time—if she hadn't already destroyed humanity by now. "Let's go, now," I said. "I'm ready."

With hazel-green eyes that held me captive, he studied my face before taking my hand. An old, but familiar sense of comfort engulfed me—one that reminded me of the way I felt when he took me to the lighthouse that night of the gala when I hadn't expected him to come for me. And somehow everything felt okay for a moment, even with the weight of the world on our shoulders.

"It's a bit of a walk. We'll need to be careful," he said, his voice strong but gentle as he glanced at McKenzie and Noah.

"I think we're gonna sit this one out. If it's good with you, we'll stay here and get some rest," Noah gestured with a flick of his head.

"Yeah, I'm sure Katrina would appreciate some privacy. I know I wouldn't want an audience if I was trying to turn into a mermaid." McKenzie ended her sentence with a small giggle I could tell she'd tried to suppress. It made me smile.

"Then let's get going." Milo looked at me, squeezing my hand. "It may be after sundown by the time we get there."

"Whatever it takes," I uttered, following him as he turned toward the door. We told our friends goodbye and left the tavern, wandering into the night.

The night was even more chaotic than the daytime. Every tavern was glowing, and the laughter of drunk men and music could be heard from every corner. People lay slumped over in doorways and on benches, and couples indulged themselves out in the open in drunken moans of pleasure.

"Quite the show, isn't it?" Milo smirked at me as I looked up at him through my lashes.

"It's something," I scoffed playfully. "I can't believe you grew up here. And yet, you're such a gentleman."

"Only when I need to be." He tilted his head, and something familiar washed over me. It felt like walking with him for the very first time along the beach in the state park of Constantine. It was as if, for only a moment, all the burdens between us no longer existed. It was just he and I, walking into something new and terrifying ahead, just like the first time.

But then *she* showed up in my head again...

"A gentleman has no place on a pirate crew, though," I scoffed.

"You're probably right there. It was quite the dilemma," he shrugged, quickening his step.

"Right," I chimed. "I'm sure you've done some really shitty things, haven't you? Worse than anything you've ever told me."

"Katrina, where is this coming from?"

"What do you mean?" I raised an eyebrow. "I mean you just killed a man in front of me. I just want to know who the man I'm with really is? Your father hid all those things away from you and your mother. How do I know you aren't hiding things from me? Just like the letter?"

Why would you bring that up? We're past that.

"Katrina," he stopped walking before he'd finished saying my name and turned to touch my shoulder. "Listen to what you're saying. This isn't you."

"It *is* me." My tone turned cold. "But is this *you*? How do I know? How will I ever really know? You're probably just like your father."

I was jolted from my dark state of mind when Milo gripped my shoulders so tightly, I nearly winced. He pulled me to the nearest wall as the sounds of glasses breaking and muffled music filled the background silence.

"Don't. Ever. Say that again," he growled through a clenched jaw. The look in his eyes was one I'd never seen—at least not directed at me—piercing and focused. He watched my eyes like he was searching for a secret message hidden within them. Then, by the nearby light of a tavern torch, I saw in the reflection of his steady, intense gaze, my own ocean blue eyes staring back into his.

I paused; my breath caught in my throat. Staring back at myself were the most beautiful, barely human eyes, framed by delicate lashes that seemed to have intensified themselves to draw all attention to my gaze. They were two moonlight lagoons, nearly glowing with the most radiant blue that rivaled the depths themselves. Like magic.

I blinked, clenching my eyes shut, and when I opened them, everything had returned to normal. I breathed a sigh of relief, but barely had time to recompose myself before Milo crashed his mouth into mine. He pulled away long enough to bring his lips to my ear, which made heat pool between my thighs.

"Damn, I hate this side of you," he whispered.

"Then why are you kissing me?" I uttered.

"Because it's still you," he said without hesitation. "And because I've been dying to kiss you for too long."

I knew then that I had to tell him about Bellamy. "Milo," I said. "I...I kissed Bellamy. But..."

"But it wasn't you?" He said. "Is that what you're going to tell me?"

"Well, yes...because that's the truth. I never would have..." I struggled to finish my sentence.

"Are you sure?" He leaned into me as someone walked past. "Because something in me isn't quite so sure. And that's why I hate this side of you, Katrina. Because I can't trust you when you're in it. I can't tell what's true and what isn't. And your siren has a way of bringing my deepest fears to light. So, I'll ask you this question, but I don't want you to answer it until you've become a siren fully and satisfied that side of you for a while. Because I want to hear the answer from *you*."

I dug my gaze into him, my brows tense and pressed together, urging him to go on. He looked at the ground, then back up at me. "Do you love me?"

"Well...yes...of course you know I—"

"No," he breathed against my lips, caressing them like velvet with his own. "Don't answer it yet."

"Fine," I said, "Then let's get going. We're wasting time here."

Milo nodded, and then walked away, turning back toward the night to lead us through the city and into the dark outskirts of town, where nothing awaited us but tangled jungle and a long hike to the middle of it.

30

WATERFALL

KATRINA

M ilo led me to a path framed by hanging moss and gnarled vines. The moonlight illuminated our steps well, shining down from a bright moon. We were silent, but the humming of nocturnal insects and summer crickets filled the air with their song. After a few long moments making our way through this tropical maze, a new sound reached our ears.

"A waterfall," I noted, as we arrived in a clearing with a lagoon in the middle of it.

"You should be safe here." Milo gestured. "I used to enjoy this spot when I was younger. Few know about it. And I doubt that's changed."

I took in the wonder around me of the greenery encircling us in this private glade. The moon's glow cut through the jungle canopy and streaked down in rays toward the glistening crystal water pooling at the foot of the cascading water. The mist from the waterfall surrounded us, casting a delicate haze that only emphasized the rhythmic golden pulses of firefly flashes over the water. But what enchanted me the most was the blue and white bioluminescent glow of the churning water from the waterfall. The water lit up like starlight with every ripple.

"So, I should just...get in?" I turned to Milo, unsure.

"It's a start," he said, helping me closer to the lagoon's edge. "Here there is no pressure. Take however long you need, Katrina, to figure yourself out."

He went to sit on a mossy log nearby at the foot of the water, while I stared down into the blue lagoon below. The water called to me, and I longed to become part of it. I felt the siren taking over. I dipped my toe in.

"Oh!" I exclaimed, in awe at the way the water glowed when I disturbed the surface.

"That's my favorite thing about it here," Milo laughed. The gentle happiness in his voice was like warm honey I'd longed to taste again. But then my siren made me scoff.

No. Shut up. Get in the water and shut up.

I dove in, my clothes billowing around me as the bubbles I created in the water lit up like silver fairy dust. For the first time, I wanted this. I truly wanted to be underwater, merging with its streams and currents. Becoming it. The water met my skin like a kiss between two long-lost lovers, and I closed my eyes, hoping to open them to a shimmering tail like the one I'd seen the night I broke the curse.

But when I opened them, I was still the same. I burst forth out of the water, drawing in a breath. Something in me still begged to be released. The siren was still there, still secretly in control in the back of my mind. I looked at Milo, confused.

"See?" I said, "It never works!"

"Keep trying," he encouraged. "Maybe it just takes time."

"I floated in the water, leaning my head back and listening to the hum of the falls nearby, my hair fanning around me like a giant lily pad. But I still had legs.

"Stop thinking so much about it," Milo said. "Perhaps you can't make it happen. Maybe you just need to *let* it happen."

I sighed. Maybe he was right, whatever that meant. I decided to soak, enjoying the feeling of the water against my body. But it wasn't enough. With slow, gentle movements, I slid out of my blouse and pants, and swam up to Milo, handing him the wet clothes.

"Can you put these somewhere dry?" I asked with a smile. "Please."

He took the sopping wet bundle from my hand and placed it on a log beside him, only to look back at me with wandering eyes, though I knew he couldn't see much with everything from my chest down below the water's surface. I studied his face, honing in on his features in the moonlight.

"You have blood on you," I finally acknowledged, noting the dark red spatters along his face and neck and dried in his hair. "From those men you..." It was hard for me to finish the sentence. He'd killed a man in front of me. He was never lying when he told me he'd done terrible things. And yet I didn't feel afraid of him. I never had. And I never would. Only safe. Even when my siren side told me to turn against him.

"I was protecting you," Milo uttered propping himself on his knee. "I couldn't control myself when I saw what they did to you." He reached down to touch my face, and I leaned forward to let him, but the siren in me yanked me back, recoiling when his fingertips hit my skin.

Don't let him touch you.

I shook my head, trying to rid myself of the vile moment that took charge so quickly. "Sorry," I muttered, "The voice in my head wants me to hate you. I don't know why."

"I have my theories," Milo said, "but I'll save them for when you're feeling more like yourself."

"But how can I? I've been here a while and I still don't know how to change. What do I have to do, drown myself?" I slapped my hands against the water in frustration, but my own words caught my attention. "Wait...maybe that's it.

Last time I changed when I went unconscious...I couldn't breathe any longer and I sucked in the water and...and I drowned."

Milo leaned forward. "Mmm. That doesn't sound like a pleasant transformation."

"It wasn't. But it makes sense," I said, thinking harder about it. "The ocean rules us. And like Cordelia said, it's more powerful than anything. So, I can't just be in the water. I have to surrender to it."

"You're going to drown yourself?" Milo lifted an eyebrow.

"Don't try and stop me," I demanded. Before he could respond, I dove underneath the water, the bioluminescent sparkles lighting up the underwater world around me, and I swam to the bottom of the lagoon. It wasn't very deep. Maybe ten feet or so, but I released my breath, letting myself sink to the bottom. Silt stirred up and smoked out the glow that comforted me, leaving me in darkness except for the surface above. I was terrified, but my siren was relishing every moment of it.

I could hear the muffled sound of Milo shouting my name. Every beat of my heart screamed for air. But siren Katrina held me under. I had to let her have control. All of it, for just this moment. As my consciousness faded, I could almost imagine a ghost of myself holding me under, pressing me against the stony, sandy bottom of this blue pool. And when my lungs felt ready to burst, I couldn't suppress the instinct to open my mouth and desperately suck in a gulp of briny water. My lungs filled with the water, burning like hell and surely stopping my heart before the blurry, obscured lagoon floor became even darker. Nothingness.

And then I opened my eyes and everything around me shone crystal clear, as though looking through polished diamond. Bubbles from the waterfall crashed into the surface in the distance, creating a roiling thrashing of brightly glowing bubbles. And I was somehow...breathing...in a way that made no physical sense. But here I was, meters deep underwater and breathing as though I stood on land.

When the strands of my hair drifted away from my face, a glimmer below caught my eye. I looked down. And just below my waist connecting to my hips was a merging of skin into ethereal scales that sparkled silver-blue like the dress I'd worn to the gala, only more beautiful, and certainly more surreal. My fins fanned out at the base like wild petals that bloomed in spring, sheer and delicate. And when I wiggled the muscles that would have been my thighs and lower abdomen, the tail flicked, surging power through the water and propelling me upward with ease. I repeated the motion, rolling my waist and hips like the motion of waves, swimming upward, until I finally broke through the surface of the water.

Relief flooded over me, as I hit the cool night air, drenched in the most refreshing sensation I'd felt in my entire life. Like I'd been reborn. And like I could finally think clearly again. The fog in my head was gone, along with the devious siren whispering on my shoulder. I was me again.

I turned to see Milo, watching me with concern, as though ready to dive in after me. "Why don't you come in and wash that blood off?" I smiled, flipping my tail up so that the two bottom caudal fins lifted out of the water, silver glowing droplets trickling off them.

When Milo didn't say anything in response, I realized how truly entranced he was. He stood to his feet, never taking his eyes off me, and slowly pulled off his leather boots. I watched him just as intensely as he unbuckled his pulled off the many layered tunics and let his pants drop to the ground. Without hesitation, he stepped gingerly into the water, the ripples glowing with each step forward.

My gaze roamed his body, admiring his rugged perfection from top to bottom. His size, his stature, his movements. In the moonlight, the veins tracing his muscles shone like subtle accents to the tattoos across his tanned skin. And the way he looked at me, even through the blood stains on his face, made me feel like no one else existed in that moment.

"You're you again," he said, dipping down further into the water. I knew it must be cold to his skin, but he didn't flinch.

"Ironic, isn't it?" I laughed. "How can you tell, though?"

"Because you no longer have that look in your eye that makes me feel like you want to rip me open."

"I'm sorry." I flicked my tail and glided toward him. "If I could take everything back I would."

"I know." He reached forward and touched me, gently feeling the side of my face that had been cut. "But I've always seen the real you."

I pressed my lips together. "So, what's your theory?" I asked.

"About what?"

"About why my siren side wants me to push you away."

"First, tell me...Do you love me?"

"More than you know," I whispered. "I would do anything for you."

Milo took my hands in his, and we stared face to face with our torsos barely above the water. "And that's why your siren side hates me. Because loving someone—truly loving someone—means being selfless and caring about someone other than yourself. And that goes against a siren's very nature." He paused and brushed away a wet strand of my hair sticking to my forehead with his thumb. "So that's how I've known all this time that the real Katrina must really love me."

"I do love you. All of you. Even the scars and hidden parts you keep tucked away in the shadows," I said, holding his gaze. "I do love you. And I'm not scared of it anymore. I'm not scared to need you anymore." I wrapped the end of my tail around his ankles. He jumped, and then reached his hand down into the water to feel the scales covering my hips.

"That'll take some getting used to," he chuckled, his smile illuminated by the moon's soft glow from above. He squinted down at the water, studying what he could see of me, and slowly brought his gaze upward, roaming over my bare stomach and chest. "You're beautiful," he added, his eyes settling on my lips.

"I'm a fish," I teased. "A magic fish."

He laughed with me, but soon lowered his voice again. "No," he sighed, "You're a goddess."

A response lingered on my lips, but I decided silence was better. I dipped my hand into the water and used it to wipe away the blood on Milo's face and neck. He watched me in the most affectionate way, letting me clean him without a sound except the water trickling off his skin.

"What's this?" I asked, noticing a thin chain looped through a tiny gold band hanging around his neck.

"I forgot I had this. It was...my mother's wedding ring," he said, reaching up to touch it, "I found it in my father's things and...and well, I took it. Maybe because it's all I have left of her. If I didn't take it, it'd be forgotten here with everything else."

"It'll be nice to have something of hers to take back with you when we finally get back home." I reached up to examine it more closely. It was so delicate—nearly as thin as a wire—with the tiniest single blue diamond set in the center. I patted it against his chest where it hung, blending in against his canvas of tattoos.

"I wonder how long it will take to get my legs back," I finally said, changing the subject as we bobbed in the water, suspended in this crisp moonlit pool.

"Not long," Milo's brows tensed. "When Valdez was ready to 'harvest' a mermaid, there was a very brief window of time she could be out of water long enough to cut off her tail. The crew couldn't let her dry too long."

The way his face fell made my heart heavy. "Stop beating yourself up for things you couldn't control," I uttered softly, pulling him nearer to the waterfall.

"I was a coward," he said. "An irredeemable coward."

"Shhh," I held a finger to his lips. "We can't hold on to the past...even if we're living in it." I looked around, taking in the serenity of our surroundings in this ethereal piece of forest. "Though some things about the past are beautiful."

"I'm learning that I can't control everything," Milo smirked sadly. "You wouldn't think it would take 300 years to figure that out." He paused, looking down at the ripples dancing past us from the waterfall's rumbling. "Can I show you something?" He finally uttered. I assured him with an eager nod.

He let go of me, and swam toward the base of the waterfall, diving down underneath it. I followed, my underwater vision as perfect as on land in broad daylight. We surfaced behind the cascades, facing the entrance to a shallow cavern hidden in the stone cliff behind the water. It was shallow enough to wade in at the very edge of the wall.

"Cool little cave," I cooed, splashing a bit of water with my tail fin.

"It was one of my favorite places to go after my mother died. I never told anyone about this spot."

"Can you carry me?" I asked, still gawking in wonder at the enchanting cave-like structure.

"Wherever you need to go." He scooped me into his arms, one arm tucked beneath my tail for support and the other behind my back. I leaned into him, keeping my grip tight as I laced my fingers around the back of his neck. He stood up out of the water and hoisted me high enough that I could reach the waterfall cave with my hands outstretched. Supporting my upper half, I positioned myself as he pushed me up to the opening.

Once secured on the stony surface, I threw my head backwards, nearly exhausted from the weight of my tail out of water. Milo climbed up with ease, and I once again found myself ensnared by him as I studied his nearly naked body with desire. But my tail was too heavy to move, and I could do nothing about it but rest against him when he sat beside me.

I nodded off for a moment or two as we sat in silence in the cave, but the night chill returning to my skin awoke me. My skin tingled, and my tail began to feel lighter—and drier. I tried to move it, but realized I was changing before my eyes, and I had maintained very little control of my lower half. The sensation of my fins ripping in half tore upward through my hips and waist, and I grasped at Milo in surprise at the pain. He gently lifted me, talking to me softly as I grimaced from the hurt. He pulled me further into the grotto, just enough so that I could lie down as he held me. And with a blinding glow that covered my entire lower half, I became fully human again.

Milo gently lowered me down into a soft mossy spot cushioned further by leaves. And I smiled, content in this haven where no one else could find us. The flowing waterfall hung like a curtain, just enough to protect our hideaway, but still sheer enough to let in enough moonlight and bioluminescent glow to see our surroundings.

The pain subsided, and I watched as the last of my scales morphed back into skin and a refreshing sensation overtook my spirit. I felt like me again. Oddly enough, lying naked, damp, in a cave in 1720 was where I felt like I'd found myself again. The siren inside me had been silenced for now. And I no longer found myself battling a voice telling me what I wanted or needed.

This time, there was no longer confusion or question about where my heart lied. I looked at Milo. I wanted him. Fully. It was always him and only him. I needed him. And I knew I could never lose him again.

His eyes wandered me, from my bare chest down to my toes. He reached for me, running his hand across my chin and down my neck, between my breasts, and down to the core of me. His fingers gently danced along my skin, lower and lower...

"Yes," I said. "I've lost you too many times. Stop waiting. Yes."

I reached forward and pulled him down to me. I watched the water rolling off his shirtless body, and I felt heat rolling in me like clouds rushing to storm. He took my hand in his and guided it to the hardness below his abdomen. I felt him, touching and pressing against his firmness, and a sensation like a wave came over me, revealing itself in my trembling breaths.

Milo pushed his lips against mine as he leaned farther over me, kneeling in the space between my legs. He coaxed from me a tender gasp that had me holding my breath as he gently nudged my legs apart.

"Katrina Delmar, my starlight, I've waited 300 years for you," he breathed. I used my other hand to help remove the soaked undergarment from his lower half. My core shook when he pushed his length against the bare skin between my thighs. He braced himself up with one hand, looking over me, and stroked my hair with the other. I ran my fingers up his back, tracing the curve of his muscles and feeling every part of him in a new way.

"In those 300 years, I've found many treasures, but never one as priceless as you. I would bury myself with you to keep from losing you again. I would seek you a thousand times to find you again and again. I would make a map of your body with the stars and follow it for eternity." He kissed me again before pulling away to snap off the ring from where it hung around his neck. He took my hand and slid the tiny gold circle onto my finger. "In this place, I confess my undying love for you. You are finally mine. And I will share you with no other."

He dipped below and tasted me. Fire blazed up in me like cannons, like the flare of a warship in the dead of night. I moaned out my pleasure softly. He held me, clinging to me like a lost treasure he'd found again. My back arched as he pulled me to him. Slowly, gently, he rolled against me until he buried himself in me. I raked my fingers through his hair and down his back glistening with sweat and seawater. He crashed against me like waves rising and falling along the shore over and over. And with my legs hooked around him, I pulled him further into me like the draw of the tide.

With a tender growl in my ear that made me whimper, he squeezed my wrists. "Trust me," he uttered against my lips that were swollen from kissing him. I closed my eyes and let myself drift in this ecstasy as I rocked my hips against his, as though we were two rolling waves breaking into each other.

"I always have. Make me your map. That only you can navigate," I shuddered between soft gasps.

Milo continued as I looked up at him once more. In his eyes I saw a look of rugged desire and unguarded passion that made me want to stay here forever, trapped in a time and place where no one knew we existed. So that we could stay like this till the end of time.

A powerful sensation in me crested, and I cried out with an ancient songful voice, as he flooded me all at once with a trembling groan. And the cave grew silent except for our heaving breaths and the ever-constant rushing of water at our backs. With a beautiful, foreign exhaustion overtaking my body, I rested my head against Milo's rising chest, and he wrapped his arm around me, tracing the skin on my chest with his fingers.

"Many are the stars, Katrina. But yours is the only light I want to look upon." He brushed his lips against my hair, and we rested together for a while in the dark of our paradise beneath the moon. I clung to him, cherishing every moment until our inevitable return to the belly of Nassau and the cruel wake of reality.

31

KNOW THE ROPES

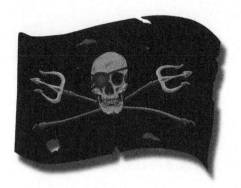

MILO

I pulled Katrina closer to me as she slept. How could she love me after what she'd seen me do? How could she yield herself to me like this after she watched me kill? I didn't understand it. But maybe there was just enough darkness in us both to balance things out.

I traced the rim of the ring on her finger with my thumb. My promise to her to be whatever she needed whenever she needed it. A protector, a friend, a lover—and even an enemy when that "other" side of her took hold. And I smiled as I realized it was just as much her promise to let me.

The night hours passed like the mist in the air from the waterfall below, fleeting and gone as quick as vapor. But it couldn't vanquish the memory of her skin against mine, her flesh between my teeth, and her hands taking hold of my body. The sweet taste of honeysuckle and sweat lingered on my tongue.

Each sensation around me seemed as tangible as fireflies, each a dreamlike mark of our time here.

"We have to go back," Katrina uttered weakly. "We can't stay here."

"I know," I rubbed her bare shoulder as she shivered against me.

I helped her to her feet, and hesitantly we both reentered the water to make our way back to the shore of the lagoon.

"I can definitely feel how cold this water is now," Katrina said through chattering teeth.

"Now you see why it took me so long to get in," I chuckled. She responded with an icy splash, and I returned the favor. Finding our clothing, slightly damp from the humid night air, we dressed and set back out toward the inn.

"How often will I have to change, I wonder?" Katrina asked as we walked, and the dim glow of the town just came into view.

"I suppose whenever you feel you're losing yourself," I shrugged.

Katrina sighed and looked ahead, quickening her pace. " I wish...I wish there was a mermaid I could talk to who could help me understand all this. There's too much to learn. And even if we find the trident, Cordelia said only a siren can use it. But that could mean anything. What if we find it and can't figure out how to use it? This is like the necklace all over again."

I matched her pace, quickening my step to stay alongside her as I thought of something that I debated whether or not to share. But I knew if I stayed silent in an effort to keep her safe, it would be a rift in the trust we'd rebuilt. Even if I was the only one who would ever know about it. I couldn't try to keep her from dangerous things. I couldn't do that to her again.

"There are mermaids aboard the *Siren's Scorn*," I uttered. "Captives. Two, if I remember correctly."

Katrina dug her heels into the dirt path below us and whipped around to face me. "Can you take me to them?"

"We'll have to be careful. And quick. We need to rest before tomorrow."

"We did rest," Katrina winked at me.

"You're making me wonder just how much of your siren side stayed behind," I joked.

"Don't worry, I'm all me," she touched the hollow of her chest. "But knowing what I am and how to use the power I have could be our biggest shot at understanding how to stop Cordelia."

I nodded. She wasn't wrong. But it was such a daunting task and there was barely enough time to do it. "It's nearly 2 AM," I said, tilting my head back to glimpse the night sky. "The harbor will be quiet. But there's always someone around somewhere."

"Something about you and me together always ends with us sneaking onto ships."

"You make a fine pirate, lass," I smirked, "But in all seriousness, if we're going to do it, we have to go now. We don't have much time."

"Then lead the way, Captain," She gestured with an open hand toward the road ahead.

I guided her back through the rat-ridden streets, where the sounds and commotions had quieted, only to be replaced with the snores and grunts of passed out drunks. By the time we reached the port, we'd lost another fifteen minutes. With uneasy eyes, I set my gaze on the *Siren's Scorn* bobbing in the tide, secured at the nearest dock. Katrina stepped forward, glancing around nervously.

"Wait," I said. "Valdez never left his ship unattended with mermaids on board. We'll have to stay hidden." I flipped the hood of my cloak over my head. "What good this'll do now that I've got a bounty on my head."

Katrina nodded, and I offered her a leg up onto the ship. Every nerve within me warned me this was a bad idea, but I couldn't deny Katrina the only chance she may ever have to learn about her nature. It also crossed my mind that perhaps, with some luck on our side, we could set the mermaids free. The ship was dark, and no lanterns hung lit. But I knew that didn't mean it was empty.

"Stay crouched low and walk along the edge," I whispered. Katrina did exactly that, and I was honestly surprised that we hadn't already been discovered yet.

Patrollers would sit on the top deck near the stern for a good view. But I didn't see anyone up there that I could tell.

I snuck to the hatch leading belowdecks, Katrina following with featherlight footsteps. My heart pounded in my head, and I fought to keep my breaths light and silent. With every creak in the wooden floorboard or every lap of a wave against the hull, I froze to listen, afraid the sound might be more than it seemed.

But, with all our caution and paranoia, we never saw another soul on board. In the belly of the ship, we descended further. The mermaid hold would be just on the other side of the brig, where I knew my younger self would be lying cold, hungry, and hopeless on moldy, piss-stained floors. A sickness stirred within my gut, and my hands quivered as I opened the door to the hold.

I could hear the muffled whimpering of myself across the wall—the cries of a boy who believed himself much too old to cry. *Me.* I squeezed my eyes shut and tried to refocus as Katrina stepped inside to join me. I motioned for her to lift the heavy cloth covering the coffin-like rectangles stacked against the wall.

As I expected, she stepped back in astonishment at the two sirens staring back at her in their watery prisons. One had fiery red hair, and the other, long locks that were nearly white.

The mermaids recoiled, thrashing violently in their containers and spilling out splashes of water through the pinstripe cracks at the top. Katrina pressed herself against the glass, letting them see her face. The white-haired mermaid slowed her movements long enough to focus, and I watched her body relax at the sight of Katrina.

"Can you hear me?" Katrina asked against the glass that separated them. The mermaid nodded. Soon, the red-haired mermaid steadied herself as well.

"I'm...I'm one of you," Katrina stammered. "I want to help you. Can you help me, too?"

The mermaids looked at each other through their transparent walls, and then back at Katrina before nodding slightly.

"There's a trident in the sea and only sirens can use it by giving up something. Do you know what that means? How would I use it?"

A sullen and broken look suddenly overtook the mermaids' faces. The white-haired mermaid pointed to her mouth and throat and made a slicing motion with her hand.

"Valdez has already cut out their tongues and vocal cords. So they can't use their song against him," I interjected, a heavy, macabre feeling creeping up on me as I knew all too well his ritual. "And they can't talk to you either."

"I'm so sorry," Katrina said to them, her eyes creasing with sorrow. "Have you at least ever seen the trident?"

Both mermaids shook their heads.

"Don't take this the wrong way," Katrina started, "but is it really true that no siren has ever tried to use it because no siren could ever be selfless enough to give it what it wants?"

The white-haired mermaid rolled her eyes and scoffed, but the redhead shrugged with a nod, pointing to her heart and closing her hands around her chest.

"You always only serve yourself," Katrina stated softly, not in an accusatory way. She thought on it for a minute, as if figuring out what that might mean for herself. "What about crying?"

I glanced at her, unsure where her question was leading.

"Do you ever cry?" She asked.

The mermaids tightened their jaws and shook their heads, gesturing a solid "no" with their fingers.

"Not even when they cut out your tongues?" Katrina pressed.

"They never cried. None of them. Cordelia is the only mermaid I've ever seen cry. And even then. Only once. When she was so broken-hearted by Valdez's betrayal that she sent the maelstrom and cursed us," I explained.

"That's why she's so powerful," Katrina muttered, taking a step toward me. "She's the only mermaid who's ever allowed herself to be vulnerable. To feel." She turned back to the mermaids. "Do you know what happens when you cry? You could get yourselves out of here!"

The sirens signaled their answer with a vague shake of their heads. And Katrina stepped back, closing her eyes for a moment.

"What are you doing?" I asked.

"Trying to think of sad things. So I can cry. I'm going to show them and set them free. I can control the water in the tanks and break the glass. If I can just—"

Suddenly a haunting melody filled the air, cutting through our whispers and halting all other noise around us. I felt as though my body was paralyzed, at the mercy of something sinister. Katrina stood unmoving, looking at me with panic in her eyes.

Like a ghost, Cordelia appeared in the doorway from the shadows, her red lips parted so that the tune flowed from her mouth. No words. No lyrics. Just a melody otherworldly. I drew my blade and glanced at Katrina just before the world around me fizzled out.

Whatever happened next was a memory I didn't have. I shook my head back and forth to fling the saltwater from my eyes as I surfaced. Katrina coughed on water a few short feet away from me. We were in the dark, floating in the harbor amidst monstrous silhouettes of ships.

"What happened?" I uttered, looking around for some clue that might help me remember.

"Cordelia used her siren song on you. She made you attack me."

"What? Katrina, I'm sorry."

"It's okay," I said. "You didn't hurt me. You just grabbed me and hauled me overboard with you."

I moved closer to her. "I'm still sorry. I didn't even realize..." I looked at my hands, disgusted with the feeling of violation I felt. I could've been made to do anything Cordelia pleased. And I despised the thought of it.

"It's fine. We're okay," Katrina panted, looking downcast. "We just...couldn't help the mermaids."

"Come on, let's get out of this water and back to the inn. We've been out long enough." I made my way through the water swiftly, eager to get back on land.

"The thought that I might be able to do that freaks me out," Katrina said, taking my hand as I helped her onto the shore. "I don't want to be able to control people."

"Then don't," I said gently. "But now you know why Cordelia wouldn't control Valdez. She didn't want his love if it wasn't real."

"I noticed when she was singing, the scale around her neck—the necklace—was glowing," Katrina stated.

I raised an eyebrow, curious to what she would say next.

"When I sang my mom's lullaby one night in my room—the same tune Cordelia was singing—I remember the necklace glowing like that. The song...The siren song isn't magic alone. I think the song is what activates the magic from their tails."

I tossed her words around in my head. She was certainly onto something, and I felt the pieces connecting.

"You know, you're making a lot of sense," I said. "And that would explain why the mermaid trade was so shrouded in mystery. The buyers knew the scales were magic...but no one knew *how* to use the magic. And when Valdez took their voices...there was nothing left but a goose chase for destroyed magic."

"And that's why Cordelia made her scale necklace. So that her song had power in either form." Katrina added, her eyes widening as she spoke.

I nodded firmly, impressed. "It seems there isn't a part of you that isn't magic," I teased, touching her thigh. "Voice, heart, tail, and everything in between."

The way she blushed through a sliver of a smile made me want to pull her to me and make love to her all over again. She was an ocean I could happily drown in forever. And with that thought, I tensed, straightening as I scanned our surroundings to make sure no one was lying in wait or following us. There was no room for unguardedness here.

When we arrived back at the inn, nearly all the lights were out except the half-burned candle on the tavern counter. It gave us just enough light to help us find our way back to our room, where we peeked our heads in quietly.

"Noah?" I whispered. "McKenzie?" No one responded.

We tiptoed inside, only to see both our friends sleeping soundly in the single bed.

"Looks like we get the floor," Katrina said.

"As we rightfully deserve," I replied. "For what it's worth, we'll be back up in just a few short hours. Might as well not get too comfortable."

We lay on the rug, bracing our backs against the wall as Katrina nestled herself into my lap. I stroked her neck with my fingertips, brushing back stray hair along her smooth skin. She fell asleep almost instantly, but my eyes wouldn't seem to close.

I stared up at the window, straining to see the stars through the glass, and I wondered what tomorrow would bring. I feared finding the trident. I didn't know what it would cost to use. I didn't know what it would demand of Katrina. And though I wouldn't burden her by showing it, I was scared of finding out.

32

SET SAIL

KATRINA

"R ise and shine, mateys!" Noah's voice startled me awake. The room was fully lit, and the sun was up long past dawn.

"We overslept!" I jolted upright, waking up Milo who lied against me.

"That's what happens when you stay out all night." McKenzie pulled her boots on as she spoke. "We were worried about you two. But we also kinda figured you wanted some alone time." She winked.

"I could say the same thing for you two. I'm sure you both just had the worst possible time here alone in this room together." I stood, adjusting my own boots over my loose pants and tying my belt around my waist.

"Look at us," Milo said, standing to his feet. "We almost look like a real crew."

"That's about all we've got going for us," Noah uttered. "I guess that makes you captain?"

"A captain's not much without his first mate," Milo said, pulling out his compass and slapping it into Noah's open palm.

"What do you want me to do with this?" Noah looked on in bewilderment.

"Just hold onto it until I need it. Consider it a peace offering. So, take care of it." Milo's voice shifted as he addressed all of us together. "Now we need to hurry. It's going to be harder than ever to take one of those ships in broad daylight."

"Can't we just take one of your father's?" I asked as we made our way down to the tavern.

"That's the plan." Milo cocked his head. "But no doubt Thane is already securing them with his own crew. He'll see me taking one as breaking the code. But we don't have much of a choice."

"Well, it doesn't matter who we piss off here if we get to leave. And right now, that's our only chance." McKenzie spoke as we grabbed some loaves of bread for a quick breakfast that we carried outside.

With jittery nerves and quick, but unsure steps we trudged to the harbor, where we watched from our own little hiding spot in the trees nearby as Milo pinpointed the ship best for the taking. It was a smaller boat, perfect for stealthy maneuvering and a quick getaway, he assured. I studied it with careful eyes, it's reddish-brown hull contrasting against the bright blue beneath it.

"That's her. The *Falcon*." Milo squinted in the sunlight. "At least the weather's on our side. These winds will carry us out of port quickly."

"So, what do you need us to do?" McKenzie shrugged with her hand on her hip.

"I'll board first in case there's anyone already there and I'll take care of it. Noah, you and I will have to raise the anchor as fast as we can. And then, I'll head straight to the helm to steer us out. Katrina and McKenzie, that leaves you two to adjust the sails as I direct."

McKenzie and I glanced at each other. I'd barely figured out the sails on the modern motorsailer back home, so I wasn't feeling very confident about manning a centuries old pirate ship. And I doubted McKenzie had any previous experience with the latter either. But figuring it out was our only option.

"Just tell us what to do," I said. "But try to use words we understand."

Milo raised an eyebrow and lifted his chin. "I'll do my best to go easy on you, but manning even the smallest schooner with a crew of four is going to be one hell of an undertaking."

The plan was easy. Loaded in an abandoned old skiff we'd found, we'd row to the schooner on the far side of the water. With heavy nets that Noah acquired from a harbor merchant stand using the last of our money, we'd do our best to look like simple fishermen, and it was unlikely anyone would notice we weren't, given the lackadaisical atmosphere of the island. We'd keep to the outside of the harbor so as not to draw attention.

Milo and Noah crafted a grappling hook from an old piece of anchor metal and rope that we would use to climb up the ship. And then it would be up to our speed and skill to get the ship out of the port before anyone who cared noticed.

With tired arms, we rowed, bracing ourselves for the climb. Sailors called out to and fro from the ships we passed, but most were too preoccupied with their own business to pay us any attention. If they did, we'd simply throw off suspicion with a wave and nod of acknowledgement.

I watched Milo, noticing how he kept a close eye on the decks of the ships within sight. I figured he was looking for Thane, but I couldn't be too sure. He seemed thoroughly focused on whatever was running through his mind.

Once at the base of the *Falcon*, we positioned our little boat near the lowest point of the hull in the midsection of the ship, and ducked as Milo carefully swung the grapple. It latched perfectly, and we steadied ourselves by holding onto it one by one. The schooner was even smaller than it looked from a distance.

Milo ascended first. It was barely even a climb for him, as the schooner's hull was only a few feet high from the water in which it floated. We waited, and once we saw Milo's hand signal over the edge of the boat, it was our turn to come aboard.

It was a short climb, and the grapple rope acted more as a handrail against the constant rolling motion beneath us as we shimmied up along the siding. Trying to hoist ourselves up without it from the base of our little canoe-boat would have been quite a challenge. I didn't realize how sore my body was until I had to use the rope to pull myself onto the ship. The twinge of ache in my arms and legs fought against me. Between sword-fighting with Bellamy, being held hostage, and transforming into a mermaid, it only made sense that the muscles in my body were straining to keep up at this point.

"Hoist the anchor," Milo ordered, running straight to the bow with Noah right behind him. They grunted as they pushed against the capstan, hoisting the weighty anchor slowly. It had barely emerged from the water, still dripping, when Milo dashed away toward the helm and pointed to the sails.

"Get the topsail up taut!" he commanded. "Haul away the rigging!"

"English, please!" McKenzie cried.

"Just pull those ropes there and loosen that one. But tie that one there!" Milo directed, doing his best to point as he adjusted the ship's rudder. "Then set the mainsail southeast a bit."

We nodded, working with nervous hands to complete the tasks.

"This one's stuck!" I shouted, frustrated with the knot I found myself wrangling.

Milo came racing over and took in the sight of the mangled rope around the hooks along the masts and hull. "Steer us out. I'll work on this rigging."

"You want me to steer?" I asked.

"Yes, go!" He motioned for me to hurry.

I rushed forward to the ship's wheel, shoving away the feeling of intimidation that clawed at me.

"I can do this," I uttered. "I can control water. Surely, I can steer a ship on it."

Looking ahead out into the open water, my heart jumped a bit at the sight of some small bits of land and sandbars peeking out in a jagged path out to sea. I'd have to carefully navigate around them, and I didn't know how fast this thing could go. With my hands gripping the wooden wheel, I turned it sharply and directed the bow in the best straight path I could envision. It was heavy, and my muscles strained to hold the wheel where I wanted it. I wondered how Milo made it look so effortless.

From my spot at the helm, overlooking the small deck, I saw Noah rushing over to help with the sails. I also noticed Milo and his strange behavior. He was almost fidgety. I could even say nervous. He kept looking back at the surrounding bigger ships that had been anchored alongside this one. The rest of his father's fleet, I assumed.

"Keep at it. There's one more thing I have to take care of," he said.

"I was starting to think you forgot," Noah snapped, yanking on the rigging with newfound ferocity and confidence.

"Forgot what?" McKenzie interrupted.

"To make sure my father's ships can never be used the same way again." And with that, Milo leapt to the stern of the schooner, pulled out a pistol we never knew he was carrying, and fired at a barrel floating up against one of the ships, creating an instant explosion. The blast forged a hole in the front of the ship in which it was placed, leaving a damaged open hull to quickly fill with water. One by one, he fired at more floating barrels like targets, till he'd splintered the sides or fronts of every one of his father's four galleons.

Amidst the rush of chaos that ensued as sailors and captains spewed curses and fired back, we picked up speed in our sails and lurched forward out into the open bay. The deep tone of warning bells signaled trouble in the harbor. I did my best to guide us through the rocky waterways, nearly tipping the boat as we reeled around a sandbar I didn't see until the last minute. The water was strong against my hand at the wheel, and it took all my body strength to keep it from slipping back. I was grateful when a strong hand took hold of the helm above mine, and I breathed a sigh of relief as Milo stepped in to take over.

"Did you plant those barrels there?" I asked as Milo steadied himself at the wheel.

"Last night after you fell asleep. But I had help." He glanced over at Noah, who quickly looked away, as if trying to play off his part in this. Milo returned his gaze to me with eyebrows furrowed. "It was reckless, I know. But we couldn't let those ships keep sailing. No one should be able to use them again, least of all Thane."

"Reckless, for sure," I chided. "But I get it. And I would've done the same," I reassured with a half smile.

"Glad you approve. Because now we have to outrun him, and I can't have you both mad at me."

I looked over my shoulder at the sight of Thane and his crew working fast to raise their ship's anchor. He watched us with narrowed eyes from his perch at the bow. Even from here, I could sense the cruelty and see the scowl on his face. I touched the tender red line of skin along my jaw, wincing as I remembered the blade slicing across it.

"This guy really isn't one to let things go, huh?" I huffed.

"He's a psychopath," Milo uttered.

With the ship sailing smoothly and swiftly under Milo's command, we wove through the last few spots of shallow water and protruding formations framing the island. Behind us, Nassau shrunk in the distance, growing farther with each passing second, smoke rising from the harbor we'd left in disarray. Now it was straight on through into the open blue before us.

With an 18th century serial killer not far behind.

33

LEADING LIGHT

KATRINA

"Do you think they'll chase us the whole way?" I crouched down, sitting on the singular ledge behind the helm.

"I wouldn't be shocked if he follows us the whole way to the Triangle. Thane loves the hunt."

"Great," I muttered. "And how long will it take us to get there this time?"

"We should average about five knots, so...maybe three days and a few hours?"

I reached up to rub my shoulders as the wind picked up and sent my hair whipping around my neck. "This time when we get there, let's stop *before* we get near the center of the Triangle," I said.

"That's the plan," Milo fidgeted with one of the knobs of the ship's wheel. "But God knows how we'll get to the trident from there."

"I have a few ideas," I said with a heavy sigh, fixing my gaze towards the horizon. I really only had one idea. And if it didn't work, we were screwed as far as I was concerned. But after everything I'd learned about myself these past few days, I was more confident than I'd ever been. And I was finally ready to face the parts of myself that scared me the most and test my limits. After a moment, I stood up and stepped down from the helm's post. "I'm gonna go check on the others. Might as well let them know how long we'll be sailing for."

"Tell them to check the weapons in the main quarters. And pick something out for each of you. Preferably something you know how to use." Milo tossed me a key ring he'd hung from his belt.

"Will do," I nodded. It wanted to smile at the feeling that we were all our own little crew, however incompetent. At least we were finally all working together.

I made my way over to the rigging where McKenzie and Noah stood looking like they'd just come off a roller coaster.

"Okay I don't know if I attached these things correctly, but we're moving so I'm gonna say it's good enough." Noah wiped the sweat on his forehead with the back of his hand.

"I think we're good for now. As long as the winds stay this way for the next couple of days."

"This isn't going to be a short trip, is it?" Noah pressed his lips together.

I shot him a grin with a look of apology. "Do you consider three days a long trip?"

He sighed with a grumble and a look of defeat. "I guess not in this century."

"Well, we'd better get pretty good with these sails because we have company." I gestured toward the horizon behind us and the ship sailing onward in the distance. It was barely a dot on the surface, but I secretly feared how quickly it might be able to close the distance between us.

"They're coming for us?" McKenzie blurted, standing on her tippy toes to get a better perspective.

"Technically Milo, but I think we're a package deal," I said. "Which is why we are gonna spend these next few days sharpening our swordsmanship skills."

I led them to the cabin and used the key Milo had given me to unlock the door. Inside, I found a much smaller cabin than I'd seen before, but it made sense given the petite size of the schooner. A hammock and square desk took up most of the room, alongside a wall rack of a few swords and pistols and an urn stuffed full with scrolls and maps. "Come on, pick something. Or two." I stepped forward, taking a cutlass down from its spot along the sword rack.

"Every minute we're here I'm still having to convince myself I didn't get sucked into a video game." Noah hesitantly reached for a blunderbuss and a short sword.

"Seriously," McKenzie spouted. "I'm pretty sure me with a weapon is more dangerous than that gang of pirates chasing us."

"Well, if they keep us from reaching the trident, we'll be stuck in this video game for the rest of our lives, so..." I raised both eyebrows at them and tucked in my chin.

"Fair enough," McKenzie shrugged, strapping a sword belt to her waist.

"Hopefully we won't have to use these," I said, "It's just a precaution."

I gripped the sword in my hand. It felt heavy and awkward, unlike the cutlass I'd held in my spar against Bellamy. I thought of him then, remembering the way he looked out at the sea like it was his home. I hoped he'd made peace with himself, wherever he was. Then I turned my attention to refocus on the sword in my grasp. I walked to Milo, carrying an assortment of swords for him to choose from.

"Did you want to add to your arsenal?" I asked with a grin.

"I suppose it can't hurt," Milo said, swiping up a sharp, barely curved cutlass from the selection and sheathing it in the baldric sling across his back, crossed with the other he already wore. "Best to never have just one sword."

I watched him for a moment at the helm. The way he handled the wheel as he breathed in the sea scent all around him, the ocean winds tousling his hair around his face and neck. The way he stood, more than a whole head taller than me, guiding his stolen ship. There was something hopeful in him that I'd never noticed before. Something beyond the hope of outrunning his enemies. But a real, deep hope that he'd always seemed to be pursuing in life was just over the horizon. Bellamy loved the sea. But Milo loved the promises it brought. Because his life had been changed by it in so many ways.

I stepped forward, settling next to him at the wheel, and leaned my head on his shoulder. He stopped and smiled at me with tender eyes that made me feel like we could outrun the whole world, just he and I, the same way we did on his motorcycle. I watched the open water in front of us as our little ship carried us along with the wind and waves. And I would've been content to stay that way forever.

The first full day at sea, we managed to create enough distance between us and the pursuing ship that we thought we'd lose them easily enough. The winds stayed strong enough to keep our pace. Unfortunately, it also meant Thane's ship was having no trouble keeping up with ours. The sea rolled in waves that kept us bobbing for hours on end, so much that my legs ached from the effort of balancing along the ever-changing surface.

We'd scarcely brought enough food for the journey in our hurry, but fortunately there was plenty of fresh water on board. We'd rotate shifts at the helm, with Milo showing each of us how to use the compass to ensure we didn't steer off course. He barely slept, I could tell. He'd disappear to the cramped cabin belowdecks for only a handful of hours at a time before reemerging to take back the wheel with tired, red eyes.

On the second night, I followed him, to make sure he rested a bit longer. It was Noah's night watch, so I knew the ship was steering soundly for the time being. He'd taken to sailing quite easily. Creeping behind the cabin door silent as the rats on deck, I watched Milo lay down on the pile of blankets strewn across the cabin floor. To my surprise, he fell asleep fast. Within minutes the only sound reaching my ears was that of his breathing and the ever-constant creaking timber of the boat.

I started to turn away, to leave him to his slumber, but a sound yanked me back. He groaned as if in pain, followed by a short whimper that made me feel weak in the knees. When I looked back at him, he was tossing himself across the blankets, twisting and turning as though trying to escape an invisible attacker. I ran to his side, shaking him awake with urgency in my voice.

"Milo," I said. "Wake up. It's alright. I'm here."

He opened his eyes and nearly leapt backward when he saw me. Between gasps of breath, he opened his mouth to speak, but seemed unable to make the words come. He sat up, keeping one leg outstretched in front of him and drawing the other up to him for a place to prop his arm. I kept my hand on his back, rubbing between his shoulder blades gently until he calmed. He pushed his disheveled hair back from his face with his free hand and then squared his shoulders to look at me.

"Was that one of your nightmares?" I asked, my tone as gentle as I could make it. I thought back to when he'd saved me from my bad dreams on the lighthouse and confessed he used to have them, too. This was the first time I'd ever seen it for myself.

He nodded, his breath returning to normal. "It's been a while. But I guess this place has taken its toll." The way he looked at his hands as he spoke, eyeing them with some semblance of disgust, I had a suspicion about what it was that might be weighing on him.

"Is it because of what happened with Thane's men?"

"It's because of me. This place has brought out the worst in me. Rather, it's brought it *back*. Because it never left. No matter how much I wanted to think it did. Here I'm a thief and a killer again. I'm the pirate I tried to forget." he muttered. "Thane's henchman isn't the only man I've killed here." His eyes burned into mine, and then with slow movements he reached into the folds of his loose shirt and out trickled the beads of a rosary. "I killed a man while fighting him, not two hours after our shipwreck. In defense. He attacked me and would've killed me if I didn't. This was his, and I've carried it with me since. I don't know why."

I studied the wooden beads, noticing the brownish-copper stains on them and the little wooden cross at the end. Blood. From a man Milo had killed. I didn't like to think of him killing. I'd pushed out the memory of him leaving Thane's men bleeding on the ground. Because I knew he'd done it for me, and my joy at seeing him again overpowered any other feeling then. And to be honest, it didn't feel real at the time.

But something was different about it now. As I sat here with him, seeing this blood-stained trinket, I soaked in the reality that the same gentle hands that touched me in love and pleasure were also the hands that had taken lives, and always had been, long before this island.

These weren't the first two men he'd killed. Even if it was three centuries past, he'd killed others before. And I knew that. And though some part of me felt sickened by it, I also knew he wasn't given much of a choice in life. And I knew I had to decide once and for all if that would change the way I saw him.

It didn't.

"I think I know why," I whispered. "Because you can't forgive yourself. And you've been holding it all inside. But you have to let go of this or it's going to weigh on your soul until it drowns you."

He shifted and blinked, as if taking my words to heart. Something in me churned. Maybe my words weren't only for him, but for me, too. Cordelia's curses had haunted me long enough. It was time I released myself from that dark burden as well.

"Cordelia told me sirens don't have souls," I added. "At least you have a soul to save."

"That can't be true," Milo said, a tension rising in his voice.

"I don't know if it is or not," I said, taking his hand. "But I do know that it's stupid to pretend we don't have things in our pasts—or presents—that we regret. But we have to either decide if we're going to succumb to it or fight it. And as long as we fight it, then we're never truly lost."

"Stay true north." His lips barely parted as he mumbled the words, a deep expression across his face as though he was recalling them from somewhere.

"What does that mean?" I asked.

"It's something an old friend once told me. And it means exactly what you just said," he offered a smile that sent warmth radiating through me like the soft red glow of a summer sunset.

"Then let's forgive and fight."

I walked with him up to the railing on the starboard side. It wasn't far, given the small size of the ship, but it was enough distance for another quick exchange of words before Milo held the bloody rosary over the side of the ship.

"If there's one thing I've been reminded here, it's that deep down, we're all slaves to the darkness inside us," Milo said sternly, watching the cross pendant dangle over the gurgling black abyss below. He bowed his head for a few seconds in silent thought, and then opened his hand. The rosary slid over his knuckles and plummeted down below. Even in the dark, the schooner was so low to the water, it was possible to catch a glimpse of the slowly sinking beads as the blood marks blossomed into the seawater around them.

I turned to him and kissed him on the lips, hoping he had truly begun to let go of his guilt, and hoping I could do the same so as not to be a hypocrite. "Now go get some sleep," I whispered in his ear before pulling away.

The second and third day was spent in a haze, merely sailing onward and keeping a close eye on our company behind. My steering shift was early morning, so I'd often spend the long moments beforehand staring out from the prow as the sea breeze wrapped its cool embrace around me and the salty morning mist beaded on my eyelashes.

On the third day, I looked down at the water, its sapphire blue glittering like fine jewels in the sunlight. I tried not to think about what might lie far below.

My siren side had been shut up for a long while now, and I hadn't heard from her since I'd succumbed to my mermaid form in the lagoon. But I almost wished she were here, now. I wished there was some way to call on her. I needed her boldness, fearlessness, and longing for the sea. Because I knew sooner or later, once we found the location of the trident, there would be only one way to get it. And it would require a dark, bottomless plunge to the sinking depths of the Devil's Triangle.

34

NOT ALL TREASURE IS SILVER AND GOLD

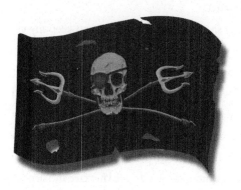

MILO

Each morning for the next three days, I would watch Katrina stand at the front of the ship. I knew she was thinking about diving down to fetch the trident. She was our only hope of acquiring it, but I didn't want her to feel that weight alone.

I'd finally accepted that Thane wasn't going to abandon his chase, and we'd eventually have to fight him off. That thought terrified me, knowing it was just us four against however many men made up his crew. And he himself was more than a formidable opponent. I knew if he were to reach our ship, we'd have quite the fight for survival on our hands. But I decided if he tried to touch Katrina one more time, I'd spill his worthless guts at the helm of his own ship and make his men watch. Even if Katrina only ever saw me as a monster afterward, I'd never let him hurt her again.

The evening of the third day, Noah had offered to steer the ship a bit longer, and the sails needed little adjustment, allowing me a few extra hours of freedom I couldn't normally afford. Katrina and I worked together in the cabin to create a plan for when we arrived at the supposed location of the trident. As we talked it over, discussing the hows and whens, I found myself losing focus as I watched the way she spoke, my gaze lingering over her rose lips as she spoke about diving down into the water.

I squared my shoulders, trying my best to keep my concentration as we leaned over the small corner table in the cabin, but something about her in that moment held me captive and refused to let go. Perhaps it was the way she spoke so bravely, and willingly intended to do whatever she needed to get the trident. Or perhaps it was her beauty alone that called to me like a siren's song. The harsh days at sea and on the island created a radiance about her that couldn't be explained. Her skin glowed with a deep sunkissed glow of warmth, enhanced by the way her dark, windswept hair framed her face and slender neck in full waves. I watched the way her chin tilted as she spoke, and I noticed the delicate dips in her collarbone. I recalled every divine curve of her underneath the loose tunic she wore. God, I wanted her right there and then.

If it wasn't those things making me lose my focus, it could only be one other—the fact that I didn't know what awaited us ahead. And I couldn't protect us. I couldn't stop what was coming.

"Can I ask you something?" I finally blurted out, interrupting Katrina as she spoke about how she would swim down and find the trident and reemerge once we'd cleared away Thane's ship.

She looked at me with a confused expression. " Yes, what is it?" She raised her eyebrows. "Go ahead."

"How much do you love me?" I asked, leaning forward. "And consider it long and well before you answer."

She looked around, obviously taken by surprise at my question. "Well," she sucked in a deep breath. "Why are you asking this? Do you think I don't—"

"No, it's nothing like that. I know you love me. But just for fun, if you had to put it into words, how would you do it?" I nodded with a gentle smile for her to go on. If she thought the question was forward, I'd make it seem like a game.

"I... I'd say I love you with all my heart. And...and I couldn't imagine my life without you. I wouldn't want to imagine that life. You are...you're everything to me." She blushed, looking down at the ring I'd given her and adjusted it gently with her fingers. "Feel better now?" She laughed.

Damn.

I never knew a confession of love could be so painful. I could only hope she was lying. Maybe there could be something else she cared for more...maybe. Perhaps she should have just fallen for Bellamy. I would've wished it. Because I was so afraid if it was true, then her answer meant something detrimental. Something I didn't want to think about yet, though I knew I'd have to face it sooner rather than later.

Later would do for now. Because right now, in this rare moment with just the two of us alone, I only wanted to pin Katrina against the wall and love her senseless. I wanted to see the stars with her one more time.

She stood watching me with her back to the wall, a longing in her eyes just as overwhelming as mine. I reached for her hand, drawing it to my lips. I kissed each one, suckling gently as I caressed my mouth across each fingertip. She drew into me, her other hand touching me gently along the ridges of my muscles. She roamed my body, leaving no area unclaimed.

"All the time in the world with you could never be enough," she said in a gentle breath.

"That's the problem, isn't it?" I whispered, tracing the perfect curves of her beneath her shirt and navigating my hand across her hips to the warmth between her legs. "I'm tired of being on borrowed time with you. So, I'm going to steal it instead."

"In true pirate fashion," she snarled softly with a mischievous gleam in her eyes. Those deep brown eyes that I would willingly drown in until my last breath.

She closed her lips over mine, teasing me and plunging her fingers into my hair. Her hands tugged at my shirt, lifting it over my head as she lowered her mouth to kiss my chest. In me, a surge of desire swelled so that I couldn't help but touch every part of her, undressing her with careful movements.

Her skin felt so perfectly delicate against my rough hands. I touched my lips to her shoulder, mouthing her softly as I worked toward her neck. She smelled sweetly of the sea. I wanted to tether her to my very soul so that we were one. And the way she wrapped me within her legs assured me she wanted the same.

Fire pulsed in my veins; my heart raced as she unbuckled my belt. I lifted her onto the edge of the table we'd been talking over, pushing aside whatever else was on it to make room for her. Gently, slowly, I moved to her. Her soft gasps against my ear made my head spin, and I whispered her name over and over so that she knew she was the master of my fate, here, now, and forever.

Our bodies might've followed the sway of the ship, with some moments slow and smooth, and others swift and deep. With each soft groan from her lips, the craving for her hammered harder in my core. I stood, holding her firm as she pressed herself against me. We were two oceans meeting, merging in riled plumes of seafoam. She gripped me, stroking my back and neck between wild kisses and teasing licks before she shattered beneath me with quaking breaths.

"Milo," she whispered, tracing the North Star tattoo on my body with her trembling fingers. At the sound of my name on her lips, I became undone, swept into a current she controlled.

The cresting desire in me grew into an animalistic need, a dam of feral thirst I could not hold back any longer. I moved faster, squeezing Katrina's fingers that had now laced themselves between mine, and a wave of bliss cascaded over me as my knees threatened to buckle.

I held onto it, treasuring the sensation that escaped me in moans, because I feared there would be little more in the way of pleasure in the hours ahead. But I refused to let that worry steal this moment from us.

Both dazed and sweat-drenched from the stuffiness of the small cabin, we collapsed together amongst our strewn pieces of clothing. As I caught my breath and regained my senses, I pulled Katrina near and nuzzled her shoulder.

"I do feel better now," I uttered into her damp hair, wishing it could last forever. Because more than anything, I dreaded leaving this cabin to face whatever came next.

35

No Quarter Given

Katrina

I smiled tenderly at Milo. These moments between us were always so quick to end, always one step away from the next threat to our lives. I couldn't wait till we just made it back home and that looming feeling could end. I fiddled with the ring on my finger, dreaming of the life we almost had—and could have again—if we could just make it back.

We redressed and climbed back out on deck, doing our best to look like we'd only been talking out the plan, but I figured our friends would be smart enough to guess that something more than discussion took place. We found McKenzie and Noah and shared our plan with them, asking them for their feedback and opinions. There was a heaviness in the air as the reality settled in that before long Thane would catch up to us. His ship inched closer every moment, and it was only a matter of time before it closed in on us.

"You two stay atop the crow's nest and fire from there. Noah and I will do our best to hold them off when they attack," Milo glanced between all of us as he spoke, addressing each of us. "We have one cannon shot. One. We'll do our best to draw Thane near the stern. And one of you will fire if you have the chance. Even if it means you blast us, too."

I shook my head, choking back a dry tightness overtaking my throat. "There has to be another way."

"I'm hoping there is," Milo said, that ever-familiar lock of hair falling over his eye. "But if we don't find it, you have to do it anyway." He glanced at us collectively once more. "Understood?"

"Crystal clear," McKenzie muttered. The dark tone in her voice was a far cry from her usual chipper self.

"At this point I've accepted we might die, but I'm not going down without a fight." Noah cradled his pistol in his hand, and there was a noble, but somber look in his eye.

I watched McKenzie after we dispersed, and I followed after her as she went to lean over the hull.

"Hey," I said, scooting up next to her with my elbows propped up in a similar manner. "Everything okay? Well—aside from the obvious."

"Yeah, I just...you know. Just once I'd like to feel like I'm brave or courageous or tough. Like you."

"Like me?" I repeated, startled by her response. "Those aren't exactly the words I would use to describe myself."

"That's because you don't see yourself, Katrina." She gestured with her hands as she spoke, her once-perfectly manicured fingernails now dirty and chipped. "You look like a badass all the time. But all anyone ever expects from me is the ditzy rich girl." She paused with a pout. "Because I *am* the ditzy rich girl."

"No," I said. "You're so much more than that."

"This whole experience has just made me realize that I can do more and be more. I just have to start looking for opportunities to do it. I tend to miss out on what I'm capable of, because I'm so busy playing the part of what I'm used to being."

"What are you saying?"

"I don't know. I just...If we get murdered by pirates, I don't want to go down crying in the corner and looking pretty. I want to know what I'm really capable of when push comes to shove."

"Then do that. Show 'em what you're made of, Kenz," I said. She smiled at me without another word, but I was sure I noticed a sparkle of confidence rise in her face.

Within moments, the air felt still, as if destruction hung in the air like a tapestry. Thane's ship nosed its way to ours, its flag already replaced with the blood red flag Thane preferred. Milo had told me about red pirate flags. No prisoners and no survivors. I swallowed a lump in my throat.

I was distracted by the ship enough until Milo darted past. He skidded to a stop and whirled around to face me. Written plain in his shining wet eyes was a look of desperation and true concern that reminded me of the way he looked when Valdez tied him to the mast and tortured him. He leaned forward and gripped my shoulder, speaking low for only me to hear.

"If things get out of control...if the plan doesn't work...you jump overboard and save yourself. Swim away. Swim far away from here and don't look back."

"Milo—" I began to protest, but he crashed his mouth into mine before I could get out the next word. When he pulled away, the worry in his eyes captivated and terrified me all at once. He was truly afraid for me. Afraid of what could happen.

"Promise me you will," he choked. "I won't let you die here."

Stunned by the moment, words stayed trapped on my tongue, so I channeled my jitters into nods to show him I understood. Shattering the tension like glass, Noah rushed in between us.

"Hate to interrupt, but we've got more company than we thought." He slapped a bronze spyglass into Milo's hand and pointed out to sea.

Milo took a look through the tube to the horizon on the left. "It's a Spanish frigate. Probably pirate hunters."

"They're coming this way, too," Noah said, taking back the spyglass.

"Aye, they are." Milo rubbed his jaw. "And that could either be a blessing or a curse. But we hold to the plan if we're attacked. The frigate's at least twenty minutes out. If we can hold off Thane until they reach us...we might have a chance if they intervene." Before either of us could respond, Milo sprinted back to the helm.

"Time to play a bit of tag," Noah uttered, leaning over the hull.

I glanced over at Thane's rapidly approaching ship, racing across the water like a freight train. He was mere minutes from catching right up to us, so close that I could hear the shouts and jeers of his men.

Our sails caught the wind, and we lurched forward as Milo adjusted the *Falcon* slightly off course. I gripped the side of the ship, digging my fingertips into the wood grain to steady myself as our ship veered and tilted with the sudden direction change. McKenzie let out a small shriek from her perch up in the crow's nest.

When the boat settled just long enough to stand upright, I made a dash for the rigging, where I began to climb up the ropes to join McKenzie. I couldn't let her get tossed around like a rag doll up there alone. The thick ropes felt like dead bones in my hands, heavy, damp, and cold, despite the bright sun overhead. I hardly noticed the thick, humid heat as the wind from so high up here whipped my skin dry. With one glance down below, my stomach flipped upside down.

I clenched my eyes shut for a second, just to shake away the sick feeling, and pushed myself upward, climbing the network of ropes to the crow's nest. From there, I could see Thane's crew clearly enough that I had to squint from the white sunlight glinting off their swords.

A barrage of threats and roars rose from the crew as they realized what Milo was doing. He maneuvered the ship forward for just a bit, only to make a sharp turn that they hadn't been expecting, and now he was sailing back in and around them. Their ship was small, but ours was smaller and faster.

As the *Falcon* curled around over and across the waves like a startled sword-fish, Thane's men followed close behind, but they couldn't match the speed of our turns.

I watched Thane at the wheel of his ship. Once he figured it out, he began to turn his vessel as though he was going to continue the chase, but at the last minute, sped right past ours, only to order his men to close the sails and drop their anchor, swinging his ship around, nearly tipping it. It swung around like a colossal, slow-moving pendulum, and though Milo had caught onto Thane's plan by now, it was impossible for him to get our boat out of the way in time.

The bow of Thane's ship whipped around, colliding into the back half of ours. The force of the blow nearly launched McKenzie and me from our post, rocking the ship side to side. We huddled in the cramped floor of the crow's nest to keep from flying out. The sound of crisp wood snapping as the ships crashed together sent a panic through my bones. They had us now.

I wondered how detrimental the damage to our ship would be. Judging by the concerned expression on Milo's face from below, it was worse than I thought. We were left afloat, still slowly swirling on the surface as the rioting water settled. Within seconds, our two vessels ended up parallel, facing opposite directions. I glanced out at sea, praying the approaching Spanish frigate would speed up at the sight of the chaos. It was closer now, but there were still minutes-worth of distance between us and them.

Thane wasted no time giving the orders to his men to take our ship. By the looks of it, his crew was made up of hardly more than ten, but it was still more manpower than we had. From their deck launched grappling ropes, taking root into our hull. I watched the scene unfold before me with trembling nerves and a hand over my pistol. McKenzie peeked over the crow's nest, a white-knuckle grip on the gun in her hands. And together we took our best aim as Thane's crew pulled our ship to theirs like a needle closing a stitch together.

A barrage of shouts and stomps filled the air as the stinging scent of gunpow-der crawled to my nostrils. I couldn't breathe, partly from the smoke tickling my lungs, but more so because my chest was tightening at the thought of Milo and Noah below facing so many attackers at once.

Half a dozen pirates swung from the rigging, leaping down with foreboding thuds as their heavy boots hit the deck. Milo fought with two swords, wielding a cutlass in each hand as he fended off the men approaching him from every side. But I knew he couldn't manage that for long. I fired my pistol with the best aim I could manage, alerting the crew to our presence. But at least I hit my target. The man gripped his shoulder where the bullet struck, and Milo used the distraction as a chance to shove him over the edge of the ship with the broad side of his sword.

"Noah, watch out!" McKenzie screamed. Noah whipped around just in time to find himself face to face with a charging crewman. He stumbled back as he met the man's sword blow with his own blade, using barely enough force to deflect the hit. If he was terrified—and I knew he had to be—he didn't show it.

I noticed Thane making his way through the fray. Slowly and steadily, he was locked on to Milo. He walked without urgency across the deck, following Milo's lead to the back of the ship. At least the plan was working so far. But I wouldn't risk him getting too close. I fired at him, but missed, instead drawing his attention upward as my gunfire whizzed right past his head. He stopped, turning around with the same calmness with which he walked before flashing a cold grin my way.

I thought he'd come for me. I thought I'd blown the plan, and if so, I wouldn't have cared. Because if Milo thought I could fire a cannon blast at him just to kill Thane, he was wrong. The pirate hunter frigate was closing in. So, I thought if I could just hold him off a little longer...

But Thane didn't come for me. He just winked at me with a wicked, sick smile curling across his lips and pulled out his sword. Even from here, I could see that it was stained with old, dried blood. He brought the blade to his face and, without taking his eyes off me, licked the crusted blood from the edge. It took everything in me not to gag at the sight. Then he turned around, bloody sword in his grip, and began walking toward Milo again. I cursed beneath my breath and fired again, this time aiming for the pirates attacking Noah and Milo, who now stood nearly back-to-back, their faces wrought with focus and exhaustion as their blades whirled.

"What was that you were saying about not going down without a fight?" I turned to McKenzie. "They can't do this by themselves. And these guns suck at long range. I'm going down there."

She grabbed my arm, nearly pulling me back as I crouched down to begin my descent down the rigging. I thought she was going to beg me not to go or tell me why it was a horrible idea. But instead, she looked me dead in the eyes and said, "I'm coming with you."

Together we shimmied down the ropes as quickly as possible, but the awkward boots and breeches offered little in the way of flexibility and movement. About halfway down, I glanced over my shoulder below. Both bloodied, our two men were losing ground. Milo's shirt was ripped in many places, and bright red blooms of blood decorated the fabric like a floral print. Noah was in no better shape.

I raised my gun to shoot from where I hung in the rigging. But as my finger pulled back on the trigger, an unforgiving resistance blocked my movement.

"It's jammed," I said, turning the pistol over in my hand to inspect it as if I knew what to do with it. "McKenzie, shoot them!" I cried.

My normally bold and boisterous roommate was anything but in that moment. Clinging to the ropes right beside me, she looked like she might cry as the wind scattered her orange hair every which way around her. She hesitated, fidgeting with the weapon in her hands.

"What if I miss?" She stammered.

"Don't think about that. They need our help!"

She grimaced, placing the pistol in her palm and aiming for the group of men fighting Noah. I could see the gun shaking in her pale grip.

"I'm going to hit Noah. I...I can't do it." Her words were peppered with strains and held back tears. Just as I was about to respond with some attempt at something motivational, the sound of swords clanging below died down.

My grip on the rigging strengthened, my hands curling around the rope so tightly I thought it might burn my palms as I directed my attention to the scene unfolding on deck. Noah had been disarmed, and a pirate held him pinned to the deck with a firm boot on his chest and a sword beneath his chin. The men ceased their battle momentarily as they waited for Thane to direct their next move.

Thane stood to speak, his penny-bronze hair framing his striking features. A sharp jawline, crooked nose, and piercing eyes full of bloodlust. He walked to Noah, his steps taunting as a dark smile stretched across his face.

"Kill the friends first. Make him watch." He pointed to Milo with the tip of his sword. "And take your time."

Just then, our ship teetered in a sudden wake, sending McKenzie and me tumbling from the rigging and slamming onto the deck below. Smoke billowed into the air, fresh from the side of Thane's ship. Cannon fire. But not from the Spanish frigate. That ship was nearly upon us, and was moving in from the east, but the cannon shot hadn't come from that direction. It came from behind.

I leapt to my feet to see the origin of the shot. My jaw dropped at the sight of the *Widow* reeling toward us, with Bellamy at the helm.

36

FIRE IN THE HOLE

KATRINA

In a whirlwind of confusion, the *Widow* edged its way carefully alongside us as Bellamy and a handful of his crew crossed over to our boat. His massive ship made our tiny schooner look like a toy sailboat as it cast its looming shadow across the deck.

Bellamy himself landed with a thud, sword drawn, eyeing his surroundings like a soldier in foreign territory. Both crews now erupted in yells and curses, a flurry of attacks flaring up all at once from all sides.

"You followed us all this way. You came to help us?" I called to Bellamy over the noise of the battle. "Why? I thought—"

"Don't ask me why!" he spat. "I don't know why I did either."

His stubbornness didn't surprise me. I'd given up on expecting him to admit he might care about something more than sailing the seas. Or that he might have feelings for a siren. But his reasons didn't matter to me right then. I was just more grateful to see him than ever.

Thane's crew was now evenly matched. Our deck was littered with bodies, some limbless or bleeding, and others already dead. I swallowed down the bile rising to my throat at the sight and cringed at the coppery smell of blood that pierced my nostrils. When I looked over at McKenzie, she seemed frozen in place.

"Come on," I said, grabbing her wrist and leading her to the bow. "Take a breath," I said, keeping her facing the water, "Don't look at it."

Inwardly, I trembled with horror, but I couldn't fall apart here. I deeply feared the outcome of this bloody battle at sea. There was nowhere to run. If Thane's men didn't kill us all, who knew what would happen when the Spaniards reached us? There was no way to end this chain of attacks but to escape it. And the only escape was a trident at the bottom of sea. A trident that could twist the very thing we were quickly running out of—time.

As I watched Bellamy's crew rush to Noah and Milo's aid, I noticed the Spanish frigate looming nearby. It turned, lining its side up with ours. We made the perfect target. Three pirate ships all clustered together in one place, heavily distracted by destroying one another. The pirate hunters would've been idiots not to take advantage of this. Looking around at the blood-soaked deck behind us, it was plain to see we'd already done most of the work for them.

"Get down." I put a firm hand against McKenzie's shoulder and urged her toward the deck floor. I dropped down and lay on my stomach next to her. I watched the war-ready Spanish frigate as the small windows along its hull slid open to give way to lines of cannons taking aim. Gray metal plates of armor covered its hull. It was so close I could hear it now. The heavy patter of the crew's boots along the deck, the twinge of ropes and sails, and the structured shouts and commands amongst the sailors. The captain was giving out orders in Spanish, and I understood easily enough.

"*Dispara!*"

Before I could blink, the side of our ship erupted in an explosion of wood chips and smoke raining down like some kind of apocalyptic piñata. McKenzie let out a wail and covered her head as debris rained down us and the ship shivered beneath us like an earthquake.

I glanced back over my shoulder. Many of the pirates from both Bellamy and Thane's crew had been knocked overboard from the blast. Milo was just getting to his feet like the rest of the men around him. He locked eyes on Thane, who was busy ripping his sword from the stomach of a squirming man on his back. Noah was still down, but I sighed with relief when I saw him slowly find his footing.

Bellamy appeared from the smoke near the cannon shot. I wondered if he had ever even stumbled when the cannon struck the ship. He walked with a calm assuredness that sent chills fluttering through me. He drew his sword, parrying a blow from an attacking pirate like it was nothing, looking around through focused eyes as if seeking his next target.

The sound of a pistol cracked through the air, followed by a jolt that sent Bellamy staggering backward and gripping his shoulder in agony. The gasp that escaped my lips was much louder than I intended it to be. I worried he would fall, but he only clenched his jaw, glanced at the blood on his hand that had stained from covering his wound. Then he charged forward, a feral look in his eye. He let out a cry, gritty and wild, maneuvering his cutlass with ferocity fitting of a pirate captain, and cut down the man who fired in one swift blow.

Another round of cannon fire from the hunters' frigate sent more pieces of the ship flying and took a handful of men down for the count. I noticed it was getting harder to keep my balance. Each awkward step to steady myself felt like the floor was shifting beneath my feet. When I glanced around once more, I quickly realized the changing angle of the deck. Barrels rolled to one side of the boat, dropping into the water below. The mast leaned in an uneasy way, threatening to snap at any moment. The *Falcon* had endured all she could take. We were sinking.

The clang of a sword caught my attention, tearing me from my observation. A pirate rushed at me, blade drawn, and on instinct I pulled out my own. He swung at me, and I stepped back just far enough to miss the blade's edge, but nearly toppled over. I begged my brain to recall everything Bellamy taught me about sword fighting, however basic. I didn't want to have to remember, though. I didn't want to fight.

The next time the man swung, I used both hands to help me brace my sword against his, and with more strength than I realized I had, I shoved forward, keeping the blade away from me just once more.

"McKenzie!" I cried, hoping she was near enough to hear. But I realized she was no longer standing beside me. Somehow, I missed her leaving my side, but now she was on the rigging, climbing up in desperation to escape an attacker of her own.

I gritted my teeth and strained against my opponent. This man would kill me if I didn't stop him from doing it first. And I couldn't accept that that may mean I'd have to kill him. Our swords danced, sparking from impacts that nearly knocked my weapon from my grip. And finally, I realized I'd have to find the strength to end it, or he would end me. With the sickest sensation swirling in my core, I recalled Bellamy's instructions. I remembered one thing he told me. That one stupid thing. *Thrust.*

I ducked one last time as the man swung at my head. All in the same instant, I closed my eyes and jutted my sword out in front of me like a spear. I should've kept my eyes open, but I couldn't watch myself impale another human.

But when I peeked back reluctantly, I saw that my sword never made much contact with the man. Instead, he stood with the tip of a blade jutting out of his chest—a sword that had entered from the back. When his limp body slid forward off the cutlass that ran him through, the person left standing behind him was Milo, panting and glowering at me with a fierceness in his eyes that made my blood run ice cold.

"Thank you," the words felt numb rolling off my tongue. It seemed as though a fog had formed in front of me, and I couldn't see through it. He'd just saved me from having to kill someone, but that didn't mean it made it any easier for him to add to the guilt he was already fighting.

He nodded in acknowledgement, then gazed out across the deck, scanning the scene. "Thane's gone. He's escaped."

He was right. I didn't see Thane anywhere. But his ship was missing. He knew we couldn't sail after him. And he'd left his few remaining men to deal with the hunters and Bellamy's crew alone. The coward.

The fog around me closed in, freezing time in its place so I could really take a long, hard look around me. But it wasn't fog. It was smoke. Real smoke that was heavy and burned my lungs and woke me to the hopeless reality surrounding me. My senses tuned in to the intense sound of men shouting, steel clashing, gunpowder exploding, wooden ships groaning and crackling as the relentless cannons roared their deathly booms. McKenzie was still trying to run, Noah didn't look like he could take much more, and Bellamy and Milo were both covered in blood not their own. This was it. These four ships would go down here. And if I stayed here a moment longer, we'd go down with them.

"I'm going down below. I'm going to get the trident." I breathed, drawing the courage to believe the words myself.

"We need to be closer to the center of the Triangle."

"Well, it's clear we're not getting anywhere else in this ship," I said, gesturing to the tipping floor below me. "I have to go find it now or we'll never make it."

The harsh look in Milo's eyes dwindled down to one of concern. "It's too dangerous. It's the deep sea."

"Dangerous is the only option we have right now." I stepped forward, meeting his gaze with an unyielding hold of my own.

He glanced away with tight lips and a creased brow. I knew he was afraid for me. And he was trying to figure out how to be okay with it. He nodded, just barely, then lowered his sword and pulled me to him with his free arm. He crashed his mouth into mine with a burning intensity stronger than the Caribbean sun above. I could taste the blood, sweat, and salt across his lips, but none of it mattered then. I kissed him back, hard and desperately. When he pulled away, he looked me dead in the eye, and he spoke to me as though guarding treasure that no one could ever find.

"You promise me you'll make it back. Even if it's a lie. You promise me..." His voice cracked with a hint of a whimper that broke me and filled my heart all at once.

"I promise I'll find you again," I uttered softly through the explosions and chaos around us, as the ship dipped lower and lower. "I always do."

With that, I turned around, racing across the leaning deck, my eyes fixed on the endless ocean. I rushed to the bow of the ship, looking ahead toward the only clear path not surrounded by smoking ships. I pulled my boots off, and next my pants, clothed only by the long tunic that draped down past my hips just barely across the top of my thighs.

With the wind at my back, I risked one more glance behind me at the sight of confused crews from all sides halting their fighting long enough to watch me with curious stares, Bellamy, McKenzie and Noah included. But Milo watched with an unsettling longing in his eyes, knowing full well what I was doing.

And with all the strength I could muster, I took a breath I knew I wouldn't be able to hold onto for long, and dove in.

37

A DEPTH SO DARK

KATRINA

The water here was murky. I braced myself for the excruciating sting of saltwater I knew I'd soon feel blazing in my lungs. I swam down as quickly as my body would allow, diving to the depths like a harpoon. I had to get deep enough that returning to the surface was impossible.

It was different this time. When I'd changed in the lagoon, my siren side *wanted* to change. She begged to drown Katrina and take her form. But now that I had her under control, every instinct in my body fought against what I knew I had to do. Thrashing, clawing my way back up, I couldn't find the strength to drown. I couldn't do it.

The surface was right overhead, glittering above me like an open skylight of hope. I closed my eyes, just begging the siren in me to take hold. She would have no problem pulling me under. I thought of Milo, McKenzie, and Noah. I thought of my parents back home. And the rest of the world. How failing might literally mean the fall of mankind. But none of that overpowered my body's desire to breathe. To be a siren, I had to be selfish. I had to think like a siren. I had to let out the part of me I'd been hiding all along.

Power. Control. With the trident, there would be no limit to what I could do with it. *Think of the things you can make them do with your song.* I relented myself to the darkest part of me. *Make the world know your name. Defeat Cordelia and take her place. Show your power.*

The idea that I might have my vengeance against Cordelia seemed to be the key. I could make her pay for all the hell she put my family through. I could torture her the way she tortured my mother and grandmothers and even me. All of the suicides and depression and nightmares could be turned back around onto her.

Get the trident and destroy her.

With that thought, a wicked grin spread across my face as bubbles floated to the surface as I fought to hold in the last bit of air in my body. I had to let go. Fully.

I opened my eyes, and the water was now nearly crystal clear. The depth still made it difficult to see more than twenty or thirty feet in front of me, but it was easy enough to make out the looming shadows of the ships overhead, thundering and rumbling like crumbling mountaintops above.

Cannons boomed overhead and shook the surface, but the further down I drifted, the more peaceful the world around me became. The last bit of light breaking through danced on the scales of my tail, glittering like thousands of diamonds. My powerful tail swept through the water effortlessly, propelling me forward and farther down to the depths. I didn't know where I was going, but I knew I had to get there as fast as possible.

The pressure beneath the sea would have been much too crushing for me in my human form, but with my siren tail and abilities, I was unstoppable. There was no depth too deep, no current too strong, and no corner of the ocean too dark. The connection between my being and the sea was undeniable and natural as breathing.

I passed sharks and rays of all sizes, schools of fish that glimmered like patterns of mirrors. I'd visited an aquarium in Arkansas once when I was younger, and I remember pressing my face to the glass in fascination at the animals, but that experience paled in comparison to swimming amongst these terrifying, magnificent creatures.

Amazingly, none of them seemed to acknowledge my presence, instead swimming calmly past me as though I belonged there as much as the starfish along the sea floor. I wished for a moment that it might be possible that I could stop and talk to them. I'd ask them if they knew where the trident was and how to get to it.

This isn't a fairytale, Katrina.

I had to force myself to remember the gravity of the situation. My siren side longed to just take her time, relax, and enjoy the time here. But I fought her desires against my true ones. Find the trident. Fast.

I knew it had to be at the bottom of the ocean. It had to be somewhere so dangerous and unreachable that even the most advanced machine couldn't reach it. But could a mermaid?

I flicked my tail up and down, pushing myself further down, until finally the white light from the surface faded, and the last echoes of sounds above dwindled. The only thing I could hear now was the soft, silent rush of water as the current and tides snaked their routes all around me.

Down, down, deeper I ventured, my vision in the dark water as clear as my sight on land. Siren night vision certainly wasn't a bad ability to have right now. For a moment, I chided myself for not having the courage to do this much earlier. If I hadn't feared this form so much for so long, perhaps I could've dove down like this and retrieved the scale before Cordelia was ever able to get her hands on it.

Stay true north. Milo's words came to mind seemingly from nowhere. Three simple words that reminded me to stay my course. To hold onto the next right step. Focusing on the past wasn't going to save anyone. It wasn't going to change things as they were. And it certainly wasn't going to matter now. All I could do was focus on the next battle in front of me—and keep going.

I studied the water around me, looking for some remnant of a clue that might lead me in the right direction. Down here, it was nearly impossible to tell left from right or north from south. But as a mermaid, I had keen senses that worked in ways I couldn't fathom. For instance, I could feel every bubble, temperature change, and switch of current direction against my skin.

So, when I paid close attention, falling fully in tune with the oceanic void surrounding me, I found I could sense an unusual pattern in the way the water flowed against the nearly translucent fins of my tail. I watched the water swirling around it. One current circulated in a way that pulled my caudal fin in one direction so subtly I might've missed it if I had been moving any faster.

The current funneled slowly into the ocean floor, twisting like a ghostly rope and the further down it went, the stronger it became. It flowed backward, against the motion of the rest of the sea, in a way that assured me it was created by something outside of nature. Where the ocean's natural undertow traveled and where this other stream led eventually met, merging like two ribbons swirling around each other, like twisting tides forming a path beyond what I could see.

I followed them, straining my eyes. Despite my siren sight, eventually the ocean's darkness became strong enough to hinder me. This was a depth far too deep for even mermaids. I could only imagine how difficult of a time Cordelia's divers would have getting down this far. This is why she wanted my help. But I knew she would find a way to do it with or without them or me. I just hoped she hadn't found it already back in the present. So, I kept on, fueled by urgency, following the gentle twisting currents that swept me along calmly as if time wasn't of the essence.

But time didn't matter here. It was a concept that didn't exist in this place. I could've been swimming for hours or minutes, God only knows. And when the spiraling currents suddenly split into three streams dancing and unraveling across each other, I knew some source of magic must be near. I swam on slowly, listening, feeling, hoping.

When my hand brushed up against something cold and solid. I yanked it away in reaction. But I quickly regained the courage to reach forward again. My fingertips met a metallic prong, and I worked my hand along the rest of it, feeling the nearly identical shape of two more on either side of it. I couldn't see it, but it was clear to me what was pulling these waters together, binding them within life, time, and space—the three prongs. I gasped in disbelief—if that's even possible underwater.

It was real. The trident was real.

I reached to grab it, feeling around blindly as I wrapped my hands around its metal rod base. It wasn't easy to uproot from its buried place in the sand beneath. With a grunt that sent bubbles bursting from my mouth, I thrashed my tail upward with all the strength I could manage and dislodged the trident from its ancient hold in the dense sand. It was all I could do to silently pray that removing it wouldn't summon some monstrous tsunami or disaster from the gods.

But nothing disastrous happened that I could tell. I smiled and swam upward, lugging the heavy scepter in both hands as I flicked my tail up and down to send me back to the surface. I wondered what awaited me there. Would the ships still be afloat? Were my friends still alive? I was almost afraid to discover what I would find waiting for me above the sea.

As I swam back toward the light, the shadow of the ships above came into focus, and the distant sound of cannon fire resumed as if I'd never left. I rushed to the surface, the water cascading over me as I broke through the barrier of sky and sea. I did my best to keep the trident hidden under the water, and I shouted for help over the sound of pistols firing and men fighting.

It was a bloody and bruised Noah who rushed to the railing of the sinking ship. He motioned for me to wait, and without much of a choice, I did. He disappeared for a moment, leaving me confused, before the sound of a boat smacking the water made me look over at the side of the tilted hull. He'd cut the ropes holding the skiff so that it dropped down over the side.

I swam to it with haste. McKenzie rushed to join Noah, and he helped her climb down into the skiff, grimacing from the strain on his sore muscles no doubt. It wasn't a far leap, as the ship was almost underwater, so it only took some careful footwork down the part of the hull that wasn't yet submerged.

"Here!" I reached over the side of the skiff and placed the trident inside. "Keep it safe."

Noah and McKenzie offered their assistance to pull me up into the boat. I gripped their arms, pushing up with my tail as best I could as they pulled me into the skiff with them. The wood scraping along my tail hurt, but not as much as the pain of transforming back once my scales began to dry. Before my fish parts became human again, I quickly reached down and plucked a scale from my own tail, wincing from the pain. It felt like ripping off a fingernail.

"Damn." Noah shook his head. "You really are a mermaid."

"Is that the hardest thing for you to believe after all this?" I asked. "Where's Milo?"

Noah glanced back up at the ship. "He should be coming."

I gripped the section of my tail that would become my thighs as it transformed back into legs. I was thankful for the long tunic I'd kept on that covered enough of me to keep from revealing everything between my legs as I lay on the boat waiting to be human again. McKenzie tossed me the pants I'd taken off earlier.

"And you were worried about not doing anything important." I smirked, taking the pants and sliding them on, relieved that I wouldn't have to continue on with a naked lower half. "I can't think of anything I'd be more grateful for right now than this."

There was a large cannon boom, and the sound of silence for just a moment. Then suddenly the clanging of swords picked up again. Milo took a running leap from the half-submerged schooner and just barely made it into the skiff as we began to drift outward. Dried blood and sweat clung to him, and all he could do was press his knuckles against his other palm as he stared at the floor of the boat in a way that worried me.

"Better late than never. We're not leaving you this time." Noah nudged Milo with his elbow as he caught his breath and settled into the boat beside him. Milo offered a smile that was genuine, but also riddled with a worn and tired fearfulness I couldn't help but notice.

"Are they coming after us?" I looked overhead at the ships bobbing there. Bellamy's ship, the *Widow,* was comparable to the size of the Spanish frigate. But judging by the battered appearance of the Spanish ship, it had been the one that had taken a beating.

"Bellamy's crew is holding them off as long as they can, but both crews are dwindling, so it shouldn't go on much longer." Milo explained, eyeing the silver trident lying across the length of the skiff.

"Now how do we make this thing take us back?" McKenzie was the one who piped up.

"Cordelia said only a siren can use it. But to do that she has to give up something so she can take control of its power." I fiddled with the scale in my hand, admiring its satin silver sheen before continuing. "I'm going to give it this. To show I'm willing to give up my powers if it means we get to go home. Besides, I never wanted to be a mermaid anyway." My heart raced with the thought of returning us all home back together, and the more I thought about it the faster my blood raced through my veins.

"How do you 'give' it anything exactly?" Noah picked up the trident, studying it with cold, focused eyes. It was at least a foot taller than him.

"I don't know," I said, standing in the wobbly skiff. Once I found my balance, I reached forward and gripped the trident at its base. It began to glow with an unearthly white haze, pulsing with the light concentrated mostly around my hand.

I held out my scale to it, not knowing what I expected, but trying to earn its acceptance one way or another. I pressed the scale against the base where the rod melded into the prongs. When that didn't work, I tried touching it to each of the prong tips, my hope shrinking a little bit with each failed attempt. But no matter what, the pulsing white light stayed, glowing rhythmically like the constant beats of a waltz.

Once I'd tried everything I could possibly think of, I looked at the others around me through eyes confounded and hopeless. The schooner was almost entirely underwater now, and Bellamy's men were retreating back to their ship. We had mere minutes before the only barrier between us and the pirate hunters was at the bottom of the sea. Though I had no idea if they'd bother coming after us, that would still leave us stuck on the open ocean in a rowboat barely big enough for the four of us with no food or water.

"I don't know what else I can do." I squeezed the scale in my hand. I had a suspicion. A dark, haunting idea why my futile attempts to sacrifice my own magic wasn't working. But I pushed it from my mind because I refused to accept that it could actually be the truth. There had to be another way...

"I do," Milo said, leaning forward in the skiff, his eyes downcast.

No. He was thinking it, too.

"The thing you love most isn't your magic, Katrina," He muttered pulling a knife from his belt. "And it isn't a thing, is it?"

"What are you doing?" I asked, noticing how he held the knife, gripping it as if ready to use it.

"Tell me what you care for more than anything." His voice draped over me like heavy velvet, darkening the air around me, while my grip tightened on the trident. Now I understood why he'd asked me how much I love him back on the ship. I knew what he was doing. And I couldn't let him do it.

"Oh my god! Look!" McKenzie shouted, pointing at the pirate hunters who were readying a cannon directly our way. The schooner was long gone under, with only a quarter of its mast jutting out of the water to mark its presence. Our only shield was gone. Bellamy was back on the *Widow*, hustling to redirect the ship and block our enemies, but there was no way he could move that thing fast enough.

"Katrina, tell me. What do you love more than anything?" Milo repeated, pulling my focus back to him.

I blinked back hot tears and swallowed the burning lump rising in my throat. I was so afraid of what would happen if I answered him. But we were out of time. I didn't know what else to do.

"You know it's you." The words dripped from my mouth weakly, cracking between each hoarse syllable.

Milo stood up, rocking the unbalanced skiff on the already choppy water, and took a step forward so that he could lean over me. He reached over around the back of my neck and pulled my face to his to kiss me. It was brief, but passionate, and I held onto the taste of him like the sweet savor of honey.

When he pulled away, before any of us could say a word, he raised the knife in his hand and swiped it across the flesh of his palm. With an unwavering stare fixated on the trident, he pressed his blood-soaked hand to the trident's prongs, and the glowing haze around it became brighter.

"No!" I screamed. "No!" I knew what he was doing. He was taking his rightful place as the thing I loved most in this world. The thing I was most afraid of losing. The thing I would never have given up, not even to save the world.

"This is the only way to get you back." He spoke as calmly as if he was simply putting a lure on a fishing hook, but in those long-familiar hazel eyes, he couldn't hide the brokenness and turmoil giving away the truth. "You've saved me, Katrina. In every way. And now it's finally my turn to save you." As he spoke, the glow around the trident strengthened, and I felt its magic surging through the scepter rod in my hand.

"No!" I shrieked. "I'll stay here with you forever if I have to. I *won't* leave you again!" I threw down the trident and let it hit the floor of the boat with a heavy, bell-like clang.

"Katrina, we have to go!" Noah screamed, gesturing to the cannon readying to blast us. "You're the only one of us who can use it! Pick it up!"

"No!" I screamed until my throat was raw, my knees hitting the floor of the boat as McKenzie and Noah each fought to hold me up on either side. But I melted in their grasp, begging them to leave me alone, screaming through wails and cries until my lungs nearly gave out. "No...no...no..."

Please no.

"Katrina! We're going to die here if we don't go back! You *know* that's what's going to happen! There's no other way!" McKenzie's tearful voice of reason raked against my core like claws.

I trembled, waves of tears breaking through my pitiful hold on them. The urgency of the moment brought back all too many fresh, horrid memories of standing at the edge of the *Siren's Scorn* that dark night months ago. When the fate of everyone I cared about was crushing me with its weight on my shoulders. Was I really to be forced to make this choice again? Lose Milo forever or doom us all?

What would it mean to give Milo to the trident? Would it kill him? Would it make him forget me? Would it take him to a place I could never find?

I stared, lost in my spiraling cyclone of thoughts as quiet tears streamed down my face. I couldn't make this choice. I couldn't do it. I shook my head, nearly choking on deep, short breaths as the hopelessness set in. McKenzie and Noah still shouted and pleaded with me, but I couldn't even understand them. I could see only darkness. Darkness as empty and void as the depths I'd just swum back from.

Just then, a strong guiding hand took mine and pried open the fingers of my balled fist. It was Milo, forcing the trident back into my grip and kneeling in front of me. I tried to pull away, to let go of the cold metal in my hand. But he held his hand firmly over mine, locking my hold on the trident in place. Each beat of my heart felt like a pickaxe in my chest as I realized there was no way to change this. The cannon would fire in seconds. Even if it missed, there was nowhere to go here in this place where no one that I'd brought here belonged. There was no other choice but this. Milo was going to make sure of it.

And I hated him for it. I hated him then, as he watched me through tangled locks of dark gold hair, falling in front of that scarred eyebrow. Then he smirked that slightly crooked smile that made me hate him more. And I smiled back, as the tears kept flowing, and I choked back the desperate wail I wanted so badly to let out.

"You just couldn't stop trying to protect me, could you?" I shook my head, barely able to see him as my tears blurred my vision. He stroked my hand reassuringly with his thumb as the trident's light became the purest white, forming a halo around us in our skiff. I could feel him shaking and it broke every part of me. I pressed my forehead to the place where our hands met on the trident. "I told you to stop protecting me...I told you...I told you..." The words broke into fractured pieces that I couldn't piece back together.

Milo reached his uncut hand forward, touching the side of my face where Thane had cut me. "That's the one thing I can never do for you, Starlight." He paused as he pressed his eyes shut for just a moment, and then looked back at me through tears of his own. "I always lose you eventually. But I find you again and again."

The light from the trident became so intense that I couldn't see him anymore. I cherished the last bit of his touch on my face and hands, and as the light shone brighter than the sun, I whispered one promise I prayed to be true as my wet lips trembled, and I felt I could barely hold myself upright anymore.

"I'll find you in every lifetime."

Cannon fire exploded, voices faded, and the white light consumed us. I opened my eyes to a blue sky.

38

ROCK BOTTOM

KATRINA

I was floating on my back, the trident still in my hand. The water around me was calm and gentle, lifting me like it intended to cradle me softly until I fell asleep. I wished I could. The cut on my face burned from the saltwater, which I didn't remember feeling when I was in my mermaid form.

I lifted my head with a jerk, righting myself in the water and still holding tightly to the trident. The ships were gone. There was no sunken schooner, no Spanish frigate, and no ship captained by Bellamy exchanging cannon fire with the others. On all sides, as far as my weary eye could see, there was only blue sea, stretching on and on. McKenzie and Noah were treading water, too, and appeared to be just gaining their senses the same as me.

But Milo wasn't there.

"What happened?" McKenzie asked.

"We're back," I said half-heartedly. "At least I think." I didn't know if I wanted to be right or wrong. My heart felt so heavy I thought it would weigh me down and sink me straight to the bottom of the ocean. If we were back, it meant I would never know what happened to Milo. And that was a reality I just couldn't face.

"At least we know your evil mermaid grandma hasn't destroyed the world yet." Noah's usual attempts to be logical and snarky just made me feel irritated. I didn't care. I just didn't care.

"No, instead we just got sent back to the present and we get to die at sea in modern times instead of the 18th century." McKenzie's comment took me by surprise, but it was what she said next that really caught me off guard. "And Milo...I can't believe he did that to get us here. This is just..."

"Yeah, I really wish I had gone a little easier on him," Noah said, bobbing in the water only a few feet from me. "I thought so many things about him and all of them...wrong." His voice cracked dryly as he dropped his gaze.

I nodded in acknowledgement. Maybe there was something underneath that stubborn indifferent exterior. But his words were worth about as much comfort as the fact that we were still stranded at sea.

We floated along, unsure of our next move, and purely at the ocean's mercy. I looked out and thought about how nothing out here on this never-ending blue expanse looked any different than it did back in 1720. The sea was unfazed by time; unchanged by the passing centuries, just as timeless as it was endless. And I could live the full life of a siren—300 years or more—and yet what would it all be for?

McKenzie and Noah talked a bit, discussing our situation and trying to figure out a way to find help or survive out here overnight if it came to that. Not even an hour had passed before they worked themselves into a panic, growing more exhausted by the second from keeping afloat for so long. I watched as the sun shifted across the midday sky, threatening to begin its descent behind the horizon in just a few more hours. I might have felt the panic, too, if I could manage to feel anything.

I was too broken to contribute. I had nothing to say, and nothing to fear. The trauma was too fresh. I didn't care how long we floated out there for. Tread water or die. I had no solution to offer. I just needed a moment to grieve. Could I just have that?

As I watched the white clouds dotting the afternoon sky, I couldn't help but feel the strangest relief at the sound of distant humming. Because I knew by the sound what approached. I could feel it in the way the vibrations in the water sent out ripples and wakes far ahead of the boat coming into view.

"Help! Help us!" McKenzie screamed, waving her hands and splashing around hysterically. Noah quickly joined her in trying to flag down the vessel.

Something was wrong. I knew long before the boat got anywhere near us that it wasn't just any boat. It was Cordelia's yacht. Time had not passed here as it had during our trip to the past. The day was right where we left it. January 10th.

"Shhh! Don't draw her over here!" I ordered the other two, my command a bit more spiteful than I meant it to be.

A raging hatred filled me when I saw Cordelia. The dark upswept hair and midnight blue pants suit made it impossible not to recognize her, even from a distance. My stomach turned and my grip on the trident grew so tight I thought it would bend the metal. And I felt relief that I could still feel something. I was glad to know I wasn't entirely numb.

Because when I thought of how nearly every bit of pain in my life had been caused by her—whether directly or indirectly—a very clear, undeniable feeling took over. And it wasn't my siren side either. No. It was just plain old me. Katrina Delmar. And the only feeling right now that could replace all the hurt and pain was the burning desire to take from Cordelia every bit as much as she'd taken from me.

39

HEAD ABOVE WATER

KATRINA

The *Belladonna* sped into view quickly, and I calculated that if Cordelia and her crew were just now arriving at the trident's location, that meant our trip to the past had only totaled a few hours in the present.

I gave a strong squeeze of the trident with my hand, thinking of Milo and still haunted by the mystery of his fate. If I thought any more about it, I might've squeezed the trident so hard it would bend in half. I'd die before letting it fall into her hands. Not to save anyone. Not because the fate of humanity was at stake. But because I couldn't bear for her to win after everything I'd given up to stop her.

"Don't let her see you!" I demanded to the others, sinking myself down into the water until only my eyes stuck out above the surface, watching the passing yacht with a watchful, vulturous stare. When McKenzie and Noah followed, I silently thanked them.

The yacht slowed a good half mile away. They were still scouting, looking for the most accurate spot they could anchor and begin their search. Even from here I could see her dive team, readying themselves and slipping on their air tanks as she stood by the railing, hunting the seas with her piercing gaze. I didn't know if she could see us from here. But when the boat engine shut off and began to drift our way in silence, I had a strong feeling maybe she'd noticed the three college kids desperately treading open water. But I had to ensure she didn't see the trident.

Her boat inched toward us like a hungry alligator. I felt the trident in my hand, sliding my fingers along its metal shaft. It had long lost its magical glow and no longer seemed capable of performing a task like transporting people to another century. Was it a one-time use thing? Or could I figure out how to activate it once again to wield against Cordelia?

My efforts to do so proved futile. I tried to manipulate any of the three—time, life, or space, but failed at every attempt. Not even a spark of magic glinted from the trident's pointed prongs. But as I studied them, I noticed how sharp they were. Like tips of a harpoon. And a thought washed over me, satiating that dark, cruel side of me that I didn't even care to fend off anymore.

"Let her see you. Distract her. Keep her talking," I said coldly to McKenzie and Noah without further explanation. And ignoring their confused expressions and remarks, I dove underwater with the trident, as I followed the call. I had somewhat of a plan.

It would've been easier with my tail. It would've made swimming beneath the boat so much faster. But I didn't have time to drown and transform. And I sure couldn't risk letting go of the trident. Besides, it would make getting onto the yacht much more difficult without my legs. From underneath, I noticed the boat's whirring propeller slowing until it came to a stop. And I knew for sure Cordelia had found McKenzie and Noah.

I surfaced on the left side of the yacht, opposite the side I'd seen Cordelia standing, and examined it for any possible point of entry. There was a ladder on the back, but it was placed high enough that the base of it was a good few feet from the water. I couldn't reach it while carrying the trident. My plan would have to go just a little differently than I'd hoped. But that was okay. It might be good to practice my siren powers on something less important before trying to use them full force.

Keeping my head just barely above water, I reached for the scale in my pocket that I'd saved from my tail earlier. I was more than grateful to see that it had survived this far somehow without floating away or falling out.

I remembered the way the scale around Cordelia's neck illuminated as she sang that song aboard the ship when she found us with the mermaids. She was drawing on its magic to be able to use her siren power, even when she was in her human form. And I was about to do the same.

I could faintly hear Cordelia talking to Noah and McKenzie, questioning them about who they were and how they'd gotten out here.

"Can you help us?" McKenzie asked.

"I suppose if I must," Cordelia reluctantly agreed. "But you're to stay in the cabin area below and not to come out during our expedition unless I approve it." I heard her order the crew to toss them both lifesavers and pull them up.

Just a little longer, guys.

I waited for someone to walk near the back of the ship. The luxurious, gleaming white yacht was at least one hundred feet, and there were a handful of divers and crew members aboard still shuffling about on deck. I eyed a male, probably in his thirties, who looked to be a worker or maybe the skipper's assistant of some kind. His lanky figure snaked its way toward the back, perhaps getting ready to drop anchor or check something on the engine. He was perfect for what I needed. I just hoped it would work.

My lips parted, and from my mouth drifted the same lulling tune Cordelia had sung. As if by instinct, the tune quickly turned into my mom's lullaby, filling the gaps with haunting notes and the poetic words I'd collected over the past year:

Lost out at sea
Do you dream of me?
By the call of the waves
I hear you and seek you
Till again the roaming sea
Brings you back to me.
Down by the shore
Meet me once more
By the light of the moon
Love me, then leave me
With the dawn rising
Haunt me forevermore

The man appeared stunned for a moment, holding his forehead as if feeling unwell. In my head I imagined him walking to the ladder. As I envisioned it, he did it. I smiled the kind of smile that holds no happiness, a wicked smile of sorts, as the scale in my pocket glowed hot.

I then directed him to drop the ladder into the water so that I could climb up, all while continuing my song and simply willing it. He obeyed perfectly, and I quickly shimmied up the ladder, dragging up the trident with me. Dripping wet and now aboard Cordelia's massive boat, I sighed with relief that my plan was working so far. And my theory about the siren song was right. My mom's lullaby was the siren song all along. And the scale was the power source from which it drew.

Next, I told the man to make his way back toward the front deck where Cordelia was standing. I followed, keeping the trident close to me and watching my back. When we reached the front, I wasted no time commanding my new assistant to quietly creep up behind Cordelia and restrain her.

He followed like clockwork, grabbing the woman as she stood at the railing shouting interrogation questions as McKenzie and Noah.

Now, make her face me. I ordered.

With a squirming and furious Cordelia in his arms, he pulled her around, seemingly struggling against her thrashing more than I would have expected.

"Let me go, David!" Cordelia screamed. "Do you understand me? Put me down now! What are you doing?"

I stepped forward, my steps leaving watery traces on the pristine polished deck as I neared her. I hummed my song softly to keep David under my control.

"Katrina," she hissed, once she stopped struggling long enough to look up and notice me. Her face instantly softened when her eyes flicked to the grand trident in my hand. "Well done, my dear. I don't think my divers could've managed such deep waters. Glad to see you didn't get crushed beneath all that pressure." She smiled.

"If you think I got this for you, think again, Cordelia." I adjusted my grip on the metal rod, twisting my palm around it to feel the weight of it. "I'd rather die than help you. Not after everything you've taken from me."

"You'd rather die?" She snickered. "Bold words. Perhaps all that pressure did get to you, after all. Perhaps that crushing darkness finally just weighed too much."

I hesitated, knowing she referred to something more than just the depths of the sea. "You're cruel, Cordelia."

"Angelfish, now, now. We've talked about this. That's no way to speak to your great grandmother." She choked out the words as the man squeezed her, one arm across her throat and the other holding her hands behind her back. The dismissiveness in her words sent fury flaring through my bones.

"I know why you're this way. You've been denied your siren form too long," I didn't know why I was wasting my time talking to her. My plan didn't include drawing things out like this. It was supposed to be quick. I was supposed to have ended this—ended *her*—by now. Why couldn't I do it?

"And just who told you that, dear? The filthy pirate you fell for? Did he tell you before or after he went on his killing spree? Or was it when you were screwing him in that cave?"

I clenched my jaw at her mention of Milo, ignoring the urge to question how she even knew about those things. "I've experienced it for myself," I said through gritted teeth, raising the trident and pointing the prongs at her.

"Then you know what it's like to have all that power just trapped within you, begging to be released and given the reins. You know what it's like to realize you were made to use it." Her eyes fluttered, beckoning me like she was trying to convince me to take a bite of the sweetest poisoned apple.

"Yes," I said, stepping forward so that the trident's sword-like prongs rested inches from Cordelia's stomach. "And it made me realize I'm stronger than I ever knew."

"Stronger?" She smiled. "And what about crueler?"

I hesitated, my arms shaking both from the weight of the trident and the fear of what I planned to do next. She kept talking, pushing me to my limits.

"Go on, Katrina," she said slyly, her words smooth, deep, and seductive like a slow song. "Kill me. Give into that side of you that's just dying to be heard. Put that trident through me like you planned to. You don't have a soul to save, after all, so why not just indulge yourself?"

I trembled all over, my breath trapped in my chest. The swaying of the ship made me even more uneasy, and I thought I might vomit but my empty stomach reassured me that wasn't possible. Cordelia continued talking, and I listened like a fool.

"My dear girl, you saw the cruelty and corruption of mankind firsthand, and yet you're still trying to keep me from putting a stop to it. Look at what they did to you. They even left you with a permanent reminder." I felt the healing scar on my face sting as Cordelia's eyes fell on it. "You saw what man does. It's no different in this century than the last or the next. They will always take and destroy what isn't theirs to own. And yet you still want to keep this world intact as it is. When we could erase all this and start anew." Her vibrant blue eyes bore into mine, and in them I saw my own reflection, holding the trident, my wet hair clinging to my skin and tangled across the scar along my jaw., thinner than I was weeks ago before I'd been forced to embark on this journey of survival. "If you'd just let it go." Cordelia whispered, gently and warmly, a sudden contrast from her earlier statements.

Her words took hold in me, and I fumbled, sorting and questioning my own thoughts. All too late I noticed I'd stopped humming. David was losing his grip on Cordelia. I rushed to sing again, forcing him to strengthen his hold. He lost his grip around her neck, but was able to restrain her from her waist, pressing her arms to her side. And I could see that around her neck, tucked into her silky blouse, was the scale necklace I could never seem to get rid of. Her most powerful weapon was now free.

"What a lovely voice, dear. But you're inexperienced. A siren's song is something that takes time to master well. If you're good enough, you can even use it on more than one mind at a time."

She flicked her gaze to the opposite side of the ship across the deck. McKenzie and Noah were just now climbing over the railing in their soaked clothing, two divers flanking them with fresh towels ready.

With her eyes fixed on them, Cordelia began singing a song of her own, like mine but more powerful, making me feel dizzy as each ethereal note reached my ears. I didn't know if it was possible to fully control another siren, but it was clearly possible for her to mess with my head somehow, just like she had at dinner.

Within seconds, the demeanor on my friends' faces changed, becoming harsh and hollow as they became entranced by Cordelia's voice. I didn't know what she planned to make them do, but I couldn't let her take them. I shoved the trident forward, touching the spear-like tip of the highest middle prong to her now exposed throat, desperate to stop her singing. But no matter how hard I tried to force my hands to plunge the trident into her larynx, I couldn't find the strength to do it.

"Looks like you need to give into your siren side a little bit more," Cordelia coaxed. "If you weren't so stubborn about keeping that halo around your head, we could've changed the world by now. Or you could've at least killed me."

Before I could think of a response, McKenzie and Noah rushed at me, stealing the trident from my grasp. I fought to pull it back, but Noah overpowered me easily and shoved me to the floor as McKenzie yanked the trident from my hands and carried it to a now unrestrained Cordelia.

"Thank you, sweetheart," Cordelia said sweetly to McKenzie as she took the trident with a smile. "I'm so glad rescuing you two paid off."

As I reeled from being slammed into the wooden deck, I looked up just in time to see Cordelia tearing the scale pendant from her neck and pressing it into the base of the trident, where it cast a white glow just like when Milo offered his blood to it. And then she grasped the rod with the other hand, making her claim as its new wielder.

My jaw dropped as I saw the scale absorbed into the trident, pulled into the metal like quicksand, and the glow brightened so intensely that I had no choice but to cover my eyes. When the light diminished, the hold on McKenzie and Noah had broken, and they both rushed to my side after shaking off their disorientation.

"What's happening?" McKenzie asked, helping me to my feet.

"She gave up the last of her magic in exchange for control of the trident." I replied, unable to look away as Cordelia relished the sight of the sea scepter in her hand.

"You didn't know how to use this, Katrina," Cordelia said, touching the tips of the prongs like they were flower petals. "Because you don't know how to channel your pain and anger into power. You're too afraid of it. You're too afraid of yourself."

"I don't want power," I croaked out dryly, my words breaking beneath the realization that I'd failed. "I just want to be left alone."

"No, you don't, dear. Being alone is the last thing you want. You want back the man you think you love." Cordelia stepped toward me, keeping enough distance between us that I couldn't reach the trident, while her glowing electricity shield sizzled as a reminder not to even try. But her sapphire eyes softened for just a moment as she continued, and I listened, my body aching and my blood racing. "Trust me, I know. That's all I wanted for a long, long time, too. But I finally realized I was wasting my time. I wasted my magic on cursing them, and I wished I could undo it for the longest. But losing my siren form made that impossible.

"Eventually, I found someone I could tolerate enough to use for my survival. A man with connections and wealth that I knew I could leverage to begin building my new life on land. I've worked hard to forget his name. Because I remember how he treated me. And how he treated our daughter, who I never wanted to bring into this world in the first place. Poor sweet Marina. She was a fool just like you. Trying to chase some man across the sea. Thankfully she came to her senses after some very vivid...dreams." She paused with a hand on her heart and a fake hint of sorrow as she spoke about the daughter I remembered reading about. I recalled the old letter I'd found last year. The one from Cordelia to Marina trying to keep her from moving to the seaside. It made even more sense now. Everything she'd orchestrated had always been for spite. For vengeance. For herself.

She continued, her features hardening again. "Her father meant nothing to me. But I suppose I played my cards well. In death he finally showed his worth. He left me everything when he died. And through the decades I used it to create the empire I have today. Because I had to."

Between the trident's silver prongs jumped wild sparks of electricity as she spoke. Without explanation, she pointed the trident down at the water.

"That's what you need, Katrina. If we're to build a better world, you need someone willing to challenge your feelings. You need to realize life isn't fair, and love doesn't create strength. Only weakness."

I blinked, watching on in confusion as power flowed from the trident, opening a rift in the seawater below.

"What are you doing?" I shouted over the roar of the water.

"I'm putting the trident to the test. It can clearly control time and space. But let's see about life, shall we? It's been said it can even bring back the dead who made the sea their grave. So, I'm bringing back someone, just for you." She winked at me coldly, and I feared what was to come next.

I stopped in wonderment, my mouth hanging open in awe as I watched the sea roil where Cordelia commanded. The rift in the sea glowed like the trident itself, and after a moment, a figure emerged—a man.

I rushed to the railing, leaning over in desperation to see if it just might be possible that she'd brought back Milo. The faintest feeling of hope fluttered wildly in my heart until it hurt. Maybe, just maybe, she wanted to let me have him back. But as the sky darkened with black clouds overhead, I clearly recognized the terrified face of Bellamy as he burst forth from the water gasping for air. And I shattered right there.

"Why would you do this?" I screamed, the cold feeling of betrayal taking hold. So many emotions flooded me, I couldn't even pinpoint what hurt the most about seeing Bellamy resurrected. It was a cruel trick on us both. "Let him rest! He's been through enough!"

Cordelia's calloused smile sent a shiver down my spine, and I rushed to grab one of the flotation devices left on the deck from when the crew had pulled McKenzie and Noah to safety. "Help me pull him in!" I cried to my friends, who hurried alongside me as we tossed Bellamy the lifesaver.

He grasped at it in a panic as water crashed over his head and the waves tossed him like a barrel. My heart broke a little at how terrifying and confusing this must be for him. Being freshly resurrected and first opening his eyes to all this.

I felt weak against the tides pulling the rope connected to Bellamy, but with Noah and McKenzie's strength added to mine, we mustered the strength to draw him in and help him up and over the side of the hull.

He gasped, coughing up seawater and holding his stomach as I helped him stand straight. It was a strange sight to see him like this, helpless and afraid, when just a few hours earlier I'd watched him leading a charge onto a ship with cannons blasting and swords drawn fearlessly. Now he looked the same way he did when I first met him months ago in the library, clad in his drenched dark jeans and black jacket, his jet-black hair cut shorter than his days as captain in his father's fleet.

"Where am I?" His voice quivered, but the sound of his voice—the familiarity of it—was enough to give me some pebble-sized semblance of comfort in the midst of everything else happening around us. I looked at him with a weighty, heartbroken stare and a well of tears fighting their way to my eyes.

"The end of the world," I said.

40

BLACK SEA

KATRINA

Cordelia had taken the opportunity to position herself at the front of the yacht, summoning the power of the trident to begin her long-awaited mission. The trident continued pulsing with power as the sky overhead darkened like ash with more clouds and thunder. Cordelia's face, illuminated by the glow of the scepter in her hands, held firm as she concentrated on manipulating the currents and rising waves through the power of the trident.

"Forty days and forty nights it took to flood the earth once. This time around it won't take so long." She spoke, more to herself than anyone around her. The divers and crewmen on her boat watched in amazement and fear as the ocean began to rise, massive hills of water rolling and lapping slowly as the ship lifted higher, until finally even they grew too fearful to stay out on deck and ran for cover in the cabin.

"Cordelia, stop!" McKenzie screamed, her lightly freckled face now spotted with tears as she watched the scene unfolding before her. Noah rushed at Cordelia but was thrown back from a force of power that leapt from the trident, leaving him writhing in pain on the deck as seawater splashed over the sides.

"Tell your friends there's no use!" Cordelia called to me, stepping up to the highest point of the prow where she lifted the trident like a prize. "But don't worry. If you're on my ship, you'll be spared. You have my favor." Her deep red lips curved into a smile that made me recoil.

I thought of my family and my friends' families. I thought of Bellamy and the heartless thing Cordelia had just done to us both by bringing him here. And then I thought of Milo and how he'd been taken from me over and over because of the woman playing God at the front of this ship. And I couldn't hold back the tears any longer. I didn't even care to save the world anymore. Clearly, I'd failed. But that meant Milo had given himself up for nothing. And that was what tore at me in ways I couldn't overcome.

Bellamy wiped away a trickling tear from my cheek as I stared emptily at the deck floor between my feet. "I remember everything," he said softly.

"Everything?" I sniffed, startled by his words. "Like, even 1720 everything?"

He nodded, his gaze being the only steady thing I had to cling to as I stood bewildered. And then I fell apart, falling into his arms as he hugged me tightly, in a tender, protective way that gave me just one tangible second of comfort and familiarity in all this chaos.

"Is he dead? Did he make it?" I cried, burying my face in his wet shoulder. "What happened to him?"

"He made it," he said. "He got away."

A wave of relief surged through me, but my heart broke all the same, knowing Milo was left behind, alone, trapped somewhere between his present and his past, and never able to return to his future. He would've continued aging through the years, and that meant he was long dead by now. His own course of history was changed forever, and I could search the world for him, but I'd never find him in this lifetime with a beating heart.

I opened my eyes as the tears became too hard to hold in, my face still pressed to Bellamy's shoulder. The waters around us crashed against the boat, relentless and fierce. The scene around me was a blur, with the white of the yacht blending fuzzily into the heavy storm grey of the sky above and the midnight blue of the water below. Like blending colors into a painting...like watercolors.

Watercolors.

An absurd thought took hold, reminding me of a power I didn't expect to call on. But as my tears flowed fast, I realized they just might prove to be my greatest strength. With a brief burst of hopefulness, I pulled back, looking into Bellamy's face.

"Get that trident away from her. Whatever you have to do," I uttered.

"Resurrected five minutes and you're already throwing me into trouble." Bellamy's voice came through a gentle teasing smile, and I pulled him in for a reaffirming embrace once more.

"You never needed any help finding trouble." I smirked weakly.

We motioned for McKenzie and Noah to come near, leaving Cordelia performing her ritual with the trident. When they joined us, I quickly relayed to them the only excuse of a plan I had left.

"She doesn't have the full power of her siren song anymore without the scale. So, without the trident she's powerless. I don't know if this will work, and if it doesn't, *none* of you come after me, understand?" The words burned in my throat, knowing what I asked of them would be far from easy.

"We're gonna die either way. Or be forced to take sides with the sea witch over there. If you need us, we're coming after you." Noah objected with his usual stubbornness, but secretly I was glad to hear it. It was nice to have him on my side for once.

"First and foremost, you have to focus on separating the trident from Cordelia. And get her into the water. I don't care how you do it."

"We'll try, but we can't get near it without getting zapped," McKenzie said.

"Then think of something. You can do it." I encouraged her with a nudge in my voice.

"So, what are you going to do once we get it away from her, exactly?" Bellamy asked me.

"I'm going to cry," I said.

Ignoring the three sets of confused eyes on me, I stepped away without further explanation, turning to face the stern. It'd be easier to dive into the sea from the back of the boat to keep Cordelia from noticing. I tugged on Bellamy's arm and led him with me halfway.

"Keep a watch on her crew. Most of them seem to be too terrified to do anything and they've locked themselves in the cabin, but I don't know how loyal to her they are. Keep McKenzie and Noah safe," I said hurriedly, noticing the waves rising higher and taller. There was no telling how much land had already begun to flood with seawater spilling into the coasts. We couldn't waste much more time.

I started off toward the stern but turned around to look back before I'd gone two steps. "Thank you for everything, Bellamy."

He nodded with a smirk. "Thank *you*, love. You're the one who's always jumping overboard for me."

I shook my head, thinking how right he was. Just once it'd be nice if doing the right thing didn't involve leaping headfirst into a raging sea. Yet here we were again.

I kicked off my shoes and climbed over the railing of the ship as it lifted and dropped with the motion of the waves. I looked down, dreading the fall into these treacherous waters. But this time, I took consolation in knowing this was the one place Cordelia couldn't reach me. She couldn't swim the depths like I could. Not anymore. Without her tail, she was forever just as helpless against the sea as any ordinary human.

But I would have to be a helpless, ordinary human, too, at least for a few painful moments. I let the tears come, because I'd need all of them. I would need every painful feeling, every heartbreaking thought, every crushing memory. As I harbored each one, I dove headfirst in, letting the rioting water push me underneath. My eyelids puckered from the sting of salt. I resisted every instinct to fight the undertow, and instead let it pull me so far under I couldn't swim back up, prompting my change the moment everything went dark.

My eyes flew open, as I resurrected in my own strange way, awakening in my transformed mermaid body. I still wasn't used to it. The muscles in my tail ached from soreness just as much as the rest of me. But I ignored the pain and swam to the surface, pressing myself to the side of the yacht so as not to get separated, and to be able to hear when the perfect time to strike presented itself.

It was difficult to hear and see, especially as lightning crackled overhead and wind continued whipping the water up higher and higher, siphoning it upward like a slowly spinning cyclone. I was grateful for the dim lights of the yacht, because without them, my surroundings would have been nearly pitch black.

I could make out the sound of voices struggling, and the spark of the trident followed by forceful thuds. I wished I could pull myself up over the railing to see what was happening, but my tail was too heavy, and I lacked the arm strength to lift myself no matter how hard I tried. I would have to trust my friends to pull through, and then I'd have to trust myself to do what I knew must be done.

After a few torturous minutes, there was silence except for the whistling wind and wild waves and the yacht's hull slapping against them. I feared that I might not be able to come back to them if I couldn't get out of this water. I would be stuck this way.

A deafening gunshot suddenly pierced the air, making me jump. Within seconds, a bright red light illuminated the air above me, orange-gold sparks raining down like fireworks over the sides of the yacht. A flare gun. Someone found the flare gun. Genius.

The splash that followed drew my attention to the front of the yacht, where against the fading of the orange flash I saw the silhouette of a woman hit the water. When McKenzie leaned over the railing above, waving the flare gun, I breathed a sigh of relief that it wasn't her I'd seen drop off the side of the boat.

"I thought of something!" She yelled proudly.

I launched forward, swimming to where Cordelia had fallen, and caught sight of the trident following, dangling for a moment by its prongs that caught on the railing before sliding off the boat's edge. I knew I had to reach it before she regained her senses and took hold of it again.

Pulsing my fins up and down fast as I could, I jetted through the water at a speed I'd never swum before. Like a dart, I ripped past the swirling currents around me and soared through the water. I dashed forward, placing myself between the trident and Cordelia as they drifted downward through the water.

I reached for the trident, leaving Cordelia below, but as I began to swim away with it in my hand, a clawed hand gripped my tail. Cordelia raked her manicured fingernails through the webbing of my tail fin, tearing through it and forcing an agonizing scream from me that sent bubbles churning to the surface.

She clawed her way upward, kicking and swimming with an ability far better than a human's. That explained how she'd survived after cutting off her tail and jumping overboard with her new legs so many years ago. But this time, I couldn't let her return to the surface.

I fought back, losing the trident from my grip as the raging tides yanked it from me. I'd find it later. But right now, I couldn't risk Cordelia getting close to it.

She swam up, her blue eyes burning viciously as she took hold of my shirt and ripped it over my head in attempt to pull me to her. As I fought the winding fabric floating around my head, she slammed her knee into my ribs. I thrashed, trying to distinguish up from down. And once I regained my equilibrium, I refocused on the venomous woman trying to kill me in this black sea.

Something darkened in me. A heavy understanding that saturated me to the core, making my bones and skin wane cold. Cordelia was never going to stop. Never. Her endless hunt for vengeance and power would never end. Until someone stopped her. And this was my last chance to do it.

I worried about the stain that what I was about to do would leave on my soul. But then I remembered I didn't have one.

41

MUTINY

KATRINA

I turned on her. I knew she expected me to swim upwards, to pull back toward the surface to get away from her attacks. But instead, I swam down toward her, the blood from my tattered fins swirling around us in ghostly crimson streams.

I clutched her shoulders, digging my fingernails into her skin so that losing my grip became nearly impossible. Against the water's pull, I swept my tail up and down in a rapid wave-like rhythm. It was a movement that still felt foreign, as my waist and core moved to maintain the force needed to drive myself down into the rising swell of the ocean that only wanted to spit us back up. But the strength of my tail surprised me and reminded me of the advantage I had.

Doing my best to dodge the scratches and hits Cordelia dealt out, I focused on holding her down, pushing her further into the ocean's belly. She fought against me like a wild animal, ripping my skin with her nails and pulling my hair so hard I felt tears stinging my eyes underwater. The raging and tossing of the ocean above grew still as it faded behind us. Our surroundings darkened into near blackness, and the crushing weight of the water grew heavier, so much that even I could feel its pressure on my chest.

I knew Cordelia was afraid. I felt it in the way she thrashed and writhed against my grip, screaming at me in threats and curses that only came out in muted bursts of bubbles. I felt the way her kicks and flails grew more desperate and tense. And whenever I began to feel sorry for her, I let an inkling of my siren side take hold so that I could harden myself to whatever empathy tried to creep its way in. I wanted to be selfish. I had to be, right now. I'd have to go to the darkest part of the ocean—and the darkest part of myself—to do it.

I can't do it. I can't.

I inwardly begged the siren in me to silence my conscience. I needed her compassionless essence to take over. Though I was afraid that once I willingly gave in, I might not be able to get myself back.

Yes, you can. She must die. I smiled coldly when I heard her voice. My own voice. *You must be more powerful. You must conquer her. You can take her place and rule the seas with the trident. After all, you've given up more than she did. You deserve to take this power.* The voice entranced me like a song, controlling my desires, and feeding the dark need in me to end Cordelia for all the wrong reasons. But perhaps that's what I needed, since I'd failed to do it for the right reasons.

With a vicious rage burning in me, a desire for power too strong to ignore, I overpowered Cordelia in our underwater struggle. I didn't know how long it would take to drown an ex-mermaid, but I would ensure this was the day I'd find out. And I couldn't have stopped myself if I wanted to.

As I swam faster and faster, forcing Cordelia down to the abyss, my true self broke through the siren's hold for just a second. And even *she* didn't hold back. The sinister memory of each suicide in my family and the nightmares that caused them rushed to my mind. Fueled by the aching thoughts, I fought

Cordelia harder each time she braced against me and dared to try escaping my grip. *Marina. Sarah. Martha. Edith. Alma. Esther. Nelda. Lydia. Mom.* They—we—suffered the same nightmares that brought us the same torment Cordelia was feeling now. Terrified, desperate, and drowning. I decided it was time for her to finally experience it fully for herself.

She reached up, clawing at me one last time as she convulsed beneath my weight. Her fingertips grated across my cheek and along my jaw, tearing open the cut on my face that had just barely begun to close. I grimaced and squeezed her shoulders harder, digging my own fingers into the meat of her flesh, and I felt as though in that moment I could've killed her with my bare hands. But I didn't have to. She stopped resisting right before she jerked violently, uncontrollably. Once. Twice. And then her hands fell away from me. Her head rolled back, and her body became as weightless as the microscopic bubbles seeping from between her red lips.

And it was over. Even in these murky depths so far below, my siren eyesight stayed sharp enough that I could see her fall away, her beautiful face unmarked by time or death. Her hair had fallen loose in our scuffle, and it floated around her now, allowing me a glimpse of what she once might've looked like as a young, carefree mermaid in centuries past. She drifted down, like a feather on a breeze, farther and farther until the darkness of the sea swallowed her whole. A part of me wondered what happened to her now, if there was anything more to her fate than becoming seafoam. I supposed it didn't matter. Because after all, we were soulless creatures anyway.

With one last glance over my shoulder at the black abyss beneath, I turned my sights toward the surface and swam back, gliding through the water as my own blood trailed behind me. I suddenly felt the sting of my wounds. The fresh bruises on my flesh throbbed, and the guilt of killing my great grandmother settled under my skin and seeped into my being. I knew I'd bear the weight of it forever, as ever present as the crushing pressure of the deep ocean.

42

WATERY GRAVE

KATRINA

When I broke through the surface, the sky still swirled in ominous billows. I drew in a breath, not out of necessity, but just an instinctual reaction from my human side. Underwater, my skin somehow absorbed oxygen from the water molecules around me. It was still a strange sensation I hadn't quite gotten used to.

But this breath was more than just breathing. It was freeing. Like reclaiming the side of myself I had to lose in order to embrace the strength I'd found in darkness. Now that darkness rested below me, left behind miles beneath the surface. At least that's what I told myself.

But my job wasn't done, because the waves still riled and tossed about, and the trident had slipped from my hands to be carried away somewhere in all this. It was probably miles away by now.

"Katrina!" I could hardly make out Bellamy's voice amongst the waves crashing. I swiveled in the water, my long, wet hair plastered to my bare chest, trying to catch sight of where I heard him call.

He dangled dangerously from the railing of the yacht, held in place by a rope tied to his waist that Noah and McKenzie were straining to keep taut against the pull of the ocean. In his grasp, veiled by misty sea spray, he held the trident. It still pulsed with blue and white electricity, sending waves of light rippling through the waves.

I watched him, thinking of how this fight was every much his fight as mine. His family had been ruined by Cordelia, even if his father certainly was just as much to blame. But Bellamy wasn't to blame. Not even a little bit. All he'd ever wanted was to belong to the sea. All he'd ever loved was cut short. Every time.

My first instinct was to rush forward and bound through the water to save Bellamy and take the trident. But then a voice returned from the depths where I thought I'd left it. It told me to take the trident and finish what Cordelia started. To make Bellamy and the others bow before me as the ocean follows my command. After all, I'd already unlocked its power with my sacrifice. I had nothing more to lose. But everything to gain. A world at my command.

Take what is yours.

A bolt of lightning struck the water in front of me, snapping me out of the trance pulling me under. I knew then that if I were to touch that trident in this state, I would lose myself forever. I would become the very thing I sought to defeat. So instead, I stayed suspended there in the waves, frozen as the whipping wind and churning water spiraled around me.

"Katrina!" One of my friends called me. I couldn't even recognize their voices. I battled the voice in my head, clamping my eyes shut as I pushed away the siren's call. I couldn't overpower it, but I could distract it. So, I shifted the focus, arguing with it until it no longer wanted to convince me to rule the seas. Instead, I redirected it, letting it speak its dark truths to me and reminding me of the monster I never wanted to become.

You left Milo behind in a world where he'll spend every day fighting until death finally claims him, old, withered and alone.

I shook my head at the painful accusation, swallowing it like bitter medicine. My siren continued. And I willingly listened.

You destroyed his life, just as your mother destroyed everyone around her. You let your heart betray him, and he'll never forgive you for that.

I swallowed a lump in my throat, opening my eyes as the tears came. Maybe mermaids were too stubborn to cry, but I was still half human, and that side of me wasn't so tough.

And now you've killed your own flesh and blood. We both knew you couldn't keep your hands clean.

My tail flicked back and forth, and my chest tightened, filling with salty, wet air as heat rose to my face like fire. I never wanted any of this.

All that destruction. All that brokenness. All that ruin. Look at the mess you've made. You're shaping up to be a fine siren.

That was it. The moment the well of tears I'd been storing up broke free, flowing, streaming from my red, tired eyes without stopping. Like a dam bursting, the release of my sorrow and anger was unstoppable. Rivers of rage poured from me, spilling over from my heart into the ocean through my tears. And when my teardrops hit the seawater below, mixing with the ocean, I felt the instant connection within. I felt a power unlike any other.

I thought of the midnight waters around me like paint beneath my paintbrush. I imagined how I might shape it, move it, and control it. And with my mermaid tears falling, I did.

Releasing a shattering cry that broke through even the loudest wave and thunder, I threw my head back, feeling the control I now had of the ocean around me. The water beneath me cupped me like a foaming throne, cresting higher until I overlooked the raging sea below. It lifted me as I screamed, the echoes of my pain commanding the tides.

I forced down the waves, opening up the water's surface like a tear in fabric. I painted the water splitting, creating a channel of air that corkscrewed all the way down to the ocean floor. In another recess of my mind, I told the sea to take the trident back, to hide it where no one—human, mermaid, or otherwise—could ever reach it again.

A section of water sprouted up, swirling like a small cyclone beside Bellamy and ripping the trident from his grip. I painted the trident far away, buried beneath the sea itself. And with that image in my mind, fresh tears still streaming down with no sign of stopping, the water wrapped the trident in its grip, twisting around it and carrying it all the way down the trench I'd created in the ocean, until it reached the floor so deep below, I could barely see it.

With a ground-shaking blast, the water forced open the sea floor, creating a grave in which the trident would lie for the rest of time. With the last of my mind's strength, I ordered the waters to bury the trident in depths even I couldn't fathom. And I watched with mixed emotions as the ocean did as I commanded.

The water violently rushed back over, closing up the split as I felt myself letting go, exhausted from the effort. I dropped down into the waves as the crest holding me dwindled and lowered. The raging storm calmed just as the sea swallowed up the trident, burying it miles below the sand to be trapped there forever by the ocean's crushing pressure.

I didn't even have the strength to move my tail to stay afloat, and my battered lungs had all but given out. My painting was finished. But I finally, finally stopped crying.

43

Jolly Roger

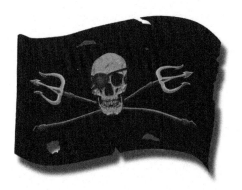

Milo

I watched on in agony as Katrina and the others vanished before me, leaving me standing in the empty skiff as cannons raged around me. I dove into the water, narrowly dodging a cannonball as it obliterated the little wooden jollyboat. And then, left without a choice but to help Bellamy as he had helped us, I swam toward the dueling ships. Because what else did I have to live for now?

As I climbed up the side of the Spaniard frigate, my thoughts riled in torment. I knew this would happen. I knew she'd be gone. But I couldn't have fathomed it would've been this hard. I knew she was back where she was meant to be, she and far away from all this. I should've been content in that alone. But I wasn't. I was completely, and irrevocably destroyed.

Katrina was right. Loving her had destroyed me. Because loving her always, *always* meant losing her.

I lost myself a long time ago, and she just took the last piece of me with her. So, I didn't even recall how I stormed the ship and struck down every enemy in my path. It was nothing more than a blur of steel and blood. And when the captain himself ran over to challenge me, I greeted him with the same relentlessness, unhindered by the wounds I couldn't feel anymore. We might've fought for seconds or minutes. It wasn't worth noting.

That is, until the moment his blade tore across my left eye. I yelped in reaction, but I couldn't even process the pain. As if to finish off the scar above it, the strike immediately left me blinded. Shades of red reflected in my good eye as thick blood leaked down my face. I knew from that moment on I'd never be the same.

With one more sweep of my sword, I dealt the fatal blow to the captain of the Spanish ship. Through muscle and bone my blade cut deep, slicing through to his spine as I drove the weapon all the way in and out his back. I watched him slide off the sword and hit the deck as the light left his astonished eyes. It was a quick, clean kill.

But there was nothing clean about the way my soul felt. And for the first time, I didn't care. So I plummeted myself further into the grime as I dropped to my knees beside the captain's lifeless body. And I drove my sword into him again and again, fresh blood spraying over me like raindrops with each strike, mixing with the crimson still running down my face. Something had taken hold that I couldn't manage to stop. And when I thought of being stuck here again in this God-forsaken place and time, I stabbed harder and faster, until the man's midsection was no more than a bloody pulp.

And then I glanced at the *Widow*, where Bellamy stood at the stern, overlooking this disaster on the seas. He'd seen everything. He'd seen the trident and Katrina disappearing and my rampage. It was more than apparent by the solemn but baffled expression he wore as his ship positioned itself to sail away.

He glanced at the dead captain, and then at me, before tipping his head my way. It seemed a nod of respect, and some kind of brotherly reassurance. And it was all I had left to cling to try to regain some sense of myself. This Bellamy would never understand exactly what just unfolded. But he would never forget it either.

When I stepped back, scarlet soaking through my tunic in blooming stains, the ship was silent. Those few who remained of this crew looked at me in disbelief, their eyes wide and weapons raised, but unmoving, not daring to approach this panting, half-blind, blood-soaked maniac standing over their mutilated captain.

"Here's your captain!" I shouted to the crew. "And how will you lot return to your king, or your governor, commodore, or whichever bastard it is you blindly obey, and bold-faced explain that you couldn't defend him or his ship?"

The men grumbled and whispered inaudible muttering to each other. I continued, my hand on the hilt of my cutlass and my other hand scooping up the captain's hat that had fallen in our duel. "I give you a choice. I drop your captain into the sea, and you follow him, or you stay and sail free under my command, and we share in the spoils evenly—spoils that make your current sailor's pay look like a pittance. What say ye?"

The seamen hesitated for a moment, looking around at the fallen bodies of the other crew members. It was silent for a time, before one man finally stepped forward with a solid "Aye. Ye fight like a devil. I'd be a fool not to sail under a cap'n who can hold his ground like that."

Soon, the rest followed, likely because there were too few of them to do anything to stop it, or because they knew there was nothing better than a sailor's wages waiting for them back home. One by one they pledged their allegiance to me, and no one dared oppose me as I nudged the captain's body off the side of the ship and into his watery grave.

"Then we repair the damage here and set sail," I said, walking the length of the deck to its center. I looked at the mast overhead, up toward the rolled-up sails. They provided a perfectly clear view above of the Spanish flag waving against the afternoon sun.

"You," I pointed to a sailor. "Cut a piece of sailcloth and blacken it with tar." The man scurried off to follow my orders, as I examined the condition of the ship and how it could be modified to better serve its new purpose.

I never wanted to be a pirate. But it was all I had left. The things I wanted and the things I deserved were always at odds. And I deserved this. Who was I to argue that a pirate wasn't as good as any other man? At least we admitted to our depravity instead of hiding it behind politics and blackmail. It was an identity that *wanted* to claim me, no matter how many times I tried to outrun it. And I was tired of running.

I made my way to the captain's quarters, where I studied the table of maps and legends and whatever other documents covered the desk in the middle of the room. With blood-stained hands, I cleared the table, sliding the papers into the floor without concern. A brown leather coin purse on the desk caught my notice, and I quickly emptied its contents. With my knife, I cut out a small piece from the leather and removed the drawstrings to fashion an eye covering. I doused my gashed eye with a splash of liquor from a flask in the room, resisting the need to groan at its bitter sting. I hardly worried about wiping the rest of the blood off me. I'd clean it up better later, when I could think straight.

I leaned on my elbows, catching my breath and clearing my head. A single teardrop managed to sneak its way out before I choked back the rest.

I don't know how long I stayed there, lost in my ponderings, before a knock at the door demanded my attention. It was the sailor from earlier, who'd returned with the tar-blackened flag. I lay the flag flat on the floor and knelt down to paint our ship's Jolly Roger. Using whitewash from the storage hold, I painted the skull, and beneath it I designed two tridents crossing instead of crossbones or swords.

"What's the name of this ship, lad?" I asked the sailor, standing up to examine my work, as though it mattered.

"La *Redenciòn*, sir," the man replied timidly.

"Fitting," I muttered under my breath.

I thanked him with a curt nod. Then I left the quarters and walked back out on deck, noticing the pale red glow against a darkening sky that came just before sunset. Tucking a knife between my teeth, I began my climb up the mast with the newly made flag in hand. And once at the top, where the ocean wind blew fierce, I cut away the Spanish banner and replaced it with my pirate flag.

The task was long finished, but I steadied myself against the foremast as my distorted gaze followed the old flag getting swept away in the wind. It drew my eyes to the horizon, where I looked out at the sea I would now roam. Nameless, damaged, alone, and forgotten by time.

I'm sorry, Katrina.

My only comfort was knowing she wasn't here to see what I'd become. But if damning myself meant saving her, so be it. My only chance to find her again someday existed solely in the care of Noah, and that did little to ease my thoughts...but it was something. I just hoped what I'd given him had made it back with him, and he had the sense to remember what I asked him to do with it.

I'd have to set out to ensure Katrina understood what it all meant by the time it got to her. Somehow, without changing the course of history, I'd have to find a way to bridge my past and her future so that we could find each other again. And with a ship and crew of my own, battered as they may be, I stood a fraction higher of a chance of accomplishing that. I didn't know how long it would take, especially with Thane still out there determined to hunt me down.

But I had all the time in the world.

44

SEASICK

KATRINA

I'd fainted from the effort of burying the trident. Right before the world around me faded to darkness, I remembered hearing Bellamy call my name, followed but the sound of a splash. But then I closed my eyes and drifted.

When I woke up, I was lying in a bed covered by fine silk sheets and blankets. The can lights above me were set just dim enough so that I could see the room's polished, hotel-like interior. To the right of me, light spilled in through the crack in the drawn curtains over the window. I sat up, rubbing my head, and thankful that I was clothed and could feel legs and toes instead of fins. I wore a simple black night chemise that smelled like rose petals. Not my style, but better than being naked.

"I'm so glad you're awake!" McKenzie's melodic voice made me jump. I hadn't even noticed her sitting in the leather armchair in the corner. "We've been taking shifts to sit with you," she said, standing up.

Her tattered 18th century clothing was gone. She looked clean and fresh, dressed it new, modern clothes. I wondered how long I'd been unconscious.

She must have noticed me eyeing her new outfit. "Cordelia's clothes," she said, pointing to herself and me. That explained my interesting attire.

"Are we still on the yacht?" I asked, trying to peek through the slit in the curtains.

"Yes," she nodded, taking a seat on the edge of the bed with me. "It's been two days. Bellamy and the skipper say we should be back to Constantine by tomorrow night." She paused to flip her freshly-washed hair back. "You should see those two going at it. Bellamy has somehow managed to gaslight him into making believe what he saw wasn't real and was just a monster storm and he hallucinated the rest. The crew doesn't seem to know right from left now and they constantly argue about what actually happened. It cracks me up. But they all at least seem to agree that their boss went overboard, so I think we're in the clear."

I tried to smile and embrace the relief that should've come with it. For a minute it even felt real. But I couldn't find the piece of me anymore that knew how to laugh. It was all too fresh. I'd lost Milo. I'd lost myself. I *killed* someone. Did McKenzie know that? She had to know by now.

She continued. "They think you drowned, too. And it's probably best we keep it that way, so you can't come out of here until we get back to Constantine."

Fine with me.

"I...I'm just glad everyone's okay." I stammered.

A softness overtook McKenzie's expression. She reached for my hand. "I know it won't be easy returning to normal for you. But I want you to know I'm here for you, and I'm sorry for all the times I've pushed you into doing things you didn't want to do. You've had enough of that." She glanced down as silence fell between us. I wasn't used to seeing her so gentle, serious, and articulate. It was almost awkward until I finally spoke.

"You saved the world, you know," I said with the best half-grin I could put on. "Only a true badass would've thought to use that flare gun." The proud smile that spread across her lips gave me hope. Hope that maybe at least one of us felt like they'd come out of this better than they went in.

"Yeah," she said, "It was pretty cool. But it doesn't come close to being a rogue mermaid." Her giggle reminded me of bubbles bursting. "Well anyway, I'll go tell the others you're awake." She stood and strode to the door, turning back to add one more thing. "Bellamy's been worried about you."

She closed the door behind her before I could even respond. I would've told her to at least give me a chance to change into something with a little more coverage than this spaghetti strap night dress before facing anyone else, but I supposed everyone had already seen everything I had to offer when they'd pulled me out of the water.

As I waited there, pulling the covers back over me when the outside air became too cold, I noticed the sensation of the thin gold ring around my finger. I spun it around with my thumb, thinking about everything that little ring encompassed, and how it would serve as constant reminder of what I couldn't get back. For a moment—just a still, sweet moment—I was back in the grotto by the waterfall, entangled with him and feeling like we had forever on our side. I blinked and all of that was gone.

Three knocks at the door made me look up. Bellamy poked his head in, his eyes settling on me almost immediately.

"You can come in," I said, resting my head against the headboard so that I was still upright even while resting.

"I told you you were going to get sick jumping in that water, love. I just didn't think it'd be 300 years later," he teased. How are you feeling?" He made his way over to me after leaving the door cracked just an inch.

"I feel okay. Just...tired." I breathed out, glancing over at the closed curtains beside my bed. "I'd like to see the view."

"Of course," Bellamy shuffled over to the curtains and drew them back, letting the room become bathed in bright light. I looked at the shimmering Atlantic Ocean, wondering how I was supposed to just go home and start the semester like nothing ever happened. I didn't know how I could, but I'd figure that out later. Bellamy stood in silence, watching the water, too.

"You know," I said, adjusting my back against the mountain of pillows bracing them, "You should probably be the one resting. I can't imagine it feels too great to be brought back from the dead."

Bellamy turned to me with a smirk. "It's not all that bad. I could barely tell the difference between being resurrected and the morning after a good, long night at the tavern. I've been far more drunk."

"I'm glad to hear it comes so naturally to you," I joked. "But in all seriousness, Bellamy, how are you really?"

He walked with slow steps back over to the side of the bed, sitting down on the mattress beside me. He looked at me, narrowing his eyes as though very focused on his response.

"How am I?" He scratched his jaw, reminding me of a cornered animal. "I woke up with a whole new set of memories that weren't there before. I remember rescuing you, and dancing with you, and fighting alongside you. I thought I was in love with you then, and it angered me so. But I don't know what I feel now. Because everything's different now. For both of us. And now I'm free. There are no curses or enemies holding me back. But I don't have a clue what to do next."

"That's okay," I leaned forward to touch his shoulder. "Neither do I."

He glanced at the ring on my finger. " I can't say I'm sorry enough, Katrina."

A weight dropped in my heart. "Funny, isn't it? We've both lost someone we love because of someone else who should've loved us enough not to take them from us." I watched the sadness cloud Bellamy's eyes, as he surely thought of Serena, and I instantly felt guilty for bringing it up. But I wanted him to know I understood in some way.

The door creaked as someone pushed it open. "Katrina?" A voice came through timid and low.

"Hey, Noah," I said with a weak smile. "I hope you've been entertaining the crew on this yacht with your beatboxing shanties."

At the sight of Bellamy's raised eyebrows and confused expression, I couldn't help but laugh a bit, and Noah chuckled along with me.

"Unfortunately, no one seems up to singing on this ship," he said, coming nearer. "McKenzie said you were awake, and I—uh—just wanted to say that I'm glad you're okay...and thank you. For stopping Cordelia. You literally stopped a disaster."

I shrugged gently. "I couldn't have done any of it without you. Don't think otherwise."

Noah nodded, and then bit his lip as though he was going to tell me something, but then changed his mind. "Okay well, I guess I'm gonna step back out on deck for a bit. Let us know if you need anything. And Bellamy, if you need a place to stay, I know of a place."

Bellamy thanked him and I waved him goodbye as he stepped back out the door, leaving us alone again. We were both quiet for far too long before it became uncomfortable.

"Noah's a good guy. He'll help you figure things out and get settled." I reassured, breaking the silence.

"I had three centuries to get settled." He looked down, a heaviness stirring in his voice. "I don't need to settle. I just need to know why I was brought back."

"Cordelia was just being cruel," I said.

"Exactly." I noticed his neck and jaw tighten. "And that's why I can't just live some mundane existence because she brought me back. I need to be something. I need to have a reason this heart beats again. I can't chase the sea like I once did. It's a different world now. So, what am I here? *Who* am I here?"

"Don't be hard on yourself," I said, wishing I knew how to take my own advice. "You don't have to know it all just yet. But please don't think you were brought back for nothing...because...because I'm glad you're here." I swallowed, hoping my pathetic attempt at encouraging him would have some power. The faint smile that formed across his face was a good enough sign that it did.

"I'll always be here for you, Katrina Delmar." And with that, he stood up and slipped out the door, and I closed my weary eyes to sleep again.

45

A SOFT FAREWELL

KATRINA

When the ship passed through the channel back to the marina in Constantine, I decided to finally come out on deck. I figured no one would notice me slip out as long as I stayed near the backside of the boat. Thankfully, I'd found some clothing in the bottom of Cordelia's dresser that made me feel a little more like myself—a simple long sleeve blouse and a snug pair of dark jeans. I made my way to the back port side, leaning over the railing on both elbows.

The boat nosed its way carefully through a path of tall reeds and dark blue water, and I wondered who was steering. As we neared the marina in the distance, I couldn't help but feel a sense of dread. When I stepped off this boat, it would feel like starting everything over again. I didn't even have my phone anymore, since it'd been lost or destroyed along with everyone else's in our initial shipwreck.

My parents were probably worried sick, I thought. But then I remembered that time hadn't passed here like it had for us. As far as my mom and dad were concerned, they'd just heard from me the day before. At least that was one less thing to worry about. But I wondered how I was supposed to find the motivation and morale to pick my classes back up when they started next week. Most students didn't have to live with the weight of killing their great-grandmother, leaving their boyfriend in the 18th century, accepting that they are part fish, and realizing there is a dark half of them that will always be trying to take over all at the same time. But that's how I would be starting my new year.

Slow footsteps caught my attention from behind. I didn't recognize them, but I didn't bother turning around either. If someone wanted to sneak attack me at this point, let them. But the voice of Noah stilled any intrusive thoughts I might've had about that.

"Um...hey," he uttered, taking a spot beside me at the railing.

"Hey," I replied.

"I'm glad you came out here." He fidgeted with his thumbs as his eyes jumped from me to the deck floor and back. "Because I've been trying to find a chance to give you this before we dock." He held out his hand and lying in his open palm was a well-worn compass. Milo's compass.

"I wanted to give it to you earlier, but it felt kinda weird with Bellamy in the room. But the night before we found the trident, Milo told me to hold onto it and give it to you when the time was right."

I reached forward with slow movement and picked up the compass. I held it in both hands as though it was a precious gemstone that I couldn't let out of my sight. Swallowing down a lump in my throat, I looked up at Noah.

"He must've known what was going to happen. All along. He knew." My words cracked. "He trusted you, you know. That's why he asked you to do it."

"He would've done anything for you," Noah said. "You were the only thing that mattered to him."

I was at a loss for how to reply. But I didn't have to because Noah seemed to understand it when the only words I could mutter out were, "thank you."

"No problem," he said, watching the dock as we approached the port toward the empty spot waiting for us at the Tesoro Del Mar Marina. "Now you should probably go back down to the cabin before anyone notices you. We'll come get you once everyone else is off."

I nodded, looking back over my shoulder to see McKenzie crossing the deck toward the cabin.

"She's probably on her way to tell me the same thing," I chuckled. "Be good to her, Noah." I managed to allow my siren side to jump in just long enough to make my eyes flash blue for added effect. Noah recoiled with a nervous smirk.

"Got it." He grinned with two upward open palms in a gesture of surrender.

Clutching Milo's compass close to my chest, I turned and made my way back to the cabin, making sure to stay unnoticed as everyone else eagerly prepared to disembark.

46

WHISTLE FOR THE WIND

KATRINA

That night I couldn't sleep. I was back in my dorm and cramping lightly from the onset of a period I felt coming—which was its own relief given what happened back in Nassau and aboard the *Falcon*. But I didn't want to be there in that dorm. I didn't know where I wanted to be. I used to be kept awake by my nightmares. But now it was reality that haunted me. And now it was 4 AM and I was exhausted from my tossing and turning and the thoughts that would never stop.

I yearned for the nights when I would sneak out and meet Milo beneath the stars, running from his unhinged captain and trying to understand the mysteries of my past. How things had changed in just a few months. I clung tightly to the blanket wrapped around me, the same one Milo had given me the first night we met, the compass tucked away in my hand as well.

When I could no longer handle the restlessness, I sat up. In the darkness, I tiptoed quietly out with a handful of paints and brushes. Next, I slipped on my shoes and jacket before closing the dorm's door softly behind me. Through the dim golden lights of the East Wing hall, I made my way onto the sidewalks and out to my car. I breathed in the familiar, homey scent of my old Jeep, grateful for at least one thing that was still the same.

I drove to the old pier, where I once stood so many times waiting for Milo. If only I could call him back with my North Star. Just one more time. What I wouldn't have given to be able to stand on that pier again this night and see him emerge from the foggy water below like before. I knew I couldn't. I knew there was absolutely no way. But I tried anyway.

As I walked through the mist, veiled by its thin white embrace, I opened my mouth and ever so softly, only loud enough for me to hear, I sang, wondering how many women long past waiting for the return of their sailors at sea had felt this same empty anguish.

"Lost out at sea
Do you dream of me?
By the call of the waves
I hear you and seek you
Till again the roaming sea
Brings you back to me."

Walking to the farthest end of the pier, I knelt down. Taking out the paints I'd brought, I spilled them onto the pier's edge, in a small puddle of seawater. The blue and white mixture swirled in a dance of chaos, until my tears began to fall, and I quietly redirected the colors into the pattern in my head. I only needed a few brushstrokes once or twice. But the rest of the shape I formed entirely with my power.

"And here I thought you'd stopped painting North Stars." I looked up with surprise at the sound of Bellamy's voice.

The full moon above gave me just enough light to see him clearly. He was walking toward me, and I quickly wiped my tears before he could get close enough to see them. "And here I thought you'd stopped sneaking up on me in the middle of the night," I teased with a sniff.

"I suppose old habits die hard." His voice was tender, and he sat down next to me, dipping his finger into the star I'd painted. "To be honest, I didn't know you'd be here. But this was the only place I could think of coming for some clarity. I'm not used to...this. To feeling. To resting." He held up his hands and looked at them as though they were foreign objects.

"I'm sure it will take some time," I said softly.

"Time," he repeated. "What a cruel thing it can be."

"Cruel is the right word." I sighed, crossing my legs and adjusting myself to face the water.

In silence we sat, the night tide crashing below us and the sea mist casting a chill over my skin. It was Bellamy who broke the silence.

"The last time we were here was right before you broke our curse. I'm sorry for who I was that night. But you pulled me back from the brink. You made me remember who I was. Thank you for that."

"You're...you're welcome." I pulled my hair over one shoulder, trying to keep it from tangling in the sea breeze.

"I lost myself after Serena's death. She was the first time I'd felt a love for anything other than the sea. A *real* love." He paused with a low chuckle before continuing.

"Serena was everything to me. When she died, nothing mattered. I couldn't stop it. I couldn't save her. The only thing in my control was the fate of my father, and I was set on controlling it. But I forgot who I was in the process. And I turned my back on everything I ever once cared about—including someone who was the closest thing I ever had to a brother."

"Milo thought of you as a brother, too. He told me that," I said, reaching over to touch his hand with a reassuring squeeze. "Stay true North. In the end you did that."

Bellamy's eyes brightened, and he tilted his head back, breathing in as though he just had a weight lifted from his shoulders. "He's a better man that I am. But even the best men break when they have nothing left."

His words worried me, and I wondered if he knew something I didn't, but I was too afraid to ask. He'd told me Milo had gotten away and made it out alive of the duel at sea. That was all I could bear to know right now.

"I know this is going to sound ridiculous, but It's almost like I can feel him. Like he's still out there somewhere, somehow, calling to me." I took out the compass from my pocket and held it up, watching the twitching needle find its way as it adjusted to point North. Some stupid part of me wanted to pretend it was showing me the way to Milo, somewhere miles away across all the oceans of the world, transcending the years that separated us.

"Maybe he is," Bellamy said. "He left you his compass."

I lifted the compass close to my face, examining its brushed metal exterior in the pale moonlight. I brushed my thumb along it and flipped it over, studying the delicately carved "H" on the back.

"May I?" Bellamy asked, scooting a bit closer. I placed the compass in his hand and watched him look it over.

"Look here," he turned the compass on its side toward me "The baseplate looks as though someone at one point tried to pry it open."

With my curiosity piqued and a terrifying hope welling up in me, I grabbed my thinnest paintbrush. I pushed its tip against the small bent lip of metal as Bellamy firmly held the compass in place. The back plate popped off to reveal a small empty space within the compass just large enough to hold something like small jewelry or a key. But there was a tiny piece of torn folded parchment instead. I picked it up, my breaths shaking and my stomach twisting in knots in anticipation.

"It just says 'Bastian Drake.'"

"Bastian Drake?" Bellamy repeated, taking the tiny paper from my fingers.

"You know that name?"

Bellamy was quiet for a minute as suspense swelled within me. He seemed to be thinking on his response. "Yes...yes, I know that name. But I'm trying to understand why Milo would've—unless..."

"Unless what?" I gripped his arm, nearly begging him to go on.

"Bastian Drake was a pirate lord who dealt in...oddities...off the coasts of Cuba. Shrunken heads, magical relics, legendary maps and rare treasures of the like. He was one of the few men more powerful than my father on the high seas. That is, until my father monopolized the mermaid trade. And by then, Bastian was willing to pay him anything for a chance at immortality."

"A siren heart." I affirmed through a soft breath.

"Exactly. We brought him one, and he promised us the Crown of the Sea in exchange. But he double crossed us instead and failed to uphold his end of the deal. Milo was there. He knows what kind of things that man has in his possession."

"Crown of the Sea?"

"Rumored to be the crown of a sea goddess, trapped in mortal form until it's returned to her. Drake managed to sink a British ship and stole its cargo. On board he found a chest with the crown."

"How exactly does Milo think this can help me find him?"

"A sea goddess, Katrina. Think of it." A smile flashed across Bellamy's face. "Find her and return her crown and she'll bend the laws of time for you. She'll *have* to help you if you break her binds."

"You say that like it's some easy task. Like all I have to do is put together a jigsaw puzzle. We're talking about finding some mythical sea goddess in a world bigger than I ever could have imagined. Even if I was to get that crown from this Bastian Drake guy, how am I supposed to know where she is?"

"You don't. But Bastian does." Bellamy nudged me. "And who said anything about you doing this alone?"

My eyes widened. "You mean you'd go with me? To Cuba...to track down some immortal pirate lord?"

"Have you not figured me out by now, love?" Bellamy straightened his shoulders. "I live for whatever adventure the sea brings me next. I'm not even supposed to be here. But now that I am, I'm not going to waste it." He put a friendly arm around me, pulling me to him as he spoke with a sly tone that grew livelier by the second, sounding more and more like his usual quick-witted self. He pointed out to the open horizon, where the morning sun had just begun to peek over the ocean. "You see, I know where Bastian is, and Bastian knows where the crown is, so now all you have to do is figure out where the goddess is."

"Solid plan." I shrugged, wrestling with the frightening sense of hope rising within me.

"Aye, isn't it?" He stood up, helping me to my feet after him. By now, a faint orange glow of the sun had broken through the morning clouds, and the fog slowly lifted.

I squeezed the compass in my hand and touched the fresh scar on my face. I knew the quest sounded far-fetched. Maybe even impossible. But that wouldn't keep me from trying. The sea's secrets were as bottomless as its depths. And it had been on my side so far...mostly. Maybe it had another surprise yet waiting to help me out one last time.

"If you really think this is what Milo meant, I'm all in," I said boldly. "I want to see him again, whatever it takes."

Bellamy's eyes narrowed with determination and a hint of mischief as he watched the sunrise.

"Then we'll bring him back, lass."

Acknowledgments

Thank you to the readers who put the wind in my sails. Seriously, because of the love you've shown my first book, I endeavored to write the next one. And I can't thank you enough for that.

Thank you for your support, your encouragement, your belief in me, and the love you've all shown for these characters that are a piece of my heart and mind.

Thank you to my husband, the sweetest of cinnamon rolls, who makes me believe in romance and true love.

Thank you to my incredible friend Sam, who cares about these characters and their stories just as much as I do.

And thank God for iced coffee, without which I would not have been able to finish this book.

Follow the Author

Thank you so much for reading. To keep up with my current works and be the first to hear about new releases (including release updates for Book 3 in the From Tormented Tides series) and special reader opportunities, follow me on social media @authorvalelane or sign up for my newsletter at authorvalelane.com

Printed in Great Britain
by Amazon

33313081R00189